Return to War

E. PAIGE BURKS

For information about this title or to order other books and/or electronic media, contact the publisher:
Infinity Flower Publishing, LLC
www.infinityflowerpublishing.com
info@infinityflowerpublishing.com

ISBN: 979-8-9861598-1-2 (Paperback)

Thank you to all of my friends and readers.
You keep me going.

PLAINS OF ADURO
AUSTIA
ABJURE FOREST
THE LIMEN
CORACINUS MOUNTAINS
FORN
FORNAX
CELO CAVUS

Tercastle Peaks
Regius Carmen
Perfides Mines
Forest of the Aife
Southern Outpost
Calamo Mare
Angulus
Festra
YMBER
Comodo River
Plains of Pacier
Sorona
Parie's Wall
Custos Obduros
Grass Mire
Dirvo
SICCITA
Eluvios River

PROLOGUE

20 years ago in Regius Carmen

ILENCE HAD FALLEN OVER THE kingdom. It was deafening, and it made the ache in Liana's chest worse. How could this have happened?

Tears crowded her eyes as she brushed dark hair from her son's face. He was still, his bloodied tunic having been replaced by clean clothing for his final trip. Beside him, on the funeral pyre, lay his golden-haired wife. Her only consolation was that their blonde-haired, green-eyed child didn't lie with them.

Finally, she stepped away from the pyre, nodding to the men around her, who held torches. The crowd gathered to witness the funeral was silent as a clergyman said words about Liana's family. One by one, the men lit the pyre.

Liana's tears spilled over as the people around her began to whisper the traditional farewell blessing. Over and over again, her heart was breaking. She should have seen this coming. She should have been able to protect her family.

She turned her violet eyes skyward, watching plumes of dark smoke rise into the morning sky, carrying away the spirits of her loved ones. An all-consuming emptiness filled her. Once again, she was alone. And somewhere out there, her granddaughter was running for her life. The thought made her stomach turn, and she clenched her teeth, bowing her head.

Jet would pay for this.

He had done many heart-wrenching, deplorable things. But this was not something she could overlook.

Liana lifted her head, feeling fury filling her. She looked toward her Captain of the Guard, Antony, who stood at her side. His dark brown eyes were wide with tears, and he blinked in surprise when she placed her hand on his arm.

"I need to see him," she whispered.

Antony's eyes widened further. "I'm not sure that is wise, Your Grace," he said, brushing at his face. "You know he will only twist your misery for the sake of his own pleasure."

Liana nodded. "That is why I need to see him now," she whispered, feeling doubt edge into her heart. "Before I lose my nerve."

Antony drew a slow breath, nodding. He motioned to his guards, escorting her silently from the ceremonial grounds.

Once they reached the safety of the castle, Liana pulled the dark veil from her hair. She wouldn't let Jet think he had won anything. If anything, he had started something that she knew he would have no desire to finish. She would have his blood on her hands this day.

The walk to the dungeons was long and every step sent a pulse of hatred deeper and deeper into Liana's heart. If she had thought that keeping Jet prisoner would drive Paraximus mad, then killing Jet would be the driving blow to her former lover. He would know that she was not what he thought she was, and that she would be coming for his head as well.

Antony and his followers paused as they reached the

door where the abomination waited for them. He offered Liana a beseeching look once more. At her curt nod, he opened the door.

Liana gritted her teeth as the door swung in, light filling the cell. She drew a slow breath as she stepped inside, feeling a guard at her elbow. Satisfaction filled her as her eyes fell across Jet. He was restrained, shackled to the wall. The chains that bound him crackled with electric magic, keeping him from moving.

Despite the fury writhing inside her, Liana still felt her stomach turn when Jet lifted his face, his onyx eyes shifting over her. A sadistic grin slid across his face, which was still splattered with blood. Everything inside her suddenly ached to break his neck, but she held her ground.

"Do I have your attention now?" Jet asked, his voice dark.

"If my attention was all you sought, then there would have been easier ways," Liana quipped. She pressed her hands together, realizing she was trembling.

Jet grunted in annoyance. "Too easy," he said indifferently. "I prefer the pain I have brought you."

Liana fought for control, feeling her fury escalate. She knew Jet could feel it pulsing through her aura, but he ignored it. It suddenly occurred to her that he was too calm for what he had just done.

"You must think that you have every move I will make calculated," she said.

Jet's glittering eyes shifted to her, narrowed dangerously.

Liana felt a small smile slide across her face. His look said volumes, and she suddenly understood his intentions. "Do you tire of my dungeons already?" she asked, hearing the condescending tone in her voice.

Jet scowled darkly. "Is a hundred years not enough for

you?" he suddenly snapped, frustration lacing his voice. "Just kill me like you came here to do."

Liana drew a slow breath, feeling the tension suddenly ease away. That was his game, wasn't it? He knew she would never let him go and that there was no escape, so he tried to force her hand. Unfortunately, he didn't know who he was dealing with. "I have no intention of killing you," she said easily.

The fury that suddenly creased his face once again spoke volumes. He said nothing as he turned his face away. It took a long moment for him to school himself into indifference again. Liana braced herself when he finally drew a slow breath.

"Then perhaps it will please you know that I enjoyed killing them," he said quietly, keeping his eyes trained away from her. "I enjoyed the way they begged and pleaded for me to stop." A soft smile pulled at his lips. "Especially the woman." Regret crossed his face. "It's a shame that the child escaped. I would have—"

"Enough!" Liana clenched her fists, feeling her jaw clench tightly. The pain was still fresh, and she took a quick step toward him.

A devilish grin was on his face as his eyes shifted to her before away again. His words had hit where he had intended.

"I will not bend to you!" Liana suddenly yelled at him. She felt tears fill her eyes. She knew she needed to get herself together. She was only playing right into his hands and doing what he wanted. She took a moment to control herself, her voice soft when she finally spoke. "You will spend the rest of your days here." She nodded at the stone around them. "These walls will be the last thing your eyes will ever see. You will not have the satisfaction of a murderer's death."

With that, she turned, walking quickly from the cell. Once Antony had shut the door behind her, she waved her hand. Golden magic wove around and into the wood of the door, sealing it.

"He may only be released by my hand," she said, looking among her guards. "No one may see him without my knowledge and permission."

The night was dark. Liana could feel her heart racing in her chest. Carefully, she blew the candle beside her out, sitting for a moment in the darkness. Jet was out of time. Doubt was starting to ease into her heart about if he would make the right choice.

Her violet eyes shifted to the door when a gentle knock sounded.

"Your Grace?"

Liana moved to her feet, crossing to open the door. She wasn't surprised to see Antony standing before her.

He bowed quickly. "He is asking for you."

Liana nodded, keeping her face void of emotion. Inside, her heart was racing. This was what she wanted. It was crucial that Jet chose to come to her of his own free will, otherwise her plan could never work.

Without a word, she stepped into the hall, following her Captain of the Guard to the dungeons. It was mostly silent, save for the soft sounds of water leaking between the rocks. Her eyes were steady as she paused in front of the door she knew well. She had spent many sleepless nights standing before it, wondering what she could do and what she could say to the wayward hellion inside.

She realized once more that her heart was racing, and she drew a calming breath. She caught Antony's dark brown eyes, nodding once. The key grated in the lock and Antony stepped back. Liana swallowed thickly as she stepped to the door, reaching for the handle. The sealing enchantment that she had placed on the door evaporated with her touch, allowing the heavy door to swing on its hinges.

It took a flash of a moment for Liana's eyes to adjust to the consuming darkness inside. She felt the pull of the void that Jet created around himself. She ignored it as she stepped inside. She noticed the way his dark eyes narrowed, catching the faint light. It was all she could see of him.

Words were hard-pressed to leave her lips as she gazed at him. "You asked for me?"

Soft scuffing let her know that he had heard her. He stepped toward her, the light from Antony's torch falling over him. Even in torn, dirty clothing, he still set an intimidating figure.

"I've been considering your offer," he said slowly. His onyx eyes were sparkling in a way that Liana didn't like.

"And?" she asked. She tried to school her voice into calm. She couldn't let Jet think he had any control over her, even though everything hinged on this moment. Her plans were nothing without him.

Jet crossed his arms, lifting his chin in a defiant manner. "What makes you so certain that I'll do as you command?"

Liana smiled then, feeling all her doubts ebb away. She had him. "Because you have no other choice," she said easily. "Once you commit to me, whether it be in word or in truth, you can never go back."

Jet's cocky manner slid into a scowl.

"You must be sure," Liana continued. "I will require all of you, and there will be no escaping for you." She knew once word reached the City of Fear of Jet's allegiance, Paraximus would stop at nothing to destroy him.

And Jet knew it, too. His glittering onyx gaze shifted away, his thoughts racing behind his eyes. "And what's in it for me?" he asked, his voice softened.

"Freedom," Liana said simply. "There will be no commands from me. You will do as I ask of your own free will. You would not be a prisoner here."

Jet's eyes narrowed as he looked back to her and Liana knew his thoughts. In the two decades that she'd kept him here, they'd come to an understanding. Initially, on nights when the darkness felt too dark and she couldn't sleep, Liana would stand outside his cell door and ruminate on her decision to allow him to live. The pain he'd caused her was endless, but one night he finally spoke to her. He'd meant it as a taunt, but somewhere along the way during those seemingly eternal and lonely nights, they had forged a tenuous thread of trust. Liana understood him now better than she supposed he understood himself. And that was how she knew that her plan could work.

Jet had never been asked to do anything of his own free will. Every move he made had been carefully planned and controlled by Paraximus. To dangle an opportunity to be free was too much for him to resist.

"Why are you so confident in me?" he asked finally, annoyance in his voice. He often reacted that way when presented with things that he didn't or couldn't understand, such as empathy.

Liana drew a slow breath, gathering her thoughts. "I'm more than happy to let you rot here in this cell," she said. "But offering you this opportunity will give you more satisfaction than it will give me."

"How so?" he demanded, suspicion lacing his voice.

"You will spill the blood of the ones you so loathe," Liana said simply. "What more could you ask for?" Her violet eyes sparkled dangerously in the faint light. "Do not think that I don't know your true nature, Jet Lamia."

Jet looked away, his brow furrowing at the thought. Liana knew him down to his core, and she knew that for years he had dreamed about having the chance to destroy her. But he had been abandoned here by his once-comrades, and she knew that the thought of revenge brought a different sort of thrill to him. Killing the ones who betrayed him would be much more satisfying, by far. He'd shared with her how he longed to feel their blood on his hands for leaving him here to rot, and he'd also shared with her how he knew that murdering his father's lackeys would drive a knife into Paraximus' gut that could be twisted as he pleased.

He looked back to her, meeting her gaze. "Fine," he said shortly. "I'll play your game."

Liana smiled benignly. "Good."

Regius Carmen, Capitol City of Ymber.
The twenty-eighth day of winter, the 851st year of the
reign of Queen Liana Estrella.
Tuesday, January 17, 2012.

L IGHT WAS TRICKLING IN FROM a window, casting happy, yellow beams across a bookshelf. Dust motes were floating through the air, as if they had no care in the world. The air was cool in the library, making it comfortable with the fire blazing in the large fireplace on the western wall. A chair was drawn away from a table, and a pile of books were scattered across the table.

A woman stood near the table, a fluffy quill pen paused halfway to her lips. She held a book in her hands, her violet eyes shifting over the words she'd written. She drew a slow breath as she made a correction, taking a slow step toward the fireplace. She was lost in thought, reading her words, when a knock interrupted her concentration. She looked up as the library door opened.

"Apologies for the interruption, Your Grace," a man said, appearing inside the door.

Liana offered a soft smile, stepping back toward the table. "Your presence is always welcome, Count Samill," she said gently. She set the book down, tucking her quill inside it to mark her place. She looked up at him, feeling her chest tighten. "What news do you bring me?"

The Count closed the library door behind him. A helmet was tucked under his arm, and he still wore his riding cloak and breeches, meaning he'd just come back from his mission. "There is currently no sign of them, Your Grace," he said, a frown pulling at his lips. "I have had my men searching high and low, and have put out the word, should someone recognize them."

Liana nodded slowly, feeling her heart drop. She looked down at her book, letting her fingertips rest against the leather cover. This wasn't what she wanted to hear, but it was what she expected.

"I'm very sorry, My Queen," the count continued. "I will keep up the search."

Liana turned to look at him then, waves of lavender hair falling over her shoulder. "That won't be necessary," she said gently, her voice just above a whisper. She didn't want to convey her disappointment, but deep inside, she was crushed. "They will appear in time."

The count seemed unhappy with her decision, but he nodded, knowing it wasn't his place to argue. "Is there anything else I can do?" he asked.

Liana drew a slow breath, forcing a smile. "Take a day to rest," she said. "If I have another mission for you, I will let you know."

Count Samill nodded, bowing to her, knowing he was dismissed. He left the library without a word, leaving Liana alone.

She sighed deeply once he was gone, pressing her

hand to her face. She'd hoped that this wouldn't have been the outcome. She'd hoped that Jet would have gotten her granddaughter to a city, found a messenger, and sent word. She'd hoped that Jet could be trusted, but doubt was filling her. Other than the bodies her men had found in the Coracinus Mountains, there was no indication that they were even in Gexalatia. There was also no way to know where he was taking her granddaughter, and that made her heart clench.

She prayed to the gods above that he was upholding his end of the bargain. She felt sick with her worry, but she knew there was little she could do. Samill Durvey had the best group of men for the job, and she knew he was taking this seriously. She could see that he was running himself and his men ragged, trying to find Nyx and Jet, and she knew it couldn't go on like this.

Liana drew a slow breath, pushing her feelings down and composing herself. She knew what her next move would be, and she knew that when Jet found out, he'd be pissed.

"They're here, Highness."

Liana nodded as she set down a teacup on a tray. The throne room was empty, save for her and the servant offering her afternoon tea. The servant exited the room quietly as three shadows appeared in the doorway. A smile pulled at Liana's lips.

"Friends," she greeted, stepping toward them to meet them in the middle of the room. Her soft voice echoed across the empty marble. She'd intentionally sent all of her courtiers away. She didn't want anyone to be privy to their conversation.

A young-looking girl was leading the group, prancing down the carpet that lined the middle of the room. She had a long, brown-haired ponytail that swung with her movements, brushing over a sword tethered to her back. She wore dark, nearly black *stuba*-leather clothing, with thin armor covering her chest, arms, and legs. Her almond eyes were shrewd, and a thin, mischievous smile pulled at her lips, belying her true age.

"Your Highness," she said, kneeling before her.

Liana inclined her head. "Otsana," she said. She wasn't especially fond of the girl—a forest sprite—as she didn't understand her guardians' motives for keeping her around, but she couldn't judge. She turned her eyes over Otsana's shoulder.

A man with dark, black skin and equally black hair stood behind her, dressed in a long black tunic and pants. His lips were pressed together lightly, his eyes a startling color of amber. Beside him was his polar opposite, a pale, snow-white woman dressed all in white. Her white hair tumbled down her back and swung loosely with her footsteps. Like her mate, her eyes were similarly startling, a bright and piercing blue. Neither spoke, but a small smile pulled at the man's lips as they stepped forward.

Liana extended her hands to the man and woman. "I trust your journey was not too arduous," she said. "I am glad to see you." She bowed her head lightly to them as they each in turn rested a hand in greeting lightly on her palms.

Otsana looked up slowly as Liana stepped back from her guardians. "My mistress says she is happy to see you again as well," she said.

Liana tried to maintain a smile, but she could feel it slipping. "We have much to discuss," she said hesitantly.

"Should we adjourn to the study—"

The pale woman suddenly stepped forward, pressing her hand against Liana's face. Her touch was hot, and Liana's breath caught in her throat as sudden images began to fill her mind. She could see Samill's men as they rode across the Calamo Mare toward the Coracinus Mountains before the image flashed to Samill standing in front of a villager, asking questions. She felt like she was seeing all the stops Samill had made in his search for Nyx and Jet. She could feel the hopelessness and frustration of he and his men as they rode across the grassy plains, no closer to finding their quarry.

Suddenly the scene shifted, showing her a dirt road. A team of dirty *asperpellis* pulling a laden-down cart and a group of travel-worn men met her eyes. Liana felt like she was flying over the scene, passing the cart and moving into the wilderness around the road. She drew a soft gasp as her eyes landed on a camp site not far from the cart and men, with a group of four sitting around a small fire. Tears sprang into her eyes as she realized that a golden-haired girl was sitting among them, her eyes so much like her father's.

"Nyx," she breathed, her heart fluttering hard in her chest.

She turned her gaze to take in the others, seeing Jet leaning back on his hands beside Nyx, staring absently into the fire. Across from them, two others sat, dragons curled around them protectively. She noticed a piece of armor lying on the ground, emblazoned with the sigil of the king of Fornax.

Liana's lips pulled into a frown. "Fornaxians?" she whispered. "What are they doing in Ymber?"

The woman pulled her hand away then, and Liana

blinked quickly, the tears slipping slowly down her cheeks as the vision faded. She held the woman's gaze, feeling softly whispered words entering her mind. *We will bring her here.*

Liana nodded mutely. She knew that the woman could feel her gratitude. Beside her, Otsana had moved to her feet, turning to look at the man.

"We must go now," she said, looking back to Liana. "We will return soon."

Liana nodded as she stepped back, bowing her head once again. "Thank you."

The man and woman nodded mutely before turning and walking toward the door. Otsana bowed at the waist to Liana before trotting after them.

Once they disappeared from the room, Liana turned her back to the door, pressing her hands against her face. All she could think about was Nyx's face. She had seemed tired and cold, but she was safe and no worse for wear that Liana could tell. Relief had instantly filled her to know that Jet had kept his word. Liana knew that the wolves wouldn't return empty-handed.

Near the Itera-Patet Road, Calamo Mare, Ymber.
The thirty-sixth day of winter, the 851st year of the
reign of Queen Liana Estrella.
Tuesday, January 25, 2012.

THE SUN HAD LONG BEEN set beyond the eastern horizon. The night was getting cold, a strong wind gusting across the plains. Jet was hunkered down in the tall grass, listening to Rian breathe softly beside him. Rian had a spyglass pressed to his eye, and his mouth was slowly pulling into a frown.

"This doesn't make any sense," he said quietly, passing the spyglass to Jet.

Jet used it to look down from their position at the campsite in the distance. A handful of large, scraggly-looking men sat around a dimming fire. Their three captives were sitting just beyond the firelight, near a cart that two massive beasts lay across.

Jet had to stifle a sigh as he passed the glass back to Rian. "That's a problem," he said shortly. "Those men know what they're doing."

Rian's brow was furrowed as he moved to his knees. He looked defeated. "You're right," he said. "Zaida and I cannot hope to take them on, even with the dragons."

Once again, Jet fought down a sigh. He and Rian had agreed that he and Nyx wouldn't get involved. He knew Nyx would be pissed, but they just couldn't risk it. She might have strong-armed him into coming with the Pangere to rescue their comrades, but there was no way she was going to make him change his mind about fighting these goons. This was all up to Rian and Zaida.

Jet moved to his feet, following Rian back over the small hill toward where they'd made camp. As expected, Rian's red dragon and Zaida's black dragon were curled in a protective circle around a fire and two girls. At their approach, Zaida jumped to her feet, her eyes worried.

"Well?" she asked. "What did you find?"

Rian sighed as he looked at her. "I'm not sure how we're going to get to them," he said slowly. "We're outnumbered, and these men know what they're doing with the dragons." He pressed his hand to his face, brushing his light-colored hair from his eyes. "We'd be totally out-matched."

Zaida's mouth was set in a hard line. She looked like she wanted to be angry with him, but instead she turned away, stepping toward her dragon. Her feelings were clearly deeply hurt at his assessment, and it looked like she wanted to cry, but Jet had noticed that wasn't her style.

"So, then, what's the plan?"

Jet turned his eyes on Nyx, seeing her watching him carefully. "We don't have one," he said, crossing toward her and sinking beside the fire.

Nyx was frowning as she looked between him and Rian. "Where do you think they're taking them?" she asked.

Jet looked up at Rian, seeing that the leader of the

Pangere was way out of his depth here. "They must be taking them to Perfide," he said finally.

Nyx looked at him, confused. "Per-fee-day?"

Jet nodded. "Mines in the mountains," he said. He glanced at Rian again. "Mines built on the backs of dragons and slaves."

Rian turned away then. Guilt was etched on his face. Just like Jet had warned, he'd led them all straight into a trap.

"How many days?" Zaida suddenly asked, stepping back toward the fire.

Jet shrugged as he looked up at her. "At this pace, a week?" he said. "Maybe more." He looked down at the fire. "The good news is that they can't travel very fast. Not with the load they're carrying. And they'll want their captives alive."

Zaida looked to Rian. "We could sneak attack them," she said. "Kill them with arrows."

Rian turned to face her, shaking his head. "They'd kill one of ours before we could kill all of them," he said. "And hand-to-hand is no good either. We don't have the numbers, and we don't know what they did to overtake Declan and Emma."

Zaida suddenly scowled, rage in her eyes. "I told you this would happen, Rian Craith!" she suddenly hissed.

Nyx jumped at the outburst, looking quickly to Jet. They'd never seen Zaida get so upset before.

Rian seemed surprised at first, but then he returned her scowl. "I asked you to trust me," he snapped.

"And I did!" Zaida returned, the fury still on her face. "And now this has happened!" She took a step toward him, clenching her teeth, a flurry of emotion on her face. "I should have never followed you here!"

Rian looked like she'd slapped him, and his face suddenly turned cold. "Then go home, Zaida," he said calmly. "Go back to Fornax."

Tears were flooding Zaida's eyes as she looked at him, her brow furrowing. "What?" she breathed.

"You heard me," Rian snapped. "If you don't think I can do this, then go home!" Anger was creasing his brow. "Go back to Mother and Father, and tell them what a failure you think I am."

Zaida drew a slow breath, the tears sliding slowly down her face. "I never said that," she managed.

Despite the stony exterior she always had, it was evident that Zaida was with Rian for life. Everyone could see how devoted the Pangere members were to each other.

"You don't have to," Rian continued. "You've always thought it. So has my father, and everyone else. So go back, and tell them to give the throne to Kaira!"

Throne? Jet could feel Nyx looking at him. He was just as stunned as she was as they traded glances.

"Don't be ridiculous," Zaida said, composing herself. She pressed her hand to her eyes, as if she was exhausted suddenly. "I will never leave you."

Rian seemed to have run out of steam also as he stared at her.

When Zaida began to speak, her words soft and in a language that Jet recognized as their native tongue. When she looked back to Rian, his face had softened. They both fell silent.

"So, does this mean you two have made up?" Jet asked, drawing their eyes.

They both suddenly looked embarrassed. "Yes," Zaida said shortly, turning away from the group. "Everything is fine."

Nyx leaned forward as Rian sighed deeply, walking to sit across the fire from her. "That still leaves the problem of how to rescue Liam, Amaya, and Ellie," she said.

Rian nodded as he looked up at her. "Luckily, we have time to figure something out."

The fire had died down and Nyx turned slowly onto her back from staring at the embers. Above them, the sky had shifted, the moons beginning to dip into the distance, indicating that daybreak was not far off. Nyx hadn't been able to sleep most of the night, a knot in her stomach.

She couldn't stop thinking about Amaya, Liam, and Ellie. She could only imagine how scared they must be and what they must think; she wondered if they thought that Rian and Zaida had abandoned them. It had taken them several days to track them down, and they'd been careful to hang back and out of sight while they tried to come up with a rescue plan. The thought made her wince to herself at how defeated they all felt, and she sighed again as she rolled back toward the fire.

"Go to sleep."

Nyx lifted her head then at the sound of Jet's English words, mildly surprised. He was lying on his back with his eyes closed, but it was clear that he wasn't asleep, and he didn't want their conversation to be understood by their companions. It made apprehension coil in her chest at what he might say.

"I'm not tired," she said softly, watching as his dark eyes flitted open. She glanced over at Rian and Zaida, seeing that neither appeared to stir from their sleep.

"Then at least be still," he snapped. "I'm tired of listening to you roll around and sigh."

Nyx frowned at him. "I can't help it," she said quietly, turning on her back and lying back down. "I feel terrible about all of this."

"We'll figure it out," Jet said easily. "We always do."

Nyx lifted her head then, surprised by his words. "I thought you didn't want to help?"

It was Jet's turn to sigh then. "We're already in this," he said. "Might as well." He sounded less than pleased.

Nyx rolled onto her stomach then, a teasing smirk pulling at her lips, but her words were silenced as a howl suddenly rolled across the open plains. She froze at the sound, the hair on her neck standing on end and a cold fear washing over her. That sound was too close. And it sounded like it came from an animal of substantial size. Her fear heightened when Jet sat up quickly.

"Crap," he said quietly.

"What?" Nyx breathed. She turned suddenly, realizing the dragons were awake and snarling, rousing Rian and Zaida from their sleep.

Rian was in a haze as he sat up, patting Raimi on the shoulder as if to soothe her. "Easy girl," he muttered sleepily. "Easy."

Again, a howl filled the early morning air, making Rian jump to his feet in an instant, reaching for his sword. Beside him, Raimi was baring her teeth, looking in the direction the calls had come from.

"There shouldn't be any wolves here," Rian said, glancing at Zaida as she notched an arrow in her bow.

"These aren't wolves," Jet said, having moved to his feet. He looked at Nyx. "Stay here with Zaida."

Nyx was on her feet as well, feeling Zaida behind her. "Where are you going?" she asked, fear in her voice.

Jet looked to Rian. "I don't think they're here for us,"

he said slowly. "I think they're here for the slavers."

Rian frowned then. He followed Jet silently up the hill where they were able to look down onto the camp. They both hunkered down into the grass, watching cautiously below.

3

Near the Itera-Patet Road, Calamo Mare, Ymber.
The thirty-sixth day of winter, the 851st year of the
reign of Queen Liana Estrella.
Tuesday, January 25, 2012.

AMAYA JUMPED NEXT TO ELLIE at the sound of a pained scream. She gasped sharply, and Liam shifted beside her. Before them, a massive shadow leapt from the surrounding tall grass, snatching one of the slavers into its mouth with a sickening crunch before disappearing again. The other men were on their feet, blades drawn, but they were no match as another beast materialized. It was a giant wolf, taller than Declan, and white in color, with a girl sitting on its shoulders.

"Get the ropes!" one of the men called, just as the girl swung from the wolf's back. She took a few easy steps, slicing into the man and dropping him to the ground.

Ellie was surprised when the girl turned toward them, and she realized she knew her. She was grinning as she swung her sword to sling the blood from it, sashaying as if she hadn't just killed a man in an easy stroke. She lifted the blade toward Amaya, and Ellie watched as Amaya squeezed her eyes shut, waiting to feel the bite of the blade, but instead, the ropes that bound her slipped away. Amaya pulled the gag from her mouth, rubbing her wrists as she looked up at their savior.

The girl inclined her head. "You should release your beasts." She turned to cut Liam free as well.

Liam gripped Amaya's hand as she reached to pull him to his feet, unable to tear his eyes from the girl. "Who are you?" he asked. They both turned sharply when another scream pierced the air, realizing that the shadow was a massive black wolf. The wolf's mouth engulfed the man's head to nearly his middle, tearing him in half, his blood dripping from the wolf's jowls.

Again, the girl smiled as if she weren't standing in the middle of a blood bath, letting her sword rest lazily against her shoulder. "There's time for that later," she said. "Free your dragons and get back to your clan."

Liam turned and ran toward Amaya, who was already at the wagon with a knife, cutting the dragons loose. The girl turned then, kneeling before Ellie.

"Hello, daughter of Willem Atturon," she said softly, gently pulling the gag from Ellie's mouth.

Ellie's eyes were wide. "Otsana," she breathed, relieved tears filling her eyes. "What are you doing here?"

Otsana used a small knife to cut the ropes around Ellie's wrists. "Looking for some fun, of course," she said teasingly. Behind her, the black wolf appeared, baring giant fangs.

Ellie watched as Otsana looked over her shoulder, as if she was listening. After a moment, she nodded. "Yes, Master," she said shortly. She turned to look to Ellie, grabbing her wrist. "Come."

Ellie was unsteady as Otsana pulled her up. She was surprised when the wolf lay on the ground and Otsana motioned for her to climb aboard. She was shaking as she did so, digging her fingers into the wolf's black hair.

"Hold on, Atturon girl!" Otsana called with a laugh.

Ellie gripped harder as the wolf launched forward into a gallop, carrying her away from the camp. She was surprised when she suddenly felt a spark of magic pulse through her hands.

"We will collect your friends and return to Regius Carmen," a wolfish voice growled suddenly, echoing inside her mind.

Ellie was surprised at the gravelly tone. He sounded like he was barely speaking words, but she could understand them as clearly as if they'd come from someone's mouth. This was the first time one of the great forest spirits—the *Silvanimas*—had spoken to her, despite this not being their first meeting. Years ago, when her mother was still alive, Ellie recalled the *Silvanimas* coming to Sorona to see her mother. Her mother was strong with the *Visus*, and they had come to ask her to scry for them. She and Bailey had spent an afternoon playing with Otsana, who was as young as they were at the time, having just come into the wolves' protection. Ellie never expected to see them again.

"Regius Carmen?" she whispered.

"Yes," the wolf answered. "Liana has sent us to retrieve all of you."

Ellie felt more relief fill her. "He has my sister," she said suddenly as the wolf slowed to a trot.

"I know," he said. "But even our power is finite."

Ellie felt her heart drop painfully.

"Ellie!"

Her head snapped up then, seeing that the sun was

finally cresting the horizon, illuminating a figure she recognized. As the wolf brought her closer, Ellie could see Rian's face more clearly. He was smiling broadly, but the dark circles under his eyes told her that he'd had just as difficult of a time as she and the others had.

A sudden, trumpeting call overhead made her eyes turn skyward to see Emma and Declan swoop toward where Ellie guessed Rian and the others were camped. He came closer as the wolf reached the top of the hill, catching her as she slid from the wolf's back. He hugged her tightly.

"I'm so glad you're all okay," Rian said, holding her out to look her over. "You're not hurt, are you?"

Ellie shook her head, glancing over his shoulder. Zaida was hugging Amaya tightly, the first real emotion Ellie had seen on her face. Nyx and Jet were standing beside the nearly dead fire as if they didn't quite know what to do. Nyx had a smile on her face as she looked over toward Ellie before her eyes turned to the massive black wolf next to her in surprise.

The wolf took a slow step toward the camp before suddenly becoming engulfed in mist. He disappeared into the cloud before reappearing, this time as an ebony-skinned man in black clothing. Ellie watched as his yellow eyes remained fixed on Nyx as he stepped closer. She was surprised when Jet suddenly stepped in front of Nyx, a scowl on his face.

"What the hell are you doing here?" Jet demanded. He could feel the *fax* twisting in his chest at the sight of the large black *Silvanima*, and he knew that was a bad sign. It remembered their trickery, too, and it yearned for revenge against them.

The man bowed then slightly, ignoring Jet, even though he could sense the *fax*'s anger. "Princess," he said, his voice deep and rumbling. "It is good to see you are well."

Nyx's brow was furrowed as she looked up at Jet. "Who are you?" she asked softly, a hint of fear in her voice. "Why did you save my friends?"

The man straightened, his yellow eyes piercing as they held her gaze. "I am called Dexter," he rumbled. "I and my mate have come on Liana's behalf to bring you home safely."

Jet sighed in disgust then, rolling his eyes and crossing his arms. "You've got to be kidding," he said sarcastically. "I had this under control."

Ellie, who still stood next to Dexter, jumped when another cloud of mist appeared behind her, a pale woman in a white gown materializing silently beside her. Otsana was just at her heel, her blade sheathed at her back.

Jet didn't like the way the white woman ignored him as she went straight to Nyx. She reached out her hand in a beckoning gesture, and Jet resisted the urge to slap it away. He watched worry creased Nyx's brow as she stared at the woman.

"This is my mate, Sinister," Dexter said then. He turned his eyes on the woman. "She speaks through touch."

Nyx stared down at her hand, feeling uncertain. She could feel the pulse of magic pulling against her, and it made her afraid of the woman. Whatever she was, she was powerful. She glanced at Jet, seeing that he looked like he'd sucked a lemon but didn't try to stop her. Slowly, she reached out her hand, feeling Sinister's cold skin against hers.

She gasped sharply as her vision swirled quickly, whisking her to another place far from here. Before her was a great hall, filled with tapestries and the fine décor of a palace. A throne stood at the front of the hall, and a woman was walking toward her. She realized the woman was speaking, but she couldn't hear the words she was saying.

Liana. The word came to her in a softly whispered voice, filling her with feelings of warmth and friendship.

Nyx took a moment to study Liana's face, realizing it was much like her own, save for deep violet eyes framed by lavender curls. Somehow, she knew that Liana had known Sinister and Dexter for a long time; their friendship stretched over centuries and Liana trusted them with her life. She heard more soft words.

We will bring you to her.

Nyx blinked then, feeling her mind come back to her body. Tears suddenly began to fill her eyes as she realized, for the first time, that Liana was truly waiting for her and wanted her home.

At the sight of her tears, Sinister offered a gentle smile, brushing one away. *Things will be all right, Princess. You are safe now.*

Nyx nodded at her silent words. She didn't think she could feel any more relieved or protected than she did in that moment.

*Near the Itera-Patet Road, Calamo Mare, Ymber.
The thirty-sixth day of winter, the 851st year of the
reign of Queen Liana Estrella.
Tuesday, January 25, 2012.*

A SMALL TOWN HAD FINALLY come into view on the horizon. Relief filled Raphael as he signaled Bartuk to descend toward the town, landing in the tall grass on the outskirts. He'd been traveling for days and he was exhausted, as was the cache of supplies Rais had given him. He slid slowly from Bartuk's back, his legs weak as he landed in the grass.

"Stay here," he commanded, looking from Bartuk to Ellena. Both dragons bowed their heads at his words, looking as if they would find a place to bed down for the evening.

Raphael pulled a satchel, filled with a few necessities, and a walking stick from the saddle before heading toward the town gate. A stark, white stone wall surrounded the settlement, protecting it from outside forces. Most likely rogue bands of the Caelin tribes. His body was horribly sore, and he was panting as he finally made it inside the wall, looking around. An inn caught his eyes, and he thanked the gods that he didn't have to walk any further.

He managed to wobble inside and collapse into a chair near the door, feeling as if he'd just run as hard as he could for days on end. It took a moment for him to catch his breath and he used the hem on his tunic to dab at sweat on his brow.

"Never have I seen a man so desperate for a drink," a woman's voice said, causing him to look up.

He tried to offer a smile as she set a large tankard in front of him, filled to the brim with ale. "Never has a barmaid misjudged a man's thirst," he countered as he reached for the tankard. He felt like he hadn't had anything to drink in days and he gulped down half the tankard before setting it back on the table.

The barmaid was still standing at the table, a hand perched on her hip. "What neck of the woods do you hail from, stranger?" she asked, looking him over.

Raphael drew a slow breath, wiping his mouth. "Sorona," he said, his eyes drifting down to the table.

The barmaid frowned then, looking down as well. "Ah," she said knowingly. "Word reached us not long after the disaster." Her brow furrowed. "Still doesn't seem to be any news of who or what razed it."

Raphael looked up at her. "What have you heard?" he asked cautiously.

She shrugged. "Some say it was a pack of Caelin warriors what had a grudge against Lord Atturon," she said. "Others claim it were hell-beasts, sent to punish the Atturons for their misdeeds."

Raphael wanted to snap at her that there were no misdeeds and that his father was an honorable man, but he caught himself. It wouldn't do to let anyone know who he was.

The barmaid leaned against the table, her eyes searching his face. "Seems like maybe you might know the truth, though," she said slowly.

Raphael shook his head slowly. "Unfortunately, I do not," he said. "I was not in Sorona during the attack." He looked up at her, seeing her eyes skirting over the thick scars that wound up his neck from under his clothing. "Mauled by a *rapere*," he said, drawing her gaze. "Nasty claws on those creatures."

The barmaid lifted her chin as if she accepted his story, but only just barely. She glanced down at his tankard. "Finish this and I'll bring you another, stranger," she said. She offered a grin that was only halfway light-hearted. "Your coin is as good here as anywhere else."

Raphael read her insinuation and reached into his satchel, producing a coin purse. "Thank you," he said as he fished out some coins to place in her hand.

The barmaid smiled a real smile then, turning to head back to the bar.

Raphael looked down at his drink then, feeling his heart racing in his chest. Word traveled fast, but no one knew the truth. He guessed that meant there were no survivors, and it made his heart ache. He would rest here for a short time, and then he would press on to find his sisters.

Ellie pressed her fingers against Sinister's soft fur, enjoying the feeling of the wind in her face. She glanced up to the dragons overhead, lifting a hand to block the sun. She then turned her eyes to Dexter and Otsana beside her. She was so glad she'd come across Liam that day in

Grassmire. Finally, she was on her way to Liana, and maybe to helping her sister.

Sinister began to slow to a trot as they neared the Itera-Patet Road. They had cut across the plains to save time and to avoid any other dangers on the road. But the daylight wouldn't last forever, and they needed to find somewhere to stay the night and eat something other than fruit and game animals.

Dexter stepped up beside his mate, looking at her. They paused for a long moment as if to talk to each other before Otsana looked over at Ellie. She raised her hand to signal to the dragon riders overhead, who landed around them.

"There is a small town just ahead," Otsana called. "A place called Kilcrest. There is an inn that we could stay the night."

Rian nodded before motioning for his Pangere to take flight. "Lead the way!" he called as Raimi launched into the air again.

Ellie held on as the wolves leaped forward, following the road but being careful to skirt it enough to stay hidden. They traveled until the sun was almost gone beyond the horizon before the lit gates of Kilcrest finally came into view.

They stopped on the outskirts and Ellie slid from Sinister's back, feeling wobbly on her legs. She looked over at Otsana as she did the same, stretching her arms over her head. The Pangere once more surrounded them, the riders sliding from their mounts as well. Rian pulled his helmet from his head and tucked it under his shoulder, stepping toward Ellie and Otsana as Nyx slid from Raimi's back as well.

"Is this it?" he asked, nodding toward the town gates.

Otsana nodded her head. "My masters and I will stay here, beyond the gates," she said.

Rian tilted his head. "Wouldn't you prefer to sleep in a bed tonight?" he asked.

"We prefer to stay away from people," she said. She looked over his shoulder at the others. "You should go on and eat and rest. We will be fine."

Rian shrugged lightly, looking to Raimi. "If you insist," he said. He pulled a bag from Raimi's back, slinging it over his shoulder. He leaned in to press his forehead against hers. She rumbled lightly as he pulled away.

Nyx watched Rian touch his forehead to Raimi's and she tilted her head slightly. "What are you doing?" she asked, drawing his attention.

"She can feel my thoughts," Rian said easily. "It's a perk of being bonded." He offered her a smile. "I was telling her to behave."

Nyx returned his grin, turning to look at the others as he looked over her shoulder. She saw Jet step away from Zayde, and she walked toward him.

"This is a bad idea," he said as she reached him.

Nyx sighed. "You say that about everything."

Jet looked down at her. "Have I been wrong yet?" he asked.

Nyx wanted to roll her eyes, but she caught herself. He hadn't been wrong, and it made nervousness sit in her chest. "The thought of sleeping in a bed sounds nice though, right?" she asked, looking at him before trotting after the Pangere, who were already walking toward the gate.

The frown didn't leave his lips as he trailed after her.

Kilcrest was much busier than he'd realized it would be as they passed inside the gate. Despite the encroaching darkness, the people were still milling about, especially around the inn near the gate. Jet watched as people paused in their conversations to look over the Pangere and he rolled his eyes. They stuck out like a sore thumb in their colors and armor.

The tavern was filled with people as they stepped through the door. Rian turned to Zaida and told her to find somewhere to sit as he walked toward the bar to secure them all rooms. Ellie was trailing behind Liam and Amaya, her eyes wide as she looked around, taking in all the people. It had been a long time since she'd been among common folk, and the ones that lived here were much different than those that she had known in Sorona.

The thought made her heart twist, and she turned away from the people around her to look for Zaida. Her eyes were skipping over the people at the table, but she suddenly paused, feeling the color drain from her face and a wave of dizziness sweep her.

"Raphael?" she breathed.

She pushed past Jet, unable to hear his protest as she pushed more people out of the way. She thought she'd seen him, but she had to be sure. Her heart was beating double-time as she craned her neck, trying to look through the crowd. Finally, she came to an opening, and tears instantly filled her eyes.

There he was, sitting at a table alone. He was tapping his fingers on the side of a large beer mug, his eyes distant as he looked in the opposite direction. She noticed how long his hair had grown and how tired his eyes looked. She also noticed the thick scar traveling up his neck.

"Raphael!" she yelled, causing the young man's head to snap up.

His eyes were wide as he jumped to his feet, hobbling

around the table to catch her as she threw her arms around him. He pressed his hand into her hair, holding her tightly. "Ellie," he breathed, his voice hitching slightly.

"I thought you were dead," Ellie managed, sobbing softly against his chest.

Raphael stepped back, pressing his hands against her face and looking her over, his brow furrowed with concern. "I'm okay," he said. "What about you? Are you all right?"

Ellie nodded quickly, tears streaming down her face. She threw her arms around him again, dissolving into more tears. "I missed you so much." She stepped back to look him over. "I can't believe you're here. I didn't think I'd ever see you again." Her eyes shifted to the scars on his neck.

He offered a small smile. "I wouldn't leave you and Bailey," he said gently.

"Ellie? What's going on?" Rian asked as he suddenly appeared through the throng, his eyes concerned.

Ellie was smiling as she motioned for him and the others to join them. "This is my brother," she said. She looked up at him. "Raphael, these are the people who rescued me."

The Village of Kilcrest, Calamo Mare, Ymber.
The thirty-sixth day of winter, the 851st year of the
reign of Queen Liana Estrella.
Tuesday, January 25, 2012.

Nyx watched as the Pangere pulled up chairs and sat at the table with Ellie and Raphael. She was happy that Ellie had found her family, but seeing them and the Pangere together made her heart ache. She hadn't found her family yet, and despite Sinister's vision, she wasn't sure if she really had any family. At least, not the way the Pangere and Ellie and her siblings were family.

She glanced at Jet over her shoulder. He seemed to read her expression as he tilted his head, motioning for her to go with him. She followed Jet to the bar, listening as he asked for two glasses and a bottle of something. She watched curiously as the bartender handed him the bottle and glasses, and Jet slid the man some coins. He was smirking lightly when he turned back to her.

"What is that?" she asked.

"This," he said, his smirk widening, "is real alcohol."

Nyx gave him a dubious look. "I thought you said coming here was a bad idea," she said slowly. He looked too happy suddenly. "And now you want to drink?"

"It is a bad idea," he said easily. "But it looked like you could use a pick-me-up."

Nyx felt the sting of his words. She wished she wasn't so transparent, but she was also grateful in a way.

"Besides," he said, shrugging, "*Vocatus* is definitely something anyone visiting Gexalatia should try."

"I dunno," Nyx said slowly, her arms crossed.

"Fine," Jet said, stepping past her toward a table that had opened up underneath a staircase that led to the rooms above them. He set the glasses down and slid into a chair, pulling the cork from the bottle. "But you're missing out."

He poured one glass as Nyx stepped closer, sliding into a chair beside him. She moved a bit closer to inspect the brown liquid. She sat back a bit when he slid the glass toward her, and she shot him a look.

"Is this going to make me regret my life decisions tomorrow?" she asked as her fingers wrapped around the glass.

Jet shrugged as he poured the second glass. "Might," he said easily.

Nyx scowled at him, feeling baited. She lifted the small glass to her nose, taking a whiff and nearly gagging from the strong smell.

"You're not supposed to smell it," Jet chided. "Just drink it."

"Does it taste as bad as it smells?" Nyx asked, her face wrinkled as she held the glass away from her.

"It's Gexalatian whisky," he said. "It's way better than the crap you call whisky on Earth." He smirked again. "This is what alcohol should really taste like."

"I feel like I shouldn't trust you on this," she said, eying him.

He offered her a smirk. "Have I ever steered you wrong?" he asked sweetly.

Nyx swallowed thickly, lifting the glass toward her lips again. She winced as she got another whiff of it. "Oh god," she said, fighting down a gag.

"Stop smelling it," Jet reprimanded again, lifting his glass to toast.

Nyx looked at him, a grimace stuck on her face. "What are we toasting to then?"

Jet's smirk widened. "To your first taste of *Vocatus*." He held the glass out to her.

Nyx felt sick as she touched her glass to his before pinching her nose to block out the smell and throwing it back. It took a moment for the taste to hit her, and she gasped, shaking her head as she set the glass down. "Agghh," she gagged, trying to wipe the taste away with her hand. She could feel it burning as it slid down her throat. "That's horrible."

Jet was watching her carefully, his own empty glass poised just above the table. "Let me know when you feel it," he said. "The first taste always hits lightweights like you the hardest."

Nyx scowled at him. "Whatever," she mumbled. She turned her head to look away, the room suddenly tipping. She threw her hands out to brace herself against the table.

Jet's smirk never wavered. "Told you."

Nyx shook her head lightly, as if trying to clear it away. "What the hell proof is that stuff?" she asked.

Jet shrugged. "Dunno," he said as he refilled her glass. "Better than the flavored water you drink on Earth, though."

Nyx shot him a look as she watched him refill his own glass. "I'm not drinking anymore of that," she said, shaking her head. The tipsy feeling was worse when she moved. She wondered how one shot could make her feel this way so quickly. She also wondered if it hit Jet the same way it hit her. In all their time together, she'd only seen him drink a handful of times, so she couldn't possibly be the only lightweight.

Jet crossed his arms on the table. "It can't have been that bad," he teased.

Nyx scowled at him. "It's horrible," she said. "I don't know how you can drink it."

"You're being dramatic," he said then, rolling his eyes. He downed the glass in front of him, setting it down with a *thunk*.

Nyx looked back down at the drink in front of her, her thoughts wandering as the first drink filled her with warmth. "Hey, can I ask you something?"

Jet turned to look at her, still leaning on the table. "Depends," he said, his voice lacking its usual bite. It occurred to Nyx then that maybe he was just as affected by the *Vocatus* as she was. And if that was the case, then who was he calling a lightweight?

"On?" she asked sarcastically.

"If it's a question I'll like or not," he said.

She looked back down at her glass then, feeling like she needed to drink it just to fortify herself to ask him her question. "It's about Sinister and Dexter," she said slowly. She glanced up at him, holding her breath. The last thing she wanted was to get her head bit off.

Jet made a displeased sound and poured another drink. "I didn't think I'd like it," he said.

Nyx frowned at him. "I haven't even asked it yet," she

said quickly.

He picked up his glass, looking over at her. "I'll make you a deal," he said, surprising Nyx. His eyes shifted to the drink in front of her and back to her face, his infuriating smirk returning to his lips. "For every shot you drink, I'll answer a question."

Nyx's frown dissolved into a scowl, but she wanted answers. If it meant one night of drinking, she thought it would be worth it. "Fine," she said. She snatched the glass off the table and downed it quickly, slamming it back onto the wood with a grimace. Once her throat stopped burning, she looked at him, seeing the humored look on his face. "What are they?"

Jet's eyes shifted toward the wall behind her. "They're called *Silvanimas*. Protector entities of some kind," he said thoughtfully. "They're ancient forest spirits." He looked back at her. "Probably born around the time the Priorae disappeared to correct the imbalance."

Nyx tilted her head. "Imbalance?" she asked.

Jet downed his own drink then, pressing the back of his hand to his mouth. "Of magic," he clarified, grimacing as if the alcohol burned. "There is always balance. No side can be stronger than the other." He looked over at her. "It's like two sides of a coin."

"Huh," Nyx said, looking down at her empty glass. "You seemed like you didn't like them."

Jet's eyes narrowed playfully. "Is that a question?" he asked.

Nyx scowled at him. "That was a statement," she snapped. She noticed the way he arched a brow at her when she grabbed the bottle and poured herself a drink. "But I do have another question." She threw the shot back, wanting to puke. It took longer for her to compose herself than the first two, and her voice was haggard when she spoke again, her cheeks feeling flushed. "What did they do to you?"

Jet's lips pressed into a thin line and his eyes darkened. He looked away, silent for a long moment. Nyx was starting to think she'd asked the wrong question, but then he ran his hand through his hair and looked back at her.

"Liana used them to trap me," he said finally.

Nyx was surprised, both that he answered and that he told her something she didn't know. "Trap you?" she asked carefully.

Jet pushed his glass toward her and she tilted the bottle to refill it. Once it was full, he picked it up, pausing with it halfway to his lips. "I'm not a good person, Nyx," he said softly before downing the shot.

"I don't believe that," Nyx said quickly, watching him. She was starting to feel like she'd been sitting next to a warm fire for too long, and her vision was getting crooked. She knew that the *Vocatus* was doing a number on her, but she had so many questions. "You've help me."

Jet leaned on the table and looked at her. "I have to," he said quietly. "I wasn't given a choice." There was something like regret on his face.

Nyx felt confusion fill her, and the drunkenness that was setting in wasn't helping. "You said Liana sent you," she said. She could feel her heart drop into her stomach.

Jet nodded. "She did."

"So how did you not have a choice?" she asked, a sinking feeling filling her. She felt like she was on the cusp of learning something that she didn't want to ever know, and it scared her. The fear was worse when Jet's eyes shifted down to her hands.

"Nyx," he said slowly, reaching for her hand. "There's so much you don't know." His brow furrowed. "If you did, you'd never see me the same way again."

"I don't believe that," she said again, her voice stronger than she felt. She gripped his hand tighter, leaning in toward him. "I know you." His eyes shifted to meet hers, mild surprise on his face. "You're not a bad person."

The corner of his lip quirked slightly. "That's something I've always liked about you," he said. "You see the best in everyone."

Nyx felt her cheeks flush suddenly. Butterflies were filling her stomach at the way he was looking at her, as if she was the only person in the room. She realized that his hand was warm as he tilted her hand up to entwine his fingers with hers. Her eyes went to his lips. "I thought you couldn't stand me," she said, her voice smaller and huskier than she intended.

His little smile grew a bit. "I don't mind being around you," he admitted.

Nyx felt her heart jump hard. "You're just drunk," she whispered, her eyes searching his. His normally sharp gaze was dulled, making it easier to read the feelings he usually hid from her.

"Maybe," he said absently.

Nyx's breath caught in her chest when he suddenly hooked a finger under her chin, tilting her head just a bit and brushing his thumb across her bottom lip. Her mind went blank, her breathing ragged as she stared at him. Her face felt like it was on fire as she looked up into his dark eyes.

"What are you doing?" she managed.

His eyes were fixed on her lips. He was so close that Nyx could feel the soft gust of his breath, the smell of the Vocatus heavy on it. He seemed like he would close the distance between them, but then his brow furrowed and he blinked quickly.

Nyx knew she shouldn't have been, but she was crushed when he suddenly sat back and let go of her hand. He looked almost panicked for a moment and he stood quickly.

"This can't happen," he said, his voice accusing as a scowl pulled at his face.

Nyx stood too, realizing her knees were shaking. She wasn't sure if it was the drink or all of the emotions suddenly assaulting her. "Jet, wait—"

"I can't be around you right now," he said quickly, turning and walking away from her.

Nyx stared after him, feeling tears welling in her eyes. The rejection she felt in that moment made the loneliness she'd felt before feel like nothing.

Zaida had just happened to look up and see Jet storm out of the inn. She'd felt her heart sink at the look on his face, and she'd excused herself to go look for Nyx. She'd found her at the table on the other side of the room, crying softly as she threw back a shot from a bottle in front of her.

"Nyx?" she asked, catching the blonde girl's attention.

Nyx looked up at her, startled, tears still running down her face. "Uh, Zaida," she said as she brushed at her face quickly. She looked up at the taller girl. "Why aren't you with the others?"

Zaida crossed her arms. "I could ask you the same," she said, disapproval on her face. Her eyes shifted down to the bottle, her frown deepening. "How much have you had to drink?"

Nyx shrugged, still sniffling. "I dunno," she said, looking at the bottle. "Why?"

Zaida sighed and slid into the chair next to Nyx, where

an empty glass was sitting on the table. She poured some of the drink into the glass and threw the shot back, feeling the *Vocatus* travel down her throat. "I saw Jet," she said slowly.

Nyx shook her head. "I just don't understand what I did wrong," she whispered, hurt in her voice. More tears filled her eyes.

Zaida rolled the glass around in her fingers. "What happened?" she asked.

Nyx shrugged as her voice became choked. "I don't know," she said. "One minute we were talking and then …" Her lip trembled as she tried to hold back more tears. "What's wrong with me, Zaida? He always pushes me away. Is it me?"

Zaida pursed her lips and poured another shot. She was terrible at conversations like these. "Jet seems … complicated," she said, measuring her words. She looked at Nyx. Complicated was not the word she really wanted to use, but she didn't think Nyx wanted to hear her assessment of Jet.

"What do you mean?" Nyx asked as she wiped at her face again.

Zaida downed her drink and turned to face Nyx. "We have a saying in my country," she said. "*Milplagis morte –* death by a thousand cuts." She watched the way Nyx's brow furrowed, as if she understood. "It seems to me that chasing him is exactly that."

Nyx looked down at her hands on the table. "But he gives me such mixed signals," she whispered. "Sometimes he likes me and I can tell, and other times …" She sighed deeply and forlornly.

Zaida reached out and caught her friend's hand, offering a small, comforting smile despite wanting this conversation to be over. "You have so much to look forward to," she said.

"You're going to meet your grandmother, you're going to meet more of your family, and make new friends, and be surrounded by people who care about you and aren't afraid to show it." She searched Nyx's gaze. "Things are going to be so much better for you. I truly believe that."

Nyx felt her heart twist in her chest. She knew Zaida was right, but it didn't make the pain abate. "You're right," she said softly. "I just need to focus on what's ahead."

Zaida offered a smile. "That's the spirit," she said. She picked up the bottle of *Vocatus* and pulled Nyx up as she stood. "Now come on."

Nyx didn't fight her as Zaida led her to the table where the Pangere and the Atturon siblings were sitting, drinking as they talked and laughed.

The Village of Kilcrest, Calamo Mare, Ymber.
The thirty-seventh day of winter, the 851st year of the
reign of Queen Liana Estrella.
Wednesday, January 26, 2012.

Jᴇᴛ's sᴛᴏᴍᴀᴄʜ ᴡᴀs ɪɴ ᴋɴᴏᴛs as he walked through the gates of Kilcrest, heading back into the vast, empty expanse of the Calamo Mare. He made an intentional detour away from where the dragons and the wolves were bedding down for the night. The moons were drifting high into the sky signaling that it was past midnight, and he could see easily with their light. The tall grass brushed at the hem of his shirt, but he didn't notice, his mind foggy.

Worthless, a voice growled softly in his thoughts.

He gritted his teeth. He didn't like the way *Vocatus* lowered his ability to ignore the *fax* that curled in his chest.

So much power. Ours for the taking.

Jet shook his head against the voice, trying to ignore it. Since he and Nyx had crossed the Limen back into Gexalatia, he'd been careful to keep the *fax* subdued with blood meals, hunting when Nyx was busy or asleep, but it had been a while since he'd hunted, and the drinking hadn't helped. He knew it was sloppy, but something about the way sadness had streaked across Nyx's face when she watched Ellie reunite with her brother made him think that sharing a drink with her wouldn't be such a bad idea. That is, until he let his emotions get the best of him.

He'd let the drink and the thought of her lips get into his head. The only thing that had stopped him was the way the *fax* had come alive when he'd leaned in toward her. It could feel the power flowing through her veins, and it wanted it. The thought that he could lose control in such an innocuous moment scared him, and he knew he needed to feed the monster. It was the only way to make the drunk feeling go away and to make the beast shut up.

He didn't have to go very far before he startled a small, ground-dwelling creature from the brush. It leapt into the grass, trying to make a run for a tunnel entrance, but Jet lunged for it, catching it easily. It squealed as he dug clawed fingers into its flesh to stop it from wriggling free. The *fax* twisted and surged inside of him, making fangs press against his lips, which he dug into the creature's neck. It didn't struggle for very long as he sucked the life from it.

Once the bloodlust faded, he dropped the creature on the ground, coughing against the metallic taste of its blood. He drew a steadying breath as he kneeled in the grass, pressing his hand against his forehead. The *fax*'s whispering was diminishing as the blood satisfied it, and the drunk, lightheaded feeling was easing. He looked down at his arms, pushing the sleeves of his coat up. The binding runes that sealed the *fax* were slight across his forearms, but they were fading quickly. He normally could have waited a bit longer, but his stupidity had complicated things.

Jet let a sigh escape him as he looked over his shoulder

back toward the walls of Kilcrest. He couldn't let his guard down again. Not until Nyx was safe with Liana.

Nyx held onto Amaya's arm as she helped her up the stairs and toward a room. She could feel her thoughts fading in and out as Amaya let her slide onto a cot. She knew Amaya was saying something, but she couldn't hear it as she pressed her face into the cold fabric of a pillow.

"Someone should sit with her," Zaida said, her voice sounding far away.

Nyx felt the cot dip beside her, and she turned her head to see three of Amaya's pink ponytail. "I'll stay with her," she said quietly. "I don't mind." She turned to look over her shoulder at Nyx.

Zaida made a soft noise and walked toward the door. "I'll bring some water."

Amaya nodded before looking down at Nyx and brushing her hair away from her face.

"Zoorrry I ruined your night," Nyx slurred.

Amaya smiled kindly. "You don't have to apologize," she said. "Zaida told me you were having a rough night."

Nyx groaned and pressed her hand against her eyes. "Don't tell the others," she murmured, her voice heavy suddenly.

Amaya made a gesture with her hand against her lips, as if locking them with a key. "I won't say a word."

Nyx grinned before pressing her face into the pillow again. She was still for a long moment and her breathing was slow and even, leading Amaya to think she was asleep. She stood and grabbed a blanket from a different cot before sliding to sit next to where Nyx slept. She pulled her satchel from around her shoulders and took a notebook from it, along with a quill and a small jar of ink. She began to write slowly in her journal, only pausing when the door to the room opened.

Zaida held a pitcher and a glass in her hand. "Water for when she wakes," she said.

Amaya nodded as she watched her cousin set them on a nearby table. "She asked me not to tell the others what you told me," she said.

Zaida didn't react much as she looked at Amaya. "That's fine," she said, moving to close the door. She then crossed over to sit next to Amaya.

"You don't have to stay with me, you know," Amaya said.

Zaida sighed deeply and looked at her. "I know," she said. Her brow furrowed in an uncharacteristic way. "I was really afraid we'd lose you."

Amaya's face softened and she reached out to hold her cousin's hand. "I'm okay now," she said gently.

Zaida patted her hand and nodded. "I know," she said. "But if the wolves hadn't come along, I'm not sure we could have saved you and the others."

"I've definitely thought the same thing," she whispered. She felt a coldness settle into her chest. She'd known that the men who had captured them were experts at what they did. If anything, she'd been more afraid that Rian and Zaida would come for them and be captured as well. "It was a close call."

Zaida turned to face her. "Promise me, no matter what, we won't split up anymore," she said, her voice soft but vehement. "We are strongest together."

Amaya nodded. "Promise."

Zaida relaxed then, the worry in her eyes easing. She leaned against the side of Nyx's cot. They were silent for a moment, but they both turned when Nyx shifted on her cot, whimpering slightly.

"No," she breathed, her brow wrinkled. "Stop." She was clearly distressed, continuing to mumble incoherently.

Amaya glanced over at Zaida. "I often wonder what she's seen," she whispered in their native Loquelan.

Zaida nodded her agreement. "Whatever it is, it's left scars in her mind," she said. Her nose wrinkled with disgust. "Being with *him* certainly doesn't help."

Amaya hummed her agreement. "Who is he anyway?" she asked quietly.

"A defector from Siccita," Zaida said, shrugging lightly.

Amaya grimaced. "I'm sure Rian was unhappy when he found that out."

Zaida nodded absently. "He was ready for a fight, that's for sure," she said. "But she defended him from Rian, saying that she trusted him with her life." She glanced at the sleeping girl again, shaking her head slowly. "I want to be critical of her, but I suppose it's because I understand how she feels."

"Rian is nothing like that," Amaya said quickly, her voice slightly offended. "Rian actually cares about all of us."

Zaida was still frowning, lost in her thoughts. "Does he?" she asked, a slight bitterness in her voice. "It seems to me that he's too busy chasing his dream, consequences be damned."

"Don't say that!" Amaya whispered sharply. "How can you, of all people, speak of him that way?"

Zaida scowled at her cousin. "Because I know him best," she hissed. "I cautioned him against this multiple times, but he'd rather believe in a supposed vision than see what's happening to us." She shook her head. "Ever since we left home, he's been acting like everything we've done is part of Eomryr Lani's plan. But I don't think it is."

Amaya leaned forward. "I think you're wrong," she whispered, trying to make her cousin believe her words. "I think you're afraid of what you don't understand."

Zaida rolled her eyes. "I think you're trying to pin things on me that aren't true," she snapped, moving to her feet.

"Where are you going?" Amaya asked, trying to keep her voice low so as not to wake Nyx.

"To check on the others," Zaida snapped over her shoulder.

She stormed from the room, closing the door quietly behind her. She wanted to be angry with Amaya, but the truth was that she was rattled; what if Amaya was right? What if she couldn't have faith in their leader because of her own fears?

Zaida shook her head to clear the thoughts away and trudged down the hall to the stairs. She paused on the top step to look down into the pub, seeing that most of the patrons had gone home for the night. Her eyes skirted over a few remaining customers, who were well past drunk, before landing on the table where Rian, Liam, Ellie, and Raphael sat. She felt her hand grip the banister tighter as they all laughed, their cheeks rosy from their drinking and their happiness.

Zaida felt her heart skip a beat when, as if sensing her lingering gaze, Rian turned his eyes on her. He offered a smile, and she turned her eyes to the wooden steps as she walked down them. She tried to forget the conversation that she'd just had with Amaya as she reached the pub level and walked toward their table.

"How's Nyx?" Ellie asked. Her voice was soft, as if she was feeling the weariness plaguing them all.

Zaida eased to sit in a chair. "She's sleeping," she said bluntly. "Amaya is watching her."

Ellie nodded. "That's good," she said. "She seemed upset when you first brought her over."

Zaida shrugged. "She didn't tell me what was bothering her," she lied easily. "And I didn't want to pry."

"So, is she really the lost princess?" Raphael asked quietly then, drawing her gaze.

"If everything we've been through is any indication, then the answer is yes," Rian said, his voice equally as quiet. He was looking pensively at his tankard.

"Huh," Raphael said, leaning back in his chair. He looked toward his sister. "She's not what I would have imagined."

Ellie shook her head, a slight smile on her face. "What do you mean?" she asked.

"I mean, she seems so …" He shrugged, looking for the right word.

"Normal?" Liam suggested suddenly.

Raphael caught his eye and nodded. "Yeah," he said slowly. "Normal."

Zaida glanced across the table at Rian, catching his gaze. She could tell from the humored glint in his eyes that he hadn't bothered to share his heritage with Raphael and Ellie yet.

"What did you think royalty would be like?" he asked then, taking a drink.

Raphael shrugged. "I dunno," he said thoughtfully. "Not like her. She seems too kind and too trusting." He glanced at Ellie. "Other nobles I've met have been a bit conceited and cold." He watched as she nodded in agreement. It seemed like he might say more, but then he winced, leaning forward into the table.

"Raphael," Ellie gasped, catching his shoulder. "Are you alright?"

He nodded, pain pulsing through his body. "I just need to rest," he said. He felt like all his strength had left him and it made soreness pulse through his entire body.

"We should all probably get some sleep," Rian said then, standing slowly. "Tomorrow will be a long day of traveling."

The Village of Kilcrest, Calamo Mare, Ymber.
The thirty-seventh day of winter, the 851st year of the
reign of Queen Liana Estrella.
Wednesday, January 26, 2012.

THE MORNING SUN FELT RIDICULOUSLY bright as Amaya pulled a window shade open. Nyx pressed her face into her pillow, trying to hide from it. She could feel how dry her mouth was as she licked her lips, and her head was pulsing painfully with each beat of her heart.

"Rise and shine," Amaya said happily, bounding toward Nyx with too much energy.

Nyx groaned. "I really can't," she managed, even her throat feeling hungover. "I just need to lay here."

"No can do," Amaya said, that same cheerful tone in her voice and a smile on her face. "But I brought you something that should help."

Nyx blinked up at her, seeing that she was holding a cup out to her. "What is it?" she asked hoarsely.

"A special concoction the barmaid said would perk you right up," she said.

Nyx sat up slowly and painfully, groaning. She rubbed her face with her hands before taking the glass from Amaya. She tilted it to look into it, seeing that it was a bright orange, but it smelled less than pleasant.

"Go on," Amaya said, crossing her arms. "Drink it all up."

Nyx didn't have the energy to fight her, so she pressed the cup to her lips and took a big swallow of the orange liquid. It was thick in her throat and made her want to puke, but she swallowed it down until the cup was empty. Once it was gone, she held the cup out to Amaya, pressing the back of her hand over her mouth as if to keep it inside her stomach.

"See?" Amaya said. "That wasn't so bad."

Nyx nodded to appease her, wishing she could just crumble back onto the cot.

"Now, get ready," Amaya continued, walking toward the door. "We'll be ready to go soon."

Nyx watched her go before looking around the room. She didn't remember how she got here. In fact, she didn't remember a lot of the previous night, and the part she did remember, she wished she could forget. She felt her heart ache as she looked over the other cots in the room, where Amaya and Zaida had clearly slept. She was dreading the rest of the day, but she splashed some water on her face before making her way downstairs.

Her footsteps were slow as she walked down the steps, looking down into the pub. She could see that the tables were already filling up with overnight guests looking for breakfast. She turned her eyes on the table in the corner everyone had gathered around the night before, and she felt her heart jump into her throat. They were all laughing and eating some sort of bread, their packed bags sitting on the floor around the table. Thankfully, Jet was not with them.

"Good morning, Nyx," Amaya called when she looked up.

Nyx felt her cheeks turn red as she walked closer to the table, seeing the slight grins and questioning looks on the others' faces.

"Sleep well?" Liam teased.

Nyx slid into a chair beside Zaida. "Yep," she said flatly. "Feel like I've been run over."

A titter went around the group as Zaida offered her some breakfast. Despite not being very hungry, she knew she couldn't turn down a meal and she forced herself to eat a bit. Her stomach roiled with every bite, but she tried to ignore it. She listened as the others spoke easily with each other, wondering where Jet had slunk off to. If she had to guess, he'd probably retreated somewhere to be alone and she didn't expect him to turn up until they met up with Otsana and the wolves.

In fact, she hoped that she didn't have to see him until then.

After the food was gone and the bill paid, they all moved to their feet and headed toward the door. Nyx was slow to her feet, looking up right as Raphael tried to stand. She was surprised to notice, for the first time, thick scars across his neck and down the parts of his arms that were bare. He moved like an old, arthritic man, leaning heavily on a cane.

He started to reach for a bag, but Ellie snatched it up quickly. "Let me carry this," she said, worry in her voice. "Are you sure you'll be alright?"

Raphael nodded, trying to smile despite the discomfort he felt with every step. "I'm fine, Ellie," he said placatingly.

Ellie leveled a look at him. "You're not fine," she said tersely. Her blue eyes were worried as she looked him over. "You're lucky to be alive."

Raphael sighed at her concern. "I can at least walk on my own," he said shortly. His steps were cumbersome as he walked slowly toward the door.

"You guys need some help?" Rian called then, paused in the doorway.

"You go on ahead," Raphael said, an easy smile pulling at his face.

Ellie's brow furrowed as if she would argue, but Nyx stepped up to her and put her hand on her arm. "I'll walk with you," she said quickly. She offered Raphael a small smile. "I don't think I'll be going anywhere quickly either."

Rian seemed satisfied and he nodded. "We'll see you there, then."

Nyx watched him disappear out the door after his group before looking over at Ellie and her brother. "I don't think we've been properly introduced," she said then, catching Raphael's eye. "I'm Nyx."

Raphael offered her a grin as he hobbled to the door. "Yeah, you were pretty far gone," he said, humor in his voice. "Raphael, Ellie's brother."

Nyx smiled a bit. "Nice to properly meet you," she said. She held the door as they made their way into the sunlight. She could feel awkwardness descending on them. "So, are you older or younger?" She glanced at Ellie. "I'm guessing older."

Raphael laughed lightly. "You'd be right," he said, finding a good hobbling pace with his cane. "What gave it away?"

Nyx returned his grin. "There's just something about how older brothers are with their younger siblings," she said, shrugging. "Especially sisters."

"You mean that overprotect vibe," Ellie deadpanned then.

Nyx giggled. "Yeah, that one."

Ellie and Raphael exchanged annoyed glances at each other before they each chuckled in return.

"What about you, Nyx?" Raphael asked then. "Any siblings?"

Nyx frowned lightly and looked down at the dirt path they were walking on. "I … I'm not sure," she said softly, the idea foreign to her.

Ellie and Raphael exchanged a look. "Sorry, I didn't mean to pry or anything," Raphael said quickly.

"Oh, no, please don't apologize," Nyx said quickly. She tried to put on a brave smile. "I just really don't know much about my family." She shrugged lightly. "I wasn't exactly told a lot about them by my aunt." She glanced from Ellie to Raphael. "I'm assuming they told you—" She glanced around nervously, "Well, you know." The last thing she wanted was for someone who shouldn't know to overhear them.

Raphael nodded. "It's hard to believe," he said pensively.

Nyx let a dry laugh escape her lips. "It's hard for me to believe, too," she said. She looked up as the gate loomed overhead. She vaguely wondered what the gates of Regius Carmen looked like.

They walked on in silence for a short while. Nyx could feel her heart in her throat at the thought that she would have to face Jet soon. She didn't know what she would say or do, or how she was supposed to feel. She was lost in her own thoughts, surprised when a shadow suddenly formed over them.

Ellie gasped, causing her to look up in time to see a

massive silver dragon circling overhead. "Bartuk!" she yelled.

The dragon trumpeted a call to her, swooping to land heavily in the grass. He lumbered toward her, nearly knocking her over as she caught his massive head in her arms.

"I'm so glad to see you," Ellie said, hugging his face tightly. Tears were forming in her eyes and the dragon made a sound that Nyx could only compare to a cross between a growl and a whimper.

Nyx was further surprised when another dragon appeared beside the first one, approaching Ellie with a similar reaction. She unconsciously took a step back as the beasts crowded around their masters, blowing hot breath across their faces and making happy noises. They were moving around like excited puppies, but in reality, they were much bigger than even the Pangere's dragons.

"It's okay, Nyx," Ellie said suddenly, drawing her gaze. "They won't hurt you." She held out her hand for Nyx, motioning her closer. "This is Bartuk and his mate, Ellena."

Nyx took a tentative step forward, feeling a tinge of fear in her chest. They were so big, they could have snapped any of them up in a single, bone-crushing bite. She locked eyes with Bartuk, watching as he lowered his head in a submissive gesture.

"Hello," she said softly, bowing her head slightly. "You're a big boy."

Ellie laughed softly, running her hands over their scales. "Do you—"

A sudden call cut off her words, and the dragons' heads snapped toward it. They each began to bare their teeth, curling around Nyx, Ellie, and Raphael. Rumbling growls were forming in their chests, which were puffing with each breath. Nyx turned to see what had startled them, unsurprised to see the Pangere and the wolves.

"Wow!" Rian exclaimed suddenly. He motioned for the others to hang back and took a step toward them. "I've never seen dragons from the north before." His eyes were lit with wonder. "They're beautiful."

Ellie patted Bartuk's shoulder, causing him to ease his stance, which in turn caused Ellena's body to relax. "Thank you," she said, letting her hand rest on Bartuk's nose. "This is Bartuk and Ellena."

Rian walked closer, his eyes still wide with amazement. "They must be quite old, to be such a size," he said, pausing a short distance away. Despite his excitement, he knew better than to approach the dragons too quickly.

Nyx only heard part of Raphael's words as she looked over the group, catching sight of Jet. She felt her heart twist hard, making her feel dizzy. She wished she could sink into the ground and disappear. The feeling was worse when he crossed his arms and avoided her gaze.

"Admire the beasts later!" Otsana suddenly called, breaking Rian's trance. "We need to move while there is still light."

Rian nodded his agreement before retreating back to Raimi and the others. Nyx started to follow him, when Ellie caught her arm.

"You can ride with us," she said quickly. She motioned to Bartuk. "It might be more comfortable and give Raimi time to rest."

Nyx didn't have to consider her words long before she nodded. Any chance to stay far away from Jet was a no-brainer. She clambered onto Bartuk's back behind Ellie, holding on as the massive dragon launched into the air. Beneath them, Raphael and the Pangere climbed aboard their mounts, while Otsana and the wolves trotted down the road. Nyx kept her eyes on the horizon, fighting the urge to look at Jet.

Celo Cavus, the capitol city of Siccita.
The thirty-nineth day of winter, the 906th year of the
reign of King Paraximus Lamia.
Friday, January 28, 2012.

BAILEY'S VISION WAS BLURRY AS she kneeled on a cushion. She felt weak and dizzy, despite the plates of food set out on the table in front of her. A twinge of pain made her lift a hand to her neck, shackles heavy around her wrists. She could feel bite marks on her skin and it made her feel sick.

"Eat, girl," a stern voice commanded.

Bailey blinked against her swirling vision, shaking her head slowly. She didn't think her stomach would hold food, and she felt too weak to try to reach for anything. She couldn't resist when a hand caught her chin and the rim of a cup was pressed to her lips. Warm broth flooded her mouth and she drank it greedily, despite the way her stomach churned. She wanted to shove it away, but her body needed it, sucking it up like water in a sponge.

Once the cup was empty, Bailey pushed the hands off

her. She felt a bit of strength return to her as she braced her hands on the table and looked up slowly. She could see the figure of a tall man standing over her, flanked by two guards in red. She wanted to hiss angry words at him, but she didn't have the strength.

"She's going to kill me," she breathed, the words feeling heavy in her chest. At his silence, she looked up at him, catching his hard stare. "Are you going to let her kill me?"

King Paraximus sneered darkly then. "What use are you to me?" he asked. "In exchange for your blood, Daya has gifted me with immeasurable strength." He lifted a hand, which crackled with energy that he seemed to channel effortlessly.

Bailey bowed her head then. "So why are you keeping me alive?" she managed. "Why not let your Dark Mistress finish me?"

Paraximus's sneer shifted to a grin. "You still have one thing useful to us," he said, lowering himself slowly so that he was at eye-level with her. There was a cruelty in his eyes that made Bailey's heart stutter. "Your connection with your sister."

Bailey wished for death right then and there, more than she had at any other time while she'd been his captive. Despite her best efforts to starve herself, King Paraximus kept her alive by force-feeding her. In between those times, he allowed Daya to feast on her blood, sucking the life from her faster than food or rest could replenish it. It was hell, being caught in this near-death state. But the worst pain was knowing that he could make Ellie suffer, too; the worst pain was knowing that no matter where she went or what she did, Paraximus would always be able to find her.

Bailey bowed her head, feeling despair crushing her. Desperation was heavy in her heart, and she turned her head slightly, seeing the handle of a dagger protruding from the belt of the soldier who had forced her to drink. An idea took hold of her, and she closed her eyes, feigning an exhausted faint toward the soldier.

The soldier was clearly surprised as he caught her limp form. Bailey didn't hear his words as she opened her eyes and snatched the dagger from his belt. Hope that this suffering might finally end filled her as she raised the dagger to plunge it into her chest. But that hope fizzled as quickly as it had come as she realized the dagger had been struck from her hands.

She winced against the pain as hot magic singed her fingers.

"Now, now," Paraximus crooned from across the table. "We can't have that." He stood slowly and motioned to the soldier next to her to take her away. "Make sure she's restrained," he ordered.

The soldier nodded as he dragged Bailey away from the sitting area where the table was and toward a room that served as her cell. Once there, he opened the door and roughly shoved her onto the bed.

Despite her best efforts to fight him, he managed to snap cuffs around each of her wrists, effectively chaining her to the bed so that she couldn't do anything to harm herself. As he made to do the cuffs on her ankles, he glanced up at her, catching her eyes. A hint of pity streaked across his gaze before he looked away.

"You don't have to do this," Bailey managed, watching him duck his head and ignore her. "If you would help me, we could both escape this place."

The soldier didn't say anything, but his fingers slowed slightly.

Bailey felt the hope streak through her again as she

watched him. She'd been pleading with him to help her since she'd first been brought to this room nearly ten days ago, after she'd begun her hunger strike. He was young and she could tell that he was upset by what was being done to her, but he'd been like a stone until now.

"Tell me your name," she said then, watching him glance up at her.

"Stop talking to me," he snapped. It was the first time he'd spoken to her and the first time he'd kept his eyes on her long enough for her to realize that, under his mop of curly brown hair, they were a soft shade of amethyst. He'd locked the final cuff around her ankle, but he stood there for a moment, his eyes turned downward.

Bailey thought for sure he would say something else, but she was disappointed when he turned to leave. She let her head fall back on the pillow, feeling tears fill her eyes. She was surprised when he paused, his back to her.

"I want to help you," he whispered over his shoulder. "But I can't." He didn't look at her. "If you think what he's done to you is cruel, it would be nothing compared to what he would do to me if I tried to help you."

Bailey drew a slow breath, feeling bitter. "You have no idea what he's done to me," she whispered. She pinned him with a glare. "What he's going to do to me."

The soldier turned slightly, sadness in his eyes. "I can't," he said. "And not because I fear death for myself." Pain creased his face. "He would torture everyone I ever loved. I would have to watch them suffer and die."

Bailey felt her stomach twist, understanding what he was saying. Paraximus didn't just murder traitors. He took everything he could from them and left them wishing they were dead. She didn't say anything as she turned her face away. She hoped that he would just leave, but when she turned her head back after a moment, he was still there.

"You asked my name," he said slowly.

Bailey narrowed her eyes at him, remaining silent.

"It's Jili." He turned then and walked toward the door, swiftly leaving the room.

Celo Cavus, the capitol city of Siccita.
The thirty-nineth day of winter, the 906th year of the
reign of King Paraximus Lamia.
Friday, January 28, 2012.

PARAXIMUS'S ARMS WERE CROSSED TIGHTLY over his chest as he gazed out of the window of his library. In the distance, he could see the moons rising high into the night sky. His thoughts were distant as he looked out over the vast expanse of Siccita from the castle window.

Daya unfurled from the statue where she had once stood, her decrepit form moving closer to him and the pale-haired girl at his feet. Her lip-less mouth pulled into a macabre smile, forcing him to look away. The girl was cowering on the floor beside him, visibly shaking, but he felt nothing for her as he watched the dark goddess slink toward her.

"Look at me, girl," Daya commanded as she approached.

The Atturon girl was weeping softly as she lifted her head, her shoulders trembling. Daya reached out a long, gnarled finger, letting a pointed claw press against the girl's neck.

"So pure," Daya murmured as she kneeled beside the girl. Her face twisted, becoming more grotesque as she grabbed the Atturon girl roughly, sinking long fangs into the flesh of her neck.

The Atturon girl's scream filled the temple, echoing off the cold stone, before fading into silence. She became limp in Daya's claws, the sight filling him with bitter rage. Just when he thought he'd have to remind Daya of her promise, she released the girl, letting her slide to the floor with a gentleness that surprised him.

She lifted her hand then, further surprising him. Her flesh, which had previously appeared to be that of a decaying body, was slowly becoming supple and smooth. The transformation moved slowly across her arm, making even her face appear less gaunt.

She surveyed her new body for a moment before turning her eyes to Paraximus. "Come to me," she commanded.

Paraximus was still repulsed down to the core by her, but he forced his body to step toward her. He didn't flinch when she took his hand and pressed it against her face.

"Come closer," she whispered, pressing a now-warm hand against his cheek. "I will give you what you desire."

He blinked suddenly from his thoughts. Despite the way the Atturon girl's blood seemed to bring her corpse back to life, her breath had tasted of putrid decay when she'd pressed her lips over his, transferring a cold magic into his body. Even now, it burned like ice in his veins, making his body feel taxed.

Daya had promised him the strength and the army to take whatever he wanted, but it was beginning to sink in that her price was high.

A soft knock on the door caused him to turn from the

window. "Enter," he commanded.

A high-ranking soldier appeared in the doorway, saluting him. "My king," he said, bowing. "The pits are ready."

Paraximus felt a small smile pull at his lips. "Good," he said. He turned his eyes back to the moons. "Send your men into the streets. I require every first-born child, not yet of age."

The soldier nodded.

Paraximus stood at the window a moment longer before turning to leave the library, satisfaction filling him. With the blood his men were procuring, it was time to start building his army.

The Calamo Mare, Ymber.
The forty-first day of winter, the 851st year of the
reign of Queen Liana Estrella.
Sunday, January 30, 2012.

NYX'S WHOLE BODY WAS SORE as she slid from Bartuk's back. They'd been traveling hard the past few days, and she could tell that Otsana and the wolves were anxious to deliver her to Regius Carmen. As she lifted her hands over her head to ease the stiffness from her back, she could see mountains looming in the distance.

"Pretty, aren't they?" Ellie asked as she landed beside her. The peaks were illuminated by the setting sun, casting oranges and blues across the faces.

Nyx nodded in agreement. "How close are we?" she asked softly.

Ellie shrugged. "Four, maybe five days, at this pace," she said, glancing over her shoulder. She excused herself when she saw Raphael slide to the ground painfully.

Nyx felt her heart jump in her chest as she stared at the mountain. The thought that she was finally so close to Regius Carmen made her feel excited and sick at the same time. She tried to let the thoughts roll away though as she turned toward the others. Her heart leapt in her chest again when she suddenly locked eyes with Jet.

They hadn't spoken since that night in Kilcrest, and the tension and silence had been noticed by everyone. Thankfully, or maybe not, no one asked what was going on, and Nyx had a feeling it was because they already knew. It was hard to keep secrets when they were all together like this.

Jet held her gaze for moment before turning away and heading into the tall grass, toward a cluster of trees.

Nyx felt her heart plummet into her feet, despite his behavior not being anything new. He never sat around the fire with them in evenings, choosing to instead slink off somewhere in the dark, but she knew he was still close by. Even though they weren't speaking, she could sense his presence, and it leant her some comfort to know he was there.

She drew a slow breath and turned to help Ellie and Raphael.

The sun was completely gone by the time they finished setting up camp and built a fire. The Pangere and the wolves had settled down by the fire to get some rest and eat, but Nyx didn't feel like joining them. She'd heard Amaya mention earlier that there was a stream just beyond the trees, and it was calling her name. She leaned toward Ellie, who was sitting beside her.

"I'm going down to the stream to wash up," she said.

Ellie looked up from the charred meat she was eating, nodding her head. "I can go with you, if you want," she offered around a mouthful of food.

Nyx gave her a slight smile. "I'll be fine," she said. "I won't be long."

Ellie nodded distractedly before shoving more food into her mouth. Nyx didn't blame her. Game had proven to be difficult to come by in the Calamo Mare. Everything was either too small or too quick; the big game had moved off to other pastures for the season. And eating fruit and sprouts all the time sucked.

She moved slowly to her feet, walking toward her pack and pulling a clean shirt from it. No one seemed to think it strange that she was leaving as she walked toward the trees in the dark. It was easy enough to find the source of the water as it flowed noisily over a bed of stones. The trees opened up and allowed bright rays of moonlight to glisten across the clear stream.

Nyx knelt slowly beside it, pressing her hands into the cold water. The cold was wonderful on her skin, and she shed her stuba-skin coat before cupping the water and splashing it across her face. It stung at first, but it sent adrenaline through her body, making her feel refreshed. She started to splash it across her arms, grateful that she could at least feel clean. After she felt like she'd been sufficiently cleansed, she pulled her old shirt over her head and let it fall to the ground before hastily pulling on the clean one.

She'd never realized before how much difference clean clothes made. After she buttoned her shirt, she quickly pulled on her coat and gathered her dirty clothing in her hands. She moved slowly to her feet, looking over the stream. It was small but trickled loudly as it wound its way into the trees. She started to turn to go back to the fire, but the flash of a light caught her eyes, making her pause.

She wondered if Ellie was looking for her, and she

walked toward it quickly. It was easy enough for her to see that the light was moving toward the water, and she jogged toward it, pushing through some low-hanging branches.

"Hey, Ell—"

Nyx drew up short, feeling her stomach flip-flop. She was stuck for a moment as she stared at Jet.

An *augarlux* floated lazily next to him, illuminating his face softly.

"Sorry," Nyx said quickly, turning to leave. She wanted to be anywhere other than there at that moment.

"Stop," he said shortly.

Nyx froze with her back to him, feeling her shoulders tense. She didn't want to talk to him or to be stuck out here like this with him. The tension and awkwardness were so thick in the air, she could have choked.

"Nyx, look at me," he said then, a hint of pleading in his voice.

Nyx felt her heart twist and she turned slowly to face him. She was surprised at the frown on his face.

"We need to talk," he said.

Nyx crossed her arms, feeling indignant suddenly. That was all she ever wanted, was for him to talk to her. But his version of talking was always some justification for why he couldn't really tell her anything. "So talk," she said hotly.

Jet drew a slow breath and rolled his eyes. "Don't be like that."

Nyx scowled at him. "Like what?" she demanded. "Angry?" She could have punched him. "I think I have every right to be angry."

"You just don't understand," he said then.

"Then explain!" she snapped. She felt a surge of painful rejection claw at her, making tears fill her eyes. "Things shouldn't be this hard."

He seemed to draw up short at her words. "You're right," he said after a moment. He drew a slow breath, as if preparing himself for what he needed to say, before looking at her. "Nyx, I have to tell you something. Something about the other night."

Nyx felt her heart jump into her throat at the look on his face. "Okay," she breathed slowly.

"Look, it wasn't what you think," he said. He seemed to be struggling for the right words. "There's something about me that you don't know."

Nyx wanted to step closer to him, to comfort him, but she felt rooted to the ground, afraid. What if she didn't like what he had to say? "Just tell me," she said softly. "You can tell me anything."

He drew a ragged breath, clearly distressed. "Nyx, there's … there's this *thing* …" He shook his head and ran a hand through his hair. "It's inside me and—"

"Nyx!"

They both jumped at the sound of Ellie's voice. Nyx turned quickly, seeing Ellie pushing her way through the trees.

"There you are," she said. "You've been gone a while and I was worried—Oh." Her eyes suddenly shifted to Jet, as if she hadn't noticed him at first. "Sorry, am I interrupting?" She turned, looking embarrassed. "I'll just see you back at camp."

Nyx felt her jaw tighten as she looked at Jet, seeing that his usual mask of annoyance was back in place. "Give me just a moment," she said quickly to Ellie. "I'll walk back with you."

Ellie nodded uncertainly before moving away to give them some privacy.

"What were you going to tell me?" Nyx asked quietly,

looking back to Jet.

Jet crossed his arms slowly, shaking his head. "It's nothing," he said then. "It's not important."

Nyx knew he was lying, but she also knew that the moment had passed. Whatever he was going to tell her, it was sealed away in a place that he wouldn't go to again any time soon. She watched as he turned as if to walk away, and she surprised herself when she jumped toward him, catching his hand.

He paused and turned to look at her, his eyes narrowed warily.

"I meant what I said," she whispered, holding his gaze. "You can tell me anything."

Jet looked down at her hand on his before back to her face. He nodded mutely, pulling his hand away gently and turning away.

Nyx didn't know how to feel as she stood there for a second before turning to catch up with Ellie. Her stomach was still in knots, because she knew whatever he was going to say, it was important.

Nyx laid on her blanket next to Bartuk, feeling the warmth radiating from his belly. He was curled protectively around her and Ellie and Raphael, his neck creating a barrier between them and the rest of the campsite. Nyx had been staring at his rising and falling mass for a while, amazed by the care he exhibited toward his human counterparts.

She noticed, too, the way his scales, nearly the size of the palm of her hand, laid flat against his body, glinting with the light of the moons overhead. It reminded her a bit of snakeskin and fish scales muddled together, but she could tell his body was strong, meant to be impervious to punctures. She could imagine that their bodies had adapted to protect against other dragons' teeth.

After lying there and admiring him for a while, she sat up slowly. She watched as he lifted his head on the other side of Ellie, looking at her with glowing eyes. She lifted her hand a bit, seeing him tilt his head curiously, before pressing her palm against his scales. He seemed unbothered as he let his head return to resting on the ground with a soft, groaning sigh.

Nyx was surprised, as she kept her hand against his skin, to realize that his belly was hot. She ran her fingers across his stomach and toward the scales on his side, noticing a significant difference in temperature. His top-side scales were much cooler. She wondered if he breathed fire like the dragons in storybooks.

She drew a slow breath as she looked up to the sky overhead, seeing stars twinkling down at her. Being this close to Bartuk made her thoughts start to wander to Hessa. Hessa was a different kind of dragon, as Nyx had come to realize, smaller and faster, like the Pangere's dragons. She thought about the first time she'd seen Hessa and how terrified she'd been.

Unfortunately, her thoughts circled back around to Savra.

Nyx could still remember lying on that stone table, watching Jet kiss her, as if his life depended on it. It left a bitter taste in her mouth. And it made his rejection at the inn hurt more. She knew he was capable of caring about another person, so why didn't he care about her?

Was that what he was trying to tell her earlier? That he wasn't over Savra?

Nyx wasn't sure if that even made sense, since he'd been the one to kill her, but she supposed that he could still mourn for what he used to have. She wondered if he missed his home, and if that would always be the one thing that kept him distant with her. Especially since he was a prisoner of war from Siccita.

At the thought, she felt sick and fear gripped her insides. How would things be once they were in Regius Carmen? Would he be allowed to stay with her? Was he trying to tell her that this couldn't work because other people wouldn't let them stay together?

She couldn't stand the suffocating feeling that overwhelmed her, and she moved quickly to her feet to get away from Bartuk and the others. He snorted at her as she stepped over his tail, as if he was unhappy she was leaving, but he let her go. She walked quickly away from the camp, grateful for the cool, early morning air. She drew in long, quick breaths, trying to keep the tears from her eyes, but she failed miserably as a wave of emotion overcame her.

She knelt slowly into the tall grass, gripping the front of her coat as pain assaulted her. She wanted to wail and scream at the intensity of her emotions, both for the ones she'd lost and the difficulty of the journey, and for the thought that she would lose Jet. Instead, she clenched her fists tightly, trying to remain silent. Her tears were hot as they crowded her eyes until she couldn't see anything anymore. She just wanted to stop existing at that moment, everything inside her feeling shattered. She never wanted any of this and she wished that she'd never existed in the first place, just so that this pain would go away.

II

The Calamo Mare, Ymber.
The forty-third day of winter, the 851st year of the
reign of Queen Liana Estrella.
Tuesday, February 1, 2012.

MOUNTAINS WERE STANDING TALL OVER the group as they stopped for a rest. The sun was throwing shadows across the plains at the foot of the mountains. A chill was seeping into Nyx as she stared up at the stark stone face hovering over them. She felt drained from the traveling and from her breakdown two nights ago. She felt cut off from the rest of the group and she felt as if the divide grew wider and wider with every step they took.

"Are you sure you're okay?" Amaya had asked her that morning as they packed their campsite.

Nyx had nodded silently, unsure if she could speak without the emotion overcoming her again.

Now, as she stared at the peaks overhead, all she felt was apprehension in her chest. She blinked from her thoughts when she felt a hand on her arm. She turned to see Amaya standing beside her.

"We're almost there," she said, offering a slight smile. "How are you feeling?"

Nyx looked up again and shrugged. "I don't know," she whispered. "Nervous, I guess." Right now, all she felt was empty. What would happen to them once they arrived in Regius Carmen?

Amaya put her arm around her and gave her a sisterly squeeze. "Not much longer," she said. "Then you'll be safe and can rest from all this."

Nyx nodded, wishing she could feel some comfort at Amaya's words. She watched as Amaya walked away to finish unpacking Declan. Her eyes drifted across the camp toward Otsana, who seemed to have a permanent frown on her face.

Otsana seemed to sense her gaze, and she stood from where she was running a whet stone across her sword, sheathing the blade and dropping the stone into her pack. Dexter and Sinister didn't spend much time in the camp, choosing to patrol so that they could rest comfortably, and they usually left Otsana behind.

Nyx straightened her shoulders as the girl approached her.

"We're two days from Regius Carmen," Otsana said once she was within earshot. "We should be met soon by an escort that will take you all into the city." She looked around, motioning to the Pangere and Ellie and her brother, before looking toward the mountain pass that loomed ahead. "Just beyond that bend is an out-of-the-way outpost. They'll send a scouting group to see who we are, and once they've come, my masters and I will part ways with you."

Nyx frowned lightly. "Won't Liana want to see you?" she asked. The thought vaguely tickled at the back of her mind that she hadn't had a chance to get to know the creatures who saved them and delivered them here, but it flitted away quickly.

Otsana offered a lop-sided grin. "She'll understand," she said. "My masters don't like to be involved in worldly affairs."

"Then why did you come for us?" Nyx asked.

Otsana shrugged. "We owed a favor."

Nyx nodded silently then. She wished she could be free like that. Just as abruptly as she'd come, Otsana left, leaving Nyx alone as she sank down onto a large rock. She looked around the campsite, watching the others go about their business, excitement punctuating their movements. She could tell they were thinking of what they would do first when they finally reached civilization. She was sure it included a good bath and some decent food. But that's not what she was thinking about.

She wasn't surprised when she saw Jet cross toward her.

He'd been less frosty since he'd tried to talk to her, but she hadn't had much to say to him. They kept their distance from each other, but it felt less tense now. He sighed as he sank to sit beside her, watching the others as well. After a moment, he turned to look at her. "We're almost there," he said quietly.

Nyx turned to look at him. "That's good," she said evenly.

He frowned at her response. "What's wrong?" he asked.

She looked away. "I'm tired," she said. She looked back to him. "I want all of this to be over."

Jet nodded as if he knew what she meant. He leaned forward and threaded his fingers together. "I don't know what to expect," he said quietly, looking over their traveling companions again. "I'm sure they'll be happy to see you, but …"

"You think they'll send you away," Nyx finished for him. She'd thought about nothing else for the last two days.

Jet shrugged. "Or put me back in prison," he said, trying to force a wry grin.

Nyx wanted to tell him that she wouldn't let that happen, but she knew that she didn't have that much power. It wouldn't matter much what she wanted once they stepped into Regius Carmen. She knew she should be upset, but she felt too numb and emotionally exhausted. She could feel Jet's eyes on her as she drew a slow breath.

"It's going to be okay," he said then.

Nyx nodded, but she didn't feel like it would be okay. She forced a ragged sigh to keep tears from crowding her eyes for the zillionth time. She wanted to talk about something else, anything other than what was about to happen, but she couldn't think of anything.

"Ho there!"

Jet's head snapped up and he moved to his feet, and Nyx turned to follow his gaze. She was surprised to see a handful of armed guards approaching them, and even further surprised when she realized they were all women clothed in dark green, long-sleeved shirts and pants, silver armor over their chests and arms. On their left shoulders was a bright yellow insignia.

The one who appeared to be the leader stepped forward, carrying a spear. She was tall and broad-shouldered, intimidating as she looked at them.

"Who are you?" she demanded. "What business do you have at this outpost?"

Nyx looked up at Jet, who looked like he would answer her, but instead Otsana was on her feet. She walked over to the guard.

"I am Otsana, ward of the great wolves, Dexter and

Sinister, and we have delivered Her Majesty's granddaughter, as she commanded." She turned then and motioned to Nyx to come to her. "This is Princess Nyx Estrella. I trust you will see her to the queen safely."

The guard frowned at Otsana before looking to Nyx. "How am I to trust the word of someone claiming to be the lost princess?" she snapped. Her eyes hardened. "She has been lost for nigh on twenty years." She raked her gaze over Nyx as if she were a disgusting heap. "What proof do you have that you are who you say?"

Otsana suddenly reached for her sword, angry. "You dishonor your queen and the princess with your words," she barked. "Do you doubt the words of the wolf gods?"

The leader lifted her spear at Otsana's movements. "We will not allow liars and traitors into our midst!" she said, causing her followers to lift their weapons as well.

Nyx gasped when Jet suddenly grabbed her arm and pulled her back behind him. She glanced behind her to see that the Pangere had pulled their weapons as well, their dragons poised to defend them. Rian stepped forward with a sword in his hand, and Zaida had an arrow notched in her bow. Just when it seemed like a fight would break out, the sound of hooves filled the canyon behind the guards.

"Captain!" a man's voice commanded. "Lower your weapons at once!"

Nyx drew a sharp breath as a horse galloped into view, at last a familiar animal in this strange place. A man was sitting astride it, a helmet tucked under his arm. He wore similar colors to the guards, but there was an air about him that let her know he wasn't a guard.

The captain immediately lowered her weapon and bowed. "Lord Count," she said, surprise in her voice. "What brings you to the Southern Outpost?"

The man slid from his horse, frowning lightly at her. "Her Majesty sent me to welcome our guests," he said. "We've been expecting you." He turned to look toward where Otsana and Jet stood, Rian close behind them. "I am pleased to see such a well-armed group protecting her, but I must confirm she is among you. Where is the princess?"

Otsana's eyes were narrowed, but she lowered her sword and looked at Nyx. She tilted her head as if she thought it was safe.

Nyx looked up at Jet, who also looked displeased. He looked down at her when she caught the sleeve of his coat uncertainly. "I'm here," he said softly. "It should be okay."

Nyx nodded before stepping around him and into the man's line of sight. She watched as his eyes widened and his lips parted with surprise.

"Your Majesty," he said, walking toward her. He kneeled on the ground before her, placing his hand over his heart. He looked up at her after a moment, clearly breathless, his voice soft. "We've searched long and hard for you."

Nyx didn't know what to say as she stared at him.

He rose slowly to his feet, a bright smile on his face. "I am Count Samill of Durvey," he said, bowing his head. "I have been sent by Our Queen to bring you to Regius Carmen." He turned to look over his shoulder, where a band of riders had appeared. "My men and I have searched for you for many weeks." His face softened. "I am glad to see you are safe and well."

Nyx still didn't know how to respond, so she nodded her head shortly. "Thank you," she managed. She watched as his eyes shifted over her shoulder and his lips pressed into a thin line, as if he'd tasted something sour. She realized he was looking at Jet.

"I had hoped it would be a much longer time before

I had to look upon your face again," he snapped suddenly.

Jet started to scowl but then his face morphed into a dark smirk. "Get used to it, Count," he said. "I think we'll be seeing a lot of each other from now on."

The Count still looked like he'd sucked a lemon, but he composed himself and turned to the captain. "Escort them to the outpost," he commanded. He tossed a smile at Nyx. "Tonight, we celebrate the return of Ymber's heir."

The outpost wasn't very far from where the mountains opened into the Calamo Mare. It was built into the side of the mountain, carved from the rocky face. Nyx was surprised by how ornate it was as they approached, and the captain signaled another guard to lower the gate. The walls were shear, stark white stone against the blue of the mountain. Turrets were positioned around the walls, and Nyx could see guards manning each one. The gate was made of metal and clanged heavily as two guards spun a massive wheel to lift it. Beyond it, two heavy and thick wooden doors were opened to allow them entry.

The air was cool as they entered the mountain hold, sunlight being reflected off the stone around them. Nyx pulled her coat tighter around her, feeling chilled. She turned to see that the Pangere were being directed toward the other end of the outpost, along with Ellie and Raphael.

"Where are they going?" Nyx asked, looking at Jet. Otsana had left to rejoin her masters, leaving them to finish the journey alone.

Jet turned to follow her gaze before letting his eyes shift over the mountain. "There must be an aviary," he said slowly. "Somewhere the dragons can be kept."

"Oh," Nyx said. She turned again when the Count rode

into the gate and dismounted. She glanced at Jet, seeing that he was watching the man with irritation on his face.

"Please, Milady," the Count said as he neared. "This way."

Nyx drew a slow breath and trailed after him, following him through a set of wooden doors that opened into a large hall filled with chairs and tables. Soldiers were drifting inside behind them, as it was clearly mealtime. Nyx was surprised to see that all of the outpost soldiers were women, while Samill's men were a mixture of men and women. The scent of the food on the tables hit her nose, making her stomach rumble against her will.

The Count turned then to grin at her. "I'm guessing you're hungry," he said.

Nyx felt her face turn red a bit as she looked at a nearby table. "I'm sure we could all stand to eat," she said quietly.

The Count nodded. "Please, have a seat," he said. "I'll have them bring you something."

Nyx sank down to sit at a vacant table, watching as Jet eased to sit beside her. She looked up at him, seeing his eyes shifting over the hall and the soldiers surrounding them. "Why is this place here?" she asked quietly, drawing his gaze.

"It's an outpost," he said, his voice soft so that only she could hear him. "It's meant to warn the city of attacks and invasions. There's probably not a large enough force here to stop an attack, but they can send a message to prepare the royal city."

Nyx nodded at his words. That didn't mean much to her and all she could think about was how uncomfortable she was. "This place feels like a dungeon," she murmured. She could feel the stares of the soldiers around them, and it made her feel like she was on display.

Jet snorted a small laugh. "It does, doesn't it?" he mused.

They both turned as the door to the hall opened and the Pangere appeared, causing a soft murmur to fill the room. Ellie and Raphael were trailing behind them, Raphael hobbling on his cane. Nyx could tell that Ellie was uncomfortable as she looked around the room.

"I can't wait for some decent food," Liam said as he slid into a seat across from them, a grin on his face.

Amaya sat beside him, setting her bag down on the floor. "Me too," she said, relief in her voice. She was looking around the room. "This will be a feast compared to what we've been eating." She looked at Zaida as she sat beside her.

"I can't wait to sleep," Zaida said. "I'm so tired of lying on the ground."

Rian eased to sit beside Zaida then, grinning at her. "What? You don't use the rocks as pillows?"

Zaida rolled her eyes at him as Amaya giggled lightly.

Nyx noticed that they still wore their armor, and all had their packs slung over their shoulders. She looked toward another door, which she assumed was to the kitchen, as it opened and the Count appeared, a guard behind him. They each had wooden tankards in their hands, enough for everyone.

"Apologies, but ale is all we have," the Count said as he sat the mugs down. He handed the first one to Nyx with a smile. "For you, Princess."

Nyx took the giant mug, looking down at the brown liquid. She'd never liked beer very much, and she figured she wouldn't like this either. She tried to keep her face blank, but she could feel her lip curling slightly at the smell. She looked around at the others, seeing that the dragon riders were delighted, each eyeing their mugs greedily.

"Before we drink," the Count said, drawing their eyes, "a toast to Her Highness's safe return!" He turned to the room and lifted his tankard, causing the soldiers around them to do the same.

Nyx felt slightly embarrassed as the others echoed his sentiment with a rousing yell that echoed through the hall. She let her mug clank against the table, watching as her Pangere friends all took deep swigs. She looked at Ellie beside her, seeing that she had a bit of a frown on her face. She could tell Ellie didn't like ale either as she took a sip. When she turned to Jet on her other side, she saw that he took a slow sip as well, but it didn't seem to be because of the taste. His eyes were fixed on the Count and narrowed slightly.

The Count, however, didn't seem to notice as he sat with them, leaning against the table. He was excited as he set down his tankard. "Your Highness, I'm very interested to hear about your trek here," he said, drawing Nyx's eyes. "We thought you would take a more direct route, but we couldn't find any sign of you."

Nyx looked to Jet quickly, noticing a slight smirk. He was pleased that the Count couldn't track them. "Uh, yeah," Nyx said, thinking about their first couple of days in Gexalatia. "Jet made sure we were safe."

The Count's eyes narrowed as he looked at Jet. "Some were beginning to question your loyalty," he said, an edge to his voice.

Jet's eyes narrowed dangerously.

Nyx was sure he had a scathing reply for the Count, but she spoke up instead. "Were you one of those, Count Samill?" she asked, an edge to her voice.

The Count seemed taken aback at her words. "I beg

your pardon, Highness," he said quickly, ducking his head. He offered a friendly smile once more. "How did you find our country on your journey?" He glanced around at the Pangere. "And how did you meet with these dragon riders?" He lifted his mug to gesture to the sigil on Rian's armor. "You are Fornaxian, are you not?"

"Indeed," Rian said. He took a long draw on his mug. "We were on our way to see the Queen, and we stumbled across a Seer, who led us to the Princess in Festra."

Samill arched a brow in disbelief. "Festra, eh? And a Seer?" he asked, a hint of doubt in his voice. "Which of you is the Seer?"

Ellie was sitting next to Nyx and she raised her hand tentatively. "I am," she said, her voice small. She glanced uncertainly at Raphael, who sat on her other side. "My sister and I ..." Emotion caught at her, but she tried to choke it back. "We are the daughters of Willem Atturon."

The Count's brow rose in surprise. "We thought you were among the dead in Sorona," he said, his eyes shifting over her. "We were deeply saddened to hear of its destruction. Do you have command of the *Visus* as well?"

"No," Ellie whispered. She clenched her fingers around her mug. "Our father did not train us to use the *Visus*." She looked at her brother. "He thought it was a curse. Maybe he was right."

The Count frowned deeply. "We will do what we can to help you," he said. "Her Majesty will do what she can."

Ellie nodded and looked down at the table, tears in her eyes. Nyx caught her hand and squeezed it gently, feeling Ellie's fingers tighten around hers. Raphael wrapped his arm around his sister's shoulders to comfort her. They each missed the way the Count looked at Jet.

He turned to look at Nyx then, as if he would ask more

questions, but then a woman appeared over his shoulder, plates in her hands. He smiled as he moved to stand. "Ah, a feast," he said as he watched the soldier and two others set food on the table. "I hope you find it to your liking, Your Highness." He bowed slightly. "I need to attend to something, but I shall return. Please, friends, eat your fill."

Nyx watched as the Pangere began to dig in ravenously, as if they hadn't eaten in months. She glanced at Ellie and Raphael, who looked like their appetites had gone, feeling the same. Her stomach was in knots, for a myriad of reasons, including the pain at remembering Melinda and her father. She wished she didn't have to sit at this table, but the rumbling in her stomach hadn't subsided.

Jet moved slowly, as if to stand, catching her eye. "Eat," he said, seeing the uncertainty on her face. "I'll be right back."

Nyx frowned as she watched him walk toward the door and disappear beyond it.

The mountain peaks blocked the setting sun, making it feel darker and colder than the open plains had been. Fires had been lit around the turrets to illuminate the fortress, and a handful of soldiers were lighting lanterns to brighten the courtyard. Jet paused briefly as he stepped into the cool air to draw a slow breath before his eyes shifted around the courtyard. When they landed on Count Samill, he walked toward the man.

Samill looked up from where he was speaking to one of his men as Jet approached. He crossed his arms and a slight scowl began to pull at his face as he met Jet's eyes. "You certainly have them all fooled, don't you?" he asked suddenly, an edge to his voice.

Jet returned his scowl. "I'm not sure what you're insinuating, *Samill*," he said easily.

The Count's scowl darkened, and his eyes raked over Jet. "You should watch your tongue, dog," he growled suddenly. "Don't think you have any power here just because Her Majesty let you slither out of her dungeons."

Jet clenched his fists, wishing he could inflict pain on the Count, but he kept his urges in check. "I didn't come here to trade insults with you," he said, fighting to keep his tone level. "You indicated we needed to talk, so here I am."

Samill looked as if he would argue, but instead he sent his man away to give them some privacy. Despite his intense dislike for Jet, Count Samill was a good man. Jet had seen that from the beginning, when he'd begrudgingly helped Jet prepare for his journey to the Limen more than a year ago.

"Her Majesty wasn't happy that you deviated from the plan," Samill said. His eyes narrowed.

Jet shrugged. "The plan went to shit when we were attacked as soon as we crossed the Limen," he said bitterly. He pinned the Count with a hard look.

Samill looked disconcerted. "There were forces at the Limen?"

"A handful of highly trained killers," Jet said. He was scowling at the thought. "Some who were familiar with me."

Samill's lips puckered. "That is …"

Jet nodded to agree with his unspoken sentiment. "I don't know what kind of magic he's toying with, but it's powerful," he said softly. "He was even able to send assassins to Earth, despite the Limen being closed."

"Impossible," Samill said, shaking his head. "No one possesses that kind of power."

Jet shrugged. "Paraximus does," he said quietly. "It's just a matter of time before he sends his forces to Regius Carmen."

Samill looked startled suddenly. "Do you think the Queen is in danger?"

Jet was silent for a moment. "Not yet," he said slowly. "If he was strong enough to invade her palace, he would have done it."

"You know the Council will want to know everything you know," Samill said slowly. "They'll expect you to provide information on your father's workings."

Jet shook his head, feeling indignant. "That's laughable," he said quietly. "I haven't seen my *father* in a hundred years. How could I possibly know—"

"Your father?"

Jet felt his heart drop painfully into his feet. He turned quickly, seeing Nyx standing behind him. Her brow was furrowed in confusion, but her eyes were wide, as if she'd been struck. "Nyx," he managed, "I thought you were eating …"

Her breaths were quickening as she stared at him, her confusion giving way to a sort of pain. "I wanted to make sure you two weren't killing each other," she managed, her voice shocked. She looked at Samill. "Is it true?"

Samill looked like he wanted to sink into the ground and disappear from this conversation altogether. Unfortunately, he couldn't, so he only crossed his arms and nodded shortly. "It is."

Jet could see her thoughts racing behind her eyes as she blinked, trying to absorb his words. "It's not what you think," he said quickly.

Nyx shook her head as she looked at him, her breaths turning ragged with her tears. "That's why … you knew things you couldn't have …" Her voice faltered and caught in her throat and Jet could tell that things were ratcheting into place in her mind. "How could you keep this from me?"

"It wasn't important," Jet said then, an edge to his voice. "You didn't need to know."

"Wasn't important?" Nyx asked, her voice breathless. "It's not important that you're the *son* of the person who wants to murder me?"

Jet stepped toward her as if to reach for her, but she flinched away. "I did it to protect you," he said softly. His dark eyes were pleading. "If you had known, you never would have trusted me."

"And why should I trust you now?" Nyx suddenly demanded. "You've lied to me this whole time! What else have you lied to me about?" She pressed her hand against her forehead, her voice a defeated whisper. "Why do you always lie to me?"

"Just let me explain," Jet said adamantly, reaching for her again.

Nyx pushed his hand away, feeling devastated. "Stay away from me," she whispered then. Betrayal was heavy in her eyes as she looked at him. "I can't even look at you right now." She looked at Samill as he stepped around Jet toward her.

"Please, Your Highness, let me take you back to the dining hall," he said, holding out his hand as if to motion the way.

Nyx shook her head, turning away from Jet. "Can you just show me where I can rest?" she asked softly. She shot Jet a hate-filled look. "I'm not hungry."

Samill nodded silently and led her toward the barracks, leaving Jet alone with his thoughts.

Regius Carmen, the capitol city of Ymber.
The forty-fourth day of winter, the 851st year of the
reign of Queen Liana Estrella.
Wednesday, February 2, 2012.

A MISSIVE FOR YOU, MY Queen," a servant said, appearing beside Liana.

She was seated at a table, sipping a cup of tea and trying to force herself to eat something, but her stomach was in knots. She had a feeling she knew what the message would be, and she nodded mutely as the servant placed it on the table for her. Her fingers were shaking slightly as she picked it up and broke the seal.

Liana read the words slowly, feeling tears filling her eyes.

The Silvanimas and a group of dragon riders were stopped at the southern mountain pass. They are being escorted by myself and my men to Regius Carmen. Her Highness, the princess, is with us.

- Samill

Liana didn't need to read any more as she sent the

letter down, pressing her hand over her eyes. Relief was strong as she cried softly. It wouldn't be long now before her granddaughter was safely home with her once more.

After she composed herself, Liana moved to her feet and summoned her handmaid. "Tell the others to prepare for a feast in two days' time," she told the girl gently. She had a smile on her lips as she looked at her servant. "My granddaughter is returning home."

13

The Southern-Most Outpost, Ymber.
The forty-fourth day of winter, the 851st year of the
reign of Queen Liana Estrella.
Wednesday, February 2, 2012.

NYX WAS SICK, DOWN INTO every fiber of her being. Samill had escorted her to the barracks, where they would sleep for the night, but she hadn't been able to focus on anything. She'd sat on the edge of her cot in silence for what felt like both an eternity and no time at all before Zaida, Amaya, and Ellie joined her. They had instantly known something was wrong, but she couldn't tell them. Instead, she'd burst into tears, wishing to any deity that would listen to let this torture end.

How could he have lied to her for so long?

She felt stupid and as if she deserved everything she was getting. She wondered if it was karma for what happened to Melinda. Was she being punished for bringing such tragedy down on Melinda and her father?

She also felt stupid because there were signs. So many signs. And she'd been too stupid to see it. How could Jet have possibly known the things he did unless he was privy to things most people weren't? And why else would Jet have harbored such resentment for Paraximus? How had she not noticed that this was so personal for him? And for good reason. His own father left him to rot in a dungeon. The people he'd led, and loved, forgot about him. No wonder he was so angry. She didn't blame him, but it left her with a thousand more questions.

It was well into the night and she hadn't slept a wink. She'd laid on her cot and let her mind roil like an ocean in a hurricane. She sat up slowly, seeing that her friends were all soundly asleep, no doubt with full stomachs and somewhat lighter hearts. She was grateful they slept so deeply as she moved to her feet and pulled on her coat.

The night air was bitingly cold as she stepped into it and closed the door quietly behind her. She walked into the courtyard, looking around. Soldiers were manning the turrets, but they looked bored as they played cards to waste time until their shifts were over. She could hear their voices as they bickered and laughed with each other. She guessed there wasn't much to do here and that there wasn't usually any excitement.

She let her eyes shift from the wall toward the door to the hall where they had been served dinner. She wasn't quite sure where she would find him, but she wasn't surprised when she felt his presence nearby before she saw him.

Nyx pressed a hand to her forehead to smooth her hair from her face as a cold wind picked up around the courtyard. "I want the truth," she whispered softly, her throat feeling raw. "All of it." When silence answered her, she turned to look over her shoulder.

Jet's eyes met hers. Despite the way his shoulders were tensed, he nodded. "What do you want to know?"

"Why didn't you tell me?" she asked steadily.

Jet looked at the ground. "It wasn't important at first," he said slowly, "but as time went on, I didn't feel like I *could* tell you. I didn't think you'd trust me anymore."

Nyx crossed her arms. That was probably true. Especially once they'd crossed the Limen and he was her only lifeline in this world. "Who are you really?" she asked.

"I am Paraximus' son, heir to his throne, leader of his armies, and the greatest threat Gexalatia has ever known."

Nyx realized she'd heard that before – from Savra. For a brief moment, she could see it. She'd always known Jet was dangerous, but she'd never really felt that danger until now. She knew that there was much, much more to his story, and it made her stomach twist. "Will I still see you the same way once I learn what you've done?"

"I don't know." Jet held her gaze steadily, and it made the pit in her stomach worse.

"What did you do?" she whispered, uncertain she wanted an answer.

Jet let his eyes shift away from hers then. "I waged war," he said quietly. "I killed people." He looked down at his hands, as if remembering a time long ago. "I spilled the blood of innocents." He drew a slow breath, his voice suddenly barely a whisper. "And I enjoyed it."

Nyx winced then, feeling sick. "You were a monster." It wasn't a question.

And Jet didn't deny it. "Yes," he said softly.

Nyx blinked, feeling tears crowding her eyes. How could she care so much for someone who was so cruel?

"Are you still a monster?" she managed, despite the way her voice quivered.

Jet was silent for a long moment. His gaze was focused elsewhere, his thoughts distant.

"Jet?" Nyx breathed, watching as his dark eyes shifted back to her.

He drew a slow breath as he held her gaze. "I hope not."

Nyx surprised him when she suddenly threw her arms around his middle, holding onto him tightly. Her tears fell silently down her cheeks. She was so tired of all of this. She didn't know what was in store for her when the morning came, but she knew that Jet had been a constant. Despite the lies, he'd had her back. He'd trained her and fought for her. He'd killed to keep her safe. She was tired of being at odds with him like this. She needed his strength now more than ever, the past be damned.

"Are you on my side?" she managed, her voice choked.

Jet wrapped his arms around her, letting his cheek rest against the top of her head. "Always," he whispered.

Jet wasn't sure if the feeling in his chest was relief, but it was definitely lighter than the guilt and anxiety he'd felt before. After he and Nyx had made up, she'd gone back to sleep for a few hours. It was now sunrise, and they were all standing at the gates of the outpost. The Pangere had been sent on ahead with their dragons, along with Ellie and Raphael, leaving Nyx and Jet with Samill and his riders.

Jet watched as a soldier approached with a muscled warhorse, which stamped its feet as the soldier held onto the reins. The soldier seemed apprehensive as she looked at Nyx.

"Are you sure you can handle him, Princess?" she asked. She was a tall woman, standing nearly a foot taller than Nyx, and she had wide shoulders, but even she seemed to be wary of the monstrous stallion beside her.

Nyx drew a slow breath as she looked at the horse. She stepped toward it, holding out her hand. The stallion's head was high as he snorted at Nyx, but then he lowered his nose, pressing his soft upper lip against her palm. The soldier seemed shocked as Nyx pressed her hand against the stallion's forehead, and the horse instantly calmed and drew a slow breath.

"Yes," she said quietly. "I'll be fine."

Jet realized he was frowning at the interaction; he thought he sensed just the faintest hint of magic, much like the first night he met Nyx, when she'd been accidentally charming the boy she liked. He watched as Nyx took the stallion's reins and stepped easily into the stirrup, mounting the massive horse. She sat tall on the stallion's back, and it made Jet's heart skip a beat. She bore such a resemblance to Liana in that moment. He didn't have time to think about it, though, as another soldier brought him a similarly stout horse.

He didn't have the magic touch that Nyx had with the beasts, but he didn't have much trouble swinging onto the horse's back. Once they were both mounted and ready, Jet lifted his head to see that Samill's horse was trotting toward them. Behind him, the captain of the outpost was watching them, frowning lightly, her eyes fixed on Nyx.

"Ah, they gave you Zephri," Samill said to her as he neared. He gestured to the stallion.

Nyx looked down at the horse and patted his shoulder. The stallion was calm beneath her touch, and Samill seemed surprised.

"It seems he likes you," Samill said, titling his head slightly. "He doesn't take to just anyone."

Nyx offered the count a small smile. "I guess so," she said quietly.

Samill let his horse sidle up next to Zephri. "He is the fastest in the stables," he commented, offering her a reassuring smile. "He will get you to Regius Carmen in no time."

Nyx nodded shortly. She knew what he really meant was that they gave her the best horse so she could escape if things went poorly. She felt Zephri shift under her suddenly when Samill turned and barked a command to his riders.

"We should make Regius Carmen by nightfall," he said as he turned his horse to lead the way.

Zephri shook his head against the bit and moved into a high-stepping trot as the riders began to move around them. Nyx realized that they were keeping her and Jet safely surrounded, and she glanced over at him as his horse kept pace with Zephri. He shot a grim smile in her direction.

"This is it," he said as their horses trotted with the rest of the group. "We'll be there soon."

Nyx felt her heart flutter in her chest, and she looked ahead at the mountain pass as they rode into it. She didn't know how she felt, except for the almost nauseous feeling in her stomach. As they fell into a rhythm, Zephri began to calm and lowered his head, his trot easing to a walk, his long legs making it feel like Nyx was sitting in a rocking chair.

After some time, the mountain shadows began to give way to the first rays of the sun as they touched the mountain tops. Nyx was surprised to see that the caps were sparkling with white snow, which was hiding glistening blue rock faces.

"Pretty, isn't it?" Samill suddenly asked, his horse once more sidling up to hers.

Nyx turned to look at him, watching as Zephri tossed his head and pinned his ears at Samill's horse. She ignored it though and offered Samill a small smile. "Yes," she said softly. She looked back up at the mountain. "I've never seen such a wonderful shade of blue stone."

Samill smiled and nodded his head. "It's quite beautiful when the sun hits it just right," he said pleasantly. "But if that impresses you, you'll be even more astounded with the Regius Arce."

Nyx frowned lightly at him. "Regius Arce?"

"Oh, the royal castle," Samill said quickly. "It's built from the stone of Montem Magnus, the great mountain." His eyes became wistful. "It is truly a sight to behold."

Nyx took a moment to study his face as he gazed thoughtfully at the mountain tops. She noticed that he had a kind set to his eyes, which were a soft, bluish green. She realized she was staring at him when he looked back at her and caught her gaze.

"But we'll be there soon enough," he said quickly. He offered her a cordial nod, suddenly seeming as if he needed to leave. "I apologize, Your Highness, but I must check in with the others."

Nyx nodded mutely, watching as he spurred his horse ahead. She wasn't sure what had happened.

"What did you say to him?" Jet said suddenly, reining his horse closer to hers. "He looked flustered."

Nyx shrugged. "I dunno," she said. "I just asked him about the mountains."

Jet made a humored noise and rolled his eyes.

"What did you think of Regius Carmen the first time you saw it?" she asked then.

Jet's brow furrowed. He tried to recall what he had seen of the city, but the memories were hazy, as he'd been under Liana's spell. "It was cold," he said finally. That was the thing that bothered him the most in the beginning.

Siccita was always warm and rarely had snow.

Nyx shook her head at his response, mildly exasperated. It seemed like a blow-off reply to her, and she didn't know if she'd ever get a serious answer.

The sun was high overhead when they decided to take a break. As Nyx slid from Zephri's back, she felt her knees wobble slightly. It had been a long time since she'd spent so much time on a horse. She took a moment to shake the feeling back into her toes as a soldier stepped forward and caught Zephri's reins.

"It helps to walk a bit," he said quietly, offering her a slight smile.

Nyx looked up at him, surprised to see that he had dark, navy blue hair and similar eyes. "Yeah, thanks," she said as she turned and walked around Zephri. She watched as Jet slid from his horse, another soldier taking it from him.

He caught her eyes and walked toward her. "Hope they at least brought lunch," he said shortly.

Nyx offered him a humored grin, crossing her arms as she watched the soldiers dismount around them. They seemed relieved as they milled around, some taking the time to break open their packs and produce food. She felt her stomach rumble then. "I guess I could do with some food," she said.

Jet turned then, as if he was going to find something for her, when Samill suddenly appeared again. He was carrying a loaf of bread and a flask in his hands.

"I'm sure you're hungry, Princess," he said, smiling brightly. "I apologize, but this is all we have at the moment." He held out his meager offering.

Nyx gave him a smile in return, watching as Jet took the flask and bread. "This is fine, Samill," she said easily. She gave a laugh. "I definitely don't expect anything fancy."

Samill bowed his head. "Please let me know if you need anything else."

Nyx nodded and assured him that she would before following Jet away from the horses and soldiers and toward a boulder, easing to sit next to him. He'd been overly helpful since they left this morning, and Nyx didn't have to wonder very hard if it was his way of trying to make things up to her. She watched as he opened the flask and waved it under his nose, taking a whiff.

"Ale," he said then, holding it out to her.

Nyx grimaced, but took it from him anyway. "What is it with the ale?" she murmured as she took a sip.

"Easy to find and cheap," Jet said as he tore off a piece of bread and offered it to her.

Nyx took it from him and shoved it into her mouth. She realized she was hungrier than she'd originally thought, especially since she hadn't been able to eat much this morning. She let her eyes shift over the mountain pass once more as she chewed the bread in her hands, feeling her thoughts shifting toward Regius Carmen. She could tell that they were close, and it made a knot form in her stomach.

"What do you think will happen when we get there?" she asked suddenly.

Jet shrugged as he handed her another piece of bread. "Hard to say."

Nyx studied the food in her hand for a moment. "Will I meet Liana?" she whispered.

Jet turned to look at her then. "Of course," he said. "Why wouldn't you?"

"I dunno," she said, still looking at the bread. "I guess I always thought queens didn't really mingle with everyone else."

Jet chuckled lightly. "You're her family," he said. "She's the one who orchestrated all of this." He motioned to Samill's men, but Nyx knew he meant everything else that had happened as well. "Don't you think she'd be first in line to see you?"

Nyx looked up at him then. "Yeah, you're probably right," she said. She frowned lightly. "Do I have other family?"

Jet drew a slow breath and looked away. "I'm sure you do," he said evenly.

Despite how measured he was trying to be, Nyx knew him better. She started to ask him what he wasn't saying, bristling at the thought that he wasn't being honest with her *again*, when suddenly a skittering sound and the sliding of rocks made her jump. She felt Jet pull her toward the soldiers and horses as the skittering became louder, and a large, hairy animal suddenly crashed down from the steep, rocky wall above them, startling the men and horses around them.

Nyx gasped as she realized the animal had landed not far from where they'd been sitting, and it was making an awful sound, as if it were in agonizing pain. She pressed her hands over her mouth as she watched a soldier draw a sword and move toward it.

"Don't look," Jet said suddenly, catching her and pulling her toward him to block her view.

Nyx realized there were tears in her eyes as the animal's bawling call filled the canyon around them before the sound suddenly stopped, echoing off the cavernous walls around them as it faded into silence. She blinked quickly, taking a moment to compose herself. For some reason, hearing the animal crying out in pain made her heart shatter.

"Are you all right, Your Highness?" Samill suddenly

called, rushing toward them.

Nyx nodded as she looked at him. "Yeah," she said, hearing the quivering in her voice. She ran her hands across the front of her pants, her palms sweating. She drew a shaking breath as she looked toward the beast, realizing the soldier who had taken her horse was the one putting his sword away.

"Just a *capra*," he called as he looked toward Samill. "Must have slipped coming down the slope."

Samill frowned lightly at the soldier's assessment. "Mount up," he said then. He looked at the soldier. "Stay near the princess, Brodrick."

Nyx didn't miss the way his eyes shifted overhead as he turned and ordered his men back to their horses. She watched as Brodrick brought her Zephri, boosting her rather urgently onto his back. "What's the rush?" she asked, turning her eyes to the *capra*.

She was surprised to see that it was almost as big as Zephri, its body covered in a thick layer of blue hair. It had massive horns that zig-zagged over its shoulders and toward its back. Blood was staining the ground underneath it from a clean stab to its heart. One of its legs was twisted unnaturally, most likely broken from the fall.

"*Capra* are very sure-footed," Brodrick said as he held onto Zephri. "Unless they're being pursued by a *petramis*."

"*Petramis?*" Nyx murmured as she watched Brodrick let go of Zephri. She looked at Jet, seeing that he was already on his horse, which was prancing nervously. "What's a *petramis?*"

Jet reined his horse forward as it pranced nervously, motioning she should follow. "Nothing good," he tossed over his shoulder.

Nyx let Zephri step into a smart trot after Jet's horse,

following him as he rode past the soldiers toward the front of the group. She didn't understand why they were in such a hurry to leave the area, but her confusion didn't last long.

A roar suddenly filled the canyon, making Nyx mash her hands over her ears. Beneath her, Zephri started, leaping to the side and jumping forward to escape whatever was making the ear-splitting noise. When Nyx finally got her wits about her, she spun Zephri around to face the pursuing creature. Her heart leapt hard in her chest as she watched a monstrous, tiger-like beast slide across the rockface, its claws leaving deep gouges behind it.

It was solid black, with bright yellow eyes, and gigantic fangs that protruded from under its lips. It didn't have fur like a tiger, though; it was encased in a thick, scaly hide, much like an alligator. Despite that, thick muscles rippled when it moved. If it hadn't traversed the rocky slope like a ballet dancer, Nyx would have thought it was extremely heavy. It didn't seem to have any trouble sliding down the slope, eyeing the dead *capra* before turning its ravenous gaze on the soldiers and their mounts.

"*Petramis*," Nyx breathed, knowing the beast immediately.

"Get away from here!" Samill suddenly called, appearing beside her. He had his sword drawn and his face was set for battle. "My men will hold it off!"

She could feel Zephri trembling underneath her, and she gave him his head, hanging on as he whipped around and lunged into a hard gallop. Just as Samill had said that morning, he was indeed swift, and he zoomed past Jet and his mare, who also took off in a gallop. Nyx let Zephri run for a long moment, hanging onto his mane as he flew through the canyon. It was like his feet barely touched the ground and soon the canyon became quiet, except for

Zephri's footsteps.

Once Nyx felt like she was out of danger, she sat back in the saddle and pulled on the reins, signaling Zephri to slow down. He was huffing hard as he eased into a high-strung canter, but he pulled against her, yearning to gallop more.

"Easy," she murmured, looking over her shoulder. She could hear the sound of hooves behind her, but for a moment she was alone around a bend. She managed to pull Zephri to a halt, feeling him twitching beneath her as Jet's mare finally appeared.

He was frowning as his mare fell into a trot, looking winded. Her neck was wet with sweat. "They really did give you the fastest horse," he said, a hint of aggravation in his voice. "I didn't think this old nag would ever catch up."

Nyx realized she was shaking as she turned Zephri toward the mare. "Was that a *petramis*?" she asked, her voice shaking lightly.

Jet nodded, turning in the saddle to look over his shoulder. "Good thing we got out of there," he said. "Those things massacre whole villages just because they can."

"Do you think Samill and his men are okay?" Nyx asked, her voice worried.

Jet wanted to shrug, but he didn't. Before he could answer, the canyon filled once again with the sound of horses, and they both turned to see Samill leading a group of his soldiers around the bend.

Samill looked relieved as he neared. "Are you both okay?" he asked.

Nyx nodded and glanced over Jet. "We're fine," she said, her voice no longer shaking. "Is everyone else okay?"

Samill's lips pressed into a thin line. "We shouldn't linger here," he said, avoiding her question. "The *petramis* was injured, but it could come back. I've left a group behind to keep an eye out for it." He reined his horse around Nyx and Jet, signaling for his men to follow, setting off in a smart trot. "We should hurry and not linger here after dark."

Nyx glanced at Jet as Zephri took off after Samill's horse, seeing the same frown on his face. She knew that something bad had happened, and she felt sorry for Samill. She guessed this wasn't how he thought their return to Regius Carmen would go. She wondered how common *petramises* were and if they only lived in these mountains.

The Tercastle Peaks, Ymber.
The forty-fourth day of winter, the 851st year of the
reign of Queen Liana Estrella.
Wednesday, February 2, 2012.

JET COULD FEEL HIS BONES rattling with each jarring step the horse he was riding took. He knew it was imperative they reach Regius Carmen before nightfall, but he felt like at this point he'd rather walk. He hated traveling by horseback, preferring even sharing a dragon with Zaida to this. After a while, his mare even seemed like she'd had enough as she slowed to a walk, clearly winded. He looked up when Nyx turned on her horse to look back at him.

"You all right?" she called, a few paces ahead of him. Behind her, two soldiers slowed their mounts as well, concern on their faces.

"Yeah," Jet said, motioning to his horse. "This old girl is just tired."

One of the soldiers immediately slid from her horse and walked toward him. "Take my horse," she said, offering Jet the reins. "I'll bring her in when she's ready."

Jet didn't argue and slid from the mare's back, trading with the soldier. Her horse was indeed in better shape, stomping its foot impatiently. Jet nodded his thanks to the soldier before turning the horse to catch up to the group.

"Do you think she'll be fine by herself?" Nyx asked, glancing over her shoulder to see the soldier walking beside the exhausted mare.

"I'm sure Samill's scouts will catch up to her," Jet said dismissively. "She'll be fine."

Nyx didn't say anything, her eyes shifting overhead to the fading sunlight. "Are we close?" she asked then.

Jet nodded.

Nyx felt her heart flip-flop in her chest. She turned her eyes toward the path ahead, feeling the butterflies in her stomach worsen as she realized it opened up as they came around a bend. Her breath hitched in her throat when Samill slowed his horse to turn and look at her.

"The Praesidio is just ahead, Princess," he said happily. He looked relieved. "Regius Carmen is just beyond it."

Nyx felt like she wanted to puke, and Zephri sensed her anxiety, beginning to prance. It didn't take long for a sharp, sheer wall to appear ahead of them. At the base of it, nestled in a circular area, was a tall fortress that appeared to be jutting from the mountain itself. A wall extended around it on either side, and a huge gate sat at the end of the road, manned by soldiers in the city's green and gold. Flags were waving in the light breeze that drifted between the mountain peaks.

Nyx's hands were tight around Zephri's reins as they reached the gate and a guard saluted Samill, allowing him and his men entrance. She noticed again that the guards were tall and broad-shouldered women, and their eyes were wide as they watched her and Jet ride into the fortress.

Once inside the courtyard, Samill halted them as another soldier approached him. She didn't carry a weapon like the others, and her armor was slightly different, leading Nyx to believe she was in charge here. Her hair was plated in stark rows across her head, a long braid falling across her back.

"My lord count," she said, pressing her hand over her heart and bowing. "I am glad to see you have returned."

Samill nodded to her from his horse. "We need a ferry, Cassie," he said brusquely.

Cassie looked up at him with a frown on her face. "You know we do not allow entry into the caves after dark," she said, a reprimand in her voice. "Why not let your party rest tonight before heading into the city?"

Samill turned then, extending his arm in Nyx's direction. "Her Majesty does not wish to wait until the morning," he said then.

Cassie turned her eyes on Nyx. She looked her over for a moment and then her face paled slightly. "Princess," she said, suddenly dropping to her knee. "I apologize."

Nyx drew an uncomfortable breath, shooting a look at Jet for help.

He simply lifted his chin, urging her to respond. He knew she was freaked out, but his eyes were calm, which reassured her that this was her place.

"Uh, stand, please," she managed, watching Cassie look up. "I agree with Samill." She looked at him. "I'd like to cross now."

Cassie bowed deeply. "As you wish, Your Highness," she said quickly. "I will prepare the ferry."

Nyx drew a ragged breath as she watched Cassie turn and bark orders to the soldiers around her. She looked over at Jet, missing the way the count's eyes narrowed in disapproval. "Was that okay?" she whispered, feeling the adrenaline flooding her body and making her hands shake.

Jet smirked lightly. "It was perfect," he said.

Nyx nodded stiffly, still feeling flustered. She looked up when Samill called for them to follow him.

They were escorted by two soldiers toward a massive cave entrance that Nyx hadn't paid much attention to when they first arrived. The mouth of the cave stretched high above their heads, giant stalactites hanging from the ceiling. But what surprised her most was a wide barge tied at the end of a rather wide dock. They were led to it and their horses were loaded onto it. Nyx realized it was big enough to support a wagon of some sort, and maybe even dragons.

Once they were aboard, six soldiers, three on each side, took their places and began steering the barge into the water. Nyx slid from Zephri's back and stepped toward the edge of the barge, feeling a cold wind blowing against them through the cave. Beneath the barge, water lapped at the sides. She gasped as, when the soldiers dipped their paddles into the water, it turned a bright blue, illuminating the cave.

She realized Jet was standing beside her as she leaned against the rail of the barge. "What is that?" she breathed, awe in her voice.

Jet leaned over to look as well. "Tiny creatures that light the water when disturbed," he said easily. "It's a rather common phenomenon."

"Bioluminescence," Nyx murmured in English then. Her eyes were wide as she watched the water spark with light and color.

Jet didn't respond as he watched her. He liked the way the glow lit her face, and the childlike joy in her eyes. He wasn't sure what he was thinking as he gazed at her, feeling his heart skip a beat. His mind drifted to what it would be like to kiss her now with her face illuminated softly in the glow. He lowered his eyes quickly before she turned to look at him, berating himself. He reminded himself of what happened at the inn, and the thought made him straighten and his brow furrow. It was time to leave these feelings alone.

It wasn't long before soft light began to illuminate the cave. Jet watched as Nyx turned to look ahead, her eyes widening as the cave opened, revealing the beauty that was Regius Carmen.

With each push of the soldiers' oars, the barge moved further into the city. On either side of the river, open land stretched into the distance. As they cleared the mouth of the cave, Nyx turned to see that mountains encased the city in a circle, keeping it nestled safely.

"Wow," she breathed, suddenly turning and making her way toward the front of the barge. She caught the edge of the railing as she took in everything around her.

Jet trailed after her, not surprised when the count accompanied her near the helm of the barge.

"This is farmland, Your Highness," he said, motioning to the open land around them. "This is where our citizens grow food for the city." He pointed ahead. "Beyond the farms are the districts where the craftsmen and millers do their work."

Nyx watched as they floated past the farmlands, docks jutting into the expanse of the river, which was much wider here than it was inside the cave. Men were milling around the docks, tying off shallow boats and moving sacks and barrels. They paused as the barge went by, seeming surprised to see all of the soldiers and horses.

After they passed the farming district, they moved toward more docks. Samill explained what each district was known for, and soon enough they were nearing the part of the city that Nyx could tell was where the elite lived. Unlike the men that had been working on the docks before, nobles dressed in fine clothing were strolling along the waterfront, ladies in beautiful dresses on their arms. Nyx watched as they paused to watch the barge go by, equally as surprised as the workers had been.

"Why do they look so surprised?" Nyx asked Samill quietly.

Samill turned to face her, smiling slightly. "They know something important is happening," he said. "The ferry never enters the city this late." He tilted his chin then, motioning ahead. "That is Regius Arce, Your Highness." He smiled at her brightly. "That is your home."

Nyx swallowed lightly, her mouth feeling dry. She leaned her head back as far as she could to take in the castle before her. It was a beautiful blue, cut right into the mountain that towered over it, much like the fortress they had entered through. It was massive and extravagant, animals carved into the rock, as well as more human images. The turrets were lit with fires, which were beginning to spread their light as the last rays of the sun fell behind the mountain peaks. Pennants hung from the spires of the castle, waving gently in the breeze. An archway stood over the dock, built high into the air, with stone guards standing on either side of it.

Nyx guessed the castle must have had at least ten floors with the way it kept climbing up the mountain, like some kind of crystal wedding cake. She wondered why in the heck anyone would ever need so many floors, but the thought fluttered away quickly as the barge met the dock with a light thud. The guards lowered a ramp, allowing Samill and his soldiers to cross onto the dock. Nyx noticed that there was a cobblestone path that led from the dock toward the archway and that it was lined with lit streetlamps. For a long moment, she couldn't move as she stared at everything before her.

"It's time," Jet said softly beside her, drawing her from her reverie.

Nyx looked up at him, seeing how confident he seemed. She drew a slow breath to steel herself and nodded, following Samill onto the dock. She watched as he was greeted by another woman soldier, her armor much like Cassie's had been. The soldier grinned widely, clasping Samill's arm in greeting.

"Welcome back, lord count," she said. "Her Majesty is expecting you."

Samill nodded and smiled easily. "Wonderful," he answered. He turned to look at Nyx. "Captain, this is Her Majesty's granddaughter, Princess Nyx Estrella."

The captain bowed low to Nyx, her hand over her heart. "Your Highness," she said, slight awe in her voice. "We are so glad for your safe return."

Nyx nodded her head. "Thank you," she said softly.

"Please," the captain said then, extending her arm for them to follow her. "Allow me to escort you inside."

Nyx didn't want to go inside, and she turned to make sure Jet was behind her. She wanted to grab his hand to make sure he didn't fall too far behind her, but she resisted the urge. He must have seen the look on her face, because he did stay close to her as they followed the captain under the archway and toward a tall staircase, which led up toward a tall entryway.

"Did they really need this many damn stairs?" Jet

murmured as they started up them.

Nyx had to stifle a nervous giggle as she glanced at him.

Once they reached the top, Nyx was surprised to see that the entry doors were also carved from stone. She was further surprised to see that they swung open easily with a gentle push from the captain. She paused as they walked toward them, pressing her hand against the cold stone.

"How is this possible?" she asked softly.

Jet leaned in toward her, a goading smirk on his face. "Magic," he answered cryptically.

Nyx scowled lightly at him, turning to catch up with Samill and the captain. She realized that beneath her feet was a plush carpet, threaded with the gold and green of Ymber's flag. It led down a rather towering and long foyer, with doors on either side. At one point, Nyx could see a separate hall and a set of stairs, and she wondered where it led to. All she could think was that this place was like a maze and she didn't know if she would ever figure it out. She was so enthralled by the massiveness of the place that she missed the pictures on the walls and the other decorations that dotted the foyer.

Jet, however, glanced up at exactly the right—or wrong—time, feeling his breath hitch in his chest. His feet stilled as he stared up at the painting in front of him, feeling his jaw clench tightly. A man was seated on a high-backed chair, with one leg thrown across the other. He wore a traditional wedding suit and his black hair was loose around his face, falling in long, straight locks across his shoulder. A crown sat on his head. His black eyes were staring out toward the observer, and his lips were quirked slightly in a pleased smirk. One hand was holding a ceremonial scepter, but the other was extended toward a woman who stood next to him. The woman was dressed similarly in traditional white, a cloak with thick, soft animal hair around her shoulders. Diamonds glistened on her dress and a tiara sat in her lavender hair, sparkling in the light. Her violet eyes were happy and a gentle smile was on her face. Instead of looking at the painter, she was looking at her new husband, love in her eyes. She, too, held a scepter in one hand, and her other was intertwined with the man's. A slow, hot rage was filling him as he stood there, lost in dangerous thoughts.

"Jet?"

He drew a sharp breath, feeling the rage dissipate as quickly as it had come. He turned to see Nyx looking up at him, worry on her face, her hand on his arm.

"What's wrong?" she whispered, searching his gaze.

"Nothing," he said quickly, shaking his head. He started to shoo her toward Samill and the captain, but she turned to look at the painting he'd been staring at. He stiffened as the emotion smoothed from her face.

Her eyes studied the man and woman depicted before her for a long moment, and each passing second made the apprehension in Jet's chest worse. Finally, she drew a soft breath and her shoulders eased.

"Is that him?" she asked gently. "Your father?"

Jet crossed his arms tightly. He ducked his chin, wishing that he hadn't stopped walking. He didn't have to answer for Nyx to know she was right.

"You look just like him," she said, glancing at Jet. She watched as anger flitted across his face, but he remained silent. She turned her eyes then on the woman standing beside him, studying her carefully. Her thoughts instantly turned to the vision that Sinister had shown her. "Is that ..."

Jet turned his head to look and opened his mouth to

answer, but a soft sound suddenly drew his gaze. His eyes fixed on someone behind her and surprise flitted across his face, so Nyx turned slowly to follow his gaze.

"That's me," a woman said, standing a few feet away from them.

Nyx stared at her for a moment. She was indeed the woman from the painting, but she looked slightly older than she had in the painting, and her violet eyes had a sadness to them that wasn't in the painting. She took a step toward them, her hands clasped in front of her, her long lavender hair swaying gently with her motion.

Jet suddenly bowed, startling Nyx. "My Queen," he said.

Nyx could feel her heart racing in her chest as she turned from him to face the woman standing before them. She didn't know what the etiquette was. Was she supposed to bow too? She'd never met a queen before.

Liana smiled gently then, her eyes traveling over Nyx's face. "I'm sure this must be strange for you," she said, her voice as gentle as her smile.

Nyx didn't know what to say as they stared at each other. She felt like she was in a dream as she held Liana's gaze. Was this her grandmother? She didn't look like any grandmother Nyx had ever seen before. In fact, she was beautiful, with a few wrinkles around her eyes and her mouth, but pale, porcelain skin. She didn't look like she was more than fifty years old.

"I've waited a long time to see you again," Liana said then. Her brow furrowed lightly, betraying her feelings. "I've missed you for so long."

Nyx felt her words strike her deep down into a part of her heart that she'd tried to pretend didn't exist. She'd always wondered about her parents and her family, even wished that she could have known them when she was younger. She thought she'd put those feelings to bed a long time ago, believing that there was no one left, but Liana's words broke the dam open, making tears flood her eyes suddenly.

Liana gasped as Nyx took quick steps toward her and embraced her, and she put her arms around Nyx as well, holding her tightly. She couldn't stop the tears that formed in her eyes, her heart brimming with too many emotions to name.

Nyx breathed in Liana's scent, trying to burn it into her brain as a comforting feeling washed over her. This was all she'd ever wanted; a home and a family and someone who loved her. Of course, she'd had that with Dorothea, but this … this felt different. She felt a connection to Liana that she'd never felt before. For the first time in her life, she felt like she was where she was supposed to be.

After a moment, she stepped back from Liana, brushing the tears from her face. "I'm sorry," she said quickly, her voice choked. She laughed a bit. "Are you supposed to hug a queen?"

Liana reached out to brush a tear from her cheek, her violet eyes gentle as she smiled. She was silent for a moment as she watched Nyx's face. "You look so much like your father," she said finally. Her smile widened slightly as Nyx looked up at her in surprise. "You have his eyes."

Nyx didn't know what to say to that. There were so many questions and so many things she wanted to know. She didn't even know what her father looked like; she used to wonder why Aunt Dee never kept photos of her parents, but now it made sense.

Liana reached for her hand then. "Come," she said, finally looking to Jet once more. "You two must be hungry after your journey." She grinned playfully. "And I'm sure you've missed your comrades."

Nyx's eyes brightened then. To be honest, she'd totally forgotten about them.

Liana nodded. "They're waiting for us in the dining hall," she said, still holding Nyx's hand as she turned to lead the way. "I'm *very* curious how you two ended up with a group of Fornaxian rebels and Baron Atturon's daughter."

Nyx glanced back to make sure Jet was following them before looking to Liana. "It's a long story," she said, slightly embarrassed.

Liana was still grinning. "And we have all the time in the world for stories."

15

Regius Carmen, the capitol city of Ymber.
The forty-fourth day of winter, the 851st year of the
reign of Queen Liana Estrella.
Wednesday, February 2, 2012.

IANA LED THE WAY INTO another massive room, where tables took up most of the space. Seated at one, near the front of the room, were the Pangere and Ellie and Raphael. Nyx felt her heart leap with joy as they turned and instantly moved to their feet to greet her. She realized that they all had bathed and wore clean clothes, and that she'd never actually seen the Pangere members in anything other than their armor and riding clothes.

"You guys clean up well," she said as they met in the center of the room.

Amaya twirled in a circle, showing off her pink, tea-length dress. "Her Majesty is very generous," she said, looking to Liana and bowing. Quieter, to Nyx, she added, "I love this dress!"

Nyx laughed and looked at Liam, Zaida, and Rian. Liam and Rian both were dressed in black pants and

boots, as well as nice shirts with blazers pulled over them. They looked like royal courtiers, suave and with their hair combed. Zaida wore a black dress that complimented her darker skin tone and her dark hair was clean and brushed, flowing loosely past the middle of her back. Amaya's hair was brushed similarly, with braids threaded into her light pink hair.

Ellie and Raphael were slower to reach them, but they were cleaned up as well. Ellie had her hair twisted in a half-ponytail away from her face and her blue dress made her startling blue eyes stand out. Raphael wore a similar outfit to Rian and Liam in a darker blue and he walked with a proper cane instead of the thick wooden stick he'd used before.

Nyx watched as Ellie walked toward her and embraced her. "We didn't like leaving you," she said.

"Yeah, but we set up the place for when you got here," Liam chimed then, a grin on his face.

Nyx returned his smile, looking past him to the feast that was set out.

"Are you hungry?" Liana asked, drawing her gaze. She waved her hand. "You should eat."

Nyx nodded at her suggestion, starting toward table. She noticed that they didn't move to follow, and she paused to look at them.

"Are you guys joining us?" she asked.

Rian shook his head. "We've eaten already," he said pleasantly. "We're going to retire for the night and give you some privacy."

"Oh," Nyx said. "Okay." She offered them a slight smile. "See you tomorrow then."

They each chimed a parting before leaving Nyx and Jet alone with Liana.

When Nyx turned to walk to the table, she saw two empty seats near the head of the table and a chair placed at the very end, which Liana eased into. She seemed happy as she watched Nyx and Jet sit on either side of her.

As Jet eased to sit across from her, Nyx could see that his face was guarded. Nyx wondered what he was thinking, but she couldn't dwell on the thought when a servant placed a plate in front of her with vegetables and meat covered in gravy. The smell was heavenly, and Nyx wasted no time digging into it. She thought it was probably the most delicious meal she'd ever had, but then again, she felt like she hadn't had anything decent to eat in a long time.

"You should eat as well, Jet," Liana said, drawing Nyx's gaze.

He picked lightly at the food on the plate in front of him, but Nyx knew it was more to placate Liana. The thought made her pause. Jet never did anything to placate anybody. Was he afraid of Liana?

She must have sensed the same thing, because, after she took a sip of wine from her goblet, she reached for his hand, placing hers gently on top of his. "You can relax," she said quietly, holding his gaze.

Jet's eyes narrowed slightly, and he sat back in his chair, pulling his hand away from hers. He turned his gaze down to the plate in a stubborn gesture, and for a moment Nyx was reminded of when she first met him. It made her yearn suddenly for an easier time, and she set her fork down, no longer hungry. An awkward silence was descending on them, so Nyx turned to Liana.

"So, you said that was you in the painting?" she asked, drawing Liana's gaze. "With Jet's fath—" she stole a glance at him, catching her words, "Paraximus?"

Liana nodded easily. "Yes, that's me," she said as if it

were nothing more than a matter of fact. "It was a long time ago, when we were married."

Nyx felt her brain screech to a halt. "Wait, you were married to that crazy guy?" she asked, disbelief in her voice. She recalled that they had been touching in the painting, Liana's hand placed in his, but it hadn't registered to her what that meant until now.

Liana offered a slight laugh at her surprise. "Yes," she said. She glanced toward the hall where the painting hung. "That was our wedding portrait." She reached for her goblet. "But, as I said, it was a long time ago."

Nyx looked down at her plate. She knew every person had a history, but this was blowing her mind a bit. "Is that why he hates us?" she whispered unthinkingly, twirling her fork across her plate. "Because you broke up?"

Liana set her goblet down, drawing Nyx's gaze. "I won't lie to you," she said gently, but earnestly. "It is one of the reasons. But there is much more to that story." She glanced at Jet then, as if to ascertain what he might have told Nyx, but he was still silent and cold toward her, much like the mountains around the castle.

Nyx looked back at her plate, realizing that there was just so much to ask – twenty years' worth of questions. She felt overwhelmed at the thought. She looked back up at her grandmother when she rested her hand on her arm.

"I will answer any questions you have," she said, holding Nyx's gaze. She smiled a sad smile then. "You must have so many."

Nyx nodded mutely.

"But tonight, I want you to rest," Liana said then. "Tomorrow there will be much buzz around your arrival, and I want you to be well-rested to face the day."

"What do you mean?" Nyx asked.

Liana seemed lightly exasperated. "I've sent the courtiers away for the evening," she said, waving her hand. "They can be busy-bodies on the best of days, and I didn't want you to be overwhelmed." She suddenly smiled again, this time in gentle delight. "And I wanted to welcome you myself. I wish I could express to you how much I've missed you and how happy I am that you're home. I'm looking forward to getting to know you."

Nyx nodded, unsure of how to respond to that. Fortunately, Liana didn't let her fish for a reply.

"If you are ready to see your rooms, I will have the ladies' maid take you upstairs," she said. She patted Nyx's arm and looked at Jet.

Nyx nodded slightly, looking over at him too. "That would be great," she said, her voice suddenly sounding tired to her own ears. She noticed that he almost seemed relieved.

Liana smiled as she waved over a servant and instructed him to summon the maid.

Nyx watched as a young girl, possibly no older than her, scampered into the room, bowing to Liana.

"You called for me, Your Majesty?" she asked, keeping her head lowered.

"Yes, Jasmine," Liana said, her hands in her lap. "Please show Nyx and Jet to their rooms." She looked up at her. "Make sure they have everything they need."

Jasmine bowed low. "Yes, Your Majesty," she said easily before lifting her eyes to look at Nyx and Jet. Her cheeks flushed, as if she were embarrassed to meet their eyes. "Please, right this way." She waved her hand to indicate they should follow her.

They both stood and bid Liana good night, and then Nyx and Jet followed Jasmine from the hall through a side door that opened into another open area which led to a staircase. Nyx was sure she was going to get lost a lot in this place.

"Her Majesty had the rooms on the second floor prepared for you," Jasmine said as they started up the stone staircase. She glanced over her shoulder. "She thought it might be easiest to help you find your way, but if you decide you'd like a different room, there are plenty to choose from."

Nyx nodded absently, glancing over her shoulder at Jet. She saw that he was looking around at the castle, and she turned slightly to face him. "Are you okay?" she asked quietly.

Jet's eyes snapped to her then. "I'm fine," he said, a bit more shortly than Nyx expected.

"You didn't look fine," Nyx said.

Jet scowled. "It just feels … weird here, okay?"

Nyx gave him a placating look and turned to follow after Jasmine.

Once they reached the landing, it opened around them, and Nyx could see that it curved around the staircase in a circle. On one side was another staircase and on the other was a hallway which led further into the castle. Jasmine directed them down the hallway. Nyx wondered where the heck they were going, but then the hall opened to a round seating area, filled with chairs, a table, and a cart with a decanter of wine. A big window offered an excellent view of the city, and a fireplace kept the room comfortably warm. It reminded Nyx of a common area in a dorm room, as there were two doors on either side of the room.

"This wing is yours," Jasmine said. She motioned to the door to their left. "Princess, this is your room, and the one opposite is yours, my lord." She then turned and pointed to a narrow staircase that was practically hidden next to the entrance. "Up the stairs is a private bathing area. The maids will prepare it for you if you wish to use it, and I will be just down the hall if you need anything else."

Nyx nodded mutely, hoping she would go away. She stole a glance at Jet, wanting to get to the bottom of what was bothering him. She watched Jasmine walk away before turning back to Jet. She was surprised to see that he had already opened the door to his room and was about to disappear inside.

"Hey, wait," she said quickly, dashing over to put her hand on the door. She felt mildly alarmed. "You're just going to leave me by myself?"

Jet seemed annoyed. "I've spent nearly every day of the last few months with you," he said, an edge to his voice. "I think I deserve some peace."

Nyx let her hand slide from the door, her feelings hurt. She stepped back from the door and nodded. "Oh, okay," she said weakly. "Have a good night."

Jet didn't seem the least bit remorseful as he closed the door without another word.

Nyx didn't like the loneliness that flooded her as she stood in the common room. She turned her back to his door and looked around. It felt weird here. The luxury made her feel like she couldn't touch anything. It was like being in a formal living room that was only used once a year for holidays.

She guessed that she should check out her room, so she crossed to her door, feeling acutely the way the carpet shifted under her feet. It was thick and tightly woven, and likely expensive. She vaguely wondered how much trouble it would be if anything was ever spilled on the carpet.

The handle to her room was cool under her touch,

the door heavy as she pushed it open. The first thing she noticed was a wave of warm air that hit her as she stepped inside. To her left was another lit fireplace and to her right was a big, four-poster bed. Beyond that was a set of double doors that she assumed led to a closet. She was surprised to see an open area where there was a mirror and lavatory. She felt slight relief at the thought that she wouldn't have to use a chamber pot or some other crude means for a bathroom. There was no bathtub, though, and she remembered Jasmine mentioning the bathing area.

Nyx crossed the room toward a tall cabinet that looked like it was meant for clothes and pulled the doors open. Inside, she found it filled with clothing as she expected, as well as drawers already filled with clean undergarments. She quickly pulled the clean clothes from the wardrobe, deciding that she needed a bath. She was very tired, all the way into her bones, but she couldn't possibly sleep until she was clean.

She was almost grateful she didn't see Jet as she opened the door and crossed to the narrow stairs. They were rough-cut stone steps, but they were smooth across the top, probably from use. Nyx wondered who used to stay in this wing as she started up them. As she came to a landing, she was surprised to see what looked like a natural spring inside of a large cave. Natural pillars of stone were holding up the ceiling, stalactites hanging from it. The light was low in the room and steam rolled from the top of the water.

A maid appeared from a doorway and walked toward her, bowing. "Would you like to use the bath, Princess?" she asked.

Nyx nodded, noticing that she wore a short outfit that looked somewhat like a robe. She looked ready to jump into the pool at any moment, but Nyx guessed that was the point.

"There is a changing area this way," the maid said, leading her toward a screen. "I will bring fresh towels for you."

Nyx drew a slow breath, feeling nervous as she stepped behind the screen. It reminded her of the first time she'd gone to the bath house with Melinda. It was so awkward, but that feeling was quickly replaced with stabbing pain in her heart.

Gods, what she wouldn't give right now to have Melinda alive.

Tears started to prick at her eyes, but she pushed her feelings down and yanked her dirty clothing off before pulling on a robe which hung on a hook, clearly set out for her to put on. It was soft, as if it were made of silk, but it made Nyx feel even more out of sorts. She'd never felt real silk before.

She walked from behind the screen just as the maid came back from the doorway she'd first come through. She was carrying a basket with rolled up towels, as well as what looked like bottles of soaps. She knelt to put the basket next to the pool.

"May I help you, Your Highness?" she asked, holding out her hand to help her down the steps and into the water.

"Uh, I'm fine," Nyx said, not wanting to be fully undressed in front of a stranger. "Could I maybe have some privacy?"

The maid nodded and bowed. "Of course, Highness," she said easily. "My name is Ava. Please call if you need me." She started to walk away but paused. "Oh, please don't spend too long in the water. Too much heat can be dangerous."

"Oh," Nyx said. She nodded. "Okay, thanks."

Ava disappeared once more into the doorway, and Nyx assumed it was servants' quarters or storage or something.

Once she was alone, Nyx took a moment to sit on the side of the pool, dipping her toes into the water. Just as Ava had warned, the water was hot, but it felt good on her aching body. She let the robe slip from her shoulders before sliding down into the hot water. It was a shock at first, but as she got used to it, it eased the soreness from her body. She took a moment to enjoy it, relishing in the feel of being comfortable for once.

So much had happened in the short time she'd been in Gexalatia. She hadn't felt comfortable in a long time. She'd been relatively comfortable with Melinda and her father, but there was always that nagging thought in the back of her head that she couldn't stay there. She felt like she didn't belong anywhere, and things had just gotten worse since they'd left Festra. She wasn't sure that belonging was what she felt here, but it helped to know that they'd reached their goal. She was here with Liana, and she didn't have to go anywhere else. Unfortunately, she knew that, even though one part of the battle was done, learning to mesh into court life would be a whole new fight.

Celo Cavus, the capitol city of Siccita.
The forty-fifth day of winter, the 906th year of the
reign of King Paraximus Lamia.
Thursday, February 3, 2012.

WE CANNOT INFILTRATE THE CASTLE yet," a woman's voice said, filling the room. It was pleasant on the ears, but at the same time, it left Paraximus with a crawling feeling.

He watched as the woman paced slowly around a table set with maps and markers. She was wearing a pale dress that drug on the ground behind her. She had black hair that had been coiled into a nice pile on top of her head, strands hanging around her pale face, framing her crimson-colored eyes. It was easy to think she was anything other than a rotting corpse reanimated.

A general sitting on his right was watching her suspiciously. "And why not?" he demanded suddenly, causing that blood-red gaze to turn on him.

Paraximus could see that it made the man feel uncomfortable, but he tried to hide it, straightening his shoulders.

"Our King has the power to summon portals," the general continued. "What is stopping him from summoning one in the middle of that wretched Liana's throne room?"

The woman turned her gaze to Paraximus then, a slight smile on her lips but murder in her eyes. "Is this one important to you, My King?" she asked as she took a soundless step toward the general.

Paraximus fought the urge to lower his gaze from hers. That was unbefitting a king, and he hated that she made his body react in fear. He gave a slight shake of his head, challenging her to do her worst.

The woman slunk toward the general, running her finger across his shoulders. "Wisdom can never be overlooked in matters like this," she said slowly. "Patience can win battles, while a lack of it can mean death." Her fingers on the hand across his back began to grow long and spindly, dagger-like nails protruding from the ends. She smirked as she dug her hand into the general's back, listening to him scream in pain, before she leaned in toward his ear. "You're a poor excuse for a general." She then suddenly yanked her hand from his body, letting him collapse to the floor.

Normally, a wound like that would have healed fairly quickly, but a black, oozing magic was flowing from her hand. The general writhed on the floor as the blackness spread across his skin, flooding his veins. The woman seemed delighted as she hovered over him, watching as the blackness slowly consumed him and he stopped moving.

"Any other objections?" she asked then, looking at the others.

Paraximus watched as the rest of his council sat meekly in their chairs, some pretending that they didn't just witness that and some clearly rattled. "So then what shall we do, Goddess?" Paraximus asked then, drawing her gaze.

"How is the army of *mortivio* coming along?" she asked then, turning and stepping over the dead man on the floor.

"We were able to procure the blood of ten-thousand first-born, Goddess," another man answered. "At Mara's direction, they will be ready before the next night of Deimos."

Daya paused for a moment, thinking. "So that gives us roughly a month," she said finally. She turned to smile in an apologetic way to Paraximus. "Creating demons takes time."

Paraximus nodded, knowing her placating ways were fake. She didn't care how long it took, because time was of no consequence to her. "We still cannot hope to overrun Regius Carmen with such a small force, even if they are demons," he said then.

Daya circled the table and walked toward him, her eyes lustful. "Don't you worry about that, my king," she said softly. "There is a way to draw your despicable son from inside her walls, where my magic cannot reach, and allow you to reclaim the *fax*."

Paraximus' eyes narrowed. "Why can't your magic reach there?"

Daya scowled suddenly and spun on her heel. "If the gods did anything right, it was giving the Priorae the knowledge to make that damned city," she spat. "Inside of Montem Magnus is a spring, said to be the place where the tears of the gods fell. The water creates a barrier that even I cannot penetrate."

Paraximus couldn't hide the scowl that pulled at his lips. He didn't realize that Daya's power could be tempered.

Was she even the fabled goddess supposed to have sprung from the blood of the gods?

"But, don't fret, my king," she said. She turned back to him. "Now that my power grows, as my form is restored, I will make you invincible."

Paraximus wasn't sure he liked the sound of that, and he stiffened as she moved toward him and sat across his knee. She lifted one of his hands to press his palm to her lips. He had to school his face as fangs grew from under her lips and she sank them into his hand, sucking his blood. After a moment, she sat back, licking her lips.

"As long as you pay your debt, I will keep my end of the bargain," she said.

Paraximus wanted to shove her to the floor, but he resisted. He felt like he'd paid his debt to her a thousand times over, and so far with no results in his favor. At every turn, his son and that little princess had managed to evade him. He was starting to wonder if she was inept and lying to him, or if she was playing a different game.

After a bit more discussion, the meeting ended and Daya slunk from the room to rest, leaving Paraximus alone with his council, all of whom he dismissed except for the captain of his guard, Ivan.

"Take the Atturon girl downstairs," Paraximus said, looking up at the man before him. He pulled a charm from inside his coat, handing it to Ivan. "Place this on her cell door. It will keep Daya away from her."

Ivan nodded and left the room.

If Daya was going to string him along, he was cutting her off. Two could play at her game.

*****

Mara watched from a shadowed corner as workers slaved in the pits below her, their hands kneading clay to make the bodies for the *mortivio* army. She held a goblet of blood in her hand as she watched their work. She didn't stir when a cold wind swirled around her.

"How was your meeting?" she asked, turning to look over her shoulder slowly.

Daya stepped toward her, crossing her arms as she looked down at their work. "The king is restless," she said, clearly unhappy. "He may have started to think that I have some ulterior motives."

Mara grinned, her smile full of shark's teeth. "Once you have the power of the *fax*, it won't matter," she said, passing her goblet.

Daya took the goblet and drained it. She stared into the distance, her mind filled with thoughts of chaos and death. Once she had the raw power of the *fax* trapped in Jet's body, she would destroy Siccita and Ymber, and anyone else who thought to stand against her.

17

Regius Carmen, the capitol city of Ymber.
The forty-fifth day of winter, the 851st year of the
reign of Queen Liana Estrella.
Thursday, February 3, 2012.

ELLIE GLANCED AT THE SEAT next to her as she slowly ate her breakfast. She was worried about Nyx, although she knew that was silly. Nyx was safe here, and she was probably resting. Gods knew she needed it more than anyone else.

"Maybe you should go see her after breakfast," Raphael murmured then, drawing her eyes.

Ellie felt slightly embarrassed. "What?" she asked.

Raphael rolled his eyes. "You've been staring at Nyx's empty chair since we sat down," he said. "If you're worried about her, go check on her."

Ellie looked down at her plate. "Okay," she said softly, pushing her food around. "I will after breakfast."

"Are you two coming to our audience with the Queen?" Rian asked then, drawing their attention. His eyes were on Ellie. "It would mean the world to us if you would share what you've seen."

Ellie thought back to her vision of Eomryr Lani, the dragon god of the sky. It was something she wasn't sure she could put into words, but if the Pangere needed more to help their cause, she couldn't turn them down. They'd saved her life, after all.

"Absolutely," Ellie said. "I wouldn't miss it."

Rian nodded with a smile. "I was hoping that would be your answer," he said pleasantly. "We are to meet in Her Majesty's throne room just before midday." He glanced at Zaida beside him. "Hopefully she will help us."

Zaida nodded and put her hand over his. "She seems like a kind and fair queen," she said. "I'm sure she will do what she can."

They all quieted as the first of the courtiers began to trickle into the dining hall. They were men and women, dressed in the finest clothes, and they eyed the group while whispering among themselves, sitting at the tables around them. Ellie felt like she wanted to shrink into the floor under their judgmental stares.

"Ellie? Raphael?"

The Atturon siblings looked up at the same time, their eyes suddenly brightening.

"Aled!" Ellie suddenly gasped, jumping to her feet.

Aled, a tall man with pale hair much like Ellie's, caught her in a big hug and swung her around, delighted to see her. "I can't believe it," he said, pressing his hand against her face. "When I heard about Sorona, I thought …" He shook his head, his brow furrowed, unable to finish his thought. He looked up then. "Where is Bailey?"

Ellie's eyes instantly fell to the floor, and she looked over her shoulder at her brother. Raphael's face mirrored hers, and Aled knew instantly that something terrible had happened.

"Oh, no," he said, shaking his head. "Is she …" He looked as if he would cry.

Ellie shook her head quickly. "No, she's alive," she said. She caught Aled's hand, realizing they were making a spectacle. "Please, sit and we'll talk."

Aled let her lead him to the table where they were sitting and slid to sit beside Raphael. They embraced like brothers who'd been apart for too long. Then Aled looked up, seeing Rian, Zaida, Liam, and Amaya looking back at him.

"This is our cousin, Aled," Ellie said then to the Pangere. "He is like me and Bailey."

Rian's eyes widened slightly. "You are a Seer?"

Aled offered a weak grin. "I don't *see* things," he said slowly. "I get premonitions." He glanced at Ellie. "My cousins' blood lines are much purer than mine, allowing them to touch the *Visus* in a way that I will never be able to do."

"Ah," Rian said then. "And what are you doing here in Regius Carmen?"

Aled seemed mildly offended. "I could ask you the same," he said, his eyes skirting over them. "Your features and accent suggest you are Fornaxian."

Rian offered an easy smile. "You would be correct," he said. "I did not mean to offend. I simply wondered if you were here to master your gift."

"I've certainly had help here," Aled said, much calmer. "But unfortunately, the knowledge I seek was lost in the fire at Sorona."

Ellie looked up at him. "What?" she gasped. "Are you sure?"

Aled saw the fear and defeat in her face. "I'm sorry,

Ellie," he said. "I've searched Her Majesty's library and I've read all there is to know about the *Visus*." He sighed shortly. "It seems Uncle Willem had the only copy of the Videns Liber."

Ellie could feel her chest tighten and any hope she might have had crumble. Of course there was only one copy of the magic book —it was a sentient creature, after all— but she had hoped that it would have saved itself and come here. She had hoped that she could use it to rescue her sister. Tears instantly flooded her eyes and she couldn't stop them. "But ... Bailey ..." She suddenly broke down into sobs.

Aled seemed startled and he put his arm around her. "Everything will be okay," he said quickly. He held her tightly against his side and looked to Raphael. "Where is Bailey? Why isn't she here?"

Raphael sighed deeply, his brow furrowed with silent despair. "She was taken to Siccita," he said softly. He pressed his hand against his eyes. "Paraximus has her."

"What?" Aled demanded harshly. "How is this possible?"

"I would also like to hear this," a voice chimed, breaking through their conversation.

Aled jumped to his feet, along with the others, except for Raphael, who moved slowly. "Your Majesty," he said bowing quickly. "Forgive our rudeness."

Liana smiled in a kind way, placing her hand on Raphael's shoulder to stop him from standing. "Please, you've been through enough," she said. "There is no need for such formalities."

They all eased back into their seats, watching as Liana joined them at the head of the table. "Now," she said, looking among them before her eyes landed on Ellie.

"What is this about your sister?"

She looked up and did her best to stem her tears. "King Paraximus took her, Your Highness," she said, her voice hitching as she spoke. "He sent men to destroy Sorona. We managed to evade them, but they still found us."

Liana's eyes were narrowed. "It's not possible for them to have crossed the wall," she said slowly. "My forces have it sealed against Siccita."

Ellie nodded in agreement. "That's because they didn't," she said emphatically. "They came through a portal."

Liana's eyes widened slightly, the only sign of her surprise. "A portal?" she said. "That … is certainly a problem." She was silent for a long moment before she looked up, turning her violet eyes on Rian. "You and your Pangere must return to Fornax."

Rian shook his head. "We can't," he said in protest. "We've been sent here for your help."

Liana once more offered a gentle smile. "It is I who is in need of your help," she said then. "And I have a feeling that, if we work together, we will achieve both our goals."

Rian seemed like he would protest more, but Zaida put her hand on his shoulder to stop him. "What would you have us do?" she asked.

Liana sat back in her chair and drew a slow breath. "Tell your father it is time," she said, turning her eyes once more on Rian. "Fornax and Ymber must unite to stop Siccita's king."

"Your father?" Ellie asked whispered, looking over at him.

Rian lowered his eyes, looking mildly ashamed. "My father is Fell, the White Dragon, and king of Fornax," he said quietly. He felt immensely guilty at the way Ellie stared at him.

"And you came here against his will, no doubt," Liana said then, drawing their eyes. "But perhaps it was fate, with the news that we've just received." She looked to Ellie before back to him. "You and your Pangere must leave as soon as you can." Her violet eyes were troubled then. "I fear we don't have much time. Tell the White Dragon that I invoke the Treaty of Kvia, and request that he stop providing Siccita with goods, namely Fornaxian war-dragons."

Rian seemed surprised then. "My father does not wish war with Siccita," he said. "He's told me so himself. And halting trade will surely enrage King Paraximus."

Liana nodded. "I understand," she said. "But use the words I've just told you. He will agree." She drew a deep breath. "Once King Fell hears of what Paraximus is capable, he will know what he must do."

"Yes, Your Majesty," Rian said, bowing his head. He looked to his followers. "We will go as soon as we can."

"Use our stores to fill your bags," Liana said. "And travel as swiftly as you can. Our time is limited."

"As you wish, Your Majesty," Rian said. "But, before we go, may we ask one request?"

Liana looked at him, seeming surprised.

Rian looked to his friends before back to her. "We'd like a chance to bid the princess goodbye."

Liana's eyes softened. "Of course," she said then. "I will let her know."

Nyx jumped awake at the sound of knocking on her bedroom door. She was groggy as she lifted her face from her pillow, realizing drool was running down her chin. She sat up quickly, feeling disoriented for a moment before she remembered where she was.

"Princess?"

Nyx rubbed her face. She didn't even know what time it was. Was it early? "Uh—yeah?" she managed. "I'm awake."

"I'm so sorry to disturb you, but the Pangere are leaving soon," Jasmine called through the door. "They wish to see you before they go."

Nyx shook her head and smoothed unruly strands of hair from her face. It took her a moment to understand what Jasmine was saying. Once she did, she jumped to her feet and moved to open the door quickly. "What?" she asked, seeing the surprise on Jasmine's face. "They're leaving? Why?" How long had she been asleep? Surely not so long that they would have already spoken to Liana.

Jasmine nodded. "Her Majesty is sending them home."

Nyx shook her head. "Why?" she asked. "I don't understand what's happening."

Jasmine offered a pleasant smile. "They are waiting for you in the courtyard," she said. "Perhaps it would be best to ask them those questions yourself."

Nyx nodded at Jasmine's words.

"Would you like some help getting dressed?" Jasmine asked. She stepped into the room before Nyx could give a proper answer and started toward the closet.

Nyx was surprised, when she opened the door, at the number of dresses. She stepped closer, watching Jasmine pull clothing out to lay on the bed for her. She reached for one of the dresses, feeling that the material was soft, but warm.

"Which color do you prefer, Your Highness?" Jasmine asked.

Nyx looked over the choices, a long-sleeved blue dress, or a similar green. She took a moment to wrap her head around having a maid and picked up the green dress. "This one," she said, holding it up.

Jasmine smiled and immediately set to work helping her put on the proper undergarments and helped her step into the dress. She nimbly laced it in the back, snug but not too tight, and used her fingers to comb the tangles from Nyx's hair and twist the curl back into it.

Once Nyx was dressed, she paused in front of the mirror, barely recognizing herself. Her hair was much longer than she remembered, and her face was clean for once. The dress also made her look like she belonged in the castle instead of making her look like a dirty fugitive. She wasn't sure how she felt about her new look, but she realized she didn't exactly have time to stare at herself as Jasmine was already waiting by the door.

"This way, Highness," she said easily.

Nyx glanced toward Jet's door as they walked into the sitting room, feeling the knot in her stomach tighten. "Have you seen Jet today?" she asked Jasmine quietly.

Jasmine paused to glance at his door and frowned. "I haven't," she said before continuing to lead the way to the stairs. "But I'm sure he's just as exhausted as you were, Highness."

Nyx nodded mutely at her words, but inside she was worried. He hadn't exactly been in the best mood when he'd shut himself in there and she wondered if he was okay. She decided to check on him after seeing the Pangere off.

The castle was winding and confusing as Jasmine led her down a different corridor and toward a set of double doors that opened into a courtyard. Overhead, the mountain was towering, casting a shadow across the city. The sun wasn't quite at midday yet, and Nyx was grateful that she could at least recognize the time by it. She blinked against a cold wind that blew through the doors and into the corridor, hearing voices outside.

Once she and Jasmine emerged, she saw her friends embracing Ellie and Raphael. She thanked Jasmine and lifted her skirt to jog toward them. When they heard her footsteps, they looked up. Nyx noticed the surprise on Rian's face as he met her gaze.

"Princess," he said, bowing. He offered an easy smile. "We hoped you would make it." He glanced over her shoulder, as if expecting someone else. "Is Jet not with you?"

Nyx shook her head, feeling her heart twist. "He won't be joining us," she said shortly. She looked them over, seeing they were wearing their armor, their bags slung over their shoulders. Just beyond them, stable hands were leading their dragons into the courtyard through a gated archway, which she assumed led to the aviary.

"You can't be leaving already," Nyx said then, hearing the slightly desperate edge to her voice. "We just got here."

Rian reached out to place his hand on her elbow in a comforting gesture. "Her Majesty has asked us to return home and deliver a message to Our King," he said gently. "We would stay, but it is urgent."

Nyx frowned lightly. "Is it about Paraximus?" she asked.

Rian nodded. "Fornax supplies Siccita with goods not found anywhere else, including dragons," he said. He glanced at his fellow Pangere. "Our mission is to stop him."

Nyx nodded, feeling her heart twisting. She stepped toward Rian and pulled him into a hug. "Please be safe," she said. She realized that once they were gone, she might never see them again. She looked at Zaida, Liam, and Amaya. "I hope to see you again one day."

Amaya grinned then. "Well, duh," she said playfully. "Throw a party, and we'll be back!"

Nyx laughed with her. "I'll hold you to it," she said. She stepped toward Amaya and hugged her before turning to Liam. "Don't eat too much fruit on your way."

Liam chuckled and held up his knapsack. "Her Majesty let us load up from her cellar," he said, revealing meats and cheese and bread. "No fruit this time!" He squeezed her tightly in a side hug.

Nyx then turned to Zaida, surprised to see the barest hint of emotion on her face. She surprised Nyx more when she pulled her into a tight hug. "Remember what I told you," she whispered so that only Nyx could hear. "Take care of yourself."

Nyx nodded, remembering Zaida's words that night at the inn, despite her drunkenness. "I will," she said softly. She looked back to Rian as he smiled and looked to his family.

"We must be on our way now," he said, slinging a bag over his shoulders.

Nyx nodded, as if giving them permission to leave, before stepping back beside Ellie and Raphael. Next to her, Ellie was sniffling lightly and wiping away tears while Raphael kept his arm around her shoulders. It was weird watching the ones who had rescued her and become her friends leave. But it seemed like an eternity and no time at all before they were astride their dragons and launching into the air.

Nyx and the Atturon siblings watched and waved as the Pangere circled overhead before turning toward the south and soaring into the distance over the mountains. Once they were out of sight, Nyx felt a weird emptiness. She felt like a large portion of the allies she had in Regius Carmen were gone, and it made her feel like she was surrounded by predators, just waiting to sink their teeth into her.

The wind began to pick up a bit, and Raphael turned to look at her. "Perhaps we should head inside," he said.

Nyx watched as Ellie nodded and they turned as if to go back into the castle, but her feet were frozen. "Wait," she said softly, watching them turn in surprise.

"What is it, Princess?" Ellie asked gently.

Nyx shook her head. "Don't call me that," she said, realizing her words sounded harsher than she intended. "I just want to be Nyx."

Ellie nodded. "Okay," she said.

Nyx wasn't sure what it was she even wanted to say. "This is probably going to sound stupid, but please don't leave me," she said, looking up at both of them. "You're my only friends here, and I—" She drew a ragged breath and looked away, feeling pathetic. "I don't want to be alone with these people."

Ellie stepped toward her and caught her hand. "We're always here for you," she said quickly. "No matter what."

"Absolutely," Raphael said, taking a step closer with his cane. "We'll help you. You won't be alone."

Nyx nodded, feeling relieved and reassured at their words. "Thank you," she said, feeling as if she wanted to cry. "I have no idea what I'm doing." She gave a watery laugh. "I've never been a princess before."

Ellie and Raphael both laughed softly, and Ellie looped her arm in Nyx's. "Let's go get warmed up," she said, looking at her brother. "And we'll introduce you to our cousin, Aled."

Nyx nodded. "That sounds good."

Regius Carmen, the capitol city of Ymber.
The forty-fifth day of winter, the 851st year of the
reign of Queen Liana Estrella.
Thursday, February 3, 2012.

JET'S ARMS WERE CROSSED TIGHTLY as he stood on a balcony overlooking the foyer. It hadn't been too difficult to find his way back to this part of the castle, but everything about this place made him feel like he was on pins and needles. Down in the pit of his stomach, he felt like at any moment he'd end up back in a dungeon cell. He tried to tell himself that wasn't true; if Liana wanted him there, then that's where he'd be, but it didn't help much.

Down below, he caught movement from the corner of his eyes, and he turned his head slightly to see Nyx, Ellie, and her brother walking into the foyer. He vaguely recalled the servant girl knocking on his door to let him know the Pangere were leaving, and he surmised that was where they had been. He noticed that Nyx's arm was linked with Ellie's, and he pressed his lips together tightly. The thought that she was finding her place among the others made him unhappy, but in a weird, slightly jealous way.

He knew he would never be accepted here, but he wondered how long he could hide from the rest of them before Liana forced him to show his face. Almost as if the thought summoned her, a voice called his name, making him turn slowly, his shoulders tense.

Liana was walking toward him, a finely knitted scarf pulled around her shoulders to ward away the chill in the halls. Her face was unreadable as she sent the servants trailing her away to give them some privacy. "You've been quite rude, Jet Lamia," she said, a slight reprimand in her voice. She gave him a wry grin. "Declining my request was not something anyone else would have deemed wise."

Jet hunched his shoulders slightly. He was prepared for her to do her worst. "I'm not your dog," he snapped. "I won't just come when you snap your fingers."

Liana's small grin never wavered. "I expected nothing less," she said. "But I did expect that you wouldn't feel so caged here." Her eyes shifted over him. He looked like he was ready to jump at the slightest provocation. "You've done as I asked." Her eyes shifted away briefly, toward where Nyx and the Atturon siblings were standing below, talking to the siblings' cousin, who had met them in the foyer. Her voice was soft. "You'll find no chains here."

Jet turned his eyes back toward Nyx and the others, his posture relaxing ever so slightly.

"I sense a change in you, Jet," Liana said then. "You're not the same person I sent to Earth a year ago." She stepped closer to him, as if to better assess him. "What's the difference?"

Jet fought the urge to scowl at her. "There's no difference," he said bitterly. It irked him when she laughed softly.

"There is a world of difference," she said easily. She surprised him when she reached out and tapped her finger against his brow. "You spend more time frowning in contemplation than you used to."

Jet felt confusion fill him, but he tamped it down. "Is this what you wanted to talk to me about?" he asked shortly. "My wrinkles?" He rolled his eyes. "I did us both a favor by declining your invitation, if that's the case."

"I actually wanted to discuss your role here," Liana said, suddenly all business. "I assume that you've been teaching Nyx as I had asked."

"Of course," Jet said sharply. "If I hadn't, she'd be dead." He felt mild satisfaction at the way Liana grimaced slightly. "She was severely ill-prepared when I found her with that handmaid."

Liana looked up at him. "Dorothea had done as I commanded," she said, an edge entering her voice.

Jet scoffed. "What a loyal servant," he said bitterly. "It's too bad she's dead now."

Liana looked startled for a moment. "What?" she managed.

"We didn't exactly have the best time leaving Earth and traveling here," Jet said. "Nyx has seen too much bloodshed already." He shook his head. "If you'd sent anyone else, she would have died too," he murmured. "Her heritage should have never been hidden from her." His thoughts drifted back to that day, so long ago now, when she'd first used her magic against Sophia's golem. "If she'd been properly taught as a child, we would have had no trouble getting here." He didn't realize that the distant look on his face gave away his thoughts.

"What did you see?" Liana asked, drawing him back to the present.

Jet didn't like that she was so perceptive. "She's strong," he admitted. "There's a power, locked away inside her, that shouldn't be possible." He glanced at Liana, seeing something akin to satisfaction cross her face, so he continued. "But she can't access it. When I saw it the first time, she was being controlled by one of Paraximus's assassins."

Fear and confusion flitted across Liana's eyes. "What are you talking about?"

"She was being controlled by blood magic," Jet said. "She was being commanded to kill me, but she turned on her handler instead." He shook his head at the memory. "Her magic was so strong and pure, it dripped like water from her fingers."

Liana's brow lifted in surprise then. "That's …" She shook her head.

Jet nodded in agreement. "She hasn't done it since," he said. "And she struggles with even basic things. But it's there." He fought a chill that was trying to descend on him. Even to this day, the monster that dwelled inside him writhed against just the thought of her power. Underneath her inept and clueless exterior, there was something unbridled and dangerous.

Silence fell over them for a moment before Liana made a soft sound, a dry smile pulling at her lips. "The balance is shifting," she said thoughtfully. "The magics always correct themselves." She slid a glance at him, tilting her head slightly. "She is the answer to what your father has tried to undo."

Jet dug his fingers into his arm at the thought. "It's too bad she'll never be able to use it," he said hotly. "It's been suppressed so long that she hardly has a connection to it."

"But you've been able to teach her some, haven't you?"

Liana asked.

Jet could feel frustration building inside him. "A child has more control over their magic than she does," he snapped. "It would be a fool's errand to try to prepare her for a fight she has no hope of winning."

Liana crossed her arms then, unhappy. "I still need you to try," she said then, her voice quiet.

Jet looked at her sharply. "What for?" he demanded. "So she can stand on a battlefield and die for a cause that was never hers to begin with? Whatever ideas of salvation you have, she's not—"

"I need her to live," Liana said harshly, interrupting him. She didn't look at him as she pressed a hand to her face. "I just … need her to live." Her voice had softened, and she looked up at him, strong emotions on her face. "She's all I have left, and I won't lose her. Not like the others." She seemed as if she was on the verge of tears. "I need her to live a long and fulfilling life, and I need you to teach her how to protect herself." She drew a slow, calming breath, but her voice was a whisper. "I won't ever ask her to step into a fight that's my fault and my burden to bear."

Jet was surprised by her words. It suddenly struck him that Liana really did care about Nyx, even though they'd spent most of Nyx's life and the last twenty years apart.

"I won't be around forever, and I want to know she will be safe," Liana said, her voice a bit stronger. "Will you do this, Jet?" She looked at him, her violet eyes telling him that there was only one correct answer. "Will you protect her after I'm gone?"

Jet stared at her for a long moment, feeling as if there was something she wasn't telling him. "Are you ill?" he asked abruptly.

Liana shook her head, drawing a slow breath. "No, but

I've seen my death," she said softly. "And I knew that you were the only one who could give me time with her. That's why I chose you."

"You've … seen your death?" he asked doubtfully.

Liana nodded. "The *Visus* touches me occasionally," she said, her voice still quiet. "Two years ago, I was granted a vision."

Jet bristled slightly. "Why are you telling me this?" he asked, his voice guarded.

Liana glanced at him, a slight smirk on her lips. "It's like I said, you're not the same person who left to Earth a year ago. She has changed something in you."

Jet frowned bitterly. "What if you're wrong?" he demanded.

Liana laughed softly. "I don't think I am."

Jet felt surprise fill him yet again. "Can your path not be altered?" he asked then, unsure of why he was even bothering. Perhaps the thought of Nyx not having her grandmother after all this time made him want things to be different for them; perhaps his heart wasn't as cold as it had once been; perhaps Liana was right.

Liana offered him a different smile then, one that was tender. "Everyone's time must come to an end," she said gently. "And I trust that, with you beside her, Nyx will be okay, in time."

Jet didn't like her answer, but it was all he needed to know. However she'd come to know about her future and whatever she'd seen, she knew it wouldn't be changed. A heavy emotion filled his chest, one that he couldn't quite give a name to, and he nodded shortly. "I will do as you ask," he said quietly.

Liana's smile didn't fade. "Thank you," she said softly. The chime of a clock suddenly filled the castle with lyrical sounds, reminding them that it was midday. "It seems it's time for lunch. I hope you'll join us."

Jet nodded as he watched her turn to walk away, their conversation ended for now. He wasn't sure what to do with the heaviness that was sitting in his chest, and he wasn't sure if it was for Liana's plight or for Nyx's.

Nyx could tell from the way Aled fidgeted that he was nervous. She thought it was humorous that she would make someone nervous. She'd never been the most powerful person in the room before.

"If you'd ever like a tour of the castle, I'd be happy to attempt to help you navigate it," he said jokingly.

Nyx offered him a grin. "I thought you would have known all the ins and outs by now," she teased.

Aled laughed. "I sometimes wonder if the Queen herself knows all the hidden places in this palace," he said.

"I know most," a voice suddenly said.

Nyx watched as Aled's face turned scarlet in embarrassment, and he bowed quickly. She turned to look over her shoulder, surprised to see that Liana was not alone. She felt her heart twist as her eyes met Jet's. She wanted to ask if he was okay, but she knew that even if they were alone, he would never admit anything had been wrong to begin with.

"I have spent most of my life in these walls," Liana continued, "save for the few years I spent in Dirvo."

"What's Dirvo?" Nyx asked curiously.

Liana gave her a smile. "Ruins now, unfortunately," she said, almost as if she was trying to change the topic. She stepped closer to Nyx. "Nyx, would you be willing to take lessons from a teacher? We have some of the best here in

Regius Carmen, and they can help you learn to read and teach you the history of Gexalatia."

"Yes," Nyx said with little thought. "I would like that." Deep in the pit of her chest, her heart was aching; she'd already had an excellent teacher who taught her to read with her mother's books. She didn't realize that her face was giving her emotions away.

"What's that look for?" Liana asked gently, her eyes searching Nyx's.

Nyx blinked quickly, surprised. "It's nothing," she said quickly, hoping beyond hope that the knot in her throat would go away quickly. She didn't want to cry anymore.

Liana didn't press her anymore, but the look on her face said she knew that there was indeed something, and it wasn't pleasant. "I will send for Master Omar, then," she said. She offered a smile. "You can begin lessons as soon as you'd like."

Nyx nodded. "That would be wonderful," she said.

Liana seemed pleased as she motioned down the hall. "Jet and I were just headed to the dining hall," she said. "You'll be happy to know that I made a special request for your first day with us." She turned and began leading the way.

Nyx let Ellie, Raphael, and Aled fall in step behind Liana in front of her, hanging back to look at Jet. "Rest well?" she asked, the question sounding lame.

Jet gave her a curt nod as he crossed his arms. "You?"

Nyx nodded as well. "Yes, thanks," she said. The awkwardness was killing her. She wanted to blurt that she felt alone and abandoned without him, but she kept it to herself as she followed after the others.

"I see you've started making friends," Jet said, walking slowly next to her.

"Yes, Aled is very nice," she said congenially. She forced a small smile. "He acts really nervous around me, though."

Jet made a humored noise. "Get used to it," he said dryly. "Everyone you meet will either be a boot-licker or a snake waiting for you to make a mistake."

Nyx frowned at his assessment. "They can't all be that bad," she said quietly as they neared the door to the dining hall.

Jet shot her a look. "I guess we'll see."

Nyx was surprised when they stepped through the doorway at the number of people inside the dining hall already. She wondered where they all came from as they milled around, the dining hall much like a cafeteria. She felt herself becoming flustered when they all began to stare at her, silence falling over them. She wondered if she should say something, but then Liana's voice filled the room.

"Esteemed guests," she said, causing everyone to look at her. "Please give a warm welcome to my granddaughter, who has finally returned to us." Liana lifted her hand toward Nyx, as if to tell her to join her.

The people gathered rose to their feet at their tables, bowing to her as she walked past them. Some seemed overjoyed at her presence and offered her words of welcome, but others seemed suspicious or unhappy. Nyx wasn't sure how she was supposed to feel as she crossed the hall and met Liana in front of the courtiers.

"I trust you won't badger her about her journey home," Liana said then, a warning in her voice suddenly, "and I assume it goes without saying that she will be treated with the respect a princess deserves."

A murmur went around the room, but Liana disregarded it.

"Now, let us enjoy this meal, which I have prepared

in my granddaughter's honor," she said, a smile plastered on her face. She caught Nyx's hand and pulled her toward their seats.

Nyx was out of sorts as she eased to sit next to Liana. She watched as Jet settled across from her and she turned her eyes on Liana, a thousand questions bubbling inside her.

"I apologize," Liana said then, as if sensing her confusion at her brusque words. "Rumors that you are not who you claim to be are circulating among them." She glanced at the other tables. "I felt it was necessary to curb any uncouth behavior before it has a chance to start."

"Oh," Nyx said softly, looking down at the plate that was set before her. Her eyes widened at the amount of food on it. Her thoughts were forgotten as her stomach rumbled and Ellie giggled beside her.

"You must be starving," she said teasingly.

Nyx smiled, feeling slightly embarrassed, but grateful for the food as she picked up her fork. "I suppose so," she managed before digging in.

The food was delicious, and soon Nyx felt herself at ease, listening to Ellie and Raphael tell stories with Aled about when they were children. She noticed that there were certain moments when one of them would bring up the third Atturon sibling, Bailey, and it would cause Ellie's brow to furrow slightly. Nyx could tell she was trying to put on a brave face, but she couldn't imagine what it would be like to have someone taken from you, especially when that someone had been with you every day of your life until that point.

"What about you, Your Highness?" Aled suddenly asked, breaking through Nyx's thoughts.

Nyx blinked quickly, caught off guard. "Sorry, what?"

she asked, feeling her cheeks turn slightly red.

"What did you enjoy doing as a child?" he asked once more, an easy smile still on his face.

"Oh," Nyx said, setting her fork down and leaning back in her chair. "Well …" Her childhood seemed so far away, as did the life she'd left behind on Earth. It was as if she was recalling someone else's memories as she searched for an answer. A fond memory struck her, and she couldn't help but smile.

"My best friend Anna and I used to go to the movies a lot," she said. "One time, we told our parents we were going to see a certain one, but instead, we snuck into an R-rated movie." She grinned to herself. "I spent the night at her house that night, and we both were petrified that we were going to get stabbed by a ghost in the closet." She started to laugh to herself but drew up short when she realized that no one else was laughing with her.

She looked around the table, realizing that Aled, Ellie, and Raphael were confused. Once more, embarrassment flooded her, along with a myriad of other emotions, including sadness. "Oh, I forgot … you guys don't know what movies are …" she managed, feeling like she wanted to disappear from the table.

"Is that something from Earth?" Ellie asked then, sensing Nyx's discomfort. "Could you explain it to us?"

Nyx felt the lump in her throat forming once more. How was she supposed to connect to any of the people here? Her life had been so different from theirs. She'd thought that finally being with her family would suddenly make her fit in, that it would be like a puzzle piece sliding perfectly into place, but she realized that was a stupid thought. She clenched her jaw to stop the tears that were pricking her eyes, moving quickly to her feet.

"Sorry, please excuse me," she managed. She didn't give any of them a chance to respond as she walked quickly from the dining hall. Once she was beyond the doors, she felt the tears crowding her eyes and she knew she couldn't stop them.

She felt like a prisoner suddenly as she looked around the foyer, realizing that she would never find her way back to her room. There were too many doors and staircases, and nowhere familiar for her to escape to; she felt trapped in a nightmare that she could never wake up from. The tears in her eyes began to roll down her cheeks and she couldn't do anything to stop them.

Nyx pressed her hands to her face, stifling a sob that threatened to escape from her. She felt like she was being crushed under the weight of the despair that had settled over her. She'd never felt as alone as she did in that moment, feeling torn between two lives, one that was taken from her and one that was being forced on her.

She drew a sharp breath when she suddenly felt someone put their arms around her and hold her tightly. She pressed her face against a strong chest, breathing in Jet's scent. She felt the tears come harder as he hugged her, and she gripped the front of his shirt in her hands. She cried until she didn't think she could possibly cry anymore, her breaths shuddering as she tried to compose herself. For once, she was grateful for his silence; there were no words that could make her feel better anyway. Just him being here was enough.

After a moment of hitched breaths, she pressed her cheek over his heart, staring at the wall. "What am I doing here?" she breathed, feeling drained.

"This is where you're supposed to be," Jet said quietly.

"I miss Anna," Nyx managed, feeling her throat closing

up again. "I miss Aunt Dee, and Melinda …"

Jet let his cheek rest against the top of her head. "I know," he said.

Nyx drew a shuddering breath. "Will I ever fit in here?" she whispered.

"Yes," Jet answered. "One day."

Nyx rubbed her face with her hands before stepping back from him to look at his face. "I wanted to go to back to my room," she said, looking around the foyer. "But I don't know where it is."

"You should go back in there with your friends," Jet said, surprising her. "Things won't get better if you don't face this head-on."

Nyx crossed her arms, feeling cold at the thought. "I can't," she said. "I'm sure they think I'm an idiot."

Jet smirked lightly. "Yeah, you did cause quite a stir," he said.

Nyx scowled up at him. "Not helping," she said shortly.

Jet drew a slow breath, his face suddenly serious. "There are a lot of people here who would love to watch you struggle," he said then, making Nyx's brow furrow. "But Ellie and her brother and their cousin are not those people." His eyes searched hers. "They are your friends, and they want to be close to you. It's good to have allies on your side."

Nyx frowned at him. "Allies?" she asked.

Jet nodded. "You'll have to discern who is for you and who is against you soon enough, but not with them," he said. "So let them help you transition to being here. Tell them your stories and let them help you learn what life is like here."

Nyx felt surprise fill her as she held his gaze. "That's … actually good advice," she said softly.

Jet seemed smug for a moment, but he covered it with annoyance. "Don't expect anything else like it," he said quickly.

Nyx couldn't stop the small smile that pulled at her lips. She drew a slow breath and let it out in a big sigh before rubbing her face with her hands. "Okay," she said, feeling as composed as she would ever be. "I think I'm okay now."

Jet nodded and turned to follow her back into the dining hall. He felt pride streak through him as he watched her rejoin the table and apologize to her friends for her reaction. She might be useless in a fight, but she would be fine here. He knew she would make a place for herself. As he slid back into his seat, he missed the way Liana's lips quirked slightly as she turned her eyes from him back to her plate, as if she were relieved to see him take care of Nyx.

Regius Carmen, the capitol city of Ymber.
The forty-fifth day of winter, the 851st year of the
reign of Queen Liana Estrella.
Thursday, February 3, 2012.

NYX DREW A DEEP BREATH as she sat at the table. She wasn't quite sure what to say to her friends, but Ellie broke the tension. "We're so sorry, Your Highness," she said quickly. "We didn't intend to upset you."

Nyx shook her head then. "No, it's my fault," she said. She looked down at her plate to gather her thoughts. "It's been such a sudden change for me, living on Earth for my whole life, and then coming here." She offered them a smile. "Please give me some time."

"Of course, Princess," Aled said kindly. "Whatever you need."

Nyx nodded, still feeling embarrassed. She glanced at Liana then. "Please forgive me for my behavior, grandmother," she said then. "I'm sure it was terribly rude."

Liana offered her a gentle smile. "You are anything but rude," she said gently. "And I'm sure I speak for everyone at

this table when I say that we would love to hear about your life on Earth." She shot the others a wry look. "Even if we don't really understand."

"Yes, absolutely," Ellie said, suddenly excited. "What is this 'movies' you spoke of?"

"Well, it's kind of like …" Nyx wracked her brain for a way to describe it. "It's like a picture, but the people are able to move and talk. And it tells a story that you can watch."

"Wow," Raphael said then. "That sounds strange."

"I guess it does," Nyx said then, smiling. "I wish there was a way for me to show you one. I think you'd enjoy it."

"What kind of stories do these movies tell?" Aled asked.

"Well, all sorts," Nyx said, feeling more at ease at their genuine interest. "Love stories, adventure stories, scary stories …" She shrugged. "There are lots of different kinds."

"And which were your favorites?" Liana asked then, drawing her gaze.

Nyx paused thoughtfully. "Love stories with a bit of adventure, I think," she said then. "The characters always seemed stronger when they finally confessed their feelings at the end of the story after fighting for each other."

Liana grinned. "I prefer those stories, as well," she said. "There are plenty of them in our library."

Nyx's eyes lit up a bit. "There's a library?" she asked.

"Oh, of course," Liana said. "It's full of books that I'm sure you will enjoy. I will have Master Omar assist you with whatever you want to learn to read."

Nyx looked down at the table then, feeling the ache in her chest. She wondered, if she shared her story with Liana and the others, if she would feel better. "I actually know how to read some," she said slowly. The pain in her heart was fresh still, even though it had been some time since they'd left Festra and so much had happened. She supposed she never really had a chance to mourn her friend, since they'd been forced to flee for their lives.

"Oh, you do?" Liana asked, surprise in her voice. "Did Dorothea teach you?"

Nyx shook her head, another stab of pain filling her at her aunt's name. "Shortly after Jet and I crossed the Limen, we met a doctor and his daughter who helped us," she said softly. "She taught me the language and how to read a bit with her mother's books." She could feel tears in her eyes. "She was my first friend here."

Liana reached out to catch her hand, searching her face. "If you'd like to see her again, I will have her and her father brought here," she said, misinterpreting Nyx's tears.

"You can't." Nyx wiped her face and drew a deep breath. "She's dead," she whispered. She couldn't look up at Liana. "And it's my fault."

Liana gripped her hand tightly, sitting back in her chair. She seemed at a loss for words for a moment and she glanced at Jet, seeing that his mouth was pressed in a thin, unhappy line. "I think it might be best for you and Jet to join me in my study," she said finally. She realized how short-sighted she'd been to think that things had been easy for Nyx and Jet in the last month.

She turned in her seat and motioned a servant to her side. "We'll be taking tea in my study," she said to the servant, who nodded and bowed. She then turned to Nyx, her eyes drifting from her face to Ellie, Raphael and Aled. "I apologize, but we must adjourn until this evening."

They all nodded, understanding on their faces.

Liana gripped Nyx's hand as she moved to stand, pulling Nyx with her. "Come," she said gently. She looked at Jet. "Come with me."

Nyx was grateful that Liana led them toward a door at the back of the dining hall, so that she didn't have to walk past the others again. Inside the door was a narrow hallway, which led to a steep stairwell. Nyx paused at the bottom of it to look at Liana as she started up the stairs.

Liana offered her a small smile. "This is one of the hidden ways I know of," she said playfully. "It's a servant's shortcut from the kitchen to the suites on the higher floors."

Nyx gave her a small smile back before following her. She appreciated her attempt at humor, but she was dreading the coming conversation. She didn't want to rehash what their trip had been like.

Liana's study must have been on the fourth floor. Nyx didn't count all of the stairs, but she felt like they'd been walking forever, and they'd passed at least four doors that must have led to the floors below. The air was colder on this level as they stepped into a hallway decorated much like the foyer and the hallway that Jasmine had led them through to their rooms. The only thing different about this floor was that there was a singular door at the end of the hall, which Liana walked toward and opened.

She gestured for Nyx and Jet to enter, and Nyx felt surprise fill her as she looked around at the room. It was grand with a tall ceiling and stone pillars. It was large, almost like a library, with shelves full of books. A hearth sat in the wall, filling the room with warmth, while a loveseat, several chairs, and a table sat close to it. Nyx noticed that another door opened into another room on the far side of this one.

"Is this the library?" she asked as she stared at all the books.

Liana laughed then. "Heavens, no," she said. She crossed toward a desk. "This is simply my study." She pulled her scarf from around her shoulders and let it rest over the back of the desk chair. "The library makes this room look like nothing."

Nyx was still in awe as she walked toward the shelves. "So this is your personal collection?"

Liana nodded as she eased into a chair closest to the hearth. "I've collected these volumes over the centuries," she said, looking up at the books. "Some of the greatest works line these walls." She smiled to herself. "At least in my opinion."

Nyx turned away from the shelves, seeing the door on the other side of the room. "What's in that direction?" she asked absently.

"My personal chambers," Liana said. "This entire wing is mine."

Nyx seemed surprised as she turned to look at Liana, seeing that Jet was still standing near the door.

"Please sit," Liana said then, her manner very straightforward. "I'm sure you both know why I've brought you here."

Nyx swallowed thickly as she moved toward a chair, feeling her stomach in knots. She didn't want to have this conversation. She sat on the edge of the seat, realizing that Jet hadn't moved.

Liana was looking at him, but he simply crossed his arms. "I'll stand."

Nyx watched as Liana looked back to her, anticipating her question. "Where should I start?" she asked meekly.

"Wherever you wish," Liana said gently.

Nyx looked down at her hands, not sure where to begin. Silence fell over them, making it harder for Nyx to find the right words.

"Tell me about the doctor's daughter," Liana prompted

then, her voice still soft and gentle. "What was her name?"

Nyx clenched her fists in her lap. "Melinda," she managed, feeling choked. "I was injured, and she took care of me." She pressed her hand over her eyes. "She taught me to read with the books her mother painted for her as a child, and she taught me some of her culture and let me join her in her village's celebrations." There was a hitch in her voice as she spoke. "She had dreams and hopes for a future …And my selfishness took all of that away."

Liana's brow was furrowed. She started to ask more questions, but Jet suddenly scoffed.

"That's not true, and you know it," he snapped then. "It was that bitch Savra who killed her."

"But Savra wouldn't have followed us there if it wasn't for me," Nyx said, tears rolling down her cheeks as she looked at Jet. "She killed Melinda to hurt me."

Jet ducked his chin, his fingers digging into his arms. "She was my responsibility," he said quietly. "I should have stopped her."

"Was she one of your former comrades?" Liana asked, turned in her chair to look at Jet. She watched as he nodded shortly. "When did you cross paths with her?"

"She and a small group of men were waiting as soon as we crossed the Limen," he said bitterly. "Paraximus must have sent her to check in with his assassins, but when they didn't come through instead of us, her orders must have been to kill us."

Liana's eyes narrowed in confusion. "Assassins?" she asked. She recalled him mentioning that earlier but had forgotten it. "On Earth?"

Jet nodded. "They were the ones who murdered the handmaid and tried to use blood magic to control Nyx," he said. "Paraximus can summon portals and he sent them to kill us a few months after I arrived."

"How could he have such power?" Liana asked, still confused. She remembered what Ellie had said about the attack on Sorona.

"My father has always done as the dark goddess, Daya, commands," Jet said. "It must come from her."

Liana pressed her lips together tightly, as if the mention of Daya's name left a bad taste in her mouth. "Daya is no goddess, even if she touts the powers of one," she said shortly. "She's nothing more than a demon of chaos in the skin of a woman."

"That doesn't change the fact that she's given him these powers," Jet said, moving closer toward the circle of chairs, his voice emphatic. "It's only a matter of time before she drops him and his army on the castle."

Liana shook her head. "That's not possible," she said frankly. She turned and motioned to a map that hung on the wall, which Nyx and Jet hadn't noticed until that moment. "The spring that lies beneath Montem Magnus is a pure source of the Creator Gods' magic. It protects the city from invasion. It's why Regius Carmen was built here, and why the city can prosper, cut off from the rest of the country."

Nyx gazed at the map, realizing it was a dissection of the huge mountain which the castle was built into, showing the floors of the castle, all the way down to a basement level where a spring was marked. Silence once more fell over them as Liana digested Jet's words.

"What happened after Melinda was attacked?" Liana asked, drawing Nyx's gaze.

Nyx glanced at Jet. "We were supposed to be put to death," she said quietly. She watched as Jet dug his nails into the back of the chair he stood over. "But we were saved by the Pangere." She looked back at Liana. "Things get convoluted, but apparently Ellie saw us in a vision and told them that they had to rescue us."

Liana seemed surprised. "How did she come to be with the Pangere?"

Nyx shook her head. "I don't know," she said. "But she saw that Paraximus was coming after us and managed to warn us."

"No, she led Paraximus right to us," Jet said bitterly. "She almost got us killed."

Liana looked at him. "How did she do that?"

"She has a twin, and they are connected," Jet said. "But since neither can control the *Visus*, Paraximus used her twin to see where we were so he could send atrox to kill us."

Liana was surprised again. "Atrox?" she asked quickly.

Jet gave her look, a bitter chuckle leaving his lips. "You seem to be surprised by all of this," he said. "How do you have no idea about what Paraximus is doing?"

Liana crossed her arms. "Everything you've told me indicates that he knew of our plan," she said, an edge to her voice. "As if *someone* tipped him off beforehand."

Jet bristled at her words, his eyes suddenly filled with rage. "Are you insinuating that someone is me?" he demanded.

Nyx was surprised by the venom in his voice. He really hated his father. She was even further surprised when Liana leaned back in her chair, her manner suddenly too relaxed. When she spoke, however, her voice was dangerous.

"Was I wrong to put my trust in you?" she asked, her words even.

"Of course not!" Jet practically barked. "I did everything you asked me to." Nyx realized that underneath the rage, there was a sort of desperation, as if, deep down, he was terrified of Liana.

At the realization, she sat forward quickly, looking at her grandmother. "I trust Jet with my life," she said quickly, her voice strong. "He would never betray us."

Liana turned her eyes on Nyx. She seemed as if she grappled with her thoughts for a moment before she nodded. "Either way, somehow he knew our plan," she said finally. "This makes things much more complicated than before." She was silent for a moment as she looked into the fire that blazed in the hearth next to her. "If he is using Daya's magic to spy on us, then we are only safe here, under the mountain's watch." She drew a ragged breath, her brow furrowing lightly. "This changes things."

Nyx wasn't sure what that meant and she met Liana's gaze when she looked away from the fireplace.

"You will begin training," Liana said to her. "Jet tells me you struggle to control your magic, so I will find you a teacher to help you. Perhaps understanding the root of your power will help you connect with it." She looked at Jet. "In the meantime, you will continue to train her to fight."

Jet didn't seem happy with her words, but he knew that there was no other option.

"Do you think Paraximus will come here?" Nyx asked quietly, her voice worried.

Liana looked at her, her face softening. "He may try to enter Ymber, but he will not enter Regius Carmen," she said reassuringly. "As long as you are here, you are safe."

Nyx hugged her middle. She hoped she could trust that Liana's words were true, but it didn't stop the fear and worry that sat in her chest.

Liana rose slowly to her feet then, facing them. "Paraximus will show us his next move in time, but for now we must have everyone believe there is no threat," she said. She seemed unhappy with the thought, but it made sense. Mass panic wouldn't help anything. She looked at Nyx. "I was planning to throw you a ball, to celebrate your safe return and to allow you a chance to be introduced to the court. Would you allow me to do so still?"

Nyx felt surprise fill her. "Uh …" She glanced at Jet, seeing him roll his eyes. "Yeah," she said softly. "Okay."

Liana smiled a genuine smile then. "Wonderful," she said. "I will make all of the arrangements." She crossed toward Nyx, reaching for her hand. "I also want to apologize to you."

Nyx frowned at her. "What for?" she asked.

"For the way I've handled things," Liana said, regret crossing her eyes. "It was never my intention for you to have experienced so much pain. I hope that in time, you will forgive me, both for what I've forced you to endure, and for the deaths of your loved ones." She drew a slow breath. "I hope that you can be happy here."

Nyx seemed surprised as she nodded slowly. "I'll try," she said quietly. Those were the only words she could find as she thought about all that she had lost in such a short time.

Liana smiled grimly. "I think it would also be a good idea for you to meet the courtiers," she said. She saw worry cross Nyx's face. "The sooner we can get the introductions out of the way, the better."

"How am I supposed to do that?" Nyx asked, the worry in her voice.

"Tonight at the dinner banquet, I will see to it that you are introduced," Liana said. She glanced over at Jet. "I expect you to be there as well, as Nyx's escort."

Jet rolled his eyes. "We have bigger problems than meeting some stuffy-shirted idiots," he snapped.

Liana turned to face him. "Nothing about what we've discussed changes the fact that right now nothing can be done," she said matter-of-factly. "I will discuss our next steps with my generals, but tonight we should behave normally." She looked to Nyx. "And you must start to integrate into court life."

"And how do we know who to trust?" Jet asked shortly. "I'm sure some of these people didn't expect Nyx to ever return."

Liana looked at him and smiled. "That's what she has you for," she said cheerfully. "From now on, where she goes, I expect you to be there as well."

Jet's eyes widened and he looked like he would argue, but a knock suddenly interrupted their conversation.

"Enter," Liana called.

A short, rather rotund woman entered the room, carrying a tray with the tea Liana had requested. "Pardon the intrusion, Your Majesty," she said as she set the tray down and bowed. "Please ring if you need anything else."

Liana offered a pleasant smile. "Thank you, Bandy," she said. Once the servant was gone, Liana looked back to Jet. "You were saying?"

Jet's face had melted into a scowl. "Fine," he relented. "I'll keep an eye on her."

Liana grinned. "Excellent," she said jovially. "Now, please sit and have tea with me." She shot Jet a look as he started to object. "It would be rude to decline."

Jet sighed in exasperation and eased into the chair he'd been leaning against.

"I should give you a walk-through of everyone you will meet tonight," Liana said then, pouring a cup of tea for Nyx.

Jet rolled his eyes, irked at being trapped for such a boring conversation.

20

Regius Carmen, the capitol city of Ymber.
The forty-fifth day of winter, the 851st year of the
reign of Queen Liana Estrella.
Thursday, February 3, 2012.

NYX WAS SURPRISED BY THE formality of the banquet Liana had put on for her. Jasmine had helped her slip into a dress that seemed way too fancy for a simple dinner, done her hair and put some makeup on her face, and made her look every inch the princess she didn't feel she was. She wobbled slightly in high-heeled shoes as she looked at herself in a mirror.

"How do you feel, Highness?" Jasmine asked, appearing behind her.

Nyx ran her hands over the beaded bodice of her dress. It laced tightly in the back and she was pretty sure if she dropped anything, it would just have to stay on the floor. There was no way she could bend in half with this thing on. "I feel like a doll," Nyx said, leaning toward the mirror to study her makeup more closely.

Jasmine had gone all-out with the eyeliner, drawing

slight, curving designs away from her eyes. She'd said it was the trend, as well as the bright eyeshadow she'd dusted on Nyx's eyelids. She'd run a bright pink pencil over Nyx's lips to stain them a pretty color and pulled her golden curls off her shoulders, save for a few tendrils around her face. Her dress was a soft blue and hugged her middle and flared around her legs. It had a fine overlay on top of the fabric of the skirt, woven with crystals that sparkled like glitter and it felt way too fancy for just going to dinner.

"You look amazing," Jasmine said, beaming. "The lords won't be able to keep their eyes to themselves!"

Nyx felt her face heat slightly. She didn't particularly want any lords looking at her. She just wanted to do what Liana had asked and meet the important people, and then take a bath and wash all of this ridiculous costume off. But she didn't say any of that to Jasmine.

"I guess I'm ready, then," she said quietly, pushing a strand of hair from her face.

Jasmine was still smiling broadly. "Your escort is waiting outside," she said happily. She walked to the door to open it as Nyx trailed behind her. "Enjoy your evening, Your Highness."

Nyx tried to return her smile. "Thank you, Jasmine," she said. She watched as her maid opened the door, and she stepped out into the common room.

"It's about time …"

Nyx turned her head toward Jet's voice, frowning at the way his voice trailed off. She was surprised to see him staring at her as if it was the first time he'd ever seen her in a dress. It made her cheeks blush, but she tried to play it off. "How do I look?" she asked, giving a small twirl.

Jet blinked several times before he answered her curtly. "You look fine. Now let's get going."

Nyx wanted to roll her eyes, but she fought the urge as she lifted her skirt to walk without tripping over it. She glanced back at Jasmine, who was still grinning madly, before leading the way toward the stairs. She could feel Jet close on her heels, and she glanced over her shoulder at him.

"You look nice," she commented.

He was wearing black shoes, black pants, and a black, buttoned coat with gold embroidery and buttons. Gold epaulets were across his shoulders, with the queen's coat of arms pressed into them. Despite looking rather dashing, the light scowl on his face sort of ruined it.

"I hate these things," he said, pulling at the front of his coat. "Stiff and hot."

Nyx stifled a small laugh. She turned her attention to navigating the stairs as they made their way down to the main floor. She was relieved to be on flat ground for a moment, her ankles thanking her, until she realized that there was the sound of people and music at the end of the main hall. She felt her stomach flip-flop.

"I'm not ready for this," she said softly. She glanced up at Jet, who seemed to feel the same.

"The sooner we get this over, the better," he said.

Nyx drew a short breath and breathed it out quickly, as if to blow away the butterflies in her stomach. She looked over at Jet when he held up his arm.

"Ready?" he asked.

Nyx could feel her heart racing in her chest, but she nodded anyway. "Ready." She looped her hand around Jet's arm, allowing him to escort her toward the sound of the party. Just before they reached the doors, she looked up at him, her hand tightening around his arm. "Don't leave me."

Jet smirked lightly. "Couldn't get away from you if I

tried."

Nyx knew that was the most agreement she was going to get, and she turned her eyes forward as he led her into the room.

A page at the door heralded their arrival, and the room seemed to become impossibly silent as they stood in the doorway. It was like everyone was frozen for a long moment, before there was a surge, and people started moving toward them.

Nyx felt overwhelmed as Jet led her into the room and people began to approach her. She turned to greet the first person, an older couple. The woman was dressed in a gown like hers, but it was embroidered with flowers, and she had feathers pinned into her hair.

"Good evening, Your Highness," the man said as they both swept her a bow. "I am Lord Caprio, Duke of Windglen."

Nyx nodded as Liana had instructed her to, recalling what she'd said about the lord. Apparently, he was one of the oldest members of the Royal Council, and highly respected. She'd mentioned that he would be a good ally. "It is wonderful to meet you, Lord Caprio," she said easily. "Thank you for attending tonight."

The lord seemed beside himself as his smile brightened. "I look forward to seeing you more often and getting to know you, Princess," he said happily. His eyes were misty as he looked at her. "You have your father's eyes."

Nyx felt her chest tighten. Liana had said that to her on their first meeting as well. "Thank you, Lord Caprio," she said. "I look forward to getting to know you and your family as well."

With that, he and his wife stepped aside to allow her to move onto the next guests. Things went like that for a solid few minutes, with her meeting a number of nobles. She noticed that most of them were older, like Lord Caprio, and she noticed that the Council members wore pins on their coats to distinguish themselves from the other guests. She also noticed that some seemed afraid to approach her almost, their eyes focused on Jet. They seemed torn between scared of him and angry.

Just as she was starting to wonder if she would ever be able to stop greeting people, the page suddenly called the room to silence, announcing the queen's arrival. Nyx felt like she could breathe for a moment as the courtiers all turned their attention toward Liana.

"Let's get a drink," Jet said as he led her away from the crowd.

Nyx let go of his arm and followed him, realizing her fingers were stiff from how hard she'd been gripping his jacket. She watched as they walked toward a table where goblets were stacked in an elaborate display, and he reached for one to hand to her. It was cool in her fingers, and she took a sip of the yellow liquid, realizing it was a sweet wine.

"What is this?" she asked as she took another sip.

"Honey wine," Jet said as he watched her. "It's a common wine here in Ymber. Easily made and cheaply produced."

Nyx tried to offer him a grin. "It's better than ale."

Jet hummed his agreement, suddenly looking over her shoulder.

Nyx turned slightly to see Liana walking toward them. She was smiling congenially, and Nyx noticed that she had two women trailing behind her.

"Good evening, Your Majesty," Nyx said, bowing to her as Liana had instructed her earlier. She said that she didn't care about formalities, but the courtiers would think it quite the scandal if she wasn't shown the proper respect.

"Hello, Nyx, dear," Liana greeted her. She leaned in to give Nyx a quick kiss on both cheeks. "You look amazing."

Nyx smiled at the complement, watching Liana look at Jet.

"And you clean up rather nicely, as well," Liana said wryly.

Jet rolled his eyes. "The sooner this is over with, the better." He didn't care one bit about decorum, and both Nyx and Liana knew he would let everyone know.

"Nyx, I'm sure you've met more people than you can remember, but I would like to introduce you to two more, if that's all right," Liana said then, turning slightly to gesture to the women. The first was young, about Nyx's age, and she wore thin-rimmed glasses. She had a kind set to her round face, and she had striking, almost magenta-colored eyes. "This is Angela. I've asked her to help you adjust to life here in Regius Carmen."

Angela bowed and smiled kindly. "Greetings, Your Highness," she said. "I'm very excited to work with you."

Nyx instantly liked her, and an easy smile came to her face. "I am, too. I can use all the help I can get," she joked.

Angela laughed politely. "I will do what I can to assist you."

Nyx nodded and looked at Liana as she turned toward the other woman. Nyx realized she was quite a bit older than she had appeared on first glance, with streaks of gray hair and wrinkles around her eyes.

"I'd also like you to meet Lady Aurie," Liana said. "She has agreed to help you with controlling your magic."

"Pleased to meet you, Your Highness," Lady Aurie said, bowing. "I hope that I can be of assistance to you."

"Thank you," Nyx said, glancing at Jet. She was

nervous at the thought of working with someone to control her magic. Deep, in a part of her brain where she didn't like to go, she was worried that she just sucked at it and would never have the control she needed. She looked back to Lady Aurie.

"I'll just apologize to you in advance," she said, trying to sound playful. "I'm terrible at magic."

Lady Aurie didn't seem the least bit fazed. "Yes, Her Majesty has told me this," she said matter-of-factly. "I have much practice in helping my students overcome obstacles."

Nyx was slightly surprised by her tone, and she nodded quickly. "Good," she said.

"If it's not too forward, Your Highness, I'd like to start working with you tomorrow," Lady Aurie continued. "There is much for you to learn and no time to waste."

"Uh, okay," Nyx managed as she glanced from the older woman to Liana. "That should be fine."

Lady Aurie nodded brusquely. "Excellent," she said. She bowed at the waist. "It was wonderful to meet you, Princess, but I will be taking my leave." She looked around, her face still void of emotion. "These things are not really for me."

Nyx could tell she would be in for a ride as she nodded. "Of course," she said. "I will see you tomorrow."

Lady Aurie nodded before turning to walk away.

Nyx looked to Liana then. "She seems…"

"Bitchy," Jet supplied suddenly.

Nyx turned to shoot him a glare. "I was going to say stiff," she said quickly, looking back to her grandmother.

Liana laughed slightly. "She can be very stern," she said. "But she is the best teacher in all of Ymber." Liana turned to take a goblet from a servant who seemed to appear out of nowhere. "She usually works with our mages to help them learn difficult skills, but she was more than happy to work with you, Nyx."

Nyx felt slightly embarrassed suddenly. "Do you think it will be that difficult for me to learn?" she asked quietly.

Liana offered her a kind smile. "Of course not," she said easily. "You'll do well under her tutelage."

Nyx felt apprehension coil inside her for the millionth time. She didn't have time to dwell on her thoughts though, as three familiar faces approached them. Nyx felt her heart soar at the sight of Ellie, Raphael, and Aled. "You made it!" she called out excitedly, moving toward them.

Ellie caught her arms and did as Liana had done, kissing either cheek quickly. "Of course, Princess," she said, smiling broadly. "We wouldn't miss this."

Raphael gave her a smile and a small hug after Ellie.

"We also figured you could use some back-up," Aled said with a grin. He jerked his thumb over his shoulder. "These people can be a bit insufferable."

Nyx was still smiling brightly. "It finally feels like a party now," she said teasingly as she looked at them. She turned when Liana appeared beside her, watching her friends bow from the corner of her eyes.

"Good evening, Your Majesty," Ellie said politely.

"Hello, dears," Liana said with a gentle smile. She looked at Raphael. "How are you feeling?"

Raphael nodded. "Much better, thanks to your healers," he said.

Nyx noticed then that he wasn't carrying a cane, and he wasn't hunched over as if he were in pain.

"I'm very glad to hear that," Liana said. She paused when another servant appeared at her shoulder, murmuring something into her ear. After listening for a moment, she smiled at them. "It appears the feast is about to begin." She motioned toward a table, clearly set for her and Nyx and their chosen guests. "Shall we?"

"I dunno about you guys, but I'm starving," Aled said then.

Nyx laughed softly, following Liana toward the table. She could feel Jet at her elbow, and even though he hadn't said much, it was nice to know he was there.

Once they were all seated, the guests around them took their seats as well. The tables were set with lovely fine china plates, with gold and green embroidered napkins. The settings looked almost too beautiful to use, but Nyx felt her stomach rumble lightly as the smell of food wafted into the room.

She was surprised to see a host of servants exiting from the kitchen and filling the dining hall, each carrying a tray or dish of some sort. They lined the room, as if taking their places to serve the dinner. Once they were all in place, Liana stood and the room came to a hush.

"Esteemed guests," Liana said, a broad smile on her face. "We celebrate this night the return of my granddaughter, only child of Kayne and Lillian Estrella, may they rest in peace," a murmur went around the room, echoing the sentiment, "princess of Ymber, and sole heir to the throne, Nyx Estrella."

Nyx felt her face flush when applause went around the room. She wanted to sink down into her chair, but she felt Ellie's hand on her arm steady her and keep her from being more embarrassed.

"Let us feast in her honor, and toast to her safe return and well-being," Liana lifted her goblet in a toast.

Nyx was surprised when the others around the room did the same. Her face turned even redder, but she reached for her own goblet, looking up at Jet. She noticed that he rolled his eyes slightly, but picked up his as well.

"To Her Highness, the princess," Liana said proudly.

A chorus of, "Her Highness, the princess!" loudly filled the room.

Nyx watched as Jet raised his glass to her, his gaze playfully cajoling as he took a sip of his drink. "To Her Highness," he said before putting his cup down.

Once more, embarrassment flooded her and she wanted to sink into the floor. For some reason, his gesture made her stomach fill with butterflies. She was glad when Liana eased into her chair, the servants finally moving forward to set the food on the table. Her stomach rumbled as she watched the servants begin to fill their plates with so much food that she didn't think she would ever be hungry again.

"Enjoy, Your Highness," the servant at her shoulder said as he bowed.

"Thank you," Nyx murmured as she picked up her fork and knife. She glanced at Ellie, seeing that her eyes were as wide as Nyx's felt.

"This is so. much. food," Ellie said as she stared hungrily at her plate.

"Don't let it go to waste," Liana said then.

Ellie didn't as she dug in, and Nyx followed her lead, feeling like the meat and gravy and bread and vegetables and fruits were the most delightful things she'd ever tasted.

Nyx didn't realize how late it had gotten as she walked slowly up the stairs. Her heart was light and her stomach was full, and her head was a bit foggy from the wine. She'd had a wonderful time dining and chatting with her friends and sharing stories about her life with them and Liana. She was in such a good mood, she almost forgot that Jet was hovering just behind her, as if to shepherd her up the stairs and to her room.

She paused as she put her hand on the banister, looking over her shoulder at him. "I don't feel ready to go to bed yet," she said as she met his gaze.

Jet seemed unhappy with her declaration. "You need to go to bed," he said shortly. "There are things to do tomorrow."

Nyx let her hand slide from the banister, the foggy-headed feeling making her want to be silly. She turned slowly away from the stairs, noting that the hallway was empty. "Let's go exploring," she said mischievously.

Jet sighed shortly. "I don't want to go exploring," he said. "You're on your own."

Nyx turned to look at him, pretending to pout. "But Liana said you're supposed to stay with me at all times," she said slowly.

Jet scowled lightly at her. "You've had too much to drink and you just need to go lie down," he said. "I know you, and you'll be useless tomorrow for your lessons if you don't."

Nyx grinned at him and turned to saunter slowly away from him, ignoring his protests. "I'm sure you've had time to find some interesting places while you were skulking around here," she said teasingly. "Show me some of them."

Jet rolled his eyes. She wasn't wrong about him having combed the castle, but it wasn't because he was 'skulking'. He always felt like he needed to know his escape routes. But an idea came to him, something that he knew would satisfy her and hopefully get her to agree to turn in so he could stop following her around.

"Fine," he said then. "I know a place you'll like."

Nyx seemed entirely too pleased as she followed him

down the hallway, back toward the dining hall. Just before they reached the dining hall, Jet made a turn down another corridor which was hidden behind a door.

"Are we allowed to be in here?" Nyx asked as she stepped through the heavy wooden door.

"Why wouldn't we be?" Jet asked as he let it swing shut behind them. "This is your home. You have every right to be anywhere you want."

Nyx didn't feel like that was exactly true, but she didn't argue with him. She was too curious about where he was taking her. She followed him down the hall and toward another door, which was already open. She saw that a steep, stone staircase descended into darkness, and she looked up at Jet.

"You're not going to lock me in a dungeon, are you?" she asked, narrowing her eyes at him playfully.

Jet gave her a fake smile. "Maybe I should," he said, sliding past her to go down the stairs. "It'd keep me from having to trail you around."

Nyx stuck her tongue out at his back before lifting her skirt and slowly making her way down the stairs. They were steeper than she'd realized, and the darkness was more encompassing than she thought possible. She was almost to a point that she couldn't see anymore and was starting to get nervous, when the sound of running water met her ears. A soft light was illuminating the bottom of the staircase, allowing her to see Jet a few steps ahead of her.

Jet descended the last few steps and turned to look up at her, seeing the curiosity on her face. The air was heavy with moisture, and the gentle sound of a lapping spring filled the cavern they had stepped out into.

"What is this place?" Nyx asked as she slowly stepped off the last stair and looked around.

"Liana would tell you this is a sacred place," Jet said as he turned slightly.

Just beyond the doorway, a spring was bubbling up out of the mountain, surrounded by large, flat rocks to make a circular fountain. It fluoresced with bright blue light, the water sparkling as it ballooned up out of the earth before falling over into a basin and running down into the stone, where it had cut an ancient channel.

"Is this the spring she spoke of?" Nyx asked quietly, in awe as she stared at the water.

Jet nodded. "This is supposedly the place where the tears of the gods fell," he said. "It's called the *Vere Lacrimae.*"

Nyx moved closer to the fountain so that she could sit on the flat rocks that contained the water. Her face was awash with the glow of the water, her eyes dancing in the light. Her lips were parted slightly as she stared in wonder, and Jet turned his gaze away quickly, his thoughts troublesome.

"If this is such a sacred place, why are there no guards?" Nyx asked then, looking toward the door they had come through. "Why hasn't a church or something been built around this place?"

Jet shrugged. "The spring feeds the entire city," he said. "It runs beneath the castle and becomes the river that brought us into the city. I guess it doesn't need to be protected when it literally turns into a river."

"How does such a small source of water make such a large river?" Nyx asked then, turning her eyes back to the water.

Jet shrugged again and crossed his arms. "Magic, I suppose," he said. Truthfully, he'd never cared or considered it before.

Nyx found herself enamored with the way the water rippled and danced, as if it were sentient and responding to her presence. She lifted her hand slowly and reached toward the water, surprised when the blue light suddenly seemed to brighten as her hand came closer. She pulled her hand back quickly, looking up at Jet.

"What was that?" she asked.

Jet took a step closer to look down into the pool. "It's responding to you," he said evenly. He sank down slowly to sit next to her. "This pool is a pure source of magic, and it can feel your aura."

"Can I touch it?" Nyx asked then, looking down at the water.

Jet looked mildly annoyed by all of her questions. "You can try," he said slowly.

Nyx drew a slow breath and reached her hand toward the glittering liquid once more. Her eyes widened as the water began to glow brightly, the blue color turning nearly white. She was startled when the water seemed to swell toward her, as if reaching for her too, but she didn't pull her hand away. After a moment of watching the small pool roil, demanding that she come closer, she dipped her fingers down into the glowing water.

She drew a sharp gasp as the water seemed to flow between her fingers, coming alive at her touch. It was cold initially, but began to grow warm against her skin.

"What does it feel like?" Jet asked. He wasn't particularly interested in sticking his hand in magic water, but he realized he was happy to watch her do it.

"It's … warm," she said, swirling her fingers slowly. "It feels …" She shook her head, as if looking for the right words. "It feels alive."

Jet realized he was grinning softly. "It is alive," he said

then, leaning forward to watch the light dance beneath the surface. "It carries the power of the Creator Gods."

Nyx looked up at him, feeling her heart flutter at the soft smile on his face. She couldn't remember the last time he'd looked at ease. She started to lean away from the fountain and pull her hand from the water, her eyes fixed on his face. She wished he could stay like that forever, content to just be with her. She also wished that there was a way she could express her thoughts to him, but no words seemed good enough as she looked at him.

Jet seemed uncomfortable as he looked up and realized she was watching him. "What?" he asked abruptly.

Nyx shook her head. "Sorry," she said quickly, looking away. A light blush crept over her cheeks. "I'm just not used to seeing you happy."

Jet felt her words sting a bit as he watched her stare at the fountain. He felt guilty suddenly, and he didn't quite understand why. "I'm not unhappy," he managed finally, seeing her look back at him.

"Are you sure?" Nyx asked, forcing a bravery into her voice that she didn't feel. "I mean, I know being with me all the time isn't really what you signed up for."

Jet surprised her when he gently took her hand in his. As much as he hated to admit it, he was only happy when he was with her. "I don't mind it," he said finally, letting his thumb brush across her fingers.

Despite feeling flustered, Nyx grinned. "I'm never going to let you forget this moment," she said teasingly.

Jet shook his head and rolled his eyes slightly. "You're lucky I don't push you in that fountain," he said, still holding her hand in his. He looked down at her fingers pressed against his before drawing a slow breath. "It's late. We should head back upstairs."

Nyx wasn't surprised by his words, and she turned to look into the water once more before nodding her head. She watched him stand and let him help her to her feet, leaving her feeling bereft when he let go of her hand.

Celo Cavus, the capitol city of Siccita.
The forty-fifth day of winter, the 906th year of the
reign of King Paraximus Lamia.
Thursday, February 3, 2012.

THE THRONE ROOM AROUND KING Paraximus was silent. The courtiers had retired for the night, leaving him alone with his thoughts. He lifted a hand slowly, watching as cold, grey magic danced between his fingers. It had been given to him by Daya, but of course, her gift had come with a price tag, as usual.

He looked down at the cut that ran the length of his arm, which was healing slowly. He knew that eventually she would take all that he had left to give, killing him, but he would see Liana's kingdom in ashes before that happened. He sat up straighter when a shadow filled the open doorway.

"I have done as you instructed, my king," a man said, kneeling before him. "The Atturon girl is secure."

Paraximus nodded as he closed his fist. "Good," he said darkly. "I have another task for you."

The man looked up, the faint light reflecting off his

dark gaze. "I am yours to command."

Paraximus grinned darkly. He stood slowly. "You may regret those words," he said as he walked down the dais to stand in front of the man. "The ones who came before you have failed me, and I have seen to it that they were given fitting ends."

The man seemed nervous for a second, but he pushed the emotion down. "I will not fail you, my king," he said strongly. "Not like the others."

Paraximus laughed then. "You are a skilled mancer, are you not?" he said.

The man looked up at him, seeming surprised. "You know I am, Your Majesty."

"And is it true that you are capable of drawing out the *fax?*" Paraximus asked stonily.

Ivan looked down at the floor. "It should be doable," he said slowly.

"Find my son," Paraximus commanded then. "Do whatever you must to bind him and bring him to me." His dark eyes narrowed. "Do not fail me like the others, Ivan."

Ivan seemed apprehensive as he rose slowly to his feet. "As you wish, my king," he said, bowing his head.

Once he was gone, Paraximus clenched his fist and looked around the room. He hated feeling trapped in this place. With Daya sapping more and more of his strength every day, he knew he couldn't possibly go after Jet. It would have been easy, before he accepted Daya's 'help', when he was stronger, but now all he felt was drained. But he didn't intend for that to last long. He also didn't intend to let Daya get her filthy claws into Jet. He knew she craved the power of the *fax*, and he would die a thousand times over before he ever let her steal that power from him.

"I see you have finally chosen someone to bring your

son here," a voice said behind him.

Paraximus resisted the urge to jump, feeling the muscles in his body tense. He recognized Daya's voice, the sound of it sending a cold chill through him. "Yes," he said, forcing his voice to remain strong. "Ivan will not fail me."

Daya was silent as she stepped forward, standing behind him and leaning in so that her rancid breath caressed his ear. "I know what you've done with the Atturon girl," she said, a deadly sweetness to her voice. "Don't think that your little enchantments will stop me."

Paraximus turned slowly, rage seeping into him. He knew she could see it in his eyes as she lifted a finger, which was suddenly a deadly point pressed under his chin.

"We don't have to like each other, King Paraximus," she said, letting the sharp edge dance over his skin. "Once I have what I desire, your debt to me will be paid."

Paraximus narrowed his eyes. If he could have killed her, he would have. "And what is that?" he asked slowly.

Daya grinned a fangy smile. "That is of no importance to you, my king," she said patronizingly.

Paraximus knew what it was she wanted. He didn't know what she needed the *fax* for, however, and frankly, he didn't give a shit what she might want it for. All he knew was that it would never be hers. It was too soon to reveal his cards, though. If she were to find out that he knew of her plans, there was no doubt she wouldn't hesitate to kill him. He had to bide his time, until he had the strength to destroy her before she could do the same to him.

"Your army is almost ready," Daya said then, stepping away from him. She walked toward his throne and sat down in it slowly, as if it belonged to her. She crossed her legs and leaned back, all too comfortable to sit in his chair. "Mara requires you to make one more sweep, and she will have all she needs."

Paraximus scowled at her. "I've given you everything I have," he said. He vaguely wondered if he still had an iota of conscience left after all. "I will give you no more children."

Daya pretended to study her nails. "Then we will take the blood from your men," she said evenly. "The blood of children is more potent, but any blood will do."

Paraximus clenched his jaw. "You will take nothing else from me, *goddess*," he spat. He surprised even himself when he mustered the strength to summon a sword, which he held to her throat. "You think you make the rules here, but you don't. This is my kingdom, and it is *my* blood that sustains you." He grinned in a dangerous way. "I wonder what would happen if I were to deny you of it."

Daya looked down at the silver sword leveled at her neck as if she were bored. She reached out her fingers and ran them down the length of it, pushing it slowly away. Her fingers split against the sharp edge, but they healed almost instantly, leaving only drops of blood, which she licked away. "You seem to be under the impression that I need you," she said slowly, an edge to her voice. "But, as I'm sure you can see, my body has been fully formed." Her eyes glinted murderously. "I take your blood as a sacrifice; as payment for bestowing my power upon you."

Rage filled Paraximus once more. He didn't say anything as he suddenly swung his sword, driving it into her neck. He watched as her blood began to pour across the front of her body, staining her dress and running down onto the floor. He gave the sword a swift yank, severing her head from her body. Her head landed with a heavy *thunk* on the floor and her bloodied body slumped to the floor. For a long moment, Paraximus felt a sense of relief as he stood over her corpse. But then a macabre smile slid across her body-less face.

Her body suddenly twitched and began to writhe unnaturally, moving to stand slowly and bending to pick up her head. She started to laugh, a horrid, gurgling sound that came from the stump of her neck as she lifted her head to return it to her body. Once she placed it against the bloodied flesh of her neck, the wound began to seal, the only sign that she'd just been decapitated the blood that stained her skin and clothing.

Shark-like teeth began to form beneath her lips, and her eyes began to glow a bloody red. Her body began to contort, much like her form when she would appear to him in the temple, becoming gnarled and stretched in an unnatural way. She lurched toward him, catching him around the neck and slamming him into the floor, pinning him there with a monstrously deformed hand.

"Do not test my power," she growled, her voice echoing as if a room full of people were speaking. She pressed hard into his body, trying to grind him into the floor. "I will show you mercy, this time, idiot king. But do not expect such next time."

Paraximus gasped in pain as she pressed down on him, his ribs cracking painfully underneath her. It was difficult to draw a breath and he pressed his hands against hers, trying to push her off of him. She seemed to enjoy watching him suffer, but after a moment she released him, her body slowly morphing back to that of a beautiful woman.

"Oh dear," she said then, looking down. "My dress is ruined."

Paraximus tried to roll up from the floor, still feeling like he couldn't breathe. He looked up at her, seeing her watching him with sinister delight. "You ... bitch ..." he managed, his voice shaking. His body was trying to repair itself, but it was so taxed by her drinking his blood that it was almost as painful as the injuries themselves.

Daya stepped toward him then, reaching down to caress his face. "It seems I must change my clothes," she said airily. Her disgustingly sweet smile widened. "Feel better, my king."

Paraximus watched from the floor as she sauntered away. Fury was raging inside him, but he knew he had to bide his time. Next time, she wouldn't be able to put her head back on.

Regius Carmen, the capitol city of Ymber.
The forty-sixth day of winter, the 851st year of the
reign of Queen Liana Estrella.
Friday, February 4, 2012.

"TIME TO GET UP, YOUR Highness!" Jasmine said cheerfully, pulling a curtain open to allow in bright rays of sun. "Lady Aurie will be waiting!"

Nyx groaned and turned her face into her pillow, trying to keep the sun from her eyes. Her head was aching slightly, and she was groggy and momentarily disoriented. "What time is it?" she managed.

"Time to get to work!" Jasmine continued. She flitted from the window to the closet and pulled open the doors.

Nyx slowly sat up and let her feet hang over the side of the bed. She brushed her mussed hair from her face, feeling like her adventure last night had come back to bite her. Just like Jet had said. She rolled her head from side to side, trying to dislodge the cobwebs in her brain as Jasmine came back with an armful of clothing.

"You'll be training today, so this should be comfortable,"

she said as she laid out the clothing.

Nyx could see that it was fairly simple, a white shirt and black pants, with a thickly padded but lightweight jacket. She hadn't seen her white stuba leather jacket since the night they arrived, and her only guess as to the reason was because the thing had been stained with blood.

"Would you like some assistance?" Jasmine said then, turning her too-eager gaze on Nyx.

"No, I'm fine," Nyx said quickly. She watched as Jasmine seemed to wilt a bit, as if she didn't like the idea of being dismissed so quickly. "But you may stay while I get ready, in case I need anything."

Jasmine smiled brightly. "Of course, Your Highness," she said. She picked up the clothes and took them to drape over a screen while Nyx slid off the bed and shuffled toward the bathroom.

On what Nyx would have thought of as a sink was a basin full of water and wash rag. Above that hung a mirror. She dipped her hands into the cold water and splashed it on her face, using the rag to pat her skin dry as she looked at herself in the mirror. Smudges of makeup were still around her eyes from the night before, and her hair was tousled from where she'd fallen asleep with it still pinned up. She started to pull the pins from her golden curls, feeling her mind wander.

"Your Highness, if I may?"

Nyx blinked from her thoughts. "Yes," she said absently.

"There was rumor that you and your escort snuck off to explore after the banquet last night," Jasmine said, a conspiratorial and giddy lilt to her voice.

Nyx felt her heart skip a beat and her hand stilled slightly as she pulled another pin from her hair. "Oh," she said, her fluster worse when the pin tangled in the yellow strands. "Um, yeah, I guess ..."

Jasmine made an excited sound and stepped toward the doorway so that Nyx could see her in the mirror. "The kitchen girls said they saw you go down to the spring," she said, the speed of her voice reminding Nyx of hummingbird wings. She surprised Nyx, though, when she sighed and a dreamy look came over her face. "I bet it was so romantic, just the two of you, in the glow of the spring ..."

Nyx finally yanked the errant pin from her hair, wincing lightly at the pain, before turning to look at Jasmine. "Oh, it's not like that," she said quickly, feeling her cheeks heat despite herself. "Jet is my friend."

Jasmine's eyes widened scandalously. "You mean you and he aren't ..." She looked confused. "But you spend so much time together, and I see the way he looks at you. Are you sure there's nothing going on between you?"

Nyx looked down at the floor, Jasmine's words like needles in her heart, and it reminded her of Zaida's words: *death by a thousand cuts.* She tried to think of an excuse to throw Jasmine off this topic, but her brain was useless, and the silence said more than she could have.

"Oh," Jasmine breathed, disappointment heavy in her voice.

Nyx could feel her heart breaking with that one word, and tears flooded her eyes. It hadn't been so long ago that he'd turned her down so viciously, and it still hurt now as much as it did then. Nyx managed to hold the tears back for the most part, wiping away a couple that managed to escape. She looked at her maid. "If I tell you something, will you keep it a secret?" she asked.

Jasmine was the epitome of 'lose lips sink ships', but in that moment, Nyx needed a friend. "Absolutely," she said quickly. "I'll never tell, I swear on my mother's grave."

Nyx was slightly bewildered at her words, but she shook it off. "The truth is, I thought there was something … I *want* there to be something, but he won't let it happen," she said softly.

"Then he is daft, Your Highness," Jasmine said quickly, obviously trying to make her feel better. "I've only known you a short time, but I can see that you are a wonderful person, beautiful inside and out. He is an idiot if he can't see that, too."

Nyx offered her a slight smile. "Thanks, Jasmine," she whispered. She realized she was still holding the last hairpin in her hands as she turned it over between her fingers. Silence fell over them for a moment before Jasmine suddenly gasped.

"You should hurry, Your Highness!" she said, practically shoving Nyx toward the screen to get her dressed. "You're late!"

Nyx realized she was practically running down the stairs as she yanked on her jacket. Her hair was tied back in a ponytail and flapped against her shoulders as she dashed down into the foyer. She tried to calm her ragged breaths as she stepped into the hall, seeing a group of people clearly waiting for her.

"I'm so sorry I'm late," she said as she neared. "I didn't realize what time it was." She looked around at the group, seeing Count Samill, two unfamiliar guards, Lady Aurie, and Jet.

"A princess is never late, Your Highness," Count Samill said then, surprising her. "The rest of us are simply early." He offered a slight smile.

Nyx straightened her jacket as she tried to return his

smile. "Either way, it's rude of me to have kept you waiting," she said. She didn't bother to look at Jet, knowing he was rolling his eyes at the Count's words. She looked to Lady Aurie. "I'm ready to get started."

Lady Aurie nodded and turned on her heel. Her dark hair was twisted up on her head and she wore a rather plain, muted red dress. "This way then," she called over her shoulder.

Nyx started after her, Jet, Count Samill, and the two guards following behind her. She glanced over her shoulder at Jet, seeing his eyes shift to her, an 'I told you so' smirk on his face. She rolled her eyes at him and turned back to Lady Aurie, seeing that she was leading them out into a part of the castle that she hadn't seen before.

It was an open courtyard, surrounded by a circle of stone. Arches leaned across the opening overhead, vines hanging lazily from the rock faces. The floor was etched with swirling designs, and in the middle was a table. As they came closer, Nyx could see that a bowl of water was set out on the table, as well as a handful of other small objects. Lady Aurie walked around the table and turned to face her across it, her back rod straight and her hands clasped in front of her. Her expression was unreadable as she looked at Nyx. In the light that filtered in from above, Nyx could see that her dark hair was a shade of blue just barely lighter than black, and her eyes were a faded green.

"Today's lesson will be somewhat shorter than others," Lady Aurie began. She motioned to the items on the table. "I will use these to conduct an assessment of your abilities."

Nyx nodded at her words, feeling her stomach twist. She watched as Lady Aurie started by reaching for a small bag, which she untied and dumped on the table to reveal smooth river stones.

"This will test how well you can connect with your magic," she said. She nodded at the rocks on the table. "I want you to lift these stones."

Nyx grimaced slightly. Sure, she'd managed to use her magic before, but it had been in times of trouble. She had a feeling she was about to be embarrassed in front of the people in the room. She nodded at Lady Aurie's request, and clenched her jaw, concentrating on feeling her magic. The warmth that she was slowly becoming used to began to fill her, drifting down into her fingertips. Once she felt ready, she lifted her hand slowly and tried to push her magic out toward the stones.

She found it was difficult, and she was straining, sweat forming on her brow with the effort. She felt like she'd finally managed to reach across the room and she moved her hand as if to grasp the stone, but then her concentration broke as exhaustion came over her. She let the magic dissolve, feeling as if she'd dropped a heavy weight. She caught herself on her knees, drawing quick breaths.

"I'm sorry," she managed, looking up at her teacher. "Let me do it again."

Lady Aurie shook her head, her lips pressed together tightly. "I've seen all I need to see," she said, surprising Nyx.

Nyx straightened, feeling her heart skip a beat and defeat fill her. "Am I unteachable?" she managed, feeling crushed at the thought.

Lady Aurie moved to place the stones back into the bag. She was much like the rocks in her hands, stoic and impossible to read. "Of course not," she said easily. "You're simply not tapped into your *anima*."

Nyx frowned. "My what?" she asked.

"Every magic user's soul is composed of two parts," Lady Aurie said. "One part is the *homni*, or the part that makes us mortal." She set her bag of stones aside. "It is our belief that we were created by the goddess Daya, and as a slight against the Creator Gods, she did not give us magic, instead cursing us to die. However, the first man was approached by a spirit. In exchange for life, the spirits imbued each of us with the ability to control the life force of the Creator Gods, which we call magic."

She walked around the table then to stand in front of Nyx. "This part is called the *anima*, and you simply have not connected with yours."

Nyx frowned, trying to take all of her words in. "So how do I do that?" she asked after a moment.

"Generally, it's something that you do innately," Lady Aurie said, tilting her head. Her eyes were narrowed slightly, as if she was unhappy. "I've only seen this type of difficulty in one whose spirit was divided, effectively cutting the *homni* off from the *anima*."

"Do you think that's been done to me?" Nyx asked, feeling her stomach churn. If that was the case, who could have done such a thing? Dorothea? She didn't want to think that the woman who raised her might have actively tried to harm her.

Lady Aurie shrugged, surprising Nyx. "It doesn't matter," she said shortly. "There is a way to repair the divide, but it won't be entirely pleasant."

Jet didn't like this at all. His arms were crossed tightly in front of his chest as he watched Lady Aurie crush herbs in a bowl. Count Samill was at his side, his two guards waiting at the top of the stairs to the chamber that led to the *Vere Lacrimae*. They stood around the fountain, the water glowing brightly in the darkness of the cave.

"I don't feel good about this," Samill said softly. He noticed that Jet dug his fingers into the sleeves of his coat harder, a bad sign.

"I'm sure this teacher knows what she's doing," Jet said quietly.

Samill nodded mutely, turning his eyes back to Lady Aurie and Nyx.

Nyx was sitting on the edge of the fountain, where she and Jet had sat just a few hours before. She watched as Lady Aurie stirred the herbs in the bowl, turning them into a runny paste. Butterflies were in her stomach as she glanced at Jet and Samill, seeing that both of them looked tense.

"Are you sure this is a good idea?" Nyx asked then. "Perhaps we should get Liana—"

Lady Aurie tapped the side of the bowl with her pestle, the sound cutting off Nyx's words. "There is no need," she said brusquely. "Her Majesty has given me permission to do what is necessary." She held out the bowl to Nyx, her eyes expectant. "Drink."

Nyx realized her hands were shaking lightly as she reached for the bowl. "What is this?" she asked as she lifted it toward her face. It smelled like dirt after a Texas rainstorm in summer, sort of damp and musty.

"This is a potion made from the leaves of the infinity flower plant," Lady Aurie said. "The infinity flower has many beneficial properties, but its leaves are especially potent."

Nyx could feel her mouth watering as if she were about to puke, but she pressed the bowl to her lips anyway. The taste hit her tongue instantly, making her want to spit it out immediately, but she kept drinking, knowing if she didn't down it all now then she wouldn't be able to do it. Once the slimy paste was gone, she handed the bowl back to Lady

Aurie, pressing the back of her hand to her lips to keep herself from gagging.

"I know it's not the most pleasant," Lady Aurie said absently. "But this is the quickest way for you to enter a receptive state."

Nyx was still trying to deal with the horrible taste in her mouth as she looked up at her teacher. "A receptive state for what?" she managed.

"To commune with the spirit," Lady Aurie said simply. "Now, no more talking. Close your eyes and relax your mind."

Nyx did as she instructed. She closed her eyes and drew a slow breath, feeling the nasty taste easing from her mouth as she drew into herself. She could hear Lady Aurie giving her calm instructions, like a yogi leading a meditation: deep breath in through the nose, out through the mouth; shoulders relaxed, back straight; continue breathing slowly. Just when she was starting to wonder if the potion would work, she felt a spark of light across her eyes, and she jumped.

"What was that?" she managed. In her head, she felt like she was speaking at a normal volume, but in reality, her body was frozen in place. "Hello?" It took a moment for her to realize that she wasn't actually speaking.

"The potion is working," Lady Aurie said, her voice sounding distant. "It's time."

Nyx wanted to ask time for what, but she suddenly felt like she was falling before feeling like she'd been doused in ice water. Her breath was stolen, and the feeling catapulted her from the final bonds of her body. When she opened her eyes, she was floating in a bright blue mass, sparks of magic dancing around her. She didn't know how, but she knew instantly it was the spring. Somehow, despite feeling like she was floating through water, she felt a wind and thought she heard the whisper of her name.

"Who's there?" she called.

Nyx was surprised when the water around her parted, revealing a yellow, sandy pathway that seemed to lead into a valley. She felt her feet touch on the sand, realizing they were bare as her toes dug into the cool sand. As soon as she was upright, the water fell away, leaving her standing in a bright, sunlit field of green grass. It reminded her of her home in Lucky, and she felt her heart twist.

A hot wind stirred around her, pulling at the thin white fabric of the short dress she was wearing. She turned into the heat, reveling in the feel of it on her skin.

"Nyx."

She turned her head at the sound, seeing a figure standing before her. "Y-you," she managed, surprised and fearful suddenly. "You're …"

The creature that stood before her was magnificent, sparkling with golden light. She was taller than Nyx, with a slim build and massive, feathery wings. Nyx recalled having seen her in a flash once before, the first time she connected with her power, but this was entirely different. She had long, straight hair and her eyes were bright, glowing the same color of gold as the light that surrounded her.

"I am," she said, her voice sounding like a ripple across a still pond. She was radiant and she exuded power, making Nyx feel afraid. "You do not need to fear me, child. I've been expecting you. I know why you've come."

"You do?" Nyx asked, her voice barely above a whisper.

She nodded. "You and I were bonded in the before-times, child," she said. "But our connection was damaged."

"Damaged?" Nyx asked, feeling her heart skip a beat. "By who?"

The spirit made a sound like a small laugh. "By you," she said.

"Me?" Nyx asked quickly, startled. "How did I damage our bond?"

"You grew and lived your life separate from me," the spirit said. "It was not your intention, I know, but it is the cause."

"So how do we fix it?" Nyx asked.

The spirit made Nyx take an unsure step back as she spread her massive golden wings. "Take my hand, child," she said, a command in her gentle voice.

Nyx was still uncertain, but she took a slow step forward and extended her fingers toward the spirit's. She could feel heat pressing against her hand from the spirit's, power flowing outward from the spirit's body. When their hands connected, a rush of fiery, fierce strength swept Nyx, sending her backwards. She felt like she was hurtled through the air, realizing she was once more engulfed in water, only this time it was real. Her body was slow to do as she wanted it to, the potion making her movement sluggish and uncoordinated. She muddled against the liquid, trying to draw a breath, fear overcoming her.

Just then, strong hands grabbed her arms and yanked her up. She coughed and sputtered as she realized that Samill and Jet were on either side of her, having pulled her out of the fountain.

"Are you crazy, you old bat?" Jet demanded angrily. "She could have died."

Lady Aurie didn't seem fazed as she watched Nyx sit on the floor, sopping wet and trying to catch her breath. "How do you feel now, Princess?" she asked.

Nyx brushed her hair from her face, looking up at her teacher. "I'm okay," she managed. She wasn't sure that she felt any different, except for the fact that she wasn't shivering from the cold. She watched as Samill moved to his feet before looking at Jet, seeing that he was still upset.

Lady Aurie reached into the pouch she'd brought with her, lifting a single stone from it. "Please, Your Highness, take this."

Jet looked ready to protest that their lessons were done for the day, but Nyx surprised him when she held out her hand calmly. She realized that the same fiery power she'd felt when hers and the spirit's hands touched was still flowing through her, without any effort on her part. She was surprised when she was able to reach out effortlessly with her thoughts and touch the cool stone. She could feel it in her mind as if she were holding it in her hand, which was a strange sensation. Without any hesitation, the stone gently rose from Lady Aurie's hand and drifted to land softly in Nyx's. Nyx closed her fingers around the stone, surprised to see a hint of a smile on her teacher's face.

"Very good."

Celo Cavus, the capitol city of Siccita.
The fiftieth day of winter, the 906th year of the reign
of King Paraximus Lamia.
Tuesday, February 8, 2012.

BAILEY WAS TREMBLING FIERCELY. SHE had her face pressed against the cold stone wall of the dungeon, but the coolness was sucked away the instant her skin touched it. Despite her trembling, she was burning up, her whole body aching. Even though it had been a number of days (she'd lost count) since Paraximus had allowed Daya to feast on her blood, she hadn't recovered as easily as she'd hoped, and now she knew she was very ill. She was starting to wonder if anyone even cared, though, since the guards still shoved food to her through the bars and disappeared until it was time to repeat the process.

She was surprised when the flame of a torch filled the darkness beyond her cell, and she managed to sit up, feeling dizzy. Her head was pounding as she watched the light come closer. She was further surprised when a face she recognized came into view.

"Jili," she managed as he paused outside the bars.

His amethyst eyes were concerned as he looked in at her. He held up a small bundle in his hand. "I've brought you medicine," he said. He knelt in front of the bars so that he could slide the small bundle to her across the floor.

Bailey fumbled for it, feeling her body protest the movement. Her head was swimming as she unwrapped it to find a glass jar plugged with a cork. Inside was liquid the color of blood. The thought made her stomach turn, but as she pulled it open the scent of fruit hit her nose. She lifted the small jar to her lips and downed the liquid. It burned slightly as it went down, but it made her spirits lift ever so slightly.

"Thank you," she said, looking back at him.

A small smile pulled at his lips, the first she'd seen. "You're welcome," he said softly. "I will bring more when I can."

Bailey nodded. She expected that he would leave, but to her surprise, he lingered for a moment.

"How are you?" he asked finally.

Bailey chuckled sardonically. "I mean, this isn't exactly a palace room, but I'm okay." She let her head rest against the cold stone wall she was propped against.

Jili nodded distractedly, the torch light glinting off his dark hair. "Good." The sound of more guards made him jump, and he looked at her, some sort of lament in his eyes. "I have to go before they catch me. But I'll be back tomorrow with more medicine."

Bailey was surprised by the way her heart dropped into her stomach as he stood. She didn't think she'd be so happy to see him, but she supposed it was normal considering he was the only person she'd interacted with besides her captors. And he was the only one of them that had been kind to her. She watched as he turned, glancing at her one last time, before disappearing from the direction he'd come.

Bailey didn't like the loneliness that filled her as the darkness returned, but at least her fever seemed to be subsiding, along with the chills that had plagued her. She realized that she was exhausted, and she closed her eyes to try to sleep. She drifted in and out of dark dreams, a restlessness sitting heavily in her chest.

After waking and falling asleep and waking breathlessly again for what felt like the millionth time, she turned and sat up straighter, pressing her head against the stone. She rubbed her face, wondering if the medicine Jili had given her was what was keeping her up. But after a moment, she started to feel like maybe she wasn't alone.

Bailey turned her head, wishing the darkness wasn't so pressing from the corners of the cell. She wrapped her arms around her middle, trying to ward the fear away, but it did little to help. Her teeth were chattering as the fear swept through her, followed by anger. She wouldn't cower alone in this dump while some thing stalked her.

Quickly, she turned toward the darkness, feeling her heart jump in her chest when the flickering of light caught her eye. She drew a sharp breath to try to steel her nerves, pushing herself to her feet against the wall. She realized she still had the small empty jar still in her hands, and she lifted it defensively, knowing it was probably useless. She took a shaking step toward where she had seen the fleeting light, realizing that there was indeed something reflecting up at her from beneath a wet and mucky pile of straw.

Bailey kneeled slowly and reached out her hand to brush the straw away. Her heart leapt into her throat as she realized that she was uncovering a familiar sight. Her hands were trembling for a different reason as she pushed the straw back quickly, revealing the worn, ancient leather cover of the Videns Liber. As her fingers brushed against it, an eye opened on the cover, glowing softly in the darkness. The Eye of the Master blinked and focused on her, acknowledging her presence, and sending a sense of comfort through her. Her father had once told her that, after the previous master no longer possessed the book, the Eye would close until it found its new master, and only then would it open and allow its pages to be accessed.

Bailey's breaths were ragged as she stared down at the magic book. "How did you get here?" she breathed. "I thought you were destroyed."

The book fluttered lightly, as if it a wind had turned its pages, falling open to reveal words. Bailey leaned down to read them in the faint light, realizing the book had answered her question. She was surprised to read that her father, as he lay dying on the floor of his study, had summoned the book and whispered instructions to it to find his daughters before commanding it to disappear. Bailey felt tears in her eyes at the thought that his last breath had been spent to send them this key to their powers.

"But why did you come here?" Bailey asked, her tears dripping onto the cracked and faded pages. "Why not go to my sister?"

The book jumped again, flopping open with a rather loud thud to another page. Bailey's eyes widened as she read the words written on it.

"This is a conveyance spell," she breathed in surprise. Her eyes drifted down the list of things she would need. It was rather short; an object to link to where you wished to go and a mirror.

Bailey felt her heart plummet. It probably wouldn't be

difficult to get an object, but getting a mirror would be next to impossible. She started to tell the book that it had come to the wrong daughter, but then the sound of jingling met her ears. She scrambled to cover the book with straw before turning to see the dim light of torch fading into view. Her heart skipped a beat as she realized it was Jili, this time bringing her breakfast.

He knelt to place the bowl in his hand on the floor so that he could push it through the bars before standing slowly. "Did the medicine help?" he asked, his voice quiet.

Bailey stood slowly and walked to the bars, grasping them in her hands. "Yes," she said, feeling exhausted and invigorated at once. "Thank you." She watched as his amethyst eyes glittered with happiness.

"Good." He didn't seem in any particular hurry as he lingered there in front of her.

"How did you get down here?" Bailey asked, glancing up the corridor toward where she knew the door was that the guards entered and exited. "Where is the usual guard?"

Jili did smile a bit then, catching Bailey off-guard. "I managed to get him to switch positions with me," he said, a hint of pride in his voice. "Turns out dungeon duty isn't as glamorous as it seems."

Bailey couldn't help the way happiness flooded her at his smile. "Did you do this for me?" she whispered, feeling tears pricking at her eyes.

Jili surprised her again when he stepped closer, his fingers brushing across hers. He was silent for a moment as his thumb traced across her knuckles. "I want to help you escape," he said finally, his words barely above a whisper. His amethyst eyes flickered to hers. "I don't know how yet, but I will find a way."

Bailey shook her head quickly. "But what about your

family?" she said, her voice just as quiet as his.

"I've already sent them on to Fornax," he said. "They will be safe there."

"And what of you?" Bailey demanded. "What if you get caught?"

Jili reached through the bars then and brushed her pale hair away from her face. "It will be worth it," he said, his eyes searching hers. "So long as you can live, it will be worth it."

Bailey was surprised and startled by his touch, and she took a step back. "You're risking your life for a stranger," she said quickly. "You hardly know me."

"I know more about you than you think," Jili said, unfazed by her reaction. "I've watched you stand up to the king's torture and Daya's bloodlust for weeks. You're strong and you have a fire for life." He shook his head, almost looking ashamed. "You make me wish that I could be half the person you are."

Bailey felt her heart twist at his words. "You are a good man, Jili," she said softly. "But I cannot ask you to do this for me."

"You don't have to," Jili said then. He turned and lifted his torch from the wall sconce where he'd placed it. "I've already made up my mind." He moved as if to leave, but was surprised when Bailey suddenly stepped forward and caught his sleeve through the bars.

"Wait," she said, her pale blue eyes wide. "If you really want to help me, I need you to bring me a few things."

Jili turned as if to ask her what she was talking about, but she pressed her fingers over his lips to silence him.

"I need these items, and for you to ask no questions," she said, holding his gaze.

He took a moment to consider her words before nodding his head. "What do you need?"

Regius Carmen, the capitol city of Ymber.
The fifty-first day of winter, the 851st year of the reign
of Queen Liana Estrella.
Wednesday, February 9, 2012.

Nyx's thoughts were drifting as she sat cross-legged on the floor. The air was cool as a breeze blew into the courtyard, the sound of vines rustling like a soft hum. It made her yearn for the rustling of tall grass and hot sun on her face and the scent of pine trees, but she pushed the thought away and recentered her mind. Her eyes were closed, but she could feel everything around her, from the small and light pulse of the stones' auras that sat in front of her, to a bright and warm, bigger aura that radiated from Lady Aurie, Count Samill, and the two guards. It was interesting to her how she could feel them all, even when she wasn't paying attention. The only person she struggled to feel was Jet.

Sometimes, she'd get a glimpse of something, a blackness that drew everything in like a black hole, but most of the time it was nothing; it wasn't even similar to any other aura she'd felt. She couldn't remember if this was how it felt when she'd first tried to connect with her spirit. She just remembered being frightened at all the new sensations. Fortunately, that experience had prepared her some.

When she'd first felt Liana's aura, it was nearly overwhelming. There was so much strength and power in her aura that Nyx had almost immediately had to leave the room. It had been too much and instantly threw her body into a fight or flight mode. That was weird to experience. She was glad that Jet had been able to help her work through it. He had told her to breathe and focus on her own aura and to draw it around her. She didn't really understand why, but it had worked, and she'd been able to be around her grandmother with no problems. Since then, it had gotten easier to control her own aura, which was both weird and innate at the same time.

So far, she hadn't encountered anyone else as strong as Liana. She wondered if that was normal, and she wondered if it was because of Liana's age or if she was just that powerful. It was also weird because Liana was the kindest person she'd ever met. It seemed disproportionate that someone so demure would be so dangerous.

"Princess, today I want to try something new," Lady Aurie's voice cut through the haze in her mind.

Nyx opened her eyes, seeing that the stones she'd felt in front of her were circling slowly in the air. It didn't take any effort to lower them slowly toward the ground, where a pouch sat, the top open. It was simple enough to direct the stones into the pouch and draw it closed with her mind. After that, she stretched her legs out and picked up the pouch, standing in an easy motion. She held the pouch in her hand out to Lady Aurie.

"What are we doing?" she asked as Lady Aurie took the stones.

"Moving objects is simple enough, but it's time to challenge yourself."

Nyx watched as the older woman walked around the table that was always set up in the middle of the courtyard. She noticed that today it had a large bowl, probably a washing bowl, sitting in the middle. As she came closer, she could see that it was filled with water.

"Scrying is something that your grandmother is proficient in," Lady Aurie said, motioning toward the water. "Abilities like scrying tend to run in families, and it would be remiss of me not to see if you possess the ability as well."

Nyx leaned against the table, bracing her hands on the edge. She looked down into the bowl, seeing her own face looking back up at her. She'd heard the term scrying before, but didn't really know what it was. "I don't really know what scrying is," she said, looking up at her teacher. "Is it just seeing things that aren't in front of you?"

Lady Aurie nodded. "That is one aspect, yes, but you could also use it to see the past, or the future," she said. A stern look came across her face. "You should always be cautious when you scry, Princess. Sometimes the waters will show you things you don't really want to see."

Nyx felt the warning in Lady Aurie's voice, and it made her swallow thickly. She wasn't sure if she wanted to learn this.

"You should always have a clear intention when you look into the waters," Lady Aurie continued. "You should know in your mind what you want the waters to show you, and you should be prepared to accept it."

Nyx was still trying to gather her courage, when a thought occurred to her. "Is this like what Ellie has?" she asked. "The *Visus*?"

Lady Aurie nodded. "Somewhere along the way, the Estrella line and the Atturon line share ancestors," she said. "But as the two lines split, the magic has evolved differently. The Atturons can only consciously access the present. Occasionally a member of their family can receive glimpses of the future, but it's not something they can control."

Nyx was surprised by this new information. Were she and Ellie and Raphael family, even if it was distant? The thought made her happy and excited, and she yearned to share what she'd learned with them.

"The *Visus* is also what allows you or Her Majesty to see things as well," Lady Aurie said, bringing her back to the present. She seemed to sense the hesitation that Nyx felt, as she was watching her carefully. "Do you wish to continue?"

Nyx blinked at her reflection in the water. Did she? What if she accidently saw something she didn't want to see? She looked up at her teacher after a moment. "I need to think about this," she said softly. "I don't know if I'm ready for this."

Lady Aurie allowed a rare glimpse of a smile to cross her lips. "That is very wise, Princess," she said, a hint of pride in her voice. "Scrying can be a heavy burden to bear." She reached for a flat, round lid and placed it over the water bowl. "I'd like for you to think about what you want to see, if you choose to do this." She looked up at Nyx, her eyes sharp. "And I want you to *only* do this with myself or Her Majesty until you are practiced enough to do it alone."

Nyx was surprised by the sharp edge to her voice. "Why?" she asked quietly.

"You are in a vulnerable state, Princess," Lady Aurie said. "You can touch the magic fully, but you are still unskilled in controlling it. You could put yourself in danger without supervision."

Nyx felt the fear fill her again, and she nodded shortly. "I understand," she said then.

Lady Aurie nodded. "We will continue with our lessons tomorrow," she said, dismissing Nyx.

Nyx turned away from her, her mind swirling as she crossed toward the door where her entourage was waiting. It was time for her session with Jet next, but her brain was busy with what Lady Aurie had told her. She barely noticed when Jet fell in-step beside her. She jumped lightly when his voice cut through her thoughts.

"Are you really going to try it?" he asked quietly.

Nyx shrugged. She glanced over her shoulder to see that Samill and the two guards were still with them. It was getting annoying. Samill had told her that it was customary for her to have a guard wherever she went, but she also assumed that Samill was keeping tabs on her. He was probably meant to keep everyone in check and pass along her progress to Liana.

"I don't know if I want to," she said slowly, glancing over at him. "What if I see something I don't want to see?"

Jet's face was serious, and it gave her pause. "That's a possibility," he said. "But it could also be helpful."

Nyx pressed her lips together tightly, still lost in thought as they made their way to the training grounds. She just wasn't sure she wanted to take that chance.

They crossed through a small grove of trees on a well-worn path which led down to the training grounds. From the top of the hill that led to the castle, Nyx could see a sprawling field, set up for different forms of combat. Beyond that were barracks, which were where the soldiers lived, and to the right of the fields and barracks was a massive dome-like shape. She hadn't seen it up close yet, but Jet had told that it was the aviary where the dragons were kept. She intended to get a good look one of these days.

A cold wind blew through her as they walked down the path toward the field. She could see that the field had been cleared and things were already setup for their session. A rack of shiny, clean swords was placed out, as well as a rack with bows. Nyx instantly thought back to the bow that Jet had gotten her in Festra. She wondered what happened to it and wished that she'd been able to hold onto it. It was a very lovely bow.

Once they stepped onto the field, Jet shrugged out of his coat and tossed it aside. Nyx didn't like this part of the day. Despite training with him before, he'd stepped up his attacks since she'd learned to access her magic. He made it seem easy to wield weapons and shields made of magic, but she still didn't think that way. It was difficult for her to anticipate what he would do because her mind just didn't think in strategies and weapons. He was trying to teach her, but most days she felt like a failure. She could study whatever he wanted her to for a hundred years and still never be good at it.

Nyx took a moment to stretch as she watched him contemplate the weapons before him. "So what are we doing today?" she asked.

Jet turned away from the weapons, a twinkle in his eyes that Nyx knew she wouldn't like. "Let's focus on hand-to-hand combat today."

Nyx tried to not let the defeated feeling get to her. Their session hadn't even started yet. Instead, she drew a slow breath and nodded shortly. "Fine," she said.

The smirk that slid across his face let her know that he

was going to kick her ass.

Nyx lifted her hands quickly, channeling her magic into her fists like he'd taught her. She always chose defense over offense because it was easier for her to try to counter him than to attack him. She watched as he took a step to the side, as if to circle her, his eyes unreadable. She guessed he was thinking of all the ways he was going to put her on the ground.

"Relax your shoulders," he commented. "You won't be able to stop an attack bunched up like that."

Nyx realized she was unconsciously hunching over slightly, pulling her shoulders toward her ears in anticipation of her body inevitably landing in the dirt. She drew in a slow breath and forced her body to relax as she took steps to mirror him.

Just when she thought she wouldn't be able to take the anticipation anymore, he lunged for her, swinging his fist. She managed to block his strike by using her magic to push his hand away, a move that surprised her. When he took another swing at her nearly in the same moment, she was able to do the same thing again. It lent her confidence as she dodged another blow, ducking under his arm. She tried an offensive strike, but he anticipated her move and avoided it.

She was breathing heavily as he took a step back from her to recenter himself. She hated how he did that; he just *knew*. It was like he could read her mind.

"How do you always know?" she asked through a panting breath.

"Know what?" he asked as they circled each other.

"What I'm going to do," she clarified.

Jet smirked. "You're easy to read," he said smugly.

Nyx felt a spark of aggravation ignite inside her, and

she jumped toward him, swinging a power-charged fist at him. Just as she expected, he dodged it, but she swung around with a kick, which she almost landed. Jet caught her foot and twisted her leg, sending her to the ground in pain.

"That was better," he said as he stood over her. "You're getting better at linking moves together."

Nyx took a moment to catch her breath as she looked up at him. "Do you think I'll ever be good at this?" she asked.

Jet made a humored sound as he held out his hand to her. "No." He caught her wrist and pulled her to her feet.

"Then what's the point?" Nyx asked bitterly. "Why do we do this every day if I'll never get better?"

Jet stepped closer to her, so that her eyes shifted to his. "Just because you aren't good at fighting doesn't mean that these skills won't save your life," he said seriously. He drew a deep breath. "Liana says she doesn't want you involved in her fight, but that doesn't mean that it won't come to you."

Nyx felt her brow furrow. She knew Liana felt that way. Liana wished that things could be different and safer. But she also knew that there was an expectation that she would lead her kingdom if Liana couldn't. She hoped that day was far in the future.

"The other thing, too," Jet said then, surprising her, "is that you need to stay alive." There was some emotion on his face that she couldn't comprehend as he looked at her. "No matter what, if something happens, you run if you can and fight if you have to." His eyes searched hers. "Do you understand?"

Nyx frowned at him. "I'm not a child," she said shortly. She didn't know why he was so serious all of a sudden. She started to turn away from him, but he caught her arm.

"I'm serious, Nyx," he said. "Promise me that you'll do

what I've said."

Nyx felt her chest tighten. Did he know something she didn't? "Fine," she said quickly. "I promise." She pulled her arm from his grip, seeing that he seemed satisfied with her answer. She held up her hands then, seeing him arch a brow. "Let's go another round."

A few hours later, Nyx was sitting in Liana's suite, sipping a cup of tea. She was sore from her training with Jet, but she tried not to let it show as she sat up straight in her chair.

"Which color do you prefer, Nyx dear?" Liana asked, drawing her gaze.

Nyx watched as Liana held up a swatch of pale pink fabric and a swatch of pale green. She looked between them both for a moment. "Can I have both?" she asked. "They're both lovely."

Liana grinned widely. "Of course," she said brightly. She turned to Angela, who was taking notes beside her. "Are you getting this all, Angela?"

Angela nodded with a smile. "Yes, Your Majesty," she said. She looked at Nyx. "It will be just as you desire."

Nyx forced a fake smile, not feeling like party-planning. She was thankful that Liana had allowed Jet to take some time to himself so that they could meet. She knew he'd be bored to tears. But she was ready for Angela to leave too, because she couldn't stop thinking about her lesson with Lady Aurie.

"What's wrong, Nyx?" Liana said then, drawing her gaze. "You seem distracted."

Nyx looked up at her grandmother, feeling her heart skip a beat. She looked at Angela then. "Might we have a moment alone, Grandmother?" she asked, turning her eyes back to Liana. "There's something I want to discuss with you."

Angela didn't seem the least bit put out as she rose to her feet and bowed. "I will start on this list straight away, Your Highness," she said with a smile. "I will take my leave."

Nyx and Liana both watched her scurry out the door, leaving them in silence. Once the door closed behind her, Liana looked to Nyx expectantly. "What's troubling you?" she asked gently.

Nyx looked down at the tea in her cup. "Lady Aurie wanted to teach me scrying today," she said softly.

Liana gave her a bright smile. "That's wonderful that she feels you're ready," she said. "You've progressed quickly."

Nyx nodded absently. "I told her I needed to think about it," she said, looking up at Liana. She was mildly worried about her reaction, but the gentle look on her face put Nyx at ease. "She said that I may have the ability because it runs in families, and because you can do it."

"She's correct," Liana said, still smiling. "It skipped your father, but it is possible that you are able to touch the *Visus*."

Nyx felt a stab in her chest at the mention of her father. "She said I could see the past, or even the future," she said softly.

Liana's smile seemed to slip some then. "Yes, if your abilities are strong enough," she said. "But it takes quite a lot of practice."

"What do you see?" Nyx asked then. "Have you ever seen something you didn't want to see?"

Liana's smile disappeared then. She seemed surprised by Nyx's question, and she took a moment to set down her own teacup on the table between them. "Yes," she said finally. "I have." She smoothed her hands across her skirt. "But it is part of having access to the *Visus*. Sometimes it will show you things that you won't want to see and for reasons that you won't understand at first, or maybe at all."

Nyx clenched her fingers around her teacup. "Why would Lady Aurie want me to try something like that?" she asked, feeling frightened.

Liana offered her a gentle smile then. "The *Visus* is not something to be feared," she said softly. "When used correctly, it can be a powerful tool."

Nyx watched curiously as Liana stood then and walked toward her desk. She pulled open a drawer and lifted an object from it, wrapped in plain white linen. Liana then turned back toward her and held the object out to her.

Nyx set her teacup on the table and walked to the desk, looking down at the linen. "What is this?" she asked as she let Liana place it in her hands. It was heavy.

"If you are able to touch the *Visus*, you can use different things to scry with," Liana said, motioning for Nyx to unwrap the object.

Nyx frowned as she saw a silver mirror peeking up at her as she pulled the cloth away. It wasn't very big, maybe as wide as both of her hands, but the silver handle and decorative design were thick, worn in some places where the mirror had been held.

"This was my grandmother's," Liana said softly. "It was given to my mother, and then to me. This is what I use to scry with."

Nyx turned it over in her hands, catching sight of her reflection. "You can use mirrors?" she asked.

Liana nodded. "This mirror in particular seems to have absorbed much of what it's seen," she said. "When you touch the *Visus* through a surface, you leave a bit of the magic trapped inside." She smiled a bit. "Because of that, sometimes the mirror shows me things I'd forgotten, at times when I need it most. I like to believe it is part of my mother and my grandmother reaching out to me."

Nyx stared at herself in the mirror for a long moment before letting it tilt in her hands to show her Liana's reflection. "Can you show me something?" she asked.

"I thought you'd never ask," Liana said, a bright smile on her face. She stepped closer to Nyx and pressed her fingertips against the surface of the mirror. "Take a look."

Nyx leaned over the mirror, staring hard into the surface. At first, nothing happened, but then the surface began to ripple softly. Her reflection began to fade away, transitioning to a place she'd never seen before. She drew a sharp breath as she realized that she was looking into a church. It was like watching a movie without sound.

The church was decorated lavishly, and the guests were in their seats. The vision shifted from showing the room to showing a man and woman standing in front of a man dressed in robes. It didn't take Nyx long to recognize the couple from the painting she'd seen her first night in the castle.

"Is this your wedding day?" she asked softly as she watched the man lift the woman's veil and leaned in to kiss her.

Liana was smiling softly. "Yes," she said. She watched Nyx's face, delighted to see her drinking in the images. "Despite what happened, it is one of my fondest memories. Can I show you another?"

Nyx nodded, not taking her eyes off the mirror. She watched as the image shifted again, this time fading to show a darkened room lit only by candlelight. In the room was a bed, where a woman was lying, propped to sit up with pillows. She had her yellow-blonde hair pulled up in a messy bun away from her face, and she looked exhausted. In her arms was a small bundle, and leaning over that bundle was a dark-haired man.

Despite their apparent exhaustion, they both seemed so happy. Nyx felt a lump form in her throat, knowing without a doubt that they were her parents, and that the bundle was her. She felt tears pressing against her eyes as she watched the scene play out, feeling the love that they expressed for each other and for her.

Slowly, she lifted her hand to touch the surface of the mirror. As the sadness washed over her, deep regret filled her. "I wish I could have known them," she whispered.

Liana felt tears pricking at her own eyes as she looked at Nyx. "I wish the same," she said softly. She held Nyx's gaze when she looked up at her. "I miss them every day."

Liana's heart wrenched when Nyx suddenly pressed the mirror against her chest, a sob escaping her. Liana quickly threw her arms around her and held her tightly, feeling her shoulders shaking as she cried.

"I'm sorry," she whispered, pressing her hand against the back of Nyx's head. A pang of hurt that she hadn't felt in a long time swept through her, and a tear slid down her face. "I'm so sorry, Nyx." But deep down, Liana knew words weren't strong enough to heal what had happened.

25

JET WAS FROWNING LIGHTLY AS he sat across from Nyx at dinner. She'd barely touched her food. She'd intentionally come down as her friends were finishing their meals and preparing to return to their quarters for the night. Her face was pale and drawn, and he knew something had happened. He set his drink down a little harder than he intended, realizing that he was prepared to lay into whoever had done this to her. The thought gave him pause. He shouldn't have been so invested, but he couldn't help it.

He glanced up at Liana, feeling her eyes on him. He noticed that she seemed distracted as well. They'd both managed to act normally while around the Atturons, but now they both were quiet and lost in their thoughts. They'd been together all afternoon, supposedly to finish planning Nyx's ball, but they didn't look happy. Liana, knowing about his condition, had ordered him to take the afternoon to hunt, keeping him out of the palace. And he didn't like being excluded.

"Are either of you going to tell me what's going on?" he asked finally.

Nyx looked up at him and then at Liana. "I don't want to talk about it," she said quietly. She set her fork down and leaned back in her seat. "I'm actually pretty tired."

Liana leaned over and touched her hand. "You should go to bed," she said. "You have a busy day tomorrow."

Nyx nodded, moving to stand. She looked up at Jet when he did the same. "You can stay," she said. "I know where I'm going."

Jet fought the urge to scowl. "I'm supposed to be with you at all times, to protect you, aren't I?" he said a bit more snappishly than he meant to. He looked at Liana, prepared for her to encourage him to sit back down, but surprisingly she simply looked back to Nyx.

"He is right," she said gently, trying to convince Nyx.

Nyx frowned lightly at her grandmother before nodding her consent. She murmured a soft good night to Liana, feeling Jet on her heels. Once they exited the dining hall, Nyx steeled herself for Jet's barrage of questions. When it didn't come right away, she looked up at him.

"Aren't you going to ask me what's wrong?" she asked, hearing the exhaustion in her voice.

Jet was silent for a moment as they reached the end of the hall and started up the stairs. Nyx felt annoyed at the thought that he was making her discomfort about him and she sighed loudly, really not having the energy for this. She started to move up the stairs quicker.

"Nyx," Jet called, making her pause.

She turned to see that he had stopped a few steps behind her, his eyes not meeting hers.

"What did she show you?" he asked then, looking up at her.

Nyx frowned in confusion and a bit of surprise. "What?" she asked. "What do you mean?"

Jet rolled his eyes. "Come on, I'm not stupid," he said shortly. "Lady Aurie asked you about scrying, so I'm sure you asked Liana about it when you were with her earlier."

Nyx felt a pang of sadness streak through her and she looked away. "I really don't want to talk about it," she whispered, feeling choked. She didn't want to cry anymore, but she knew she would once she was alone in her room and tucked safely under her sheets. She couldn't stop thinking about her mother and father's faces as they gazed down at her. Before she knew it, the tears were rolling slowly down her face.

In an instant, Jet was on the step below her and he pulled her toward him as she crumpled into his arms, sobbing softly. The guilt that plagued him was heavy in his chest. He pulled her up the remaining stairs and guided her toward the sitting room in their wing of the castle. He let her slide onto the couch and eased to sit beside her, watching as she leaned over her knees and cried. After a long moment, she was able to compose herself.

"I just don't understand," she said as she drew a ragged breath. Her face was flushed, and her eyes were puffy as she rubbed at them. "I never did anything wrong. Why did everyone have to be taken from me?"

Jet looked down at his hands, which were folded in his lap. "I can't answer that," he said softly. "I wish I could."

Nyx wiped at her eyes more, looking mentally, emotionally, and physically exhausted. "She showed me my parents," she whispered then, her lip trembling. "She showed me the day I was born." She shook her head as more tears fell down her face. "I'll never get to meet them. Liana has these memories that she can look back on, but I never even got that." She leaned back in the seat. "I don't really even know what happened to them. Aunt Dee said that they were killed in an accident, but now I know that's not the whole story."

The guilt was worse in Jet's chest. He knew the story. He'd been there. And since getting to know Nyx, he wished he hadn't. In this moment, he would have given anything to change history, and it just added to the list of reasons why he needed to keep her at a distance. Once she found out what he'd done, that he'd been the reason they died, she would hate him, and he didn't know if he could live with that.

Silence fell over them. Nyx was lost in her own thoughts. She didn't expect much from Jet, because he wasn't exactly the comforting type, but she realized that she was okay with the quiet. He didn't need to say anything for her to feel comforted.

She moved to her feet, turning to look at him. "Thank you for sitting with me," she said softly.

Jet nodded mutely.

"See you tomorrow?" Nyx asked.

Jet nodded again before watching her turn and disappear into her bedroom. He let his head lean against the back of the couch. This was difficult and getting more so by the minute.

Nyx didn't sleep well. She kept waking from disturbing dreams that she couldn't remember, and she felt more exhausted by the time the sun finally started to fall through the window. The sadness from the day before was still crushing. She wondered if she should just stay in bed.

Eventually she rolled out of the sheets, knowing that Jasmine would be in soon to get her ready for the day. She didn't really want to explain anything to Jasmine, so she hurried to the bathroom to wash her face and try to make herself look normal. It didn't really work, but it was the best she could do.

Once Jasmine finally arrived, Nyx felt like she was sleep-walking through getting dressed. She barely heard a word that Jasmine said, agreeing mindlessly with her when she asked questions. If Jasmine noticed, she didn't let on. Nyx realized that she didn't care, and that was a strange emotion to her. Was this what depression felt like?

When she walked out of her room, she saw Jet waiting for her in the sitting area. He didn't say anything, but his eyes held hers for a moment more than necessary, and she knew that he was trying to gauge if she was okay. She looked away to hide the fact that she wasn't, even though she knew that he could tell. They walked in silence to the bottom of the stairs, where Samill and his two guards greeted them.

"Good morning, Highness," Samill said brightly. "Are you ready for your session with Lady Aurie?"

Nyx forced a smile. "Of course," she said, her voice hoarse.

Samill instantly took notice. "Are you feeling well, Your Highness?"

Nyx nodded quickly. "Just had some trouble sleeping last night," she said easily. "I'll take a nap this afternoon and feel better."

Samill nodded. "Let me know if there is anything I can do for you," he said.

Nyx nodded again. "I will," she said. She turned to head down the hall as Samill fell into step beside her. She looked up at him, noticing that there was a nervous air about him.

"Are you excited for your ball tomorrow night?" he asked.

Nyx glanced away for a second. She'd totally forgotten about the ball with yesterday's events. Today it felt like the worst possible thing in the world, but she forced a tight smile anyway. "Absolutely," she said. "I've never been to a ball, so this will be a new experience for me."

Samill smiled brightly. "That surprises me," he said. "I'm sure you must have attended parties or other such events on Earth."

Nyx nodded. "Yes, but never as the guest of honor," she said.

Once again, Samill seemed a bit nervous. "If it's not too forward, Your Highness, I'd like to ask for a dance," he said then.

"Oh, okay," Nyx said, confused by his demeanor. "That would be great."

Samill smiled again, and this time Nyx wondered why he was so happy. "Wonderful," he said brightly. "I can't wait."

Nyx nodded and tried to be happy, too, but really she was just confused. Fortunately, they had reached the courtyard where Lady Aurie awaited them, so she didn't have to wonder about it long. Nyx felt her heart skip a beat as she saw the water bowl laid out again today.

"Good morning, Your Highness," Lady Aurie said with a bow.

Nyx nodded a greeting, her eyes shifting to the bowl.

"Did you decide if you wanted to try scrying today?" Lady Aurie asked, following her gaze.

Nyx stared hard at the bowl, feeling her stomach flip. She wanted to know what she could see, if anything at all.

Perhaps she could see more of her parents. That thought gave her some hope, and she looked to Lady Aurie. "I think I do want to try," she said.

Lady Aurie smiled a bit and nodded her head. "Very good," she said, turning to walk around the table. She motioned for Nyx to step up to the table as well. "Take a moment to center your mind. Once you're ready, think about what you'd like to see."

Nyx closed her eyes and took a few deep breaths in and out. It was easy to find her center today; her brain was empty from the mental exhaustion she felt. After a few more breaths, she realized that she could feel the pulse of the magic in her veins more clearly than any other time before. It was warm and lent her some strength, but it also left the feeling of gold and light in her mind. It didn't really ease the sadness, but it was some comfort to know that the light was still there.

She could feel her aura surrounding her, creating a light shield around her. She could feel the auras of the others around her, and it made a map of colors in her mind. Each person in the room had a different color-feeling to them, and she could have easily guessed who was standing where at any given moment. It still was stark to her that all she felt from Jet was almost-empty blackness.

"Are you ready to look?" Lady Aurie asked, breaking through her thoughts.

Nyx drew another breath and pulled her thoughts back to herself. She wondered what she should try to see, and the church from Liana's wedding vision was the first thing that came to her mind. She took one more breath before opening her eyes and looking at her teacher.

"I'm ready," she said.

Lady Aurie nodded, motioning to the bowl. "Place

your fingers into the water," she said. "Feel your magic flowing from you to the water, and back."

Nyx did as she instructed. The warm magic flowed out of her hands and into the water, creating a light sheen. She was surprised by the way the water passed energy back to her, feeling alive.

"When you're ready, ask for what you want to see."

Nyx stared into the bowl, feeling her body and the water communing. The water was happy, but felt old, older than even the stones she practiced with. It occurred to her that water must have memory. It had been around for so long and seen so many things as it fell from the sky and flowed across the ground.

As if sensing her thoughts, the water swirled lightly, the sheen across it growing brighter. Nyx took that as her cue and blinked against her reflection. "I want to see the place Liana married," she whispered, so quietly that almost no sound was coming from her lips.

The water swirled a bit more before suddenly becoming impossibly still. It was smooth like the surface of Liana's mirror, and Nyx gazed into it, surprised to see what appeared to be the inside of a castle. She frowned lightly as she realized the image was moving, as if she were walking.

She passed through a door and into a hallway, finding another door that opened into a flight of stairs. Cold suddenly pressed into her through her fingers as the vision took her down the first step. Fear started to grip her, but she realized she couldn't stop. She watched as she descended further down the steps, the darkness more and more consuming.

Nyx realized her breathing had quickened and her heart was racing. There was something at the bottom of the stairs that was strong and pulling her toward it, and she was terrified. The terror worsened as she realized she was stuck, unable to stop the vision. "No," she whispered. "No, I don't want to see anymore."

She thought she could hear the sound of Lady Aurie's voice, but it was nothing but a soft drone in the back of her mind. The vision kept pulling her down the stairs into the dark and the thing at the bottom began to whisper her name. The fear she felt escalated and her heart leapt into her throat. She struggled to pull herself away from the bowl, but she was rooted to the spot, as if whatever had her in its snare was keeping her from escaping.

She screamed against the cold magic that was suddenly drifting across her hands, realizing that whatever she'd connected with was reaching back. The terror reached a crescendo as she realized she was at the bottom of the stairs, one final door between her and whatever had her caught in its trap. The door started to open, and she felt cold fear at what she might see. A last wave of panic overcame her and she forced all of her strength into her fingers, a pulse of hot magic exploding from her hands.

She felt concussed for a moment, her ears ringing and her vision blurry. Her mind felt disjointed. It took her a long moment to come back to herself and when she did, she realized she was lying on the ground, clutching her hands to her chest. Her breaths were ragged and hard, and her heart was racing. Scared tears were pooling in her eyes as she blinked several times to clear her mind, feeling her thoughts sharpen as the seconds passed.

"Nyx, look at me!" Jet demanded, as if it was the millionth time he'd said that. When she focused her eyes on his face, she saw relief cross his eyes. "What happened? What did you see?"

Nyx was trembling as she lay there, turning her eyes

back to the table. She saw Lady Aurie standing in front of her, concern on her face, and Samill and one of his men were on the opposite side of her. She turned toward Jet then, reaching for him desperately as he put his arms around her. "I don't want to see anymore," she whispered quickly, feeling the tears sliding down her face. Her voice was trembling. "I don't want to see anymore."

Nyx was sitting on the floor next to the fireplace in Liana's quarters. She wasn't listening to what Liana and Jet were saying as she stared into the flames. Apparently one of the soldiers had run to get Liana when they realized something was wrong. She pulled the blanket around her shoulders tighter, the chill that had tried to overtake her earlier having never left her. She felt like she could practically sit in the flames and still be cold.

She felt her ears tune in to Jet and Liana's conversation, catching the tail-end of Liana's words: "I couldn't see what she saw. I tried, but it wouldn't show me."

Nyx turned to look over her shoulder, seeing that her grandmother looked slightly distressed, and Jet had his arms crossed tightly.

"What if it was a ploy by Paraximus?" he asked bitterly. "What if he's trying to find a way to get around the spring's magic?"

"It wasn't your father," Nyx said then, drawing both of their gazes. Her voice was level and without emotion. She didn't know how she knew, but she did.

Liana turned toward her and took a step closer to her before sinking into a chair. "We can't know that for sure," she said gently. "Especially since you never saw what it was."

Nyx turned back toward the fire. "I can't explain it, but I just know," she said. "It didn't feel like another person." It was something strong and powerful, but the more she thought about it, the more she was starting to feel like it wasn't malicious. Whatever it was had been trying to speak to her, not harm her.

Liana drew a slow breath and looked over to Jet, who was frowning lightly. "Nyx, dear, perhaps you should go rest for a bit," Liana suggested kindly. She moved to kneel next to Nyx, brushing a strand of hair from her face. "You look exhausted."

Nyx realized that Liana's touch comforted her, and it made her feel safe. She glanced over Liana's shoulder to Jet before nodding slightly. "Yeah, that sounds like a good idea," she whispered.

Liana moved to stand and Jet stepped toward her, both catching her arms to help her to her feet. Her legs were trembling, and she felt like her limbs were made of jello. She leaned heavily against Jet, feeling him put his arm around her shoulders. As his warmth began to seep into her, she realized her eyes felt impossibly heavy all of a sudden. She didn't even make it a step before her mind slipped into darkness and she collapsed.

Jet caught her quickly and lifted her into his arms. She was breathing evenly against his chest, and he looked at Liana, seeing the worry on her face. "She's asleep," he said. "She used all the energy she had trying to break free."

Liana took a step toward him, reaching out to brush Nyx's golden curls from her face. Her violet eyes were soft. "She needs time to recuperate," she said softly. "The last two days have been hard on her, and I'm not sure she's really recovered from your … travels." She looked up at Jet then, seeing that his face was guarded. "Take her to her room and stay with her."

Jet seemed like he wanted to protest, but Liana shook her head.

"She needs you to be there when she wakes up," she said quietly. "You give her strength."

Jet let out a short sigh and turned to carry Nyx to her room. He hoped Liana was right.

26

Regius Carmen, the capitol city of Ymber.
The fifty-second day of winter, the 851st year of the
reign of Queen Liana Estrella.
Thursday, February 10, 2012.

Nyx groaned lightly as she stirred from her sleep. She opened her eyes slightly, seeing that it was dark out and she was lying in her own bed. Confusion filled her as she sat up slowly. She turned her head, feeling startled as she realized that she wasn't alone.

Jet was sitting in a chair next to her bed, and he had leaned forward when she sat up. "It's about time," he said, an annoyed edge to his voice.

Nyx pressed her hand against her forehead, feeling a slight headache pounding behind her eyes. "What happened?" she asked. "How did I get here?"

"You fainted," he said. "Liana made me bring you here and asked me to sit with you."

Nyx drew a long, slow breath, turning to look out the window, seeing stars twinkling in the night sky. "How long have I been asleep?" she asked distractedly.

"A while," Jet said. "It's well past midnight."

Nyx frowned slightly, turning to let her legs hang over the side of the bed closest to him. She was still wearing the outfit Jasmine had picked out for her earlier that morning, minus her boots. She ran her hands across the legs of her pants in a nervous motion. Despite having slept for more than ten hours, her mind still felt like her vision had just happened.

"What's wrong?" Jet asked, watching her carefully.

"I can still … feel it," she whispered. Those words didn't quite describe what she felt, but it was close. "Like it's still happening, but not."

Jet's brow furrowed. "Maybe that's just the residual magic," he said. "It should pass."

Nyx clenched her fists against her knees, wanting to tell him that she didn't think it would, but instead she nodded. "Yeah," she said quietly. "Maybe." She felt a pang of hunger fill her then and she looked at him. "I'm hungry."

Jet moved to his feet. "Come on," he said, walking toward the door.

Nyx hastily grabbed her boots and pulled them on before trotting after him. She realized the castle was oddly quiet, but it was kind of nice. She followed Jet down the stairs and into the dining hall.

The lights were dim, only a few lit here and there, and the room felt too large and empty. Their footsteps echoed a bit as Jet led the way to the back of the room, toward a door where Nyx had seen the servants come in and out. She realized there was a lot of this castle she had never seen, let alone even considered or thought about. Jet held the door open for her and she stepped inside a small room filled with plates and silverware and napkins and other such things.

"What is this room for?" Nyx asked.

"It's the scullery," Jet said as he stepped past her. "The servants prepare their trays here and bring the dirty dishes back here."

"Oh," Nyx said, realizing there was indeed a wash basin on the far side of the small room, as well as an area that could have been used for prepping plates or stacking them to be washed. She noticed that Jet crossed to the other side of the room and shouldered open a swinging door. She followed behind him, feeling warmth hit her face.

She knew this must be the kitchen. It was quite large, with ovens and open firepits. The fires were barely cinders, but Nyx could tell that it hadn't been long since they'd died down for the night. She could see bread and other foods set out on a cutting table for the morning, and she took a step toward the table.

"Do you think they'd mind?" she asked, motioning to the bread.

Jet scoffed slightly. "Of course not," he said easily. "You're the princess. You can do what you want."

Nyx didn't like the way his words felt, as if she should just take whatever she wanted with disregard for others, but she took a small loaf of bread and pulled the end off of it and popped it into her mouth. As she turned around, she saw that Jet had pulled open what looked like an ice box and was rummaging around in it.

"What's that?" she asked as she stepped closer.

"Cold storage," he said. He glanced up at her, a slight smirk on his face. "You know, a refrigerator?"

Nyx narrowed her eyes at his teasing. "I didn't think Gexalatia had refrigerators," she said as she took another bite of her bread.

"It's not like the ones on Earth, but it gets the job done," he said as he straightened and used his foot to nudge the door shut. In his hand was a glass bottle. He set it down on the kitchen island.

"What's this?" Nyx asked as she leaned over it.

"Milk," Jet said as he pulled a cork from the top. He handed the bottle to her, watching her wave it under her nose.

It smelled like milk, but inside the bottle it was a slightly blueish color. She tried not to think about it too hard as she lifted it to her lips and took a sip. She was surprised that the taste was very much like milk from back home. As she set the bottle down, she noticed that Jet had pulled two stools toward the island so that they could sit.

Once they were seated, Nyx tore a chunk of bread from the loaf and held it out to him. He took it wordlessly, picking a small piece off the end and eating it. They sat in silence for a moment, eating their bread, when Nyx suddenly remembered the Count's question from earlier in the day.

"Hey, can I ask you something?" she said then, looking over at him. To her surprise, he looked at her as he reached for the milk bottle, his eyes curious. "The Count asked me for a dance at the ball tomorrow."

Jet was silent as he watched her pick at her bread, his fingers brushing the neck of the milk bottle in a distracted way.

"He was acting all weird about it," she continued. "Is it a big deal or something?"

Jet made a humored sound before he took a sip of the milk. "He wants your permission to court you," he said finally. He watched as her eyes widened in surprise.

"What?" she asked quickly. "Court me? Like a boyfriend or something?"

Jet still seemed amused. "Something like that," he said,

crossing his arms on the table. He didn't like the way his gut twisted at the thought, but he kept the feeling to himself.

Nyx looked stunned for a second. "I said yes," she said quickly. "I didn't know that's what he meant."

Jet shrugged, trying not to let his feelings get the best of him. "It's not a big deal," he said. "It's just one dance." He vaguely wondered if he was trying to reassure her or himself.

Nyx felt flustered as she turned to look back at her bread. "Yeah, you're right," she said softly. "It's just one dance." But deep down, she was nervous and slightly nauseous. She didn't know if she wanted anyone to court her. She also picked up on the way Jet had tensed, as if he was unhappy.

They sat in silence for a while and Nyx picked at the bread, no longer really hungry. She hated that Zaida's words just kept coming back to haunt her. Finally, she looked up at Jet, seeing that he was leaning on the table, staring across the room. She wanted to ask what he was so lost in thought about, but instead she pushed the bread away and moved to stand.

"I'm tired," she said, feeling his eyes shift to her. "I'm going back to bed." She hated his silence as he simply nodded and she left the kitchen.

Nyx was glad to have had time to sleep in the following morning. Liana had informed her a few days ago that she should skip her lessons today because of the ball, but after yesterday's events and the day before that, it seemed like a great idea. She wasn't anywhere near ready to practice using her magic again. Plus, her brain still felt fried from experiencing so much emotion in the last two days.

Thankfully, the weird feeling from the day before had faded some, but it was still in the back of her mind, nagging at her. She tried to ignore it as she got ready for the day, hoping that the last-minute preparations would distract her.

As she pulled on a soft cotton dress and her shoes, a knock sounded at her door. She pulled her hair back from her face as she walked toward it to open it, weaving her golden curls into a braid. She was surprised to see Ellie when she pulled the door open.

"How are you today, Nyx?" Ellie asked quickly, her blue eyes concerned. "Are you feeling well? Is there anything I can do for you?"

Nyx felt her heart twist a bit. "I'm fine, Ellie," she said with a smile. "Thank you for checking on me."

Ellie seemed a bit nervous as she stood there, threading her fingers together. "I don't want to seem impudent," she said softly. "I just hadn't seen you in a few days, and I was worried."

Nyx nodded. She could only imagine how Ellie must be feeling; she must think that Nyx didn't value her friendship. "I'm sorry," she said. "These past two days have been … weird." She tried not to think about them too hard as she stepped through the door. "Why don't you come with me to meet with Liana? We're going to see how the preparations are coming along for tonight."

Ellie smiled then, cheering up immensely. "I would like that," she said. She stepped back as Nyx closed her bedroom door, falling into step beside Nyx as they walked toward the stairs. "Where is Jet?"

Nyx shrugged. "He said something about a meeting," she said, trying to remember what he'd told her. "I think it's about the guards for tonight or something."

"That sounds boring," Ellie said with a soft laugh.

Nyx agreed silently. "What about Raphael and Aled?" she asked.

"Raphael has been doing treatments with Liana's healers," Ellie said. "They last most of the morning and I usually don't see him until lunch time. And Aled is meeting with one of the lords to assemble a group to go to Sorona."

Nyx paused as they reached the bottom of the stairs. "Sorona?" she asked in surprise.

Ellie nodded. "We've been talking about going back," Ellie said then, her voice meek. She seemed bashful as she looked up at Nyx. "It's our home."

Nyx felt her heart drop into her feet, but she forced a smile. "I understand," she said. "I hope that you and Raphael are able to return."

"But it won't be for a while," Ellie said quickly. "Aled has a lot to do, and Raphael is really not well enough to travel yet."

Nyx felt some relief, and she guessed it must have shown on her face.

"So we can spend lots of time with you before we leave," Ellie continued quickly.

Nyx nodded. "I would like that."

Just then, a voice called her from the end of the hallway. They both looked up to see Angela walking toward them. "Princess, we're ready for you in the ballroom," she said pleasantly.

Nyx smiled. She was getting tired of faking happiness. "We were just on our way," she said. They both followed Angela into an area of the castle she wasn't very familiar with, soon arriving at large, open doors.

Nyx didn't know she could be more impressed with Regius Carmen until she saw the ballroom. A grand, winding staircase draped from the entrance down to a platform and split into two separate stairways before opening into a massive room. Large, round stone pillars, decorated with gold accents and intricate carvings, held up the ceiling, which arched over a smooth, pale grey granite floor. A massive crystalline chandelier hung overhead, dangling from the stone ceiling like a bedazzled stalactite. Small, coiling dragons and bright blue and black birds fluttered across the pale stone, flashing glittering, magical wings. Servants bustled around, arranging flowers and table decorations, or using the colors she'd chosen to accent the room. At the far end of the room, tall stone doors opened out into what looked like a garden.

"Wow," Nyx breathed.

"Do you like it?" Liana appeared beside her, a smile on her face.

"Your Majesty," Ellie said with a bow. "How are you today?"

Liana nodded her head. "How is your brother?" she asked.

Ellie smiled. "He's feeling so much better thanks to you," she said. "We are forever in your debt."

Liana put her hand on Ellie's shoulder. "Nonsense," she said. "If anything, I am in your debt." She looked to Nyx as Ellie's cheeks turned red a bit.

Nyx offered Ellie a smile as well. "It's true," she said gently. She thought back to the moment that Ellie and the Pangere had saved her and Jet. "I wouldn't be here without you." She could tell Ellie was embarrassed, so she decided to change the subject. She turned and gathered her skirt so that she could twirl around and stare at the ceiling. "Are those real?" she asked, motioning to the creatures flitting about.

Liana laughed, motioning for them to follow her down the stairs. "Just an enchantment to make the art come alive," she said gently. "It can be changed at any time, so if this is not to your liking, we can make it whatever you desire."

Nyx watched as two tiny dragons curled around each other, almost tying together in a knot, before slithering away. "Could you turn the ceiling into a night sky?"

"Certainly," Liana said. She raised her hand and with a wave the scene changed to a black velvet sky with diamond stars. Intermittently, shooting stars would cross the view.

Nyx grinned broadly as she watched the display, noticing that the servants working around the room had paused to admire it too. "That's so cool," she said.

Liana's smile never wavered. "There is much more to see," she said, leading the way into the room.

Nyx noticed that the arches and edging of the stone pillars were glimmering, as if coated in gold. Bright green banners with the Estrella house sigil hung across balconies on either side of the room, framing the stone doors to the garden. As they came closer, Nyx could see that the garden was a large terrace that overlooked the city below, which was glowing in the sunlight, the river sparkling like it was full of diamonds. She followed Liana toward tables, which were set around the edge of what appeared to be a dance floor.

"Are you pleased with the settings?" Liana asked.

Nyx stepped toward one, placing her hands on the ornately carved chair. Pale green and pink tablecloths were laid perfectly across the tables. Shining silverware sat in perfect settings around pale china plates. Nyx guessed that everything here was real, and really expensive. Even the chairs were backed with velvet, and plush cushions were on the seats.

"This is so amazing," Nyx said. She turned to look at the identical tables. "Where do we sit?" She half expected to see a head table like at a wedding on Earth.

Liana motioned to a balcony. "There," she said.

Beyond the railing Nyx could see a long table. It appeared to be set the same way, except two tall chairs were placed at the table. A wide staircase wound up to the balcony. "Why so far away?" Nyx asked.

"It is customary," Liana said, still smiling gently. "The royal family always has the best seat in the room, so that we may see the festivities."

Nyx frowned lightly. "Does that mean we have to sit there all night?"

Liana shook her head. "Heavens no," she said. She brushed a loose strand of lavender hair from her face. "I'm sure you will have many offers to dance, if you choose."

Nyx felt her face turn red as she thought about handsome men lining up to dance with her. It was weird for her to be the most popular person in the room.

Ellie noticed her fluster and grinned. "Have you had any requests yet?" she asked.

"Well, kinda," Nyx said, her fluster worsening. "Count Samill asked for a dance with me yesterday."

Ellie's grin widened. "That's so exciting," she said. She caught Nyx's hands. "Everyone is going to want to have a dance with you."

Nyx felt her stomach twist. She didn't like the idea of being swarmed by people she didn't know.

"You always have the option to decline," Liana said then. "It is more than acceptable for you to choose who you want to dance with and who you don't."

That made Nyx feel somewhat better, but there was still a knot in her stomach.

"You and Ellie should start getting ready," Liana continued. She smiled brightly. "There's still plenty of time, but you should let Jasmine and the handmaids pamper you."

Nyx turned and looked to Ellie. "Will you join me?" she asked. Pampering sounded great and she wondered what it included.

Ellie smiled and nodded. "Of course, Princess," she said happily. "I'd be delighted."

Liana turned to Nyx then and hugged her. "I will see you both tonight. Enjoy being spoiled for a bit."

Angela reappeared then from where she'd been standing on the edge of the room. "Please come with me, Your Highness," she said. "I will take you and your guest to the spa."

Nyx glanced at Ellie as they followed Angela. She led them back down the hall and toward another wing that Nyx was unfamiliar with. A doorway led to a set of stairs, much like the ones that went into the hot spring in her wing. They were smoothly worn stone steps and they descended down. As Nyx and Ellie followed Angela, Nyx could smell the scent of water, as well as bath salts and oils. She started to feel excited as they finally reached the bottom of the stairs.

The room opened up around them, revealing a cavernous room filled with steam. To one side were hot springs and to the other was a wide doorway that seemed to lead into another area. Candles were lit all around, giving the room a calm and soothing vibe, as well as filling it with a floral scent. A servant appeared as they entered, a smile on her face.

"Sasha, are things prepared for the Princess?"

The servant nodded. "Of course," she said gently. Nyx noticed that she had kind brown eyes, and her dark hair was swept up in a tight bun. "Right this way, Your Highness." She motioned toward the opposite room.

"Enjoy yourselves," Angela said with a bow before walking back up the stairs.

Nyx and Ellie followed Sasha through the wide doorway, seeing what looked like massage tables set up around the room. There were at least ten, and they were all prepared with clean white linens and small pillows. Next to each was a woven basket, filled with bottles of lotions and oils.

"We weren't sure how many guests to expect, so we made sure to prepare all the stations," Sasha said then. She pointed to a screen in a corner. "You both may change there. When you're ready, choose a table and the girls will be with you. If you need anything in the meantime, please let me know."

Nyx felt uncomfortable as she looked at Ellie and they walked toward the screen. It was quite large, and behind it was an area where several people could change into robes at once. Nyx turned toward Ellie once they were out of sight. "Have you ever done something like this before?" she asked softly.

Ellie shook her head, her cheeks turning a bit red. "No," she whispered. "I hope it's good."

Nyx agreed. "Are we supposed to take all our clothes off?" she murmured, reaching for a robe.

They both were startled when two more servant girls appeared. They both bowed and the taller of the two addressed them. "Do you require assistance?" she asked.

Nyx and Ellie exchanged a glance. "Um, we've never done this before," she said hesitantly.

"Oh!" the servant gasped. "Don't worry, Your Highness, we are at your beck and call." She smiled broadly. "I am

Meg and this is Kala. We will help you both undress."

Meg stepped toward her and began to undo the strings on her bodice, while Kala did the same for Ellie. Once they were both in their undergarments, the girls stepped back.

"You can undress to your level of liking," Meg said with a smile. "Once you're ready, come choose your station and we will begin your massages."

Nyx pulled the robe around her shoulders, glancing quickly at Ellie. "Are you going to undress?" she whispered.

Ellie shrugged. "I guess," she said with a nervous laugh. "I'm sure they do this all the time, so it won't be a big deal."

Nyx agreed mutely, watching as Ellie turned away to give her some privacy. They each finished stripping down before tying their robes tightly around themselves. "Ready?" Nyx asked.

Ellie nodded with a small smile. "Ready."

Jet glanced out the window, seeing that it was getting dark. He looked down at the formal suit that a manservant had brought to him, feeling his nose wrinkle. The fabric was stiff around the collar. He hated that. There was nothing about this event he was looking forward to, starting with the fact that it was a logistical nightmare.

With so many people in attendance, it would be difficult to keep Nyx safe from anyone looking to hurt her. Something that hadn't escaped him in the time that they'd been here was the fact that there were some who didn't believe she was who she said she was or didn't like that she'd come home since it meant one more person between someone else and the throne. The biggest threat to consider was Liana's cousin, Canus Seren, the Duke of Austia.

Canus seemed like a mild-mannered man, ready to

accept his role and happy with his position, but Jet didn't feel like the man passed the smell-test. He seemed to know too much about what was going on around the castle, despite the fact that he only spent the winter in Regius Carmen before returning to his home in Austia. He also was quite powerful; he had a lot of wealth and was well-known amongst the Caelin due to his business: breeding, buying, and selling raperes.

At first, being a breeder of the creatures didn't seem so glamorous, but there was more to it than that. Austia bordered the Plains of Aduro, where most of the Caelin tribes had migrated to when Ymberians began to gentrify the country. The building of Paries' Wall played a small role in that, but for the most part it was lords being awarded lands by the regency and pushing the native peoples from their homes. Because of this, the Caelin had an alliance with Austia. In exchange for commerce, they supplied Canus with the finest breeding stock, in turn making his raperes the most desired in the country. Caelin tribesmen raised their mounts to be bold and fearless, not to mention there was a certain level of prestige in owning a Caelin-bred rapere.

All that in consideration, Jet knew that he needed to keep an eye on Canus. If anyone had the motive and manpower or money to organize a coup or assassination, it was him. And he would be in attendance tonight, along with his daughters, Serefina, Rosalinda, Francesca, and Isabella. Apparently, the reason Jet hadn't seen them around the castle previously was because they'd been visiting other relatives.

He felt apprehension as he pulled on a shirt and buttoned it. Tonight really needed to go well. Nyx deserved it. He could tell she was struggling. She hadn't been herself since learning about her family's ability to scry, a deep sadness sitting just below the surface. Jet realized that, along with learning how to use her magic, she was learning things about herself that she didn't know before. She was learning truths that were buried and secret, and he clenched his jaw at the thought.

She had asked him before if she would still see him the same after learning all he'd done, but he knew that she wouldn't. She'd be horrified and angry. He hadn't been a nice or pleasant person in the past. His hands were soaked in blood, so stained that it would be impossible to forget, or forgive. And, despite his actions being at his father's behest, he couldn't lie and say that he hadn't wanted to participate. He just hoped that someday she could forgive him.

Jet drew a slow breath as he pulled on his coat, trying to push the thoughts away. He needed to focus to get through the night, and it was time for him to meet Nyx to escort her to the ball.

He took one more look at himself in the mirror before crossing to the door and stepping into the sitting room. Liana had informed him that Nyx would be getting ready in a different wing of the castle this evening, one where she could be doted on by her maids. He was supposed to meet her in the main hall.

His mind was still distracted as he trotted down the steps, thinking about the security meeting earlier in the day. Count Samill had led the meeting, along with Liana's captain of the guard, Antony Twile. Antony had served Liana for many, many years, and he took all security matters seriously. Jet knew that they were probably being too cautious because Antony's men were well-trained. He had just resolved to try not to worry about anything as he stepped off the last stair into the foyer. He walked toward the main hall, stepping through the archway that led to the stairs. He turned his eyes down the hallway, seeing quite a few faces that he didn't recognize.

Guests were already making their way to the ballroom, some coming down from other wings in the castle and some having just arrived. Jet stood to the side and surveyed them as they went by. This was obviously a big to-do, and it seemed anyone who was anyone had come. He noticed that there seemed to be more young men in the castle than normal, but he also considered that maybe he was being paranoid. All of these nobles couldn't have possibly shown up here with their sons thinking that one might catch Nyx's eye.

A twinge of jealousy filled him. He'd have to keep a close eye on all of them. He was so distracted by the thought, imagining how he could fend off any interlopers, that he hadn't noticed that the guests at the end of the hall had stopped and were making way for someone. A hush fell over the guests, and Jet turned his head to see what was happening. His heart jumped as he saw what they did.

Nyx was walking slowly down the hall, escorted by a handful of guards and her maids. She was wearing a seafoam green ball gown that flared around her. Instead of the off-the-shoulder style that most young women he'd seen were wearing, her dress covered her shoulders, lace sleeves over her arms. The top part of her dress hugged her middle, the neckline swinging just low enough that he could see the sparkle of a necklace against her collarbone. Her golden curls were swept up away from her face, diamond hair pins catching the light every so often around a simple and elegant tiara. There must have also been diamonds sewn into her dress because she sparkled with every step she took. She seemed slightly embarrassed by the attention she had garnered, her cheeks dusted with a light blush.

Jet realized two things then. One, he wasn't going to be able to keep other males away from her, and two, she was definitely the most beautiful woman he'd ever seen. His mind blanked a bit as she came closer, her eyes catching his and a soft smile pulling at her lips. Once she was close enough, he bowed to her.

"Good evening, Princess," he said as he straightened. He held out a hand to her. "Are you ready?"

Nyx seemed slightly surprised by his behavior, and her eyes narrowed as if she was trying to determine his sincerity. She didn't skip a beat though as she took his hand and let him loop her hand around his arm. "I am," she said.

As they walked down the long hallway toward the ballroom, her guard detail in tow, the nobles around them stopped and allowed them to pass, bowing as she went by. Jet let his eyes shift over them, seeing that they were all focused on Nyx. Most seemed enthralled with her beauty, but a few were frowning lightly.

"I hate how they're all staring at me," Nyx said softly, glancing up at him. "It's like they've never seen a girl in a dress before."

Jet was practically scowling at all the attention. "It's only because they've never seen such a beautiful girl in a dress before. They need to put their eyes away." The words escaped his lips before his brain had a chance to censor them. He barely caught the last sentence on his tongue before it slipped out: *because you're mine.*

Nyx's cheeks turned a darker shade of red. "Jealousy isn't a good look for you," she managed, trying to sound teasing even though she was clearly flustered.

Jet wanted to snap that he wasn't jealous, but he didn't trust himself to speak, and the simple fact was that he was.

He was insanely jealous, and he needed to get himself together.

They finally reached the entrance to the ballroom. A page stood at the entrance to the staircase, and he heralded her arrival by announcing her loudly to the room.

Nyx's eyes widened as the people already gathered stopped and turned to watch her and Jet come down the stairs. She took careful steps down the stairs. In her mind, she was imagining herself missing a step and faceplanting in front of everyone. At the thought, her hand tightened around Jet's arm.

Jet glanced down at her then, his jealousy easing as he saw the nervousness on her face. He wracked his brain for something to say that didn't sound dumb. "You look like you feel better," he commented quietly as they reached the landing where the stairway split.

Nyx nodded. "I do actually," she said in the same soft tone. She'd fallen asleep at some point during her and Ellie's pampering session, and it had been the most restful sleep she'd had in a long time.

Jet thought she might say more, but they reached the bottom of the stairs and a familiar face greeted them.

"Good evening, Your Highness," Aled said, bowing to her. He was smiling brightly. "You look amazing."

Nyx returned his smile. "You don't look so bad yourself," she said.

Aled gave a nervous laugh. "It's amazing what a bath and change of clothes will do," he remarked. He turned slightly. "If my cousins are here, they should be waiting for you in the loft." He motioned toward the balcony. "Her Majesty invited us to sit with you."

"Oh, wonderful," Nyx said happily.

"I'm making my rounds, but I will join you shortly,"

he said. He bowed once more and wandered away to greet some other people he knew.

Nyx watched him go before feeling Jet pull her toward the stairs to the loft. Liana had explained to her that they and their chosen guests would dine at their table, and during the dinner, it was customary for the attendees to come up and introduce themselves. She realized that most of the people that were crowded around were unfamiliar to her.

"Are all of these people nobles?" she asked Jet softly.

Jet shook his head. "Most are, but some are commoners," he said. "Rich merchants and the like who can afford to attend."

"Ah," Nyx breathed. "Seems like there's a ton of people here."

Jet shrugged, trying to act nonchalant. "It's a big deal, I guess."

They finally reached the stairs and Nyx let go of Jet's arm to gather her skirt in her hands. She was surprised to feel his hand on the small of her back as they went up the steps together, and she glanced over at him. "Why are you touching me?" she asked. She meant for her tone to be playful but it came out almost annoyed.

Jet seemed to be caught off-guard. "It's called being polite," he retorted. "It's also so you don't bust your ass on the stairs."

Nyx frowned at him but accepted his reason. She had to admit that she was glad he was helping her; she was wobbly in heels on a good day, and with the billowing skirt of her dress, it was a lot more difficult to keep her balance.

Once they reached the top of the stairs, Nyx felt her feet slow. Sitting at the table, which she thought would just be for her and Liana and her friends, was a man and four women, about her age, whom she didn't recognize. Ellie and Raphael were nowhere in sight, so she guessed they hadn't arrived yet. She watched as the man stood when he caught sight of them. Much like Liana, his eyes were a shade of violet. He had what she assumed was lavender-colored hair that had faded to a silvery grey with time. He seemed to be about Liana's age, although it was hard to tell. The women around him all stood as well, each revealing the same shade of violet eyes.

"Princess," he said as he came toward her and bowed. He was smiling brightly. "It is wonderful to finally make your acquaintance."

Nyx nodded shortly. "Yes, of course," she said, feeling put on the spot. The way he was looking at her, as if they had met before, was throwing her off as well. "I'm sorry, you are?"

The man frowned. "How terribly rude of me," he said. "I am Canus Seren, Duke of Austia, and Her Majesty's cousin."

Jet's eyes immediately narrowed as he looked at the duke. He hadn't expected the man so seem so ... innocent.

"My favorite cousin, to be exact."

Nyx turned to look over her shoulder, seeing Liana crest the stairs. She was being escorted by a page, who took his leave once she was safely on the landing. Liana was beaming as she walked toward Canus, her arms outstretched.

"How are you, love?" Canus asked as he embraced her and kissed her cheek.

"I'm fine," Liana said, stepping back to look him over. "How was your trip?"

Canus returned her smile. "Droll," he said with a laugh. "The Duchess is as dry as day-old bread."

They both shared a knowing laugh over his assessment of whoever he'd been to visit before Liana turned toward Nyx and motioned for her to come closer. Nyx could feel Jet behind her as she stepped forward.

"Canus, this is my granddaughter," Liana said, her voice soft and her smile bright. "She has finally returned to us."

Canus was smiling much like Liana. "I see much of your father in you, Princess," he said gently. His eyes shifted over her face as if she was a familiar sight. "And hair like sunshine, just like your mother." He glanced at Liana. "Let's hope she didn't inherit Kayne's sharp tongue."

Liana still smiled, but a hint of sadness flitted through her eyes. "Kayne certainly was not afraid to speak his mind," she said as she looked to Nyx. "Have you met the girls yet?"

Nyx shook her head. Her stomach was churning uncomfortably with the mention of her parents.

Canus turned then and motioned for the women behind him to join him. "These are my daughters," he said with a smile. "My eldest, Serefina, my second-eldest, Rosalinda, and the two youngest, Francesca and Isabella."

Nyx noticed that they each bowed in turn. Serefina stepped forward after the introductions, a bright smile on her face. Just like her father, she had deep violet eyes, but unlike her father and her sisters, she had bright red hair, which was twisted up away from her neck.

"I'm so happy to finally meet you, Your Highness," she gushed. "I've heard so much about you."

Nyx nodded stiffly. "Yes, I'm happy to get to know some of my family as well," she said, forcing a smile. Despite Serefina's happy demeanor, Nyx felt a mean-girl vibe from her. She glanced over at Serefina's sisters, seeing that they were much more demure. She guessed that Serefina was the leader and the others just did as they were told.

"And who is your escort this evening, Your Highness?" Canus asked then, drawing Nyx's gaze. His eyes were studying Jet. "I don't believe we've met."

Jet gave him a curt smile. "We haven't," he said. His arms were crossed.

"Canus, this is Jet," Liana said then, her voice quiet. Her eyes were watching Canus' reaction closely. At the first sign of rage and disgust, Liana stepped toward him and put her hand on his arm. "You know of my deal with him," she murmured.

Canus managed to wrench his eyes from Jet and turn them to Liana. "This feels like playing with fire, My Queen," he hissed softly.

Nyx felt her hackles rise slightly, and she took a step closer to Jet. She glanced at him, seeing the surprise on his face when she reached for his arm.

"This is my choice," Liana said firmly. "And I will not be undermined, not even by you, Canus."

Canus seemed even more unhappy, but he took a moment to compose himself before nodding his head. "Have you come before the Council yet?" he asked, turning back to Jet. He looked entirely displeased as he saw Nyx holding on to Jet's arm, as if she were claiming him.

"Your Council hasn't called on me," Jet said easily. "And even if they do, they'll be disappointed. I have nothing to offer them."

Canus was scowling and looked like he wanted to argue Jet's point, but Liana stilled him.

"Let's discuss this another time," she said gently. "Tonight is about Nyx." She glanced at her granddaughter.

Canus drew a slow breath before nodding. "Of course, Your Majesty," he said then. "Forgive me."

Liana patted his arm before stepping toward the table. "Nyx, dear, will the Atturons be joining us?" she asked as she walked toward her seat at the head of the table.

"I believe so," Nyx said, glancing over her shoulder into the gathering crowd. She wondered where Aled had meandered off to, as she couldn't easily pick him out of the throng.

"They'll be here soon enough," Liana said with a smile. She motioned for Nyx and Jet to sit. "Come, let's have a drink. Dinner will begin soon."

Nyx glanced up at Jet as he led her toward her seat on Liana's left. He was silent as he helped her into her chair, but Nyx could tell it was because he was fuming. He moved to Liana's right to sit down, noticing that Canus was sitting in the chair beside him. Nyx watched as they exchanged disgusted glances before resolutely ignoring one another.

Liana didn't let the awkwardness linger, however, as she lifted her wine goblet. "A toast," she said then, smiling brightly. "To Nyx's safe return."

Nyx and the rest lifted their glasses to her toast. Nyx was horribly uncomfortable as she took a sip of her wine and looked around the table. The three youngest Seren girls seemed uncomfortable as well, but Serefina was glancing boldly around the table, first to Nyx as if to size her up, then to Jet. Nyx didn't like the way her eyes lingered on Jet for longer than necessary.

Liana began to fill the air with conversation about Canus' travels, but Nyx wasn't listening. Her thoughts were jumbled, starting with the pit in her stomach at the mention of her parents and ending with the desire to tell Serefina to mind her own business as she continued to stare at Jet. She guessed he wasn't having the best time either as he rolled his eyes when their gazes met. Nyx had to fight the urge to smile as relief filled her. At least she wasn't the only one who felt out of sorts here.

"Your majesties and guests," a page suddenly appeared at the top of the stairs, bowing at the waist, "may I present Lady Ellie Atturon and Sir Raphael Atturon."

Nyx felt a genuine smile pull at her face as she stood, seeing Ellie and Raphael. Ellie was dressed in a light blue ballgown, her pale hair twisted around her face, while Raphael wore a complimenting suit. Nyx noticed that he wasn't carrying his cane and he looked like he was standing up straight. She also noticed that the slight bit of scaring that peeked from under his high collar was fading.

"I'm so glad you made it," Nyx said as she crossed to them and hugged both of them. She supposed they could see the relief on her face, because they were both smiling brightly.

"Sorry we're a bit late," Ellie said. She glanced at her brother. "Someone was taking a while to finish getting ready." She gave him the stink eye.

Raphael rolled his eyes at his sister. "It's not my fault," he said. He looked to Nyx. "I couldn't find the right shoes." He motioned to the boots on his feet.

Nyx laughed then. "You both look great," she said, turning. "Come sit down."

Ellie and Raphael were both grinning as they approached the table. Ellie noticed the other guests, and she felt her smile slip a bit as she noticed that she was getting a rather hard glare from a red-headed girl.

"Hello," she said, bowing slightly. "I am Ellie Atturon, and this is my brother Raphael." She glanced at the other girls and then at the man, watching as they bowed their heads to her.

"This is my cousin, Canus, and his daughters," Liana

said then. She didn't move to stand, but she was smiling. "I'm happy you both could make it."

Ellie smiled brightly at Liana. "We wouldn't miss it," she said, glancing to Raphael.

"Will Aled be joining us as well?" Liana asked.

"Yes," Ellie said as she sat in her seat. "He was visiting with some of his acquaintances before the festivities begin."

"Very good," Liana said. "Then I suppose it is time to begin our dinner." She stood slowly and walked toward the railing of the balcony, overlooking the crowd below. As she stood there, the crowd began to hush, all eyes on her. "Welcome, my dear guests and thank you all for attending." She was smiling as she addressed the crowd. "Tonight we celebrate the safe return of my granddaughter, Princess Nyx Estrella, daughter of Kayne and Lillian Estrella, and heir to the throne." She turned to glance at Nyx over her shoulder. "Let us feast and rejoice in her honor!"

A cheer rose from the crowd, and Nyx felt like she wanted to sink into the floor. She could feel her face turning red. The embarrassment was worse when Liana turned toward her.

"Would you like to say a few words, Nyx?" she asked.

Nyx felt her heart jump into her throat. She had no idea what the heck she was supposed to say, but she felt like it would be rude for her not to. She moved slowly to stand, joining her grandmother at the railing. When she looked down and saw the massive crowd below, she felt her head start swimming.

Liana noticed the way her face paled, and she put her arm around Nyx's waist. "Just thank them for coming," she said gently in Nyx's ear. "That's good enough."

Nyx nodded. She cleared her throat. "Um, thank you all for being here," she said, hearing her voice echo around the room as if she were speaking into a microphone. "I hope you all have a good time."

With that, another cheer rose from the crowd. Liana patted Nyx on the back, laughing softly. "That was good," she said.

Nyx still felt horribly embarrassed. "Are you sure?" she managed as they turned away from the railing.

Liana laughed again. "Anything a princess says is good enough," she said. "And the more you do it, the better you'll get."

Nyx felt her stomach drop. "I'll have to do it again?" she managed.

Liana still seemed humored. "Not tonight," she said, hugging Nyx lightly. "But in the future, you will need to address your people." They paused before they sat down, and Liana motioned to everyone at the table. "But tonight, we will all enjoy each other's company and let the worries wait for tomorrow."

Celo Cavus, the capitol city of Siccita.
The fifty-third day of winter, the 906th year of the
reign of King Paraximus Lamia.
Friday, February 11, 2012.

BAILEY WAS TREMBLING AS SHE sat near the cell door. She watched the guards carefully, knowing that their rotation was almost done. Her heart clenched at the thought of Jili helping her. She hoped that he would come through for her, but she tried to tell herself that she would understand if he changed his mind. It was a huge risk for him to take for her; she was a stranger to him, and she wasn't sure that she could do what he had promised for someone she didn't know.

She leaned her head back against the wall and tried to calm her racing heart. She knew she needed to be patient. She could feel the pulse of the book hidden under the dirty hay, and it leant her some comfort. She'd read over the spell a million times it seemed like; she wasn't sure how she could be any more prepared.

Finally, she heard the jingling of keys and the clanging of doors, and she knew that it was time. Her whole body was tense as she waited for Jili to appear around the corner to her cell. She tried not to jump to her feet when she finally saw him. He seemed slightly breathless as he met her at the bars.

"I couldn't find a mirror large enough," he whispered, his eyes downcast. He pulled a small, square mirror from a pouch in his belt to show her. "This is all I have."

Bailey felt her heart drop. She wracked her brain for a moment. "We need a reflective surface," she breathed. She looked quickly around the dungeon, her heart skipping a beat as her eyes landed on a jug of water across the room. She grabbed Jili to get his attention. "Jili, the water!"

Jili turned to see the jug and crossed quickly to grab it. He pulled the keys from his belt and unlocked the door. The sound of the latch sliding open echoed heavily through the cavernous dungeon, making both of them freeze.

"Do you think anyone is coming?" Bailey breathed.

Jili listened for a long moment then shook his head slowly. "No, I think we're clear," he said quietly. He stepped into the cell and turned to hand her the jug of water. He was surprised when he was met with her arms thrown tightly around his middle.

"Thank you," she breathed. She looked up at him. "I don't know if this will work, but I can't tell you how much it means to me that you're willing to try."

Jili's lips quirked slightly. "Don't thank me until we're out of here."

Bailey nodded and released him, taking the jug from him. She walked toward where she'd kept the book buried in the straw. As she pushed the dirty hay away from it, she heard Jili gasp softly.

"How did you get that?" he whispered.

Bailey shrugged. "It came to me," she said. "I thought it was destroyed, but here it is." She glanced at Jili as he knelt next her, watching his eyes widen as he saw the eye on the front of the book open. Bailey turned the cover over, and the book rustled suddenly, responding to her touch and flipping open to the spell she needed.

Bailey took a moment to read over the spell again, for the million-and-one-th time, before looking to Jili. "Let's hope I can do this."

Nyx was regretting that she had promised the Count a dance.

He was standing at the top of the stairs, one of many in a long line of guests who had come to offer their praise to her and Liana after the dinner ended. The food had been delicious and she was certain she'd nearly eaten herself into a coma, that is, until Count Samill appeared. He looked dashing, his sandy-blonde hair combed nicely and his high-collar suit making him look taller. Nyx was fairly certain he was even puffing his chest out a bit.

"Good evening, Your Majesties," he said, sweeping them a low bow. He looked to Nyx. "Your ball is wonderful."

Nyx nodded and smiled. "Thank you, Count Samill," she said politely. She glanced at Liana, who was giving her a subtle 'go over there and talk to him' look. She tried not to grimace as she moved to her feet and stepped toward the Count.

"If it's all right with you, Princess, I would be honored to lead you in the first dance," he said with a kind smile.

Nyx glanced over her shoulder toward Liana, but instead she caught Jet's eyes. She felt her stomach flip-flop at the way he was scowling lightly. She realized, though, that all eyes were on her, and everyone but him was expecting her to accept the Count's offer. She thought she even caught a glimpse of jealousy on Serefina's face.

"Of course," she said finally, forcing a smile. "That would be wonderful."

Count Samill seemed to relax a bit then, and his smile was much more easygoing as he held out his arm to her. "Shall we?"

Nyx took his arm and tried to ignore the way her heart was racing as he led her down the stairs and toward a dance floor, where a thousand eyes were watching them. She felt so self-conscious, and she turned to look at Samill so she didn't have to look at anyone else.

"I hope I don't embarrass you," she said softly, watching him look down at her. "I'm still learning the steps."

Count Samill gave her a reassuring smile. "I'm sure you'll do wonderfully, Your Highness," he said. "As far as I can tell, you're a quick study." He chuckled lightly and Nyx couldn't keep from grinning in response.

Once they came to the floor, Samill led her into the middle of it. The first dance was customary for the guest of honor to lead, but Nyx didn't like being in the middle of the floor in front of all these people. It made her feel bare.

Samill bowed to her and she bowed slightly in response before the music started and he caught her hands and pulled her toward him. Nyx realized she was shaking lightly as she glanced around the room, seeing all eyes still on her, most of them belonging to young men who looked eager to catch her attention. She could feel the grimace on her face as Samill led her around the floor.

"You're doing well, Your Highness," Samill said, breaking her thoughts.

Nyx tried to offer him a small smile.

"Don't be nervous," he said, giving her hand a gentle squeeze. "Your dancing is just fine."

Nyx nodded slightly. What he didn't know was that she'd done this step with Jet countless times, back on Earth when they would go dancing. The thought that she'd rather be dancing with Jet flitted across her mind, making her cheeks flush slightly. She couldn't wait to bail back to her seat on the balcony once this was over, and she knew that relief was in sight as the song started to wind down. The sound of applause began to echo around the room, and Nyx pulled her hand from the Count's, intending to escape.

As soon as the song ended, though, and before he even had a chance to ask her for another dance, she found herself swarmed by gentlemen, each vying for her attention to ask for a dance. She felt like it was open season and she'd become the prey, and she was cornered. She wasn't sure how she would navigate her way out of this, and she could feel her face becoming redder as she began to feel overwhelmed. Just when she thought she would have to shove her way through the crowd and run from the floor, a hand suddenly pressed against hers.

Her movements were instinctive as her fingers wrapped around the ones pressed into hers. She didn't consciously register who she was clinging to, but something felt familiar and safe about the gesture. She turned as she realized she was being pulled away from the group, feeling her breath catch in her throat.

"Jet," she breathed as he pulled her against his chest. She watched as his eyes shifted around to the others, as if to warn them to back off, before he expertly maneuvered her onto the dance floor, another song having already started. It was easy to fall into step with him.

"You always need rescuing, don't you, little princess," he said, a slightly smug edge to his voice.

Nyx's face was hot as she offered an embarrassed smile. "They just all came out of nowhere," she managed. She noticed that others were filling the dance floor around them, and she was relieved that the attention was off of her, even if only for the moment.

Jet made a humored sound. "Insects to a flame," he murmured.

Nyx tilted her head lightly. "What?" she asked.

Jet turned his eyes on her, and something about the way he was looking at her made her heart jump into her throat. "Everyone wants you," he said. "And the ones that don't want you, want to be you."

Nyx felt her face flush slightly and she looked away. "That's ridiculous," she said.

Jet suddenly turned her, forcing her eyes to meet his as she spun back to him. "It's the truth."

Nyx felt breathless as she gazed up at him. She could feel his hand pressed against her back and smell the scent of his breath. Her eyes drifted toward his lips before she forced herself to look away, feeling stupid. Why did he still make her want him? Hadn't he made it clear to her that he didn't feel the same way?

"So," she managed, "does that mean I have to dance with all of them?"

Jet smirked. "You can do whatever you want, little princess," he said. "It's your party."

Nyx felt her heart flip at the way he called her 'little princess'. She hadn't heard him call her that in a long time. It reminded her of a time that felt distant and far away. She didn't realize that her thoughts were running away with her until he pulled her toward him as the song ended.

"What are you thinking about?" he asked as he paused, his eyes searching hers curiously.

Nyx looked up at him, wondering if she should tell him. She started to, but they were interrupted by a tall young man who had seemingly appeared out of nowhere.

"Your Highness, I am Deren Harding, may I have this dance?" he asked quickly, smiling brightly.

Nyx looked up to Jet, her eyes pleading, watching as he held her gaze. She hoped that he would take the hint and send the young man scurrying away, but instead his grip on her hand loosened.

"Princess," he said, bowing slightly.

Nyx narrowed her eyes at him, realizing that his lips were pulling in a smirk. He was doing this on purpose. She fought the scowl that tried to cross her face, turning her eyes on Deren.

"Of course," she said politely, taking his outstretched hand.

Deren seemed ecstatic as he led her onto the floor. Unfortunately, his excitement seemed to get in the way of his thoughts, because the first few steps of their dance were incredibly awkward and silent.

"So," Nyx said finally, "tell me about yourself."

Deren looked surprised. "Have you not heard of my father?" he asked.

Nyx felt her opinion of him instantly sour. "No," she said shortly. "Should I have?"

"He's only the richest merchant in Regius Carmen," he said boastfully. "He owns a hundred ships – the largest fleet in the continent."

Nyx arched a brow at him. "And what of you, Deren?" she asked, realizing he was trying hard to impress her with his daddy's money. "What have you accomplished?"

Deren's eyes darkened slightly. "I stand to inherit his wealth and his business, of course," he said curtly.

Nyx wanted to roll her eyes. She didn't ask him any more questions, instead letting her eyes wander across the floor. She felt her heart skip a beat when Deren turned her, causing her to catch sight of Jet at the edge of the dance floor. There was something in the way he was watching her that made her stomach turn in knots, a yearning in his gaze that she'd never seen before. At that moment, she could have let go of Deren and walked away from him without a second thought – and the idea was very tempting – but the spell was broken when Jet's attention was drawn away from her by Serefina.

She realized that she wasn't paying attention to Deren at all as she kept trying to turn her head to keep Jet and Serefina in view. From the glimpses she got, she could see Serefina smiling charmingly up at Jet, who seemed to be trying to ignore her. Nyx wondered how long he was going to stand there and let her pester him, but she didn't have to wonder long when she turned in time to see him step away from Serefina and disappear into the crowd. She felt her heart sink as the song ended and Deren let go of her.

"Thank you for the dance, Your Highness," he said with a bow. Nyx could tell he was preparing to ask her for another dance, just as another young man appeared.

"Your Highness," he said with a bow, "I am Topher of House Warner." He glanced at Deren, who seemed to realize that he was nobility and deferred to him. "I would be honored if you would grant me a dance."

Nyx looked at him for a moment, noticing that he was just about as tall as Deren, but had a wider, stronger build. He had dark blue hair and amethyst-colored eyes, and he carried himself with a poise and confidence that Deren lacked. The thought crossed her mind that it might be a good idea for her to get to know some of these people, so she nodded.

"I would be delighted," she said, offering him her hand.

Topher smiled, leading her back into the crowd on the dance floor. As they fell into step with the others, he looked at her. "I was so pleased to hear that you had finally returned, Princess," he said, surprising her slightly.

"You were?" she asked before she could stop herself.

"Oh yes," he said quickly. He seemed somewhat bashful. "For so many years, your existence was like a fairytale. No one was sure if you were even still alive. The queen kept your whereabouts a closely guarded secret and very rarely spoke of you, except to mention that one day you would come home."

Nyx was surprised to hear that.

Topher grinned broadly. "You are a legend that has come to life for most of us. All anyone could talk about the past few days was seeing if you were truly real."

Despite knowing he didn't mean it that way, his words struck her in a place that made her feel gross. Was she just a sideshow for these people? She tried to imagine how she would feel if she were in their shoes, seeing the fabled lost princess after all this time, and it made her feel worse. This was her life, not some gossip fodder for the bored nobility. She wanted to be seen as a person, not as some oddity to be paraded around.

"Well, here I am, and I am definitely real," she said, her tone a bit harsher than she intended.

Topher noticed the edge to her voice, and his brow furrowed as he immediately began apologizing to her. "I do not mean to upset you, Princess," he said quickly. "Please forgive me."

Nyx turned her face away from him, wishing that she could just go back to her room. She would love to crawl under her covers and pretend that the rest of the world didn't exist for a while.

But she knew that wasn't going to happen.

She forced a smile then and looked back to him. "No apologies necessary," she said, knowing she needed to salvage this dance. She felt her face ease into a genuine smile as she looked at him. "Being here is just as strange for me as it is for you."

Topher relaxed, and she was surprised by how handsome his smile was. "I suppose it is," he said easily. The music began to wind down, and he bowed to her, holding her hand. "I would very much like to hear more about you, Your Highness." He offered another smile. "Perhaps one day soon."

Nyx returned his smile. "I would like that," she said. She bowed her head. "Thank you for the dance."

Topher turned to leave, and Nyx realized that she was not being accosted for another dance. She started to wonder why, but then she turned to see Samill approaching her and realized that his presence, much like Jet's, must have scared off the rest. She thought back to what Jet had said to her the night before, about him asking permission to court her, and she realized that it must be official in some way now, since she allowed him to lead her in the first dance. The thought made her heart skip a beat.

"How are you fairing?" Samill asked as he came within earshot of her.

Nyx used the back of her hand to brush at her temple, realizing she was sweating lightly. "I think I could use a drink," she said, glancing around the room.

"Of course," Samill said obligingly, motioning into the

crowd.

Nyx watched as a servant appeared, carrying a tray of champaign flutes. The thought of champaign made her mouth feel even more parched, but Samill surprised her when he leaned in and murmured something to the servant, who promptly vanished back into the crowd. Nyx turned to look up at him curiously, further surprised when the servant almost immediately reappeared, a water glass in hand.

"Oh, thank you," Nyx said as she took the glance from the servant. She shot Samill a wry look as she took a sip. "How did you know I would prefer this?"

Samill flashed her a grin then. "In the short time I've spent with you, Your Highness, I've never seen you ask for anything other than water," he said simply.

Nyx tilted her head slightly. "You surprise me," she said, watching his eyes dance with mirth.

"It's my job to notice things," Samill said.

"And what else have you noticed?" Nyx quipped, her eyes narrowing playfully.

"That you enjoy dancing," Samill answered, surprising her further. "Even though you claimed earlier you didn't know the steps, the practiced way you followed me said otherwise."

Nyx's face flushed. She didn't know if it was because she'd been caught out or if it was because he really was paying attention. "I'm sorry," she said quickly, feeling the need to explain herself. "I was just nervous."

Samill laughed softly then. "Please do not apologize, Princess," he said, stepping closer to her. He leaned in conspiratorially. "Your secret is safe with me."

Nyx took another sip of her water, emptying the cup. She watched as Samill reached out to take the empty glass from her, and she chewed the inside of her lip lightly when his fingers brushed against hers. She watched as he turned to a passing servant to place the empty glass on a tray, noticing how straight his shoulders were and how poised he was. As he turned back to her, her eyes traveled across his face to meet his. He paused for a moment, seeming surprised, and Nyx felt her face turn red again.

He'd caught her red-handed admiring him. But instead of making things awkward or belittling her like she'd started to become used to, he smiled and held out his hand. "Care for another dance?"

Nyx's face brightened and she accepted. It was a nice change to be with someone who seemed to actually enjoy her company.

Jet drifted along the edge of the room, his eyes finding Nyx without any difficulty. He tried to keep on the move to stay away from Serefina. He wasn't the least bit interested in dealing with her, and she was persistent. He'd found that if he lingered in one spot for too long, she somehow managed to find him.

He did pause, however, as he stepped around a large pillar and looked toward the dance floor. He could see Nyx standing with Count Samill, and he felt his chest tighten as he watched Nyx look up at him, practically batting her eyelashes. The jealousy that flared inside him was hot and fierce, and he turned away.

It wasn't fair.

Watching her flirt with Count Samill wasn't fair, but neither was the way he'd treated her. His logical mind knew that. But the rest of him wanted to punch something. He tried not to dwell on the feeling as he watched Nyx and

Samill walk onto the dance floor together.

Nyx had lost count of the number of dances she'd let Samill lead her in. All she knew was that she was getting tired, her dress feeling like it weighed a zillion pounds. As the most recent song ended, she looked up at Samill.

"I need a break," she said, feeling breathless.

Samill's eyes were slightly worried as he nodded. "Of course," he said quickly. He noticed that she was fanning her face with her hand. "Are you hot? Perhaps we could step outside for a moment?"

Nyx nodded, the thought of cold air on her face sounding refreshing. She allowed Samill to lead her toward the open garden doors, realizing that she hadn't had a chance to explore the garden yet.

Just as she'd suspected, the winter wind felt good on her face as she and Samill stepped out onto the terrace. She took a moment to revel in the feel of it before she caught sight of the garden below. She gasped, walking toward the terrace railing to stare at it.

Below them, beautiful hedges lined a stone pathway, winding into the garden. Lanterns were lit along the path, reminding her of Christmas lights. Softly glowing insects fluttered around the lanterns, drawn to the light and the warmth. The whole garden fluoresced with light and life, reminding her of a fairy garden.

"Wow," she breathed, listening to the sound of fountains bubbling beyond the hedges. She turned her eyes over the garden, further surprised by the sight of the city in the distance.

Just like the night that she'd arrived, the river was glowing softly as it wound from the mountain and through the middle of the city. It was quite the sight to behold, stark peaks surrounding the edges of everything. It was the first time that Nyx had truly seen the safety that the mountains provided.

"It's beautiful, isn't it?" Samill said softly beside her.

Nyx nodded. She hadn't seen anything so captivating since the night Melinda had taken her to the temple in Festra.

The thought gave her pause, making a lump form in her throat. She looked down at her hands, clenching them against the stone of the terrace railing.

Not to her surprise, Samill tentatively reached for her hand. "Are you alright?" he asked, seeing the way her brow furrowed.

Nyx tried to be smooth as she pulled her hand away, clasping them in front of her. She forced a smile. "Yeah," she said quickly, fighting the pain in her chest. "Just tired."

Samill didn't seem to buy her excuse, but he didn't pry. "Would you like some water?" he asked.

Nyx nodded, relieved at the thought of some alone time. She watched as he turned to go inside. Once he was gone, she stepped down the terrace stairs quickly and into the soft, glowing darkness, wanting to get lost. She could feel tears trying to well in her eyes, and she took hard, deep breaths to try to keep them at bay. The lump in her throat was worse the more she tried not to think about Melinda.

The sound of the party became distant as she wandered deeper into a maze of tall hedges, the quiet of the night surrounding her and lending her some comfort. Her footsteps slowed as she came around a tall hedge, surprised to see what was hidden behind it.

Rows and rows of bright, blooming and glowing infinity flowers filled the night. They wrapped around a circular courtyard, in the center of which sat a large fountain. Their soft light was different than the light from the lanterns, casting a glow across the water of the fountain and making it appear to glimmer softly the way the spring did beneath the castle. Nyx moved toward it, curious for a moment if it was the same living water.

As she passed the flowers, their light flared and their petals turned toward her, reaching for her. Some of them began to release small, glowing tufts, which reminded her of the fluff of a dandelion. The tufts floated lazily on the air, making it feel like the night was filled with falling glitter. It was beautiful and calming as Nyx reached the edge of the fountain and eased to sit on the wide stone.

She carefully reached her hand out to touch her fingertips to the water, mildly disappointed when it didn't react the way the spring had. It was cool to the touch, however, and she realized that her breathing had slowed, and her mind was slowing down. She let her fingers drift through the cool water as she looked around at the glowing flowers, wishing that she could just stay in this moment alone for a while.

Almost as if summoned by her thoughts, a shadow appeared on the path, and she felt disappointment fill her. She stood slowly, expecting to see Samill materialize from the darkness with the glass of water he'd set off to find. Instead, her heart jumped into her throat as the soft glow reflected off of Jet's dark hair.

"Jet," she managed softly, trying to hide her surprise. "What are you doing out here?"

"I could ask you the same thing," he said as he stepped closer. His eyes drifted around, taking in the infinity flowers. "Where's your date?"

Nyx felt her face turn red. Was Samill her date?

"I asked him to give me some space," Nyx said quickly, drawing his gaze. She wondered why she felt guilty suddenly, and she glanced back toward the ballroom. "Just needed a break."

"Hm," he said, watching her carefully. "You two were looking pretty cozy on the dance floor." His tone was almost accusing, and it occurred to Nyx that he sounded jealous, just like he had earlier.

Her brain was spinning, wanting to tell him that it wasn't like that and that he didn't need to worry, but before anything coherent came to mind, he stepped toward her and sat next to her on the edge of the fountain, close enough that his shoulder was almost touching hers. Instantly, whatever excuses she'd thought she'd need to offer him vanished, leaving her wondering why he made her feel so insane and so complete at the same time.

Nyx looked over at him, watching as he let a slow breath past his lips, his eyes drifting over the garden again. "They're pretty, huh?" she asked, looking at all the infinity flowers, still glowing brightly around them.

"Hm." He nodded slightly. "They're alright."

Nyx fought the urge to roll her eyes at his response. A cool breeze began to kick up around them, and a chill shook her. She glanced at Jet when she realized he was shrugging out of his coat. She felt her cheeks turn hot as he turned toward her and pulled it around her shoulders.

"You don't have to do that," she said softly.

"I know," he said, his fingers lingering on the lapels of the coat as he straightened it around her. He was close enough to her that his knee was brushing hers.

Nyx felt her heart flutter in her chest. If this was a movie, it would be the part where he pulled her toward him and kissed her. She knew she shouldn't, but she wanted that to happen. And the worst part was that she knew, in her heart of hearts, that he did, too.

Her mind flitted back to that moment that seemed so long ago now, when he'd nearly kissed her in the inn. The pain and embarrassment she'd felt tried to flood her, but she managed to push it down by looking away from him and shattering the moment. As she sat there, she could feel the tension increasing between them. She glanced at Jet, noticing that he had turned his face away from her and his brow was furrowed.

She hated that this always happened. She was more than ready for some answers, and she knew that she'd been on the cusp of learning the truth once before.

"Jet, I need to ask you something," she said quickly, before he could scurry away from her like he always did.

He frowned lightly as he looked at her. "Okay."

"Do you remember that night, right after we left Kilcrest?" she asked, watching his face. She saw recognition and something like regret flash across his eyes. "There was something you were trying to tell me."

Jet drew a slow breath and leaned away from her.

"What was it?" Nyx pressed. "What were you going to tell me?"

Jet shook his head and turned slightly, as if he was going to leave. "It was nothing," he said. "There was a lot going on, and I was worried about nothing."

Nyx knew he was lying, but she pushed the thought down, along with the feeling to yell at him that he just needed to tell her what was going on. "I meant what I said," she whispered. "You can tell me anything. I won't judge you."

A sarcastic smirk crossed his face then, as if he didn't believe her. "Okay," he said, an edge to his voice.

"I'm serious," Nyx said quickly, offended by his attitude. "I don't care about who or what you were in the past. I know who you are now."

Jet rolled his eyes and started to stand, but he was surprised when Nyx caught his hand quickly. He held her gaze, feeling his stomach tighten at the look on her face.

"Don't walk away from me," she managed, her voice tight with emotion. "You know that I—" She caught the words that she really wanted to say, glancing away from him. "I care about you." Her words were rushed as she followed up with, "You're my friend."

Jet was silent for a moment, his eyes traveling down to her hand on his. His heart was telling him that he should just be honest with her, but his mind was telling him that was a bad idea. He wanted to be whoever it was she thought he could be, but he knew that deep down it was a lie. He could never escape the past. He started to pull his hand from hers and tell her to leave him alone about it, but a sudden, creeping sensation began to come over him, making his muscles tense. He knew that she sensed it too from the way her eyes shifted around, her fingers tightening around his.

A bright light suddenly began to pour out of the fountain, which was starting to roil and slosh against the stone. The infinity flowers around them brightened as well, responding to a surge of powerful magic.

Jet had pulled Nyx toward him once the fountain started to glow, and she was holding tightly to his arm. They both watched as the water began to grow choppier, like waves on an angry sea, before it suddenly became completely still. The light that was rolling off of it became so bright that they lifted their hands to shield their eyes before it was suddenly gone just as quickly as it had come.

Nyx blinked quickly against the change, her eyes widening as they readjusted to the darkness. She heard the sharp intake of a breath, and she gripped Jet's arm harder as two forms struggled to pull themselves out of the water, as if they were surfacing from a deep pool. Once they gained their footing, they sloshed toward the edge of the fountain. The light had faded from the water, but the infinity flowers were still blooming, and Nyx watched as a girl brushed her wet hair from her face, her deep blue eyes glowing softly.

"What the hell?" Jet breathed, voicing her thoughts.

As she stared in surprise at the girl, a realization hit Nyx. She let go of Jet's arm, seeing that he'd realized the same thing she had. She took a step forward, seeing her and the man next to her pause, as if they'd just noticed that they weren't alone.

"Bailey?" Nyx managed. She watched the girl's glowing blue eyes widen. "You're Bailey, aren't you?"

Bailey drew a shuddering breath before nodding slowly. "How …?" Her voice was trembling, and Nyx imagined it was from the cold and their sudden appearance in the water.

Nyx reached out her hand then, watching Bailey look at her warily. "I can take you to your brother and sister," she said softly.

Bailey's eyes widened as she met Nyx's gaze. "Where are we?" she managed.

"Regius Carmen," Nyx said. "You're safe."

Tears suddenly filled Bailey's eyes, mingling with the water on her face. She glanced over her shoulder at the man behind her. "We did it," she gasped. "We did it."

28

Regius Carmen, the capitol city of Ymber.
The fifty-third day of winter, the 851st year of the
reign of Queen Liana Estrella.
Friday, February 11, 2012.

ELLIE WAS DANCING WITH ALED. She laughed as he spun her in a circle, realizing this was the most fun she'd had in a long time. Her afternoon with Nyx had been so relaxing and it made the ball feel like a treat. She'd even gotten requests to dance from a few of the nobles before Aled had snagged her, claiming that this was his favorite song.

The song ended and Ellie and Aled laughed as they bowed to each other. "Thank you for the dance, my lady," he said playfully.

Ellie giggled a bit. "It was my pleasure, good sir," she said, mimicking his tone. She followed him from the dance floor. "Did you happen to see where my brother scurried off to?"

Aled shrugged as he caught a waitress and took two glasses of champagne. "He probably had to sit down," he said as he offered her a glass. "I know he's been feeling better, but it still seemed like he was getting tired."

Ellie agreed as she took a sip of her drink. "He's been doing so well with Her Majesty's healers."

Aled nodded as he swallowed a mouthful of drink. "It was very generous of her to let her healers help him."

Ellie didn't say anything as she looked down at her glass. The past was flooding back to her, reminding her that her sister was still in Paraximus' evil clutches. Instantly, the happiness she'd felt was gone, replaced by guilt and worry.

Aled seemed to notice as he stepped closer to her. "Are you okay?" he asked. He seemed to know where her thoughts were as he reached out to touch her arm. "Thinking about Bailey?"

Ellie nodded as tears threatened to fill her eyes.

Aled rubbed her arm. "Me, too," he admitted quietly. "I think about her every day."

Ellie looked down at her glass, staring at the bubbling liquid. She didn't want to cry, but she could feel that the tears were there to stay. She started to look up at Aled and tell him she needed a moment, when suddenly something like the feeling of cold water doused her.

She turned her head toward the terrace, feeling almost as if there was a beacon beyond the doors. She realized that the initial coldness was fading, and now she felt something different; something she recognized. "Bailey," she breathed.

"Ellie? What—?"

Ellie shoved her glass at Aled. "I have to check something," she said urgently. She turned and pushed her way quickly through the crowd and to the terrace door. She didn't notice how cold the air was on her face as she raced into the darkness.

She could hear voices, but pure instinct drove her

as she ran down the steps, following a glittering trail of infinity flowers. She rounded a thick hedge, feeling her heart instantly drop into her feet.

"Bailey!"

The other Atturon sister lifted her head as she was being helped out of the fountain. Their eyes met, and each sister ran toward the other.

Ellie grabbed her tightly as they embraced. "How are you here?" she managed, tears flowing down her face. "How did you escape?"

Bailey held tightly to her sister. "You won't believe me," she said as she stepped back a bit. It was then that Ellie realized she was clutching a book in her arm.

"What?" she breathed. "How?"

Bailey shook her head, wet strands of hair flinging around her face. "I don't know," she said. "But it did."

"Let's get inside before you both freeze," a voice said, drawing the twins' gazes.

Ellie realized then that there was a man with Nyx and Jet, and he was sopping wet like Bailey. And he was wearing Siccita's colors. Ellie turned her eyes on her sister and Bailey read the question in her gaze.

"He's my friend," Bailey said softly. "He helped me."

Ellie seemed to accept that as two guards came into the courtyard and Jet immediately began giving them orders. She put her arm around her sister, not caring about her dress getting wet as they followed one of the guards away from the garden.

Liana looked over the railing of the balcony, feeling Canus stand at her shoulder. She turned to offer him a smile, which he returned as he sipped at his drink.

"Looks like everyone is having a great time," he said, his eyes focused on the dance floor.

"Indeed," Liana said, watching the partygoers below.

Canus turned to look at her. "Am I finally allowed to ask what you were thinking when you agreed to let Jet out of prison?" he asked.

Liana looked at him. "I needed his skills," she said frankly. "I wasn't sure that he would cooperate at first." She turned her eyes back to the party below. "But now I know that my instinct was right." A slight smile pulled at her face.

Canus turned to face her, leaning against the balcony rail. "What instinct is that?" he asked.

Liana was still smiling as she looked at him. "They say that only fire can temper steel," she said softly. "But we both know that chalargentum, the strongest and most unbreakable metal in Gexalatia, is tempered by the cold."

Canus tilted his head, humored. "And who is tempering whom, dear cousin?" he asked, understanding that she was talking about Nyx and Jet.

Liana's smile grew a bit. "That, Canus, remains to be seen," she said playfully. "But I do know that he has kept her alive, and she has changed something in him." Her eyes darkened. "Despite everything that my former spouse tried to do to him, he's changed."

"I will trust your judgement on that," Canus said, sipping his drink with a frown.

Liana knew that was the best she could expect from him and she turned her eyes back to the dance floor. From their vantage point, she could see Ellie talking to her cousin, and the younger Seren sisters following after their oldest sister like puppies. She watched them for a moment, noticing that Serefina was trying her best to catch the eye of a young noble. She didn't envy Serefina or her sisters.

Liana started to mention to Canus about finding his daughters husbands, when suddenly a cold feeling began to creep down her spine. Her brow furrowed and her eyes caught sight of Ellie pushing through the crowd toward the balcony doors. She felt her heart catch in her chest. Where was Ellie going in such a hurry? She'd seen Nyx and Count Samill step out onto the terrace, and now her senses were telling her something was happening.

She turned and motioned to a nearby guard. "Find my granddaughter," she said, her voice soft but commanding. "She went onto the terrace."

The guard nodded and jogged away, signaling to one of his comrades to follow. As they disappeared down the stairs, Canus looked at her.

"What was that about?" he asked.

Liana turned away from him, a page stepping toward her to escort her down the stairs. "I'll let you know when I know," she said brusquely. She tried not to seem in a hurry as she descended the stairs, not wanting to alert anyone else to what she thought she sensed.

Just as she reached the main floor, a man approached her, smiling widely. "My queen," he said, bowing. "It is wonderful to see you've come down."

Liana smiled brightly at him. "I'm so glad you could come, Lord Rana," she said, leaning in to allow him to kiss both her cheeks in greeting. The joy she felt at seeing him was real, but her thoughts were distracted. "I apologize, but I need to attend to something."

Lord Rana, ever the gentleman, bowed his head. "Of course," he said easily. "Hostess duty calls. But I will save you a dance." He offered her a wink, which made heat rise in her cheeks.

It had been a long time since she'd been attracted to

anyone – nearly twenty-five years since her husband had died. It used to feel like a betrayal to his memory to even think of being with someone new, but when she'd had the opportunity to get to know Lord Rana last year, after the death of his wife, she knew that there was something worth exploring there.

However, the fluttering feeling in her chest was dwarfed by the concern she felt for Nyx's safety. She knew what she'd felt was an influx of magic; she just didn't know what it was or how it could have come here with the spring's protection.

Just as she reached the edge of the ballroom, one of the guards reappeared and crossed to her quickly. "What is it?" she asked, seeing the distracted look on her face.

"The princess has asked for you to join her in your study, my queen," she said softly. "There was … an incident."

Liana frowned at the guard. "Is she injured?" she asked quickly.

The guard shook her head. "No, Your Majesty," she said. "No one is injured, but you must see for yourself."

Liana didn't like how tightlipped she was being, but she knew it was probably for the best, seeing as they were surrounded by nosy eavesdroppers. She nodded slightly. "Very well," she said. "Has Brodrick escorted them there?"

The guard nodded. "Yes," she said. "He's taken them out of sight of the guests."

Liana nodded once more. "Thank you, Freira," she said. "Come with me." She turned and started toward a door at the far end of the ballroom that led into a servants' area, which allowed them to cross into the main hall without being noticed by anyone. Liana's heart was in her throat as she led the way up the stairs, toward her quarters.

Jili pulled his soaked clothing over his head and tossed it to the floor. The red cloak that he'd worn was a dark crimson, like the color of blood. His blood, if he was ever caught. He tried not to think about what he'd just potentially sentenced himself to, instead trying to calm his racing heart. He wasn't in Celo Cavus anymore. He was here, in Regius Carmen.

He was here with Bailey.

Jili's heart fluttered lightly at the thought. He hadn't doubted her abilities, but he'd never seen anything as magical as the portal that she was able to open with the water that she had poured on the floor. It had shone so brightly, a white light that was blinding, but he hadn't hesitated when she'd grabbed his hand and pulled him into the puddle after her.

What had stolen his breath away was the way the puddle had dropped out from under his feet, sending them plummeting into the white light. The light had swirled around them, flowing like water, and just when he thought he couldn't hold his breath anymore, it had spit them out into the fountain.

A sharp knock on the door of the changing room made him jump and reminded him that he had some explaining to do. Well, mostly Bailey, since she knew more than he did, but he needed to be there with her. "Coming," he called. His stomach twisted in a knot at the thought of facing the queen, but he knew he couldn't drag his feet any longer. He straightened the tunic that he'd been given, knowing he was as ready as he'd ever be. He walked to the door and pulled it open, not surprised to see Jet – the spitting image of King Paraximus – standing on the other side.

When he'd first seen Jet, standing near the fountain next to the blonde-haired girl, he'd nearly fainted in fear. He thought for certain that it was King Paraximus and that he and Bailey had been caught. For a long moment, he'd thought they were going to be tortured and killed, but then he'd realized that things weren't quite right. The garden didn't look familiar to him, and the air was freezing cold, not at all warm and muggy like it should have been. And when the blonde-haired girl—the princess—had spoken to them, that's when he realized they were safe.

Once the guard had brought them into the castle, they'd been escorted upstairs to living quarters. Jili assumed it was where Bailey's sister had been staying, because she took Bailey into a room to help her change out of her wet clothes. A servant had appeared with clothes for him as well, and that's when he stepped into another room to change. Of course, he hadn't been able to escape Jet's gaze until that point, and it was that same look on Jet's face now that made his heart skip a beat.

Fear flitted through him as he looked at Jet, who was scowling lightly. He was too young to have witnessed the General at the peak of his might, but he had heard the stories. He was grateful for the fact that there was a guard standing behind Jet, otherwise he had a feeling that the General would have had more than just questions for him. Jili was quiet as he and Jet stared at each other.

It seemed like there were a lot of things Jet truly wanted to say, but he finally settled on, "I don't trust you." The rest of his message was implied, though. *Step wrong and you're dead.*

Jili was tense. "I don't trust you either."

Jet's eyes narrowed slightly before he nodded curtly. "This way."

Jili watched as the guard with Jet fell into step behind him, a hand resting on the sword at his hip. He wanted to tell them that they didn't have to worry about him, but he understood. He would have been wary too.

They walked down the hall toward a door, where he knew Bailey had been taken. When they reached it, Jet pushed it open, revealing a large sitting room. A fire was blazing in a hearth, heating the room and illuminating rows and rows of books. Jili stepped inside the door, ignoring the way Jet was watching him as his eyes landed on Bailey's pale blonde hair.

"Bailey," he said, crossing toward her quickly and reaching for her. "Are you—"

Jili drew up in surprise when she turned, a ballgown flaring around her. He started to ask her why in the hell she was dressed like that, but then he realized that something wasn't quite right. He pulled his hand back, feeling his stomach flip as he realized that this girl wasn't just her sister, she was Bailey's identical twin. He guessed that because it had been so dark and there had been so many things happening, he'd hadn't noticed at first.

"I'm Ellie," she said softly. Her eyes were watery as if she'd been crying. "Are you the one who saved my sister?"

Jili felt his face flush slightly. "Well, I wouldn't say that …" he murmured. He was surprised when she suddenly threw her arms around him to hug him.

"Thank you," she said, holding him tightly. "Thank you for what you've done."

Jili's face was hot when she let go of him and all he could muster was a small nod. He looked up when another door in the suite opened, another lavishly dressed woman appearing. He recognized the blonde-haired girl that had been standing next to Jet, but in the light he could see her features clearly. He was struck by her sunlight-colored hair and deep emerald-green eyes, but his stupor didn't last when he saw Bailey emerge from the room behind her, dressed in dry clothes as well. Her eyes lit up as she saw him, and she crossed to him quickly, catching his hand.

"Are you okay?" she asked.

Jili nodded. "Just glad to be dry," he said.

Bailey didn't have to force the smile that pulled at her face. She turned toward Ellie. "I'm assuming you've met my twin sister," she said, glancing at him.

Jili nodded, watching as Ellie's eyes welled with tears as she looked at Bailey.

"I can't believe you're really here," she said, wiping at her face.

Bailey's eyes began to water too, but mostly from the relief she felt. "Where is Raphael?" she asked then, glancing around the room.

"I sent someone to fetch him," Nyx said then, drawing her gaze. She looked at Ellie. "I still don't know how you knew." Before she and Jet had barely even had a moment to sneak Bailey and Jili away without causing a scene, Ellie had come running from the ballroom, her eyes wild as she searched the garden for her sister.

Ellie looked at her twin, some kind of knowing passing between them. "Don't you know that twins share souls?" she asked, her voice only half-playful. "I would know when my other half was near."

Bailey reached out to catch her sister's hand and squeeze it tightly. She knew what Ellie meant; she'd felt her sister too the moment she'd stepped out of the fountain and the surprise had worn off a bit. But it had always been that way for them. One could always know where the other was intuitively. Their father had said it was their bond, and

Bailey knew that was probably true, but she knew now that it was the *Visus* too. And she knew that their connection and their link with the *Visus* was why the *Videns Libre* came to her and brought them here.

Nyx met Jet's gaze as she stepped toward him. "Where is Liana?" she asked softly.

"She's taking care of the party," Jet said. He glanced back to Jili and Bailey, his brow furrowed unhappily.

"Are you worried?" Nyx asked.

Jet let a soft breath pass his lips. He hated that she could read him so easily. "If she could bring herself here, who's to say that Paraximus couldn't do the same?" he said finally.

"I would say that's not going to happen," Liana's voice chimed suddenly, making them both to turn toward the door. She and Raphael were entering the room. As Raphael's eyes landed on Bailey, he immediately rushed to her.

"How can you be so sure?" Jet asked as he crossed his arms.

"Because your father cannot touch the white magic," she said simply, although there was an edge to her voice.

"My father has more than proven that his magic doesn't obey what we thought we knew," Jet snapped.

Liana looked unhappy for a moment before she turned to look at Bailey. "Well, be that as it may, he won't be coming to Regius Carmen tonight," she said, a slight edge to her voice. "But I am curious to know how you came here, Bailey Atturon." Her violet eyes shifted to the man beside her. "And your friend."

"Yes, how did you escape from King Paraximus?" Ellie asked quickly, her eyes worried.

"Somehow the *Videns Libre* came to me," Bailey said, glancing at the book she clutched in her arms. She hadn't let it out of her sight since they'd come through the fountain. She looked at Jili, who was sitting next to her. "I found it beneath the straw in the dungeon where I was being kept …" Her voice softened and she swallowed thickly, as if she were afraid. "King Paraximus had me taken there to keep me from Daya."

Nyx shot a look at Jet, knowing she'd heard him mention that name before. His eyes were dark and his jaw was set as he stared at Bailey.

"Daya?" Raphael asked then, shaking his head. "The goddess of death?"

Bailey nodded and shivered lightly. "She is real," she said softly, fear in her voice. "She was using my blood to strengthen her body." She looked to Liana. "King Paraximus has a deal with her. In exchange for the blood of either me or my sister, she was to grant him power, and he was to use the other to spy on Regius Carmen." Bailey looked at Ellie, seeming relieved. "Thankfully, I was the only one he had, otherwise I might not be here as he may have very well fed me to her."

Ellie held tightly to her arm, tears springing into her eyes. "That's why he tried to find me," she whispered, remembering the day that Bailey had been forced to see her.

Bailey nodded. "She has given him some of her strength, but if he gains more and gains a way to control the *Visus*, he'll be too powerful to stop," she said.

"Well," Liana said, her voice betraying her surprise. "That's …" She was at a loss for words, and it made Nyx uncomfortable. Liana always seemed to have an answer for everything. But behind her violet eyes, Nyx could see her thoughts roiling. She finally turned her gaze to Jili. "And who is this that you've brought with you from Siccita?"

Bailey's face softened as she looked at Jili. "This is Jili," she said. "He was supposed to guard me, but instead he chose to help me."

Jili placed his hand over his heart suddenly and bowed to Liana. "I am a dead man if I ever return to Siccita," he said quickly. "I no longer serve King Paraximus, and I only wish to stay here with Bailey." His amethyst eyes were worried as he looked up at her. "I was only a low-level soldier, but I can provide you with information in exchange for my freedom."

Liana smiled gently then. "Please be at ease," she said. "I trust the *Visus.* I would not have brought you here if you were not worthy."

Jili's face softened with relief and he bowed again. "Thank you, Your Majesty."

Nyx glanced at where Jet stood silently across the room, his face unreadable. Nyx wished she knew what he was thinking, but she had no doubt it wasn't good and it made fear creep into her heart.

Liana drew their attention when she stepped closer to Bailey. "You've given me much to think about," she said, glancing between Bailey and Jili. "But I can tell you're both exhausted."

Bailey nodded. "Yes, a comfortable bed would be wonderful," she commented as Ellie held onto her arm. "After so many nights sleeping on the floor."

Liana turned her eyes to Ellie. "You should take your sister to rest," she said. She then looked to Raphael and Jili. "Raphael, I believe the room near yours is empty. Would you show Jili to it so that he may rest as well?"

Once the siblings and Jili were gone, Liana lowered herself into her chair, her brow creased with worry. It was only then that Jet shifted from his spot, his eyes guarded.

"Are you sure it's safe for him to be here?" he asked, his voice quiet.

Nyx felt her heart jump as she realized what he'd been thinking. What if Jili had come here to hurt Liana? Or even her?

Liana pressed her fingers against her chin. "I will have guards posted along the hall," she said quietly. "I meant what I said about the *Visus*. It does not make mistakes." She looked up at him. "But perhaps it would be safer for you to stay with Nyx tonight."

Nyx felt her heart twist with worry. "Do you think it's true?" she asked then. "What she said about Daya? That she is giving Paraximus her power?"

Liana stole a glance at Jet then, seeing the way his jaw clenched. "I had my doubts when we first spoke of it, but now ..." She drew a slow breath and looked to Jet again. "What do you know of this?"

Jet scowled softly. "It's no secret that he's been using Daya's power for centuries," he said quietly. He turned toward the fireplace, his eyes distant as he stared into the flames. "Where do you think all of those hell spawn came from?"

Nyx frowned. "Hell spawn?" she breathed. She watched as Liana's face smoothed, her eyes darkening as if recalling whatever he was referring to, and it occurred to her that there was a history between them that she could never begin to understand.

"My father is powerful, but he doesn't have the strength alone to turn the dead into *cariosus*," Jet continued. He stole a glance at Liana, some twisted twinkle of delight in his eyes.

Liana's gaze hardened. "You still relish in your father's acts of savagery," she said, the barest hint of disgust in her voice.

Jet turned his eyes away from her. "It's in the past," he said, as if whatever shared memory they had would vanish with his words.

Nyx didn't like the way his hint of cruelty made her stomach twist. He'd warned her that the things she'd learn wouldn't be pleasant but watching him take enjoyment from his past acts made her want to crawl out of her skin. Liana's next words broke her out of her thoughts.

"It may well be in our future," she said sharply, almost accusingly. "And whose side will you stand on then, Jet Lamia?"

Nyx felt her heart twist. Why would Liana ask that question? Wasn't Jet on their side now?

Jet rolled his eyes. "I've done everything you've asked of me," he said dismissively, as if she were stupid for even bothering to say that to him.

"Except swear your loyalty," Liana quipped.

Jet instantly scowled at her. "That was never part of the deal," he snapped, a dangerous edge to his voice.

Liana laughed sardonically. "I would never ask you to swear fealty to me, your sworn enemy," she said sharply. "I know you'd rather see me dead than ever commit to such a thing."

Nyx stared at her grandmother in shock, unsure of what she was witnessing. The last thing she wanted was to see things between Jet and Liana go bad. She almost wanted to tell both of them to cut it out.

"I won't swear to your stupid state either," Jet retorted. "Your councilmen can kiss my a—"

"Swear it to Nyx," Liana said calmly, cutting him off.

Jet's brow rose in surprise, his expression no doubt mirroring Nyx's. He looked just short of saying, "huh?" but the word never came out.

Liana held his gaze patiently.

"She knows I'll keep her safe," he managed then, his voice uncharacteristically small.

"I need to hear it," Liana said evenly. "I don't care how you feel about me or what your plans for me are in the future." Her eyes darted to Nyx then, a deep sadness in them. "I need to know you'll protect her."

Jet stared at Liana in silence for a long moment. Nyx thought for sure he was trying to come up with a way to get out of her request, and the thought made her chest ache. Did he resist because that was his nature, or because he didn't want to be bound to a promise he couldn't, or wouldn't, keep?

Finally, he seemed to accept what she was asking, and he turned his dark eyes on Nyx. She felt her face flush when he stepped toward her and held out his hand. Her fingers were trembling as she let them rest against his. He looked down at her hand in his and drew a slow breath, letting his thumb drift across her knuckles.

"I swear to you, before the Creators and on pain of death, that I will always keep you safe," he said softly. His eyes flicked to meet hers. "Do you accept?"

Nyx's breath was stuck in her throat as she nodded. Jet had never been so sincere before. "Yes," she managed after a moment. She couldn't hold his gaze and she looked down at her hand in his. Not surprisingly, he released her, turning to look at Liana.

"Happy?" he asked, his voice dripping with sarcasm as he crossed the room.

Liana gave him a humorless smile. "Yes," she said, echoing his tone. "Thank you so much." She drew a slow breath, seeming relieved. Her thoughts turned inward as she looked at the fire, weariness pulling at her features. "You two should go rest." Her voice was distant. "Tomorrow will be … busy."

Nyx looked at her for a long moment, imagining that security would increase, and so too, probably, would her training with Jet. "Will you be alright?" she asked finally, focusing on her grandmother's face.

Liana looked at her and offered her a kind smile. "Don't worry about me, child," she said gently. "Go on to bed, and I will see you both at breakfast."

Nyx didn't feel right leaving her, but she nodded and moved to her feet, her ballgown billowing around her. She followed Jet as they walked toward the door to Liana's suite. The air felt cold in the hall as they stepped into it, and Nyx remembered then that she was still wearing Jet's coat. She pulled it tighter around her, wondering if the cold was from the stone walls, or something deeper.

Jet walked beside her in silence, lost in his own thoughts. They didn't speak as they reached their shared living room, and Nyx paused to look up at Jet.

"Liana said you should stay with me tonight," she said slowly.

"I know what she said," Jet quipped, his voice lacking the bite he intended.

Nyx scowled at him. "If you don't want to all you have to do is say so," she said shortly. "No need to get snippy."

Jet sighed. "Let me change my clothes," he said. His eyes drifted over her, and Nyx felt her heart skip a beat. A hint of the way he'd looked at her when she'd walked down the main hall tonight flickered across his face. "You should change, too."

Nyx nodded silently and turned to go into her room. Once she was inside, she stepped toward the mirror.

Jasmine had been kind enough to leave a nightgown folded on the boudoir, and Nyx let her fingers drift over the fabric. It was thick and felt comfortable.

She slowly pulled at the clasps on her dress, her mind roiling. She didn't understand everything that Jili and Bailey had told them this evening, and the idea that some evil goddess was lending Paraximus her power had sounded like pure fiction from the first moment she'd heard Jet and Liana talk about it. But now, it sounded like a terrifying reality that she hoped didn't actually exist.

Finally, she felt lighter as her ballgown slipped to the floor. The fabric of her nightgown was indeed much more comfortable, and she realized that she felt tired suddenly. She tossed her dress over the screen for Jasmine to take care of it later before walking to her bedroom door. She wasn't surprised to see Jet sitting on the couch in the living room, waiting for her.

She noticed that he'd changed into soft pants and a t-shirt that looked comfortable, but his shoulders were tense as he stared across the room. He glanced at her when she stepped around the couch into his line of sight.

"So," she started, twiddling her fingers nervously. "Are we going to have a slumber party here in the living room, or what?"

Jet arched a brow at her. "Is that what you want?"

"No," Nyx said, eyeing the couch. "I'd rather sleep in my bed." The thought of laying on the hard couch or the even harder floor made her grimace slightly.

Jet stood slowly. "Let's go then," he said, motioning to her room.

Nyx felt her face start to turn red as she turned and shuffled into her bedroom. It was weird to be alone with him, and in her bedroom no less. She felt self-conscious as she climbed onto her bed and watched him shut the door. He took a moment to look around before easing into a chair near the door. Uncomfortable silence fell over them.

"Aren't you going to lay down?" Jet asked after a moment, irritated that she was just sitting there staring at him.

"Oh, um, yeah," Nyx said, flipping the covers back and pulling them over her lap.

She paused before she laid down, realizing that her hair was still pinned up. She could feel his eyes on her as she pulled at the hair pins, allowing coils of yellow curls to cascade across her shoulders. Once she was done, she turned to set a handful of diamond pins on the bedside table and then leaned back into her pillow. Despite the awkwardness of his presence, it didn't take long for her body to start to feel tired, but before she closed her eyes, she looked at Jet.

"Can you turn the light off?" she asked, her voice sounding exhausted to her own ears.

Jet gave a half smirk before lifting his hand and waving it, a soft burst of magic causing the candles around the room to snuff out.

Nyx blinked for a second against the darkness, the soft glow of the fire in the hearth illuminating the room a bit. She closed her eyes and tried to will her mind to sleep, but the stillness only made the thoughts from earlier return. She wanted to ignore them, but one was too pressing and persistent.

"Jet?" she breathed after a moment.

"Hm?"

"Have you ever seen her?" she asked quietly. She couldn't see his face very clearly in the dark, but she could tell his arms were crossed and he was looking away from her. He knew exactly what she was talking about.

"No," he said, his voice quiet as well. "I never wanted to."

"Are you afraid of her?" Nyx asked then.

Jet didn't answer right away. "Yes," he said softly.

Nyx felt the weight of his answer hang in the air, and it made her feel afraid. There were so many more questions she had, but she didn't think she wanted to know the answers right now. She lifted her head slightly, drawing his gaze. "Will you lay here with me?" she whispered.

She guessed he must have heard the fear in her voice because he didn't fight her request. Instead, he stood slowly and walked toward the bed, sitting on the edge. He took a moment to fluff the pillow next to him before stretching across the bed and laying on top of the covers. He folded his hands across his middle and sighed softly.

"Thank you," Nyx whispered then, feeling her eyes becoming heavy.

Jet turned to look at her, somewhat annoyed, but also somewhat humored. "Go to sleep."

Nyx smirked a little as she pulled the covers higher over her shoulders and pressed her cheek into the pillow. It didn't take long for her to fall into a deep sleep.

29

Regius Carmen, the capitol city of Ymber.
The fifty-fourth day of winter, the 851st year of the
reign of Queen Liana Estrella.
Saturday, February 12, 2012.

Nyx was walking slowly down a corridor. It was cold, and the air was stale, as if the walls hadn't seen sunlight or a proper dusting in too many years. She thought for a moment that she recognized the faded pattern of the rug beneath her feet, but the feeling flitted away as the sound of a voice caught her attention.

"Come to me."

Nyx felt her footsteps slow, and she realized she was looking down the hall into murky darkness. "Where are you?" she asked, her voice echoing in the emptiness.

"You know where I am," the voice answered. "Come to me."

Nyx didn't move, feeling afraid. "I can't see you."

"You will," the voice assured her. "Come to me."

Nyx shook her head, feeling trapped and alone. "No," she said, taking a step back. The darkness surged forward suddenly, and Nyx turned to try to run from it. She felt like she was moving through water as she tried to escape, the dark barreling down on her.

"Come to me!" the voice bellowed.

Nyx suddenly felt herself falling, the darkness engulfing her as the floor fell away from beneath her.

She drew a hard breath, her eyes flying open as she sat up quickly. She looked around, realizing that she'd been dreaming. It had felt very real, though, and her heart was racing still. It took a moment for the fear she'd felt to subside, leaving a deep, unsettled feeling in her chest. She looked around her bedroom, seeing light tumbling across the floor.

She remembered then that Jet had been with her, and she turned her head, surprised to see that her bedroom door was open. Beyond the door, she could hear voices, and she slid out of the bed to find out what was happening.

In the living room, Jet was sitting on the couch as Jasmine and another maid set out a rather large breakfast on the table in front of him. They had laid out two plates and set out two teacups. Beside them, a rolling cart was laden with fruit and pastries and pretty much any other breakfast food she could have imagined.

"Oh!" Jasmine looked up, smiling brightly. "Good morning, Your Highness."

Nyx nodded toward her, eyeing the food. "Good morning," she said distractedly.

"Did we wake you?" Jasmine continued. "We were trying to be quiet."

"No," Nyx said, easing to sit on the couch next to Jet. She continued to look over the spread. "This looks amazing."

Jasmine was still smiling. "Her Majesty asked that we

deliver this to you," she said. "She also requested that you join her in her study once you've had a chance to eat."

Nyx felt her stomach flip-flop as she looked at the floor. She was nervous about where they would go from here, but she knew that she needed to let Liana worry about that. She didn't say anything as Jasmine poured her and Jet some tea.

"Do you need anything else, Your Highness?" Jasmine asked after she set the tea kettle on the table.

Nyx glanced at Jet, seeing that he looked bored, and she shook her head. "No, we're fine," she said. She watched as Jasmine and the other girl bowed before taking their leave. Once they were gone, Nyx immediately grabbed a pastry and took a huge bite of it. She glanced at Jet as she chewed her mouthful. "Want some?"

Jet rolled his eyes and shook his head.

Nyx shrugged as she chowed down on the pastry. She leaned back into the couch, looking across the room. Fleeting visions from her dream flitted across her mind's eye, and she felt déjà vu. She wondered where she had seen that place before, but she couldn't place it. She knew that would bother her all day.

"Did you sleep okay?" she said then, glancing over at Jet.

He shrugged dismissively. "Did you?"

Nyx shrugged too.

They sat in silence for a bit. Nyx couldn't eat any more as she thought about what Liana might say. Finally, Jasmine and her helper returned. While the other girl began to pick up their mostly untouched breakfast, Jasmine trailed Nyx into her room to help her dress. Nyx chose pants and a comfortable top to go with her boots. She knew there wouldn't be any reason to wear a dress. She was surprised though, when Jasmine pulled a box from the closet that she hadn't seen before.

"What's that?" she asked.

Jasmine set the box on her bed and opened the lid to reveal an elaborately stitched coat. "I was asked to make sure you wore this today," she said with a smile.

Nyx stepped toward it and reached out to feel it, realizing that it had the same smell as the stuba-leather coat that she'd worn in Festra. "Is this stuba?" she asked.

Jasmine nodded, still smiling. "It appears to be of fine craftsmanship," she said as she looked at it. "Sewing stuba-leather is no easy feat."

Nyx pulled the coat from the box, seeing that it was just her size. It was light in her hands, and when she pulled it on, it was comfortable and not too heavy. It was a soft green, reminding her of the color of Earth's summer grass, and she stepped in front of the mirror to admire it.

"Do you like it?" Jasmine asked, her smile saying that she already knew the answer.

"Yes, very much," Nyx said as she turned to face her handmaid. "I'll have to thank Liana when I see her."

"Oh, it wasn't from Her Majesty," Jasmine said as she turned to put the box away.

Nyx stared at her in surprise. "It wasn't?"

Jasmine shook her head as she placed the box back in the closet. When she stepped back out, she looked to Nyx. "Count Samill requested it for you," she said plainly.

Nyx felt her face turn red suddenly. Both from embarrassment and the thought that Jet would be very unhappy.

She didn't miss the way Jet frowned when she walked into the living room. She fussed with the buttons on the green coat before smoothing the front of it and looking up at him.

"Nice coat," he said shortly.

Nyx held his gaze, trying to read past the furrow in his brow. "Samill gifted it to me," she said slowly.

Jet's face blanked then, and Nyx knew it was because he was trying to hide his disgust. "Looks like your relationship is progressing then," he said dismissively.

"Relationship?" Nyx asked, feeling her face starting to turn red.

Jet smirked. "You let him have the first dance last night," he said, ticking it off on his fingers. "You spent most of the night dancing with him, effectively keeping any other suitors at bay, and now you're accepting gifts from him." His eyes were dark and bitter. "Looks like you've accepted his courting."

Nyx felt her stomach flip over. She wasn't sure if it was from butterflies or Jet's obvious irritation. She wasn't sure if she wanted to be courted by Samill, but then the thought of his easy smile flashed in her mind. She looked up at Jet and forced her own smirk. "I suppose it does," she said then.

He scowled then, but Nyx didn't care. If he was going to take out his aggravation on her, she might as well deserve it. She turned, feeling bolstered but knowing he would knock her down several hundred pegs during their training later.

"Come on," she tossed over her shoulder. "Liana is waiting for us."

Jet didn't say anything, but Nyx could practically feel the bitter anger seeping off of him. She knew his mood would be worse when they started down the stairs and she noticed Samill and two of his guards waiting in the foyer for them.

Samill smiled up at her as she came closer, and it made

Nyx's heart skip a beat. "Good morning, Your Highness," he said, bowing slightly. "I hope you were able to rest well last night."

Nyx nodded as she stepped off the last step. "I did," she said easily. She noticed that his eyes skimmed over her green stuba-leather coat, and he grinned broadly.

"I see you're wearing the coat I sent you," he said, his voice pleased. "Is it suited to you?"

"Oh yes, it's lovely," Nyx said, holding out her arms. "I was surprised to receive it, but I will wear it a lot."

The pleased light in Samill's eyes never wavered. "I'm glad to hear it," he said. He then held out his hand and motioned for her to lead the way. "We should get to Her Majesty's suite."

"Of course," Nyx said, sparing a glance over her shoulder to Jet. She was mildly delighted at the way his lips were pursed. As she walked down the hall toward the stairs that led to Liana's suite, she felt justified in letting Jet suffer a bit. After the way he'd treated her, he deserved it. Let him stew in his jealousy. Not to mention, Samill was hardly an unpleasant man to look at or spend time with.

The thought of what might be possible with Samill made her heart jump again. What if she grew to care about him? What if things became serious? Despite the excitement and the possibilities, something formed in the pit of her stomach, making her feel like her new thoughts about Samill were wrong. And it didn't take a genius to know what she was feeling; she didn't really want to be with Samill, because what she really wanted was to be with Jet and to have him want her, too.

She felt like the wind had immediately been sucked from her sails, and she was glad that they were nearly to Liana's suite. She noticed a guard at the door as they approached, a woman with dark, navy hair and keen eyes.

"Princess," the woman said, placing her hand over her heart and bowing. "The Queen is expecting you."

Nyx nodded and tried to give her a thankful smile as she opened the door for them. She looked around as she walked into Liana's study, the scent of books and the crackle of the fire reaching her. It normally would have calmed her, but not this time.

Liana was standing near a desk, looking at some papers on top of it. When they walked into the room, she looked up and smiled gently. She crossed the room and gave Nyx a gentle hug. "Good morning, dear," she said. "How did you sleep?"

Nyx returned her embrace, breathing in her scent and feeling comforted. "Good, I think," she said as Liana released her.

Liana was smiling still as she held Nyx at arms' length. "You have a new coat," she said then.

Nyx grinned lightly and nodded. "It was a gift from Samill," she said without thought.

Surprise crossed Liana's face, and she looked over Nyx's shoulder to shoot Samill a playful, withering look. "That was very kind of you, Count Samill," she said.

Nyx glanced over at him, seeing that his cheeks were tinged slightly pink with embarrassment. He looked like he would offer some sort of excuse, and Nyx realized that Liana was being protective of her. Before Samill could form a coherent sentence, Nyx looked to her grandmother.

"I'm glad to have a new one," she said quickly. "It's even in my favorite color." She smiled at Liana, who sighed shortly.

"We will speak later," Liana said, her eyes shifting to Samill. "There is etiquette to follow if you wish to court my granddaughter."

Samill seemed thoroughly embarrassed, and he bowed low. "I apologize, My Queen," he said quickly. "I did not mean to offend. Forgive me."

Liana laughed a bit then. "There is nothing to forgive, Samill," she said then, crossing toward him. "It's just that what may be common knowledge for us may not be so for Nyx."

Nyx wondered what that meant, and she glanced at Jet, remembering the way he'd ticked off her crimes this morning. He was glaring at the back of Samill's head, but he must have sensed her eyes on him. He glanced in her direction before stalking over to sink into a chair.

"There were no problems last night, I trust," Liana said then, turning her attention to him.

"Nope," he said shortly. He motioned vaguely toward Nyx. "That one snores like a damn beaver, though."

Nyx's face flushed a bit and she scowled at him. "I do not," she said stiffly.

Jet arched a brow at her. "How would you know?" he challenged. "You were asleep."

Liana made an annoyed sound before sinking to sit in her chair. "You two are like bickering little children," she said mostly to herself. She reached for a cup of tea sitting on the coffee table in front of her. She looked up to Nyx and Samill. "Sit." She motioned to the two-seater couch across from her.

Nyx moved to plop onto the couch, crossing her arms and glaring at Jet. She glanced over at Samill as he eased to sit beside her, suddenly feeling self-conscious. The couch was very small, and he was sitting very close.

"Nyx, we need to brief you on what is happening with Paraximus and the threat from the south," Liana said then, her tone all business.

Nyx frowned lightly. "Okay," she said, her voice quieter than she meant. "What do I need to know?"

"Well, quite a lot actually," Liana said slowly, a worried look on her face as she looked at Samill.

Nyx turned to look at him as well, seeing that he was mirroring Liana's look.

"Samill, would you like to begin?" Liana asked.

Samill nodded. "Of course," he said. He turned to look at Nyx. "I'm going to give you a lot of information, so stop me if you have questions."

Nyx nodded mutely.

"I spent some time talking to Jili and Bailey this morning," Samill began. "Jili was able to fill me in on a lot of the workings of Paraximus' castle guard. He knew very little about what was going on elsewhere, only that there are rumors among the men that Paraximus is using blood magic to create an army, which he will bring here, to Ymber."

"What kind of blood magic?" Liana asked. She knew it came from Daya, but knowing what the evil goddess was creating would help to a degree.

Samill shook his head. "I don't know," he said. "Jili didn't seem to know much more than that either."

"Is it what you mentioned last night?" Nyx asked then. "The care-ie-o-sus? What even are those?"

"The living dead," Liana said. "They are mindless creatures that kill and eat anything in their path. They do not distinguish between friend or foe." She drew a slow breath. "It could be, or it could be something much more dangerous," she said softly. "But we will be prepared for whatever he tries to bring to us."

Nyx threaded her fingers together tightly as she

watched Liana turn to Jet, not feeling put at ease by her words. What could be more dangerous than basically zombies?

"What do you know?" Liana asked him.

Jet shook his head. "How could I know anything about what he's doing?" he said shortly.

Liana looked like she expected his answer. "Can you make a guess?" she pressed.

Jet turned his eyes toward the fireplace. "I cannot," he said quietly. "Other than it's probably something he was given by Daya, and there's a good chance that you can't assemble an army large enough or strong enough to combat it. Not without your own twisted magic."

Liana didn't look happy, but she still didn't look like he was telling her anything she didn't already know. "What is your advice?" she asked then.

Jet made a sarcastic humored sound. "Run." He glanced at her then. "If he comes here and breaches the mountain, there's nothing you could do to stop him."

"Hm," Liana said, her eyes appraising as she looked at him. "That's not really an option." She turned back to Samill. "What is your advice?"

Samill drew a slow breath. "Well, as you very well know, Paraximus made a push last time to come around the coast." He glanced at Nyx before standing and walking toward a map on the wall. "He brought ships from the Eluvios and sailed around to the bay." He pointed to the top of the map, north of where Regius Carmen sat. He turned his eyes on Jet. "He landed on the Plains, as I'm sure you recall, Jet."

Jet scowled and there was a hint of something in Samill's voice that made Nyx's heart clench.

"Is that where you were taken prisoner?" Nyx asked quietly, looking at him.

Jet's scowl didn't ease, and that was all the answer she needed as she looked back to Samill.

"Our victory was only because of Our Queen's quick thinking, forming her plan to subdue Jet, and because Aduro is a central spot to Austia, and the forest that the Aife call home," Samill said.

"Who are the Aife?" Nyx asked.

"A race of women warriors," Liana said, drawing her gaze. "Tall, strong, and mighty, with a culture primed for more than a thousand years for battle."

"Oh," Nyx breathed. "Like Amazons."

Liana and Samill didn't seem to know what she was talking about, but Liana nodded. "Yes, perhaps like your Amazons from Earth culture."

"And Austia ... that's where Canus is from?" Nyx continued. "Where he breeds the raperes?"

"Yes, precisely," Liana said, smiling. "You catch on very quickly."

Nyx wished she had time to revel in Liana's compliment, but she knew there was something Samill hadn't gotten to yet. "So what's the problem this time?" she asked. "Will he try to come to Aduro again?"

Samill crossed his arms and shook his head. "I don't think so," he said quietly. "If his army is large enough, he could come through Parie's Wall."

Nyx frowned, looking from him to Liana. "Won't the wall stop him?" she asked quietly.

Samill shook his head and Liana drew a slow breath. "With a massive enough army, and despite the enchantment placed on the wall, it will be nothing," Liana said. "If his army is made of Daya's hell creatures, then it won't matter where he attacks first. He'll destroy everything."

"He might even summon a portal on top of us," Jet said

then, his voice cutting. "Who needs walls when you can just open portals?"

Nyx felt her heart drop into her feet and a knot formed in her stomach. Sudden hopelessness swamped her. "What do we do?" she whispered, feeling her throat tighten. She wasn't sure if she wanted to cry or vomit.

Liana gave her a small smile. "The best we can," she said then. She looked to Samill. "It's time to call the people to service. I leave the preparation to you."

Samill nodded.

Liana looked back to Nyx, an apology in her eyes. "I had hoped this day would be far off, but I want you to accompany me to meet with the tribal elders," she said. "We must ask them to stand with us, for the good of Gexalatia."

Nyx wasn't sure what that meant exactly, but she nodded. "I'll do what I can," she said softly.

"Good," Liana said. "We'll leave in three days' time."

"I just can't believe you're really here," Ellie said. She had her arm threaded through her sister's, clinging to her tightly. They were sitting in the living room that joined Ellie and Raphael's room, a fireplace blazing across from them. Ellie had hardly been able to sleep a wink the previous night, afraid that if she closed her eyes then Bailey would disappear.

"I almost can't either," Bailey said. She leaned her head against the top of Ellie's, feeling her twin's emotions.

"I'm so sorry," Ellie whispered, her voice choked. "I shouldn't have left you."

Bailey turned to look at her quickly. "Nonsense," she said sharply. "If you hadn't run, we might not have made it." Her thoughts went to dark places. "If we had been together, one of us might have been fodder for …" She couldn't finish her sentence as her stomach turned, making her feel nauseous. She didn't even want to imagine what might have happened to her sister if they had been together.

Ellie sensed the darkness that clouded Bailey's mind, and she grasped her hand. "It's done now," she said softly. "You never have to go back there."

Bailey held her sister's hand tightly. "I'm not so sure," she whispered, meeting Ellie's gaze. "I'm not so sure that we won't have a part to play if we are to stop Daya."

Ellie's brow furrowed. "What can we possibly do?" she asked softly, worry in her voice.

"We must learn to use the *Videns Libre*," Bailey said, her voice steady. "We must be ready to do what we can to stop her."

"But today, you must rest," a voice said from behind them.

Both girls turned at the same time, unsurprised to see Raphael. He walked toward them, barely limping anymore.

"I can't believe how well you've healed," Bailey said with a small smile. She moved to stand and walked toward him, throwing her arms around him. "I was so afraid we'd lost you."

Raphael returned her embrace. "I would never leave you," he said as he hugged her tightly. "I'm just sorry I wasn't there to keep you safe."

Bailey stepped back from him. "I'm just glad I met Jili," she said. Her eyes shifted over his shoulder. "Where has he gone to? He was with you, wasn't he?"

Raphael nodded. "Count Samill asked to speak with him," he said.

Bailey's brow furrowed slightly, her eyes unhappy. "What did the count want?" she asked, an edge to her voice.

Raphael shrugged. "He said he had some questions. I didn't pry."

Bailey nodded mutely, still frowning as Raphael stepped toward the couch to sit next to Ellie. She glanced down the hallway briefly before turning to face her siblings.

"You care for him very much, don't you?" Ellie asked then, a small smile on her face.

Bailey's cheeks flushed instantly. "Well, of course, I mean, because he helped me," she stammered.

Raphael grinned at her as Ellie laughed. Bailey could tell he was about to tease her, but suddenly his eyes shifted over her shoulder. She turned quickly, her face flushing darker as Jili suddenly appeared.

"Speak of the devil," Raphael murmured so that only they could hear. He grunted lightly when Ellie elbowed him in the ribs.

Bailey ignored them both as Jili came closer. He looked tired still, but a smile pulled at his face as his eyes met hers.

"The count didn't drill you too much, did he?" Bailey asked hopefully.

Jili shook his head. "No," he said easily. "I expected his questioning and told him what I knew."

"About Paraximus and Celo Cavus?" Bailey asked.

Jili nodded. "I'm sure he will have many more questions as time goes on," he said. "But for now he said we should just rest."

Bailey offered him a small smile. "Yes, that's a great idea," she said. She looked to her siblings. "Just stay away from these two." She nodded toward them with a grin, seeing that they had the sense to look slightly embarrassed.

"Do you have any siblings, Jili?" Ellie asked then.

Jili shook his head. "No, only my parents," he said. He walked around the couch the three siblings sat on and eased heavily into an armchair across from them. He grinned a bit. "But obviously I missed out."

Ellie smiled. "Only in some ways," she said, glancing at her brother. "But in other ways you're lucky."

"Yes, you don't have two little birds chirping at you constantly," Raphael said teasingly, looking at his sisters.

Ellie leaned into him. "We chirp because we care," she said dramatically.

Raphael laughed and met Jili's gaze, seeing that Jili was smiling as well. "We haven't had breakfast yet," he said then. "Would you like to join us?"

Jili's smile grew some and his eyes shifted to Bailey. "I would love to."

30

Regius Carmen, the capitol city of Ymber.
The fifty-fourth day of winter, the 851st year of the
reign of Queen Liana Estrella.
Saturday, February 12, 2012.

NYX WAS LOST IN THOUGHT as she sat on a bench, overlooking the training field. The thwacks of wooden swords were lost on her as she stared at the dirt. Things felt insurmountable, and her heart was heavy.

"Hey."

Nyx looked up sharply, seeing Jet standing over her. He held her gaze for a minute, as if he was trying to decipher her feelings.

"Do you want to talk about it?" he asked finally.

Nyx shook her head and stood, picking up a bow that was sitting next to her on the bench. "No," she said softly. "I'm still trying to wrap my head around it all."

Jet nodded. He eyed her. "Going with a bow today?" he asked.

Nyx gave him a look. "I was decent with it before, so I wanted to see if I still know how to use it," she said.

Jet shrugged. "Okay," he said. He turned his shoulders, motioning for her to lead the way toward the targets.

A row of wooden cutouts and large bales of hay were set out across a course. A handful of soldiers were training, practicing distance-shooting. Nyx and Jet walked up to a free line of targets, and Nyx pulled an arrow from the quiver on her hip. She took a moment to roll the stiffness from her neck before she notched the arrow and drew the bowstring. She tensed slightly when she felt Jet's hand on her elbow.

"Not so high," he said evenly as he tipped her arm into the right position. He reached for her forward hand, his fingers curling over hers to help her line up the shot. "Keep both eyes open."

Nyx's heart was thundering in her chest at his touch, and she realized she was holding her breath. Her body felt hot as she realized he'd leaned in to see down the sight like she was, bringing his face close to hers.

"Inhale slowly," he said then.

Nyx drew a slow breath through her nose.

"Exhale through your mouth," he continued, "and when you reach the end of the exhale, let go."

Nyx breathed out slowly and evenly, feeling the slight muscle twitches in her body pause as she reached the end of the breath. Without hesitation, she let go of the arrow, watching it sail across the field and strike a wooden dummy with a resounding smack. As she lowered the bow, she heard Jet laugh softly.

"Damn, he never saw it coming," he said.

Nyx blinked as she looked at the dummy, realizing her arrow had struck it squarely in what would have been the crotch. She pressed her hand over her face, feeling embarrassed.

"Next time, aim up a bit," Jet said.

The sun was starting to arch downward toward the mountains by the time they were done training. After shooting practice, Nyx had done a few rounds of hand-to-hand with Jet. She was sitting on the ground now, her back against the bench she'd been sitting on earlier. Her stuba coat was draped over the bench beside her, and she used the back of her hand to wipe sweat from her face. She looked up when Jet appeared in front of her, holding out a flask to her.

"This better not be ale," she said shortly, taking it from him.

Jet grinned slightly before he moved to sit next to her. He looked at her as she took a long drink from the flask. "You did better today," he commented. "You're getting better at using your magic to bolster your attacks."

Nyx set the flask against her leg, wiping a stray drop of water from her chin. "Well, it feels more real today," she said shortly. She glanced at him, seeing that his eyes had shifted away and were distant.

"I guess it does," he murmured.

Nyx watched him for a second, seeing that he was lost in another time. "What are you thinking about?" she asked then.

Jet blinked from his thoughts. He started to say something, but Nyx interrupted him.

"Don't say nothing," she said quickly. "You've been staring into space too often lately. Tell me what's on your mind."

Jet rolled his eyes and made a humored sound. "I don't think you really want to know," he said finally.

"Why?" Nyx asked, bristling slightly. "Do you think I can't handle it?"

Jet looked at her, a smirk pulling at his face. "I was thinking about how it would feel to finally rip out my father's throat."

Nyx felt her heart jump, and she was sure her face paled a bit.

"But, I was also thinking that it's the only way to keep you safe," he said, his face serious then. "If I can stop him, you'll be safe."

Nyx's face softened and her heart ached. "As long as you stay with me, I know I'll be safe," she said.

Jet's eyes shifted down to the ground, and Nyx felt her chest tighten. "Nyx ... I ..." He stopped, as if the words were stuck in his throat. "There are so many things I want ... no, need to tell you," he managed finally, his voice soft and uncharacteristically worried. "But these things, they're ..." He shook his head, lost for words.

"The things that would make me see you as a monster?" she asked, her voice barely a whisper.

Jet's gaze rose to meet hers. He didn't have to say anything for her to know it was true.

"I already told you," she whispered. "I don't care about those things. I know who you are now." She could tell that he wanted to believe that, but, at the end of the day, he didn't. "You can trust me with anything."

"You have no idea how much I wish that was true," he said softly. He turned his face away then, his attention drawn to someone coming down the hill from the castle. A scowl immediately began to pull at his lips. "Oh look. It's your boyfriend."

Nyx felt her face flush as she followed his gaze, seeing Samill crossing the field. He smiled when he caught her gaze.

"Good evening, Princess," he said happily.

Nyx returned his smile as she looked up at him from the ground. "Good evening, Samill," she returned pleasantly. "How are preparations going?"

Samill nodded. "Very good," he said. "I'd be happy to tell you more about it if you're interested."

Nyx felt apprehensive at the thought, but she thought maybe she should take him up on the offer. She would need to know these things sooner or later. "Sure," she said, glancing over at Jet, who was watching Samill warily.

"Perhaps over a meal?" Samill asked, a hopeful lilt in his voice.

Nyx didn't respond right away, feeling her face turning red. Was he asking her on a date? "Um, yeah, sure," she stammered. "Maybe over dinner or something?"

Samill looked pleased. "Yes, that would be wonderful." He surprised her again though, when he pulled off his coat, revealing loose-fitting clothing. "But I actually was hoping I might catch you in time for a sparring lesson before dinner," he said. "I know it's getting late and you've been training all day, so if you're not up to it, I understand."

Nyx looked at Jet uncertainly, seeing that he was giving Samill a glare. When he caught her eye though, he shrugged. Nyx took that as his way of telling her to do what she wanted. She wondered for a moment if Liana had asked Samill to test her, and the thought offended her slightly. Did Liana and Samill think she'd been doing nothing all this time? She looked back to Samill.

"I guess I can give it a go," she said as she got to her feet. She sounded more confident than she felt, but she was determined to erase any doubts from his or Liana's minds. "But I haven't sparred with anyone other than Jet before."

Samill was still grinning. "Then let's see what you've learned."

Nyx drew a deep breath and rolled her shoulders, loosening her muscles. She was tired from her earlier session with Jet, but adrenaline started to pump through her as she squared off with Samill. She was nervous and she wondered if he was going to be hard on her. She noticed that he didn't pick up a weapon, so she surmised that they would be doing hand-to-hand. She glanced over her shoulder when Jet got to his feet as well and stepped toward her.

His back was to Samill as he leaned in. "He likes to leave his face open."

Nyx frowned at him, wondering how he knew that.

"Also, go for the ankles." Jet gave her a little pat on the shoulder and a small smile that Nyx couldn't place before stepping out of the way.

Nyx looked at Samill, seeing that he had stepped toward the middle of the dirt arena. He looked like he was sizing her up, but in a less deadly way than Jet usually did. Nyx lifted her fists slowly.

"Ready?" Samill asked.

Nyx nodded, feeling her stomach tighten with anticipation. She kept her eyes trained on Samill as he lifted his hands as well, seeing that Jet was right – Samill didn't bring his fists all the way up to his cheeks, instead letting them rest below his chin. Nyx wasn't sure how that would help her yet, but if she was smart, she could use that to her advantage.

Samill came toward her then and swung a fist at her, making her twist away from him. Since he was taller than she was, he moved slower. She knew that staying out of his reach wouldn't be difficult, but taking him down would be. She could hear Jet's words in his mind: *let your opponent do the work. Tire him out.* He'd told her that once, right before he threw her into the sand after letting her exhaust herself in an attempt to land a blow on him.

Nyx's eyes tracked Samill as he made another lunge at her, seeing that his footwork was slow. This time, she spun under his arms and pushed her magic into her hands, dealing a charged blow to his middle. Nyx could tell she had winded him as he stumbled back, pain on his face as he tried to catch his breath.

Instantly, Nyx felt terrible for hitting him. "Are you okay?" she asked, a hint of panic in her voice. She worried that she'd hit him too hard in her fervor to prove herself.

Samill nodded and braced his hands on his knees. "I just wasn't expecting that," he said, clearly trying to power through the winded feeling.

Jet made a snickering sound and Nyx looked over her shoulder, shooting him a glare. After a moment, Samill seemed like he had caught his breath. He straightened, his face set with determination.

Suddenly the tone of the session changed.

"I won't underestimate you this time," he said, making Nyx's heart skip a beat with fear.

He was faster as he stepped toward her, swinging at her. Nyx gritted her teeth as she realized that he'd been going easy on her in the beginning. He didn't think she was as skilled as she was. The thought bolstered her some, and she focused on what she was doing.

Her body felt like it was moving of its own accord, her muscles and mind remembering the things that Jet had taught her. She lifted her arms and pushed her magic into them, creating a sort of shield. It blocked Samill's blow, but the force of his hit still pushed her back a bit. She quickly regained her footing, dodging him as he came at her again.

She managed to spin away from him and to the side, so that he was moving away from her.

Now with his back to her, he was an easy target. Nyx dealt a kick to the back of his leg, sending him to the ground. Once again, muscle memory propelled her as she spun her body, her foot aiming for the side of Samill's face. She didn't make contact though, as he anticipated her move and caught her, flinging her into the dirt.

Nyx felt her heart lurch, slightly afraid as Samill pinned her. He seemed pleased with himself as he looked down at her.

"Do you yield?" he asked, a smug smile creeping across his face.

Nyx felt anger flare inside her chest. She'd seen that look on Jet's face too many times to count, and it filled her with bitterness. Jet might get away with it because she couldn't beat him, but she wouldn't let Samill do the same.

She could feel her hands digging into the sand beneath her. She could see Jet in her peripheral view as he crossed his arms, and she glanced at him, seeing that his face was unreadable. Despite his stoic look, she felt like she knew what he was thinking. He wasn't surprised that she lost. Her anger was bolstered by the thought, and she gripped a handful of sand.

"I do not," she said, suddenly flinging the sand into Samill's eyes.

He reeled back and released her, and she rolled to her feet away from him. She grabbed a wooden sword from the rack next to her, leveling it at Samill's face. It took a moment for him to clear his vision, and when he did, he looked disappointed as he stared down the practice blade at her.

"That was dirty," he said, clearly unhappy.

Nyx took a step closer to him. "Fights aren't always fair," she said, echoing words Jet had said to her before. She felt a sudden rush of power as she pushed the sword toward him. It suddenly felt good to stand over him, with her sword to his throat. She knew, had it been a real blade, she would have cleaved him apart with ease.

The thought made her heart twist as she realized that she had just imagined killing Samill. She quickly released the sword, letting it land heavily in the sand, feeling terrified of her own thoughts, but she didn't have a chance to apologize as sudden, fierce pain twinged behind her eyes. She spun away from Samill, gasping as a feeling like that of a hot knife piercing her temple sent her to her knees.

She thought she could hear Jet and Samill calling for her, but just like the day that she tried scrying with Lady Aurie, her mind was consumed with something else. This time, though, instead of the feeling of watching a dream, she felt like something was wiggling around in her brain. It felt like something was invading her body, and there was nothing she could do to stop it.

You hunger for blood, a voice suddenly echoed in her mind. Its words were even, as if it were stating a fact. *To have power. To stand over your enemies.*

Nyx could feel tears rolling down her cheeks as she pressed her hands into the cool sand. The pain was still intense, but when the voice spoke, it ebbed some. She forced herself to focus on the feel of the rough grains on her skin. Maybe if she could refocus her mind, she could take control back.

You can't ignore me, the voice continued. *We are linked. You will come to me, and I will give you the power you need to save the ones you love, like Melinda. If you possessed my strength, she would still live. With me in your hands, no more shall die.*

Nyx shook her head, her fear and the pain starting to ease. Slowly, it was being replaced by a feeling that she couldn't place but that was weirdly familiar. She realized that the voice wasn't threatening her, it was beckoning her.

"I don't know how to find you," she breathed.

I will show you the way.

Nyx's body suddenly moved without her help. It felt like when she'd been controlled by Sophia's magic, as if she were a passenger in her mind, but this time she wasn't afraid. The magic that coursed through her felt warm and alive and as natural to her as any part of her body. She stood and lifted her hands, her golden magic running from her fingertips. It dripped into the sand of the training arena, before flowing forward of its own accord and twisting into thick, spiraling shapes. Something was beginning to grow up from the ground, and suddenly Nyx felt the grip that had overcome her release her, leaving her with only the familiar feeling of the magic pulsing strongly in her veins.

She gasped softly as she staggered back, feeling Jet catch her as the magic continued to spiral and form the walls and spires of an immense castle. Her mind felt drained as she stared at the stone structure that she'd somehow created, and her ears started ringing as her knees buckled.

"Get her inside," she heard Samill say, an edge to his voice. "I'll speak to Her Majesty."

Jet didn't say anything as he lifted her into his arms. Nyx turned to look up at him, her mind hazy and sleep pulling at her.

"What did I do?" she whispered.

For the first time that she could recall, Jet looked concerned. "I don't know."

Regius Carmen, the capitol city of Ymber.
The fifty-fourth day of winter, the 851st year of the
reign of Queen Liana Estrella.
Saturday, February 12, 2012.

NYX'S SKIN WAS HOT, EVEN through her coat, as Jet carried her into the foyer. He knew it was from her magic. There was a hot pulse just beneath her skin, and it took everything in him to ignore the way the *fax* curled away from it. It shifted between being afraid of her purity and the desire to consume her power. It whispered softly in his mind, which made his heart twist. She was too strong, and too much of a trigger for the beast. She was dangerous to him. Thankfully he was distracted when Liana appeared, nearly running down the hallway.

"What happened?" she demanded as she reached them.

"You should ask Samill," Jet snapped at the accusation in her voice. "She was sparring with him." He tried to focus as the whispering continued in the back of his mind.

The man appeared over Liana's shoulder, his eyes worried. "I don't know what happened, Your Majesty," he said quickly. "Something just came over her."

Liana pressed her hand against Nyx's face. Her lips were pursed slightly, but her face began to smooth as she stood there, feeling the heat of Nyx's magic. She looked up at Jet, and he knew what she was thinking.

"Was it like before?" she asked softly.

Jet nodded. "Magic like water." At his words, the *fax* twisted in his chest, trying to surge forward. He barely managed to stifle the wince that shot across his face. It was taking everything in him to ignore the monster.

Liana's brow furrowed and she turned to look at Samill. "Take her to the infirmary," she said, an order in her voice.

Jet felt his fingers tighten around her. "I can take her there myself," he snapped, surprised by the edge in his voice. For a second, the *fax* was still, and Jet felt fear at what that meant.

"I need you to show me the … structure," Liana said then. When Jet still didn't look like he'd hand Nyx over to Samill, she placed a hand on his shoulder. When she spoke next, her voice was soft but commanding. "Let Samill take her."

Jet's jaw clenched, but he stiffly released her as Samill lifted her sleeping form into his arms. He didn't like the way he felt at all as Samill disappeared down the hall with her – both because of her absence and also because of the way the *fax* was suddenly twisting with ire.

"I can feel the disturbance in your aura," Liana murmured once they were alone, drawing his gaze. "You can't be around her right now."

Jet clenched his fists. "I have it under control," he said darkly.

"Do you?" Liana asked. Her eyes shifted down to where his nails were leaving bloody divots in his palms.

She let her fingertips drift across the sleeve of his coat, revealing the faintest hint of black runes on his hands.

At the sight of them, Jet spun on his heel and marched toward the door he'd come in through. He could feel Liana behind him.

"When did you hunt last?" she asked, lingering a few feet behind him.

"Just a few weeks ago," he said, pausing inside the door. The thought of blood on his lips made him want to puke. He hated it. "I'm fine."

"You're not fine," Liana said.

Jet was silent. He knew she was right.

"Let's go outside," Liana said then, motioning to the courtyard and the training field.

The air was cool as it hit Jet's face, and he inhaled deeply, trying to force the *fax* to become still.

"You cannot lose control," Liana said as she followed him.

Jet paused and turned to face her, seeing that she was watching him calmly, her hands folded in front of her. "I do have it under control," he snapped. His voice turned accusing. "I did have it under control, until she decided to start doing weird shit."

Liana didn't say anything, her eyes watching him pensively.

Jet crossed his arms tightly at her stare. "I can't predict when she'll set it off."

Liana's eyes narrowed, his words catching her off-guard. "What do you mean?"

Jet looked away and sighed in irritation. He didn't want to let the words pass his lips, but he knew she wouldn't leave him alone now that it was out there. "It … craves her power," he said quietly. He shook his head as his thoughts swirled in his head. "It was like with the golem. So much power. So much strength." He could feel the *fax* shift at the thought. "The *fax* desires it. I can't predict when she'll trigger it."

Liana's brow creased. "You will hunt weekly, then," she said, her voice firm.

Jet scowled, but Liana held up her hand to silence him.

"You cannot be a danger to her," she said evenly. "The creature must be kept quiet at all costs."

Jet clearly didn't like her words, but he didn't argue with her. At his acceptance of her instructions, Liana looked toward the hill that hid the training arena. "Show me the structure," she said then, letting her hands fall to her sides.

Jet led the way from the courtyard and to the top of the hill where the pathway wound down to the training field. Once it came into view, he paused, hearing Liana gasp softly. Below them, the sand of the training area had been turned to stone, a massive castle rising into the air. All around the newly-formed statue, the sand had been carved away, as if a builder had scraped it together to create the statue. Two deep grooves snaked away from the statue, toward where Nyx had been standing when she released her power.

"Dirvo," Liana murmured as she stared at it. Her face was slightly pale. "How could she have done this?"

Jet felt the same question tugging at him as he stood there and stared at it. Despite the fact that Dirvo now lay in ruins, the castle before them was an exact replica of it in its prime, with towering spires that reached toward the clouds. Jet had never seen Dirvo as anything other than ruins, its destruction having taken place nearly a thousand years earlier, long before he was born.

"I think the bigger question is why," Jet said, glancing at her. "And who."

Liana looked at him, her eyes widened. "Paraximus?" she whispered.

Jet shrugged. "She connected with something that day when she used the water to scry," he said, recalling the day that she had sat before the fire and told them it wasn't his father. "She said it wasn't him, but what else could it be?"

Liana didn't like the way her stomach twisted with anxiety. "I think we need to find out more," she said. She looked up at him. "But first, you need to hunt and she needs to rest."

32

The Temple of Daya, Celo Cavus, Siccita.
The fifty-fifth day of winter, the 906th year of the reign
of King Paraximus Lamia.
Sunday, February 13, 2012.

MARA POURED SCALDING WATER INTO a tub, watching
it run over her mistress's skin. Daya didn't seem to
notice the heat, her eyes focused on a point across the room,
lost in thought. Her milky-white skin, which had been
smooth and supple when she'd had the Atturon girl's blood,
was now beginning to lose its glow and slight wrinkles were
beginning to appear. Mara didn't let her gaze linger for too
long, though, knowing her mistress was in a volatile mood.

"Mara." Daya's voice echoed around the stone room
softly.

"Yes, Milady," Mara said, setting her pitcher down and
kneeling beside the tub. "How may I serve you?"

Daya's eyes never moved from the wall, and her voice
was distracted. "When will our army be ready?" she asked.

"Soon, Milady," Mara answered. "The mortivio are
growing nicely. Perhaps one more cycle and they will be

ready."

Daya nodded. The timeline didn't bother her; when one was immortal, a moon cycle was nothing. No, the problem was that, without the Seer's blood, her body was deteriorating faster than she expected. Not even the blood of altar girls could sustain her for long.

"My body won't last much longer," she said absently. "I need the power of the *fax* to survive on this plane."

Mara picked up a rag and began to lightly scrub Daya's shoulders. "What would you have me do?" she asked.

Daya was silent. Truth be told, she wasn't sure yet. She wasn't sure how to lure Paraximus' son to a place where she could take him. As long as he was in Regius Carmen, he was shielded by the Creators' magic, and unreachable to her. But she knew it was only a matter of time. When the time was right, she would consume him and use the *fax* to take over this dreadful world and everyone in it.

Before she had a chance to express her thoughts, however, the door to her chamber suddenly slammed open. Mara jumped to her feet, her teeth bared as Paraximus and a handful of his guards stepped into the room.

Daya turned to look at him, unbothered. She grinned at the blazing hatred in his eyes. "To what do I owe this interruption?" she asked, not moving from the tub.

"What have you done with the Seer?" Paraximus growled furiously. "Where is she?"

Daya watched passively as his guards surrounded her. She chuckled lightly as she turned her eyes back to King Paraximus. "I should be asking you the same," she said easily. Her face began to twist into a shark-toothed smile. "You are the one who kept her from me."

Paraximus gritted his teeth and pulled a sword from his side. "Don't play dumb with me, bitch." He stepped toward her quickly, as if to ram his sword through her chest.

Daya, however, had other ideas. Her body morphed quickly, her limbs shooting out to grotesque lengths. She lunged forward toward Paraximus, crawling on all fours like a human spider. Before he could drive his sword into her, she caught him around the neck and slammed him against the wall.

Seeing their king in peril, the handful of guards leapt to his defense. Daya snarled as she turned her head, preparing to slaughter them all, but pausing as Mara easily stepped between them and her mistress. Just like Daya, her body was beginning to morph, rows of razor teeth appearing and her limbs lengthening to monstrous proportions. Unlike her mistress, her hands became tipped with long, dagger-like claws, which she used to spear the guards who rushed toward her. She struck them down easily, bathing the room in their blood while sinking her fangs into their flesh.

Paraximus could do nothing but watch and listen to their dying screams as Daya turned soulless eyes on him.

"Is this how every interaction is to be between us? Both of us reveling in blood?" Daya asked, leaning in toward him. "Or shall I kill you now, Idiot King?"

Paraximus winced and dug his nails into the flesh of her hand. "You cannot kill me yet," he managed through gasping breaths. "You have taken blood from me as payment."

Daya brought her disgusting mouth close to his face, breathing putrid air into his nostrils. "Do not mistake me for those weak creator beings," she hissed, fury in her words. "Promises mean nothing to me."

Paraximus smirked darkly. "But blood oaths do," he quipped.

Daya let out a roar of aggravation. She reared back and

slammed Paraximus into the wall before releasing him. He was right and it vexed her to no end. Blood magic kept her from smashing his head in. Slowly, she forced her body to retract into the form of a woman once more, her eyes still blazing with hatred as she watched him writhe on the floor.

"Neither of us wish to be bound by this agreement," she said as she stepped toward him. "What do you desire from me to end this arrangement?"

Paraximus gasped and struggled to sit against the wall. His eyes blazed with hatred as well, but he seemed somewhat pleased by her offer. "First tell me what you did with the girl," he demanded.

Daya rolled her eyes and turned away. She stepped through the blood on the floor as if the squishing of it under her bare feet was commonplace. "Do you truly believe that I would have taken my source of youth and disposed of it?" she asked in a haughty voice. "If it were up to me, I would have kept that girl alive for years, just to feast on her blood. Besides," she turned slowly to look at him angrily, "I was not the one who kept her behind a spellbound door."

"Am I to believe she simply escaped?" Paraximus demanded, managing to pull himself to his feet.

Daya's face twisted with cruel humor. "Perhaps she had some assistance."

Paraximus's eyes darkened and his thoughts turned inward as rage played across his face. He was silent for a moment, and Daya had a feeling that this blood bath wouldn't be the only one tonight. Finally, he turned his eyes back to her, resolve in them. "Give me your power," he said shortly. "All of it. And I will consider our blood oath fulfilled."

Daya tilted her head curiously. "All of my power?" she asked, sadistic humor in her voice. "Is that truly your wish,

King Paraximus?"

He seemed as if he would hesitate, but instead he squared his shoulders. "Yes." He flinched lightly when Daya suddenly waved her hand, a jagged blade appearing in her fist.

Slowly, Daya dragged the blade across her wrist, causing fetid black blood to ooze from the wound. "Then drink," she commanded. "If you desire what is mine, consume me." She watched as Paraximus's face paled slightly. She thought for a moment that he would turn her down, but then he stepped toward her.

His boots squelched in the ick that covered the floor, but his eyes were fixed on her oozing wrist. Daya held out her arm as he came within reach, her eyes darkening with mirth as he gripped her wrist. He seemed to hesitate once more, but then he pressed his mouth over the wound. Daya grinned again as she felt him sucking at the ooze that flowed from her veins.

"Now our pact is finished, King Paraximus," she said. She watched as he released her and turned away as if he would vomit. Her grin widened as he suddenly stumbled to his knees, spasming as her blood flowed through him.

Runes suddenly began to glow across his skin as he collapsed to the floor. A scream tore from his throat as her magic shredded through his body. Glee filled Daya as she watched him thrash in agony. The next few moments would decide his fate; if he survived he would have her powers, but not without a price. Either way, she reveled in seeing his misery.

After a while he began to still on the floor, his breaths hard and ragged. The runes were still coating his skin, which was pale and covered in a light sheen of sweat. Daya took a step toward him and kneeled slowly.

"I'm almost disappointed," she mused as she listened to him gasp softly. "I was quite hoping my power would be too strong for you."

Paraximus groaned. "Bitch," he managed.

Daya grinned. "But there is more," she said, leaning closer to his ear. "The same magic that you used to bind your son now binds my magic to your pathetic body."

Paraximus gritted his teeth at her words.

"And you know what that means, don't you, Idiot King," she said, her words a statement and not a question. "Just like your poor child, you will consume blood, or the magic will consume you."

Paraximus's eyes shot to her, filled with hatred.

"Oh, come now," she said pityingly. "Was this not what you wanted?" She patted his cheek. "A small price to pay to have vengeance."

Paraximus looked like he would have more choice words for her, but suddenly the runes began to glow and agony creased his face again.

"Looks like you should feed," Daya said, pleasure in her voice. She rose to stand, watching as he gasped and clenched at his chest. "The good news is Mara has brought the feast to you." She motioned to the bloodied bodies of the guards that Mara had slaughtered and laughed.

At the mention of her name, Mara appeared beside Daya, her chin and the front of her dress covered in crimson. "Come Mara," Daya said to her. "Our time here is complete."

Regius Carmen, the capitol city of Ymber.
The fifty-sixth day of winter, the 851st year of the reign
of Queen Liana Estrella.
Monday, February 14, 2012.

Nyx's brain felt fuzzy as she struggled her way to consciousness. The first thing she noticed was that she was cold and she began to shiver fiercely. The second thing she noticed was that she was in a hospital wing. She tried to lift her head to look around at the empty beds around her, but sharp pain shot through her head. She pressed her face into the pillow beneath her head and pulled the thick blanket over her tighter. She couldn't remember ever feeling so cold in her entire life. It felt like her body couldn't shiver hard enough to even begin to warm her again.

"Easy there," a voice said.

Nyx felt another blanket pulled over her, and she cracked her eyes to see a woman standing beside the bed. She wanted to ask who the woman was, but her jaw was trembling too hard.

"The shakes will subside with time," the woman said,

easing to sit on the edge of the bed and rubbing Nyx's shoulders over the blankets. "The coldness is a byproduct of too much magic expenditure."

Nyx turned to press her face back into the pillow. Her thoughts turned back to the training field. Her memory was fuzzy. Was it a castle that she'd seen? She tried to remember, but it felt far away.

"Nyx," Liana's voice was gentle, a hint of concern in it.

Nyx turned her head toward her grandmother's voice, seeing her walking quickly toward her. She was still trembling fiercely as Liana reached her and pressed her hand against her face. Her hand felt impossibly warm and Nyx pressed into it.

Liana sat on the edge of the bed, shushing her softly like a mother would a small child. "You're okay," she said softly. "You'll feel better soon." She leaned closer, putting both of her hands on either side of Nyx's face.

Nyx felt the pulse of warm, gentle magic from her grandmother's hands. It started in her cheeks and flowed slowly into her, easing down her neck and into her chest. Her tight muscles began to relax as the hard shivering subsided and she drew ragged breaths, her body aching slightly. Even though the quaking in her body had subsided, she still felt bone-deep exhaustion.

"There," Liana said as she leaned back. "You'll need time to rebuild your strength, but this should help."

Nyx's eyelids felt heavy as she relaxed into her pillow. "Wh … wha …" She tried to speak, but the words felt clumsy and thick.

"There is time for that," Liana said softly. "Please just rest now."

Nyx didn't have to be told twice as dark sleep consumed her. Her dreams were empty, only a pitch blackness in her mind. She didn't know how long she slept, but it was the soft sound of chimes that woke her.

When she opened her eyes again, she was alone in the infirmary, and it was dark. There was moonlight twinkling beyond the windows, and as she lifted her head, she realized she was alone. She pressed a hand to her temple, feeling a light throbbing there. Fortunately, the intense shivering from before was gone, but she still felt drained. She started to wonder where everyone was, but suddenly the soft sound of chimes met her ears again.

She turned her head quickly, seeing what looked like fireflies dancing across the floor and toward the infirmary door. She frowned in confusion, but she felt the urge to follow them as their golden light drifted out the door and into the corridor. Her legs were shaking as she moved to her feet, and she staggered a few steps, catching herself on the railings of the empty beds before finding her balance.

The light from the fireflies was fading and she felt a sense of urgency as she walked quickly toward the door. She caught herself on the frame, glancing up and down the hall, barely catching the light of the fireflies disappearing around a corner. She followed after them as quickly as her unsteady feet would carry her, catching herself on the wall as she rounded the corner. The golden fireflies were bouncing slightly, as if waiting for her, before another chime rang out softly and they disappeared into a door.

Nyx staggered toward the door, frowning as she put her hand on it. She'd never been in this part of the castle before, and she had no idea what was beyond the heavy wooden door. Slowly, she pushed it opened, darkness greeting her. She blinked several times to allow her eyes to adjust, suddenly seeing the flash of golden sparks again. She walked quickly into the room, the scent of dust and paper hitting her nose. She paused as she let the door swing shut behind her, realizing she was in a massive library. It was covered from ceiling to floor in rows and rows of books, with shelves jutting from her left and right. It reminded her of a library she'd seen once in a movie – impossibly huge and filled to the brim with anything she could think of. Her admiration was cut short, however, when the chiming sound came again, this time the golden sparks illuminating a shelf in the distance.

Slowly, she walked toward the light, seeing it start to dim as she came closer. Confusion filled her as she finally stopped where the sparks had disappeared, and she looked at the bookshelves on either side of her, wondering why she had followed them there. Was she supposed to be looking for something? And if so, what?

Her eyes flitted over the books slowly, her muddled brain trying to read the writing on the spines. Just when she thought she would need to give up, a book that didn't look like the rest stood out to her. It was leather-bound like the others, but instead of writing on the spine, it only bore the outline of a rose pressed into the leather. She carefully slid it from between the books and held it in her hands. That same rose was pressed into the cover, large and dark, and she felt her heart skip a beat. Was what she was looking for in this book?

She turned slowly, running her fingertips over the cover, feeling the etching beneath them. Something about it felt familiar and inviting. She walked back toward the main entrance of the library and saw a desk near a large window that overlooked the city. She stepped toward the desk and set the book on it, slowly turning the cover.

The book creaked and cracked, as if it hadn't been opened in many, many years, but the words were still crisp as she held the book in the moonlight.

Slowly, she let her eyes drift over the scrawled words on the first page, feeling her brain deciphering them. "The Story of …" she whispered. She paused on the last word, realizing it was very foreign to her. Slowly, she tried to sound it out. "… glad-i-an-ima …"

The book suddenly flared with light, the words becoming bright and golden. The book suddenly felt warm, like it was alive, and it took everything in her not to throw it away from her. She gasped as the pages began to flutter, an unnatural wind blowing her hair back as the book seemed to be flipping to the page it wanted her to see. The bright writing inside the book was nearly blinding, but it suddenly stopped. Nyx gasped as the chiming sound suddenly filled her ears again, and she dropped the book on the table, trying to read the glowing words. Her brain felt like it was being overloaded as things she didn't know how she knew began to fill her mind, as if she were reading the words easily.

She saw images of a woman with pale purple hair in a cave, her clothing sopping wet and her hair clinging to her face as she struggled out of a pool of water. Once she was on dry land, she turned her eyes toward a massive doorway cut into the rock. She seemed wary but confident as she walked toward the doorway and pressed her hands against it. Instantly, her golden magic began to illuminate runes on the door, and suddenly the rock dissolved, leaving the way open for her. The woman stepped forward into a chamber, where a shaft of moonlight was beaming down onto a pedestal. Atop the pedestal was an object. Nyx couldn't quite tell what it was, but as the woman stepped into the chamber, Nyx heard the voice that had been plaguing her more clearly than she'd ever heard it before.

"Come to me."

Nyx willed the woman to walk closer, feeling her heart racing in her chest.

"Come to me."

The woman took slow, guarded steps, and Nyx could feel that something was about to happen. Her heart hung in her chest as the woman reached out a hand to grab the object—

"Nyx? What are you doing?"

Nyx jumped at the sound of the voice pulling her from the vision. The book in front of her slammed shut, the golden light gone. She blinked quickly, feeling an odd mixture of sadness … and rage as she turned her eyes toward the library door.

Jet was standing in front of a window, the cold night air blowing in and across his face. The city glistened below him, and the river wound its way across the landscape, glittering with its own light and the light of the moons. Jet had been sitting by Nyx's bed most of the day after he'd returned from hunting as Liana had commanded. Liana had told him that she'd woken at some point while he'd been gone, but that she'd told Nyx to rest more. It had been hours since then, and Jet had finally decided that he needed to get up. He'd walked to the end of the corridor and opened the window, needing to breathe in fresh air. He hadn't realized how late it was, and he also hadn't realized that he wouldn't be alone.

Liana appeared at the top of the stairs near him, dressed in her night clothes. An augarlux floated next to her, illuminating her face. She pulled her robe tighter around her shoulders as she saw him near the window.

"How is she?" Liana asked softly as she came toward him.

Jet shook his head. "Still sleeping." He hunched his shoulders as she leaned on the window sill beside him.

"I suppose it's for the best," she said quietly.

"Doesn't any of this bother you?" Jet demanded, turning his dark eyes on her. "That something is trying to take control of her."

Liana looked at him, her brow furrowed in a way as if she was trying to decide if she should be angry with him. "Of course it does," she said, the edge in her voice. She looked back out the window, helplessness flashing across her eyes. "But I can't see what it is." Her voice was a worried whisper. "I don't know how to stop it."

Jet felt her helplessness. "So what are we supposed to do?" he asked.

Liana shook her head. "I don't know."

Silence fell over them as the night air blew through the hallway. Jet didn't like the feeling that was settling in his chest. How was he supposed to keep her safe if he didn't even know what he was trying to protect her from?

The sudden sound of a door shutting caught his ears and he turned quickly to look at Liana, seeing that she had turned toward the source of the sound. She glanced at him over her shoulder. "Perhaps she's awake?" she said cautiously.

Jet stared down the hall, listening for any other sounds before taking slow steps toward the infirmary. Something didn't feel right to him, and he walked faster. As he rounded the corner toward the infirmary, a sudden flare of magic filled the air, making the hairs on his neck stand up. He froze momentarily to look at Liana, seeing that she was at his elbow.

"What the hell was that?" he demanded.

Liana looked equally disturbed and she stepped past him, leading the way. "It felt like it came from the library."

They both were nearly running as they reached the library door and Jet shoved it open quickly. They both drew up short as a hot wind and golden magic were swirling around the room. Jet felt his heart lurch in his chest as he saw Nyx sitting at a desk, golden light cast over her face as a book hovered in front of her. He stepped quickly into the room, calling her name.

The book suddenly snapped shut and she looked stunned as she sat still for a moment. But then she turned her eyes toward them and Jet felt his heart plummet to his feet. Her jaw clenched as she moved to her feet. She waved her hand and summoned a golden sword, rage filling her emerald eyes.

"I almost had it, Jet Lamia!" she screamed as she lunged toward him and swung the sword as his chest.

Jet dodged her blade, making sure to put himself between her and Liana. "What the fuck!" he yelled as she made another swing at him. "What are you doing?" He could tell that something had taken over her. She never addressed him like that, and there was a hard set to her face that wasn't hers.

Her anger was palpable though as another crazed scream came from her. "I was almost there!" She swung the sword at him again.

Despite her uncharacteristic fury, most of what she was doing was uncoordinated and lacked any finesse, making it easy for Jet to use his magic to block her, pushing her off balance. As she staggered to the side, he stepped toward her, his instincts taking over. This wasn't her, and whatever had her in its grip had access to power that he knew he couldn't stop if he didn't get her under control now. He needed to disarm her before it was too late. Guilt plagued him, but he did what he knew was the right thing: he swung his fist at her, catching her across the cheek and knocking her to the floor. As she landed on her back, he kicked her right hand, making the sword slip from her fingers and the grip on her magic release. Before she could channel the magic into her fists, he knelt over her, catching her hands. She was oddly strong as she struggled against him, her emerald eyes blazing with a fire that he'd never seen in her before.

"I'll kill you," she hissed between clenched teeth. "I'll kill you!"

Jet scowled at her. "Shut up," he snapped, pressing her harder into the floor. "Snap out of it!"

Liana appeared at his side, her hand pressing against Nyx's face. Nyx turned her eyes on her grandmother, and the sudden fury started to ease almost as quickly as it had come. Her eyes welled with tears and her struggling began to slow.

"I'm sorry," she breathed as she looked at Liana. The tears were thick as they rolled down her cheeks. "I'm sorry, Grandmother."

Liana shook her head and shushed her softly. "There is no need to be sorry," she said gently. "We are just concerned about you."

Nyx shook her head, the tears still coming fast. "No," she managed. "I'm sorry I can't save you."

Liana pulled her hand back quickly, her eyes wide. "What?" she breathed.

"I can't save you," Nyx gasped through ragged sobs. "I can't save you!"

Jet turned to look at Liana, seeing that her brow was furrowed with sadness and pain. "Hey!" he snapped, causing her to look at him with watery eyes. "Now is not the time! Stop her!"

Liana blinked quickly, nodding shortly. She focused her eyes back on Nyx's face and pressed her hand to her temple. "Sleep," she whispered, pushing her magic into Nyx. "Just sleep."

Nyx's struggling suddenly began to weaken and her eyes grew heavy. Her sobs quieted as her eyelids fluttered shut and she was still on the floor. Jet realized he was panting softly as he slowly released her, making sure she was definitely out. He rested his hands on his legs as he looked at Liana.

"What the fuck was that about?" he demanded.

A tear rolled down Liana's face as she stared down at Nyx. "She saw what I did," she whispered, her voice steady despite the emotion on her face.

"And what the hell is that?" Jet demanded again. Why was everyone always speaking in riddles?

Liana clenched her jaw briefly as if to rein in her sadness. "My death."

Jet blinked quickly. Their previous conversation when he and Nyx had first arrived flashed through his mind. He had so many questions but he knew she wouldn't answer any of them as she rose to her feet and crossed the room toward the desk.

Her eyes were distracted as she looked at the book lying on top of it. "Take her back to the infirmary," she said distractedly.

"What are you going to do?" he asked as he moved to his feet.

"I need to see what else she saw," Liana said as she picked up the book. "Then maybe I can understand what's happening to her." She turned to look at Jet. "Do not leave her side under any circumstances until I get back."

Jet wanted to ask her where she was going, but he knew she wouldn't tell him. He simply nodded and lifted Nyx into his arms.

Regius Carmen, the capitol city of Ymber.
The fifty-sixth day of winter, the 851st year of the reign
of Queen Liana Estrella.
Monday, February 14, 2012.

LIANA WAS STANDING IN FRONT of the *Vere Lacrimae.* She was watching it bubble and ripple as it fluttered up from the earth and ran down into the mountain channel. Beside her was Lady Aurie. She could feel Lady Aurie's displeasure as she held the book against her chest.

"I do not think this is wise," Lady Aurie said quietly, her voice guarded. "What if this opens you to something untoward, Your Majesty?"

Liana glanced at her, giving her a slight smile. "That's why I have you here," she said. "Am I wrong to trust in your abilities?"

Lady Aurie sighed and her displeasure deepened. "Of course not, Your Majesty," she said with a slight bow of her head. She glanced at Liana then. "When you are ready, I suppose."

Liana nodded and turned to sit on the edge of the flat

stone circle. She drew a slow breath as she centered her mind and clutched the book in her hands. She lifted the book toward her lips. "Show me," she whispered softly. "Creators, show me what I need to do to help her."

With that she fell backwards into the bubbling water. Lady Aurie drew a quick breath and stepped toward the edge of the spring, gripping the flat stone. She watched as the water flared bright blue around Liana as she sank into impossible depths. She didn't know how long she was supposed to wait, but she watched the magic swirl around Liana, splaying her lavender hair around her. Liana didn't move as she sank further, and Lady Aurie started to worry she would float too far for her to reach her, but then Liana's eyes flashed open.

They were bright and glowing violet as she suddenly surfaced from the bubbling and roiling magical water. She coughed slightly as she reached for Lady Aurie who grasped her hand and pulled her out of the water. Liana set the book on the edge of the spring and drew some quick breaths.

"What did you see?" Lady Aurie asked, watching the glow in Liana's eyes start to dim.

Liana took a moment to catch her breath before straightening as the light completely faded. Her face was set as she looked at Lady Aurie. "I know what must be done," she said, her voice slightly breathless. "I know what it is. I know what we must do." Her voice caught slightly and her brow furrowed with pain. "No, not us ... Nyx. I know what Nyx must do."

I hope you enjoyed this book. Would you do me a favor?

Like all authors, I rely on online reviews to encourage future sales. Your opinion is invaluable. Would you take a few moments now to share your assessment of my book on Amazon or any other book review website you prefer? Your opinion will help the book marketplace become more transparent and useful to all.

Thank you!

About the Author

E. Paige Burks is a graduate from Texas A&M University with a degree in Agricultural Communication and Journalism. She is also a three-time award winning author, mother, and licensed veterinary technician.

When she is not writing fantasy and love stories, she enjoys tacos, singing out loud, cuddling with her cats, and taking long naps.

E. Paige Burks lives in Houston, Texas with her family and a bunch of animals!

Check out her other titles:

Return to Royalty
A Gexalatian Tale Series Book One

Return to Gexalatia
A Gexalatian Tale Series Book Two

The Heart of the Guardian

Jewels for Gemma

A special preview of

Return to Power

Book Four

of

A Gexalatian Tale Series

Prologue

The Past

THE WIND WAS WARM AS IT blew across the gardens of Regius Carmen. The scent of the infinity flowers was soft and sweet. The summertime air was comfortable, but it was fleeting. Summer never lasted long enough. Especially the summer evenings. The sun had begun to set already.

"Your Highness?"

Violet eyes shifted at the sound of her maid's voice. She rose slowly to her feet, her lavender hair fluttering in the soft breeze. She could see the concern on her maid's face. "What is it?" she asked gently.

Her maid bowed. "You have a guest."

She felt her cheeks flush. She knew who would be calling.

She nodded to her servant. "Please let him know I will be in shortly," she said.

Her maid bowed, before leaving her.

She drew a slow breath, trying to calm her pounding heart. It had been some time since she had seen the prince, and it made her feel giddy. Something about him was so alluring. She knew she had fallen in love with him, and she wasn't sure how it had happened. Their meetings, initially, had been brief, but then he began to visit more frequently. She could tell that he was beginning to have feelings toward her as well.

She smoothed the front of her gown, before turning

and following the path toward the castle. She felt her heart skip a beat as she looked toward the entrance, seeing his dark figure in the doorway. She paused as he stepped into the waning sunlight.

He was beautiful as he smiled at her.

He descended the steps slowly, his pitch-colored hair swinging around his face. It was tethered back in a ponytail, which swung in straight locks down his back. His dark ebony eyes found hers as he stepped onto the garden path.

"Your Highness," he said, bowing at the waist.

"Prince Paraximus," she said, inclining her head. She met his gaze as he stepped toward her, catching her hand in his.

"Liana." Her name was a reverent whisper as he lifted her hand to his lips. He kissed her softly. "I have missed you."

Liana felt her heart ache in her chest. "I have missed you, as well," she said softly. She let him loop her hand around his arm. The closeness of his body was comforting. "To what do I owe this visit?"

Paraximus grinned as he turned to lead her inside. "Am I no longer allowed to visit you for my own selfish pleasure?" he teased.

Liana felt her face blush. She had known that was why he had come. There was no business going on at the moment.

She was surprised when, as they reached the doorway to the castle, he turned to face her. He caught her hands in his.

"I haven't been able to think about anything other than you," he said softly. He watched as her violet eyes widened with surprise. "We've been together so often recently, and I have made up my mind."

Liana felt her heart twist in her chest when he suddenly sank down to his knee. She barely had time to react as he produced a golden band from his pocket.

"Marry me, Liana," he whispered. He watched as her violet eyes widened in disbelief.

She was silent for a long moment, staring at the band in his fingers. This was more than she could have ever hoped for from him. She looked into his ebony eyes, a smile suddenly sliding across her face. She nodded slowly.

"Yes, my love," she whispered. "You know I will." She gasped when he suddenly rose to his feet, catching her into his arms. She drew a sharp breath as he held her tightly.

"I love you," he whispered, pressing his hands into her lavender hair.

Liana felt her heart leap. He had never told her that he loved her, but she had always known.

The city was brightly colored as the day of their wedding came. Liana watched out the window of her room as the citizens gathered in the streets, ringing bells and singing songs in celebration. She smiled to herself, pressing her hand over her lips.

This was all so much more than she could have ever imagined.

She didn't think things could be any more perfect.

There was a soft knock on her door, and she looked up as her maid entered. She bowed at the waist. "Are you ready, Your Highness?" she asked.

Liana was still smiling softly as she turned, nodding her head. "Yes, Lucinda," she said quietly. She followed her maid into the next room, which had been arranged with a platform and large mirror for her to dress in front of. Her lace wedding gown was hanging on the far wall, waiting for her.

Lucinda chatted excitedly as she helped Liana put on her dress. Once she laced her up, she paused. Liana's eyes shifted to her in the mirror. She was surprised to see tears on the older woman's face.

"What is it, Lucinda?" she asked softly, worry creasing her brow.

Lucinda smiled, brushing at her tears. "I knew this day would come," she said softly. "Ever since you were a tiny babe, I knew you would grow into a beautiful woman." She wiped at her face. "It has just come so fast."

Liana's face softened. Lucinda had been her maid since she was a child. She couldn't imagine her life without her. She turned toward her, surprising Lucinda when she pulled her into a hug. "You have always been more important to me that you could ever know," she said. She smiled. "I am happy to share this moment with you."

Lucinda's tears were renewed. "Your mother would be very proud of the young woman you've become," she said.

Liana felt bittersweet tears fill her eyes. Her mother had passed away when she was in her teens, leaving Lucinda to care for her. She had never known her father, since he had died shortly before she was born.

She drew a slow breath as she turned back to her reflection, unable to talk about her mother. She wished that she was here to see her get married, but nothing could change the fact that she wasn't. Lucinda seemed to understand her silence, as she rubbed her arm soothingly, before moving her to sit in front of a vanity.

Lucinda twisted her lavender hair into beautiful ringlets, before dabbing light makeup on her face. Once she was finished, she opened a wooden box that sat on the vanity. Inside was a silver tiara. Diamonds sparkled brightly in the light. She set it carefully in Liana's hair, before pinning in her veil.

Once she was ready, Lucinda smiled at her, seeing her violet eyes widen as she looked at herself in the mirror.

"Are you ready?" she asked.

Liana nodded, her fingers brushing the veil lightly. She had never imagined herself in a wedding dress, and the sight was incredible. She rose slowly, allowing Lucinda to help her into her white slippers. After that, she gathered the train of the dress into her hands.

Liana walked slowly from the dressing room toward the chapel. She could hear the bells chiming the hour, and she drew a long breath as Lucinda set her train down and stepped inside the foyer to pick up her bouquet. Everything felt surreal as Liana took it in her hands. She looked up as the wedding march began to play, feeling her heart skip a beat.

Lucinda smiled at her as she looked to the pages that opened the door for her. She leaned in to kiss Liana's cheek gently. Liana smiled at her, before taking a step into the light of the church. She looked at all the people gathered there, recognizing many of them, before she turned her eyes to the end of the aisle.

Paraximus' dark eyes were gentle as he watched her walk slowly toward him. As she came closer, he smiled lovingly at her. He took her hand, helping her up the steps of the dais they stood on.

The cleric said a prayer before he looked at them, smiling. His words seemed a blur as he read passages from his book and soon he turned to Liana, asking her to recite his words.

Her voice was soft as she did so, her violet eyes never

leaving Paraximus' face.

"Do you take this man to be your husband?"

Liana's cheeks flushed and she glanced away, before back, feeling embarrassed suddenly. "I do," she whispered.

The cleric did the same for Paraximus.

"I do," he said gently. He returned her smile as they gazed at each other.

"You may kiss your bride."

Liana gasped as Paraximus stepped toward her, catching her in his arms. He pulled her against him, dipping her as he pressed his lips against hers. When he set her back to her feet, she was laughing softly.

The rest of the day was a blur for her as they celebrated and laughed and danced well into the evening with their guests. Finally, as the festivities seemed to wind down, she looked at Paraximus as he led her from the dance floor.

"You look tired, my love," he said, brushing her face.

She nodded as she leaned into his touch.

He smiled softly. "Shall we retreat to our room?"

Liana's face flushed. She had never shared a room with anyone, let alone a man. She nodded though, letting him take her hand.

After they bid their farewells, he took her from the ballroom, leading her down the hall to the suite that had been prepared for them. It was dark and quiet as he opened the door for her, scooping her into his arms to carry her over the threshold.

Liana laughed as he set her down, watching as he closed the door behind them. She liked the way his hands felt on her face as he caught her for a deep kiss.

"I love you, Liana Estrella," he breathed against her lips.

She looked up at him, frowning slightly. "I believe it's

Liana Lamia now," she said. She gasped in surprise when he suddenly caught her around the waist, carrying her to the bedroom.

He was gentle as he set her on the bed. "You're right," he said slowly, grinning at her. He watched as her face flushed when he unbuttoned his blazer, laying it on the bed next to her.

Liana watched as he leaned down to kiss her again, and she let her hands catch around his neck, threading into his pitch-colored hair. She could feel him pressing his body against hers, and she knew where this would lead. She was nervous and excited at the same time. She had waited for this moment for a long time. Her face flushed darkly, her violet eyes meeting his.

"It's okay," he said, easing to sit beside her on the bed. He brushed her lavender hair from her face. He kissed her gently. "We'll take it slow."

Liana nodded mutely, searching his eyes. His gaze was gentle and loving, and she reached out to brush the long strands of dark hair from his neck. She had thought about this moment more often than she cared to admit, and she wanted it to be perfect.

Her heart was thrumming in her chest as she reached out, running her hands down his strong chest. She could feel the hard sinew of his muscles and his racing heartbeat beneath her fingertips. He was just as nervous as she was, but he covered it better. She swallowed thickly, pulling at the buttons slowly. She could see her hands shaking, and she mentally berated herself.

This man was her husband now.

She looked up into Paraximus' dark eyes, feeling her nervousness abate some. "You are my husband," she whispered. "I won't be afraid when I'm with you."

He smiled, his dark eyes glittering with his happiness. "And I will always take care of you, my wife," he whispered.

Castle Dirvo was stunning as it rose against the sky, sitting on the edge of a cliff overlooking the bay. As the time had passed, the ancient stone had become white-washed and bleached with the salt and the sun. It was tall and proud as its spires rose into the sky.

Liana felt her heart ache as she gazed at the castle from the window of her carriage.

She had left her only home in Regius Carmen, and Dirvo was to be her home now. It was where her beloved husband lived with his family, and it would be a new experience for her. For so much of her life, she had been alone, having been raised mostly by Lucinda. It seemed strange to be losing the only home she had ever known, but she knew she was gaining so much more.

"It is beautiful, Your Highness," Lucinda said softly, looking at her.

Liana smiled, nodding. "It is," she said.

"You will be very happy here," Lucinda said gently.

Liana's violet eyes were wide as she looked to her maid. Lucinda was smiling gently in a motherly fashion.

"I know you are nervous, but you will be happy here," Lucinda said. "I can see how much you love King Paraximus, and it isn't right that you have been away from each other for so long."

Liana turned to look back at the castle, letting Lucinda's words settle in her head. It was odd to hear her refer to him as king, but with their union they had decided to unite Siccita and Ymber and become the first rulers of a united Gexalatia. "I hope that you are right," she said thoughtfully.

"It will be different to be away from Regius Carmen."

Lucinda nodded. "Yes, but it will be a good change," she said. "You were lonely in Regius Carmen."

Liana pressed her lips together tightly. She didn't like to think about that. It was true. Despite being surrounded by her court and some cousins, she had no close family to speak of. She had no one that she called a friend, and it left her to her own devices most times. It was a lonely life.

But everything had changed for her when she met Paraximus. She had seen him several times when they were children, when his father would come for yearly meetings with the Council. She remembered vaguely that she had been glad to have a friend her own age, but she was discouraged from playing with him. It wasn't ladylike, or so Lucinda had told her. As they had grown older, her studies and her duties kept her more and more busy, until she saw him for what felt like the first time.

Liana had been asked by one of the Council leaders to meet him. It was strictly political, since she would soon be asked to sit in on the Council's meetings, and she had agreed. She just hadn't expected the meeting to go the way it had.

He was definitely the most beautiful man she had ever seen as he had stepped down from the dragon he was riding. His long hair was tethered back from his face, swinging around his shoulders. His dark eyes were captivating as he had looked at her, smiling gently.

She remembered his face from the earlier years, but she hadn't expected the way that her heart was racing in her chest. As he approached her, she realized that her palms were sweating, and her cheeks were slightly flushed.

He had bowed before her, taking her hand. "Queen Liana," he said, kissing the back of her hand.

Liana had bowed in return. "Prince Paraximus," she said politely. She felt flustered as he stared into her eyes for much longer than she felt was necessary.

"It is good to see you again," he said softly.

Liana had offered a small smile. "And you as well."

The pleasantries had continued as they walked into the foyer, but Liana couldn't keep her eyes off of him. She had never felt so captivated by anyone. She had wondered for a long time if it was just her, but she knew he felt it too when he returned a few months later, his visit lasting for much longer than a business trip would have. He had spent every free moment he had with her, and it was something that she was unused to. However, the night that he told her that she was the most beautiful woman he had ever met was the night she knew. She was hooked now, and she knew that her heart belonged to this man.

She felt a blush color her cheeks as she blinked from her thoughts. Dirvo was much closer now, and she looked to Lucinda, feeling nervousness twist inside her.

Lucinda caught her hands, squeezing them reassuringly.

They were silent as the gate was lowered to allow them entrance, and they began to traverse the streets of the castle. The citizens were beside themselves with joy, crowding the carriage and cheering her arrival. It was clear that they were celebrating in her honor, as the streets and homes they passed were decorated with bright colors and festive flowers.

Liana didn't know how to respond to them initially, choosing to smile and wave. She had never been subjected to such treatment, and she had never been celebrated in such a manner. It made arriving at the entrance to the palace both comforting and bittersweet.

She felt her heart catch in her throat when she saw

Paraximus walking down the steps. His pitch-colored hair was untethered, swinging freely around his face, and he was dressed down in a simple shirt and breeches. He was beaming with delight as he reached the carriage as it stopped, throwing open the door for her.

Liana was all too happy to see him, and she was out of the carriage in an instant, wrapped safely in his strong arms. He held her tightly, breathing in her scent.

"My love," he whispered, his fingers combing through her hair. He kissed her lips softly. "I have missed you terribly."

Liana felt her face flush. "I have missed you," she said quietly. His sentiments felt so foreign, but so delightful at the same time. She wasn't used to having someone dote on her so much, and she definitely wasn't used to being so emotional. For some reason, though, she felt tears suddenly crowd her eyes.

Paraximus' brow furrowed and he caught her waist gently. "What's wrong, love?" he asked, his pitch-colored eyes worried. He brushed at the tears that were slowly rolling down her cheeks.

Embarrassment flooded her. She had no idea why she was crying, and she was just as surprised as he was. She shook her head, looking up at him. "Nothing is wrong," she whispered, feeling her heart twist as she wrapped her arms around him. "Nothing could be wrong when I'm with you."

A small smile slid across his face as he brushed his knuckles across her cheek. "You missed me."

Liana looked into his eyes. Of course she had missed him. Hadn't she said that? But then realization struck her. She was crying because she missed him; because she hadn't realized how much she needed him until he wasn't with her.

"I'm sorry," she whispered.

He laughed softly, lifting her chin so that she was looking at him. "There is no need to apologize, my love," he said. He wrapped her arm in his. "Let's go inside." He grinned. "Daruth and Valindra have been dying to see you again."

Liana swallowed thickly as she looked toward the palace. She had met both of his siblings when they had come to their wedding, but it had been the first and the last time. His brother Daruth looked much like their mother, with gray hair and light eyes, while his sister Valindra took after their father just as Paraximus did.

She let Paraximus lead her up the entry way steps and into the palace. It was grand, with arching ceilings. The scent of the ocean was somewhat drowned out as they stepped inside. The air was cool, but there was a feeling of home that came over her.

Her violet eyes drifted over everything as he led the way, finally coming to rest on the large doors to the throne room. It was similar to the one in the palace at Regius Carmen, but it was just different enough to be beautiful in its own way. She looked to Paraximus as he pressed his hand against the door, pushing it open slowly.

Liana's eyes widened in surprise as she saw that the room was full of courtiers, and they bowed as she entered. She looked at her husband in surprise, seeing him smiling at her. "What is this?" she asked.

He took her hand, leading her to the foot of the dais where two thrones sat. "This is where we will rule together, my love," he said gently. He held out his hand, helping her up the steps and to be seated. Then he turned to address the crowd.

"Thank you all for coming," he said. "Let us celebrate the arrival of our queen, and my dear wife, Her Highness

Liana Lamia."

A cheer rose from the crowd, a party falling into swing. Music began to play, and the people around them began to smile and dance and celebrate her arrival.

Her eyes shifted to Paraximus. "You did all this for me?" she asked.

"Only the best for you, my love," he said. He kissed her softly, taking her hand. "Would you share a dance with me?"

Liana looked into his eyes, feeling an unexpected warmth fill her. Would the rest of her days be like this? She nodded as he led her onto the floor.